DAVID WILLIAM PEARCE

A TWINKLE IN THE EYES OF GOD

A MONK BUTTMAN MYSTERY

Black Rose Writing | Texas

The author grants the final approval for this literary material.

First printing

ISBN: 978-1-68433-413-1
PUBLISHED BY BLACK ROSE WRITING
www.blackrosewriting.com

Printed in the United States of America
Suggested Retail Price (SRP) $19.95

A Twinkle in the Eyes of God is printed in Chaparral Pro

A grateful thanks and acknowledgement to Eric, Renee, Jenn, Elle, Michelle, Karen, Erik 7, and John of the Barnsian Nobility for making me a more thoughtful writer and to Cappi Birnberg for her enthusiasm and support.

A Twinkle in the Eyes of God

1

I was supposed to be at the beach.

Instead, I was in a small dilapidated church in the middle of nowhere keeping Lucian, or what was left of him, company while Agnes and Rebekah went for the sheriff.

In the quiet, we sat.

Well, I did.

Lucian was dead.

He was set against the front of the pulpit, his legs splayed out, and his hands by his side. Under the cross of Calvary, he'd been stabbed to death.

Murdered.

Among the twelve rows of pews, the twelve windows, and the eyes of God, we waited. I didn't know how long he'd been dead, but it couldn't have been long. The process of decomposition had not yet distorted his features, though his corpse's odor was on the cusp of ripe.

A dapple of light crept across the floor.

I pondered the late Lucian DeBerry, the man of God who would deliver a needed righteousness to the land God had so joyously given. I knew this because he'd told me. I looked up at the savior fixed upon the weathered cross above him, then back at Lucian. Soon he would less resemble himself than a figure from nightmares: bloated, black, and a feast for maggots.

The Oklahoma dust danced in the filtered light.

Outside I could hear the faints chirps of birds flitting this way and that, oblivious to the two of us. I thought that fitting. Only a week ago, the two of us had been arguing over the nature of God, of belief. He was, as I expected, charming, talkative, and thoroughly engaged in turning me to his way of thinking. I found the personal touches, the use of my name, and the deep interest in my physical and spiritual well-being, affecting. I wasn't buying, but I enjoyed the spiel. I could see how those lost or looking would find comfort in his words.

He was, he assured me, God's messenger.

I rose from the pew.

Lucian looked smaller now that the light was gone from his eyes. The dark clothes, caked with blood, clutched at his thin frame. I noticed his shoes were untied. Images of James and Boyer filled my head. All dead.

All killed with knives.

My stomach continued roiling with whatever bile it contained. I'd have to think of something else.

The beach, I should be at the beach.

I left the dead man.

On the porch of the decaying church, I found a box to sit on. Lucian was on his own. I didn't need any more flashbacks of bloody murder.

The sky was bright and high as the horizon stretched far beyond the edge of the plateau upon which the church had been built all those years ago.

When would the girls be back?

How many more would die?

I had to think of something else!

2

It was a glorious summer day, and I was right where I wanted to be. The lawn chair comfortably cradled me as I sat in front of my little bungalow. Shaded by the palms and Jacaranda trees, I nursed a glass of iced tea and thought how my simple life over the last six months had changed.

Life was good!

For the first time, in a long time, I had enough money, love, and affection, that they no longer led me by the nose, or other body parts, into foolishness. I still did the occasional errand for Aeschylus and Associates, but no more sleuthing, and there was enough work here at the bungalows to keep me busy. Though, in truth, I spent more time at Agnes' house. As for love, between Agnes and Judith, I had more than I needed. Still, it was nice to have some time to myself. It was the perfect day to do nothing; the perfect aspiration for a nobody like me.

"Well, look who's making an appearance, Monk Buttman."

"Joanie, my one and only." She was standing over me, my one-time lover; the woman I longed for before Agnes stole my heart.

"I have a hard time believing that with all the women you've been running around with lately." A beautiful smile graced her lovely face though she looked unusually thin. "And as usual, there's no chair for a lady."

"Au contraire, my lovely." I got up and retrieved a second yard sale lawn chair from inside my front door. Like the one I was sitting in, it had seen its share of miles and butts, depending on how you looked at it, but it was still sturdy. "I have one right here for you. You can't say Monk Buttman doesn't know how to treat a lady."

"No, you definitely can't say that." She sat down.

Even though our so-called romance ended a while ago, I often felt the same ache and realized how much I missed her. With my living with Agnes and her relationship with Mikal in full swing, we didn't see each other very often.

"What's on your mind, and while I'm up, can I get you something to drink, although now that I think of it, I don't have a whole lot here, sorry. Tea?" I pointed to the glass by my chair.

"That's fine. It's probably too early to start drinking heavily."

"Probably and all I have on that front is whiskey which I know you don't care for."

"It's nice to know you haven't completely forgotten my likes and dislikes."

"I don't think that's possible." I left her long enough to find a clean glass, ice, and tea.

She was lost in thought when I returned. I sat down and watched her as she took a drink and ran her finger along the rim of the glass. "You even have ice this time! I feel so special," she said, after a minute or so.

"Like I said, my one and only. What's up?"

"It's nothing, I just have a lot of things on my mind right now."

Isn't that a contradiction?"

Joanie turned to me. Dark circles held her eyes. "I suppose. How's Agnes? I assume you're still with her or have you moved on to the rich woman?"

"Agnes is as happy as a clam," I assured her, and why not? I keep her house clean, I reorganized her closets and storage; I cooked for the woman, although she likes to help a little more these days, and for the last two weeks I'd been fixing up her house. "As for Judith, she's in Michigan. Her father's sick, so she's staying with him for the summer."

Joanie didn't really care for either of them.

I met Agnes and Judith on the same day; the same day I witnessed Desiree Marshan kill Todd Boyer. Happenstance or good fortune landed me in both their beds and to my delight, I was still on good terms with both. Agnes was the more stable relationship of the two, while Judith was more of a sometime thing. I knew at some point I'd have to give up Judith, either when she tired of me, or when Agnes pitched a fit and demanded I choose between the two of them. Until that time, I promised myself not to think too hard about it. Flawed reasoning, perhaps, but it allowed me to sleep at night.

"It still surprises me that Agnes lets you screw around with the rich woman, but what do I know?" She said mostly to goad me.

I thought Joanie would like Agnes, but whenever I tried to get us together with her and Mikal, she hemmed and hawed, so I stopped bringing it up. Plus, I knew Agnes felt far more threatened by Joanie than Judith. Agnes knew I'd been in love with Joanie and worried I might be tempted back. Joanie disapproved of my relationship with Judith and believed Agnes should be more vitriolic in *her* disapproval. Neither understood the bond I had with Judith, one that formed during the mess with Judith's now legally separated husband, Martin, and in some ways neither did I, but Judith was fun, incredibly beautiful, and if she occasionally wanted my company, I wasn't going to say no.

I shook my head as Joanie stared at me. "Yes, and since we've beaten that horse to death, why don't you tell me what's wrong? You look exhausted, you're too thin, and that's saying something for a town that prizes skinny women."

Joanie leaned back in her chair and sighed. "I'm worried... about everything. That's what's wrong. I don't know what's going on with Mikal, my singing career is going nowhere, I have no money, and I have this terrible feeling I'll have to move soon."

"That's quite a list. I thought you and Mikal were doing good. He's been around a lot, and I heard he's even living with you. That's not working?"

Mikal was supposed to be the man Joanie had spent a lifetime looking for. He was good looking, a musician and arranger who was always working, as far as I knew, and would take care of all of Joanie's past problems with men. I wasn't surprised when she hit the wall with him, that seemed to happen with every man she'd ever met, including yours truly, but I kept that to myself.

"It's working ok, it's just not what I expected, that's all. He does live with me, when he's in town, but he comes and goes all the time. I thought he made more money, but a lot of the projects he's passionate about pay little and he says there are more than enough hacks in this business to do all the boring crap he has no interest in, even if it pays better." She took a drink. "I don't mind him living with me. Actually, I kind of like it, but the place is too small for the two of us, and it's not like I can afford a bigger place... And if I have to be honest, with the singing gigs I have or don't have, without Mikal's help, I couldn't afford where I live now. I don't want to move, but with Bennie being sick and Ardis leaving, I don't see how I can stay. I'm not paying much as it is, and technically, this place is supposed to be for seniors. Who knows what the next owners or managers are going to want." She glowered at me.

"What?"

"You don't have to worry if you get the boot you just have to make nice with Agnes. Maybe that's when she'll lower the boom on you fucking the rich woman."

I grimaced at that. "Yeah, I heard Bennie was sick. Ardis says they have him in hospice care. It's too bad. Bennie was a funny guy to be around. She said she expects to move down to San Diego to live with her daughter after

Bennie passes away." Benjamin and Ardis Madison had owned this place forever and in their later years operated it as a home for seniors with limited incomes, so the majority of the bungalows had to be rented to seniors. "I'll ignore the jab at Judith."

"You spoke to Ardis?" She seemed surprised that I would. "Really? Maybe that explains the odd remark she made to me a few days ago when I talked to her about this."

"What remark was that?"

"She said I should, and I quote, talk to that nice Mr. Buttman." Joanie tightened her eyes as she looked at me, "So what about it, nice Mr. Buttman?"

"Well, if you must know—"

"Yeah?" She was glaring at me.

"No, interrupting!" I took a moment for some phony umbrage. "Anyway, while you and Mikal were in San Francisco, I was doing a few things for Ardis, and we had a chat. She was wondering who would take over after she left and I agreed it was a concern. Not everybody wants to do this sort of thing, and she didn't want some overly officious tightwad running the place. You really need someone who likes and understands what it takes to work and deal with seniors. You know they can be difficult sometimes, set in their ways—"

"Monk, get to the point!" Not only did she shout at me, but also smacked my arm.

"Wow! You know you don't have to be such a grump!" I rubbed my arm for effect.

"Monk!" She raised her arm, ready to smack me again.

"All right…what was I saying? Oh, yeah. I suggested that maybe *you* might be interested. You already know everybody here. You could move into Ardis' bungalow, which would give you more room, the rent is part of the package so it wouldn't be an issue, plus there's a reasonable stipend. I thought, given your circumstances, it might be a good fit."

"Really?"

"Yeah, really."

She had a rather disbelieving expression on her face. "Why didn't she say all this when I talked to her?"

"I don't know; why does the sun rise in the East?"

"That doesn't answer the question," she said, her eyes looking past me. The wheels were spinning. "Do you think she'd go for that?"

"I think she would." Joanie finished her tea. "Feeling better?"

A light smile found her beautiful face as some of the worry disappeared. "Maybe."

"As for Mikal, if he makes you happy then maybe all those foolish dreams you've been carting around need to be put away. It's ok to enjoy what you have."

"Maybe. Thanks, Monk, I appreciate it." She got up and put the chair back inside the bungalow. I gave her a hug and watched as she motored over to her little oasis here at the Moonlight Arms, a name I never understood.

"Anytime," I said to myself. With that, I returned to my chair and my tea.

My reverie was short-lived.

My new phone, the one that replaced the perfectly functional one Agnes and the promoter Mr. Jones had given me, began its endless chirping. Reluctantly, I pulled it out of my pocket and pressed my finger to the icon on the screen. My splendid isolation from these invasive inventions had been taken from me by all the bisecting interests of business, family, and crazy girlfriends who felt the urgent need to keep tabs on me. Bedazzled by regular sex, I caved and was now unhappily tethered to this miserable device. I still didn't like that I was now so easily monitored by God knows who.

"This is Monk."

"Dad, is that you?" The voice on the other end sounded just like my daughter.

"Becky?"

"Yes, it's me." My daughter was calling me. "Can I ask you something?"

I had an odd feeling of unease. "Sure." I tried to remember the last time my daughter wanted something from me. Our relationship, such as it was, tended to meander between indifference and uncomfortable silence with the occasional stop at possible reconciliation, which never quite worked.

"Mom told me you were coming out this summer; are you?"

"I was thinking about it." That's about as far as I had taken it. I was forever making plans to see people I never actually got around to seeing. It was enough that Agnes kept dragging me to the old man's farm. "Will you be there?"

"That's why I called. I don't know. Farrell wants to join this new religious community he's found, and I wanted to talk to you about it. I..." In the background, there was a voice she responded to. "I'm on the phone, can't it wait?" I couldn't tell if it was the voice of someone I knew. "I don't need you pressuring me about this..." The voice I couldn't quite make out was saying something. "Dad, can I call you back in a few minutes?"

"Sure."

The line went dead.

Rebekah, my only child, my only real link to a distant past only eight years gone, was calling me for advice, or what I assumed was advice.

Me!

I spent the better part of the afternoon processing that thought. To say our relationship was fraught was, in itself, problematic, mainly because we never really had a relationship to begin with. The problem was of my own making. Angry at being exiled from my cushy life as a punk teenager after James was killed, ashamed of being a coward for running as he lay dying, and then being confined and constrained by the orthodoxy of my mother's conservatism that pressured me to be a responsible member of society, I took my disenchantment out on Astral and Rebekah by yelling at them, ignoring them, or by burying myself in the details of farming which I didn't even care for.

Rebekah returned the favor by whining at me when she wasn't ignoring me. Badgered by an exasperated Astral, we would play nice for a time until she felt better and then return to our petty ways. By the time I'd left, after being dumped by Astral for the preening Judah, Rebekah had run off and married Farrell Jenkins. In the intervening eight years, we saw little of each other. Only once did we spend any substantive amount of time together, that being when she came out for the gathering at the farm. I'd promised to go but vacillated until it was too late.

I am, at times, a petty man.

Rebekah came down to see me, and we talked for the first time in a long time. As usual, I promised to come out to see her but never did. Like the farm, I found the thought of going back to Virginia pointless and made excuses so I wouldn't feel too bad when I didn't. Now that I think of it, she probably didn't believe me anyway. It was just polite small talk. Of course, by then she was a grown woman with her own problems, chief among them her inability to get pregnant.

Farrell had dismissed her idea of seeing a medical specialist insisting that God would take care of them. I considered Farrell to be a moron, but she believed deeply in the sanctity of marriage and meant to see the hard times through with patience and love and the good graces of God. I found this perplexing, but having been a party to the religious indoctrination of her formative years, I did my best not to be too big of a hypocrite in my concern.

Besides, I knew she wouldn't buy my side of the argument.

I waited, but she didn't call back. In a moment of weakness, I called her, but the line was busy. With the afternoon sun beating down, I gave up on my chair and tea, locked up my quiet little bungalow and joined the teeming masses populating the interstate system on my way back to Agnes.

• • • • •

The door to JD Financial, where Agnes worked, was locked. I was late. With that in mind, I went next door to Johnny D.'s and made my way to the bar for a drink. Rey, the octogenarian bartender, nodded to me and poured a glass of whiskey over ice. On the TV, providing the only illumination in the place, was a game, show from what looked like the Seventies. Rey put the drink in front of me.

"Thanks, Rey."

"No problem, Monk. Agnes is with Johnny, she should be out momentarily," he said with no expression whatsoever.

Together we watched as Charles Nelson Reilly and a middle-aged woman played the $25,000 pyramid. I don't think Rey had any interest in what was on. In the many times, I'd come in, waiting for Agnes or having nothing better to do, I could discern no evident pattern in what Rey would watch. One moment it was animals, another moment might be sports, and in yet another soap operas. I don't know that he even watched them. They were just there, mute fluttering images of an imagined world. Maybe at his age, it was enough. I became engrossed in the program, although I don't know why, and didn't see Agnes come out of Johnny's office.

"There's my ray of Sunshine," she bellowed.

We both turned. Rey flashed a smile at Agnes while I shook my head. "You know I don't like you calling me that," I whined.

She wrapped her arms around me. "Tough! It's who you are." She then planted a big kiss on me, and I returned the favor. I don't think Rey cared or noticed. "Sorry, I'm late, but I had some things to go over with Johnny before we take off tomorrow."

"Tomorrow? Where are we going?"

Agnes looked at me, bemused. "We're going to the farm this weekend. You know that!"

"I thought that was next week," I had no interest in going to my father's commune.

"It's not, and you know it's not, so stop the phony surprise. Are we eating here?"

"No, I have some cod marinating back at the house. It's good for you."

"So is seeing your family. Now we can both be miserable together. Finish your drink and let's go."

Rey smiled from across the bar. I didn't care for the smile.

"I need your help here, Rey!"

"Have a good trip," he said. Evidently Rey wasn't going to save me. With no other excuses available, I escorted my significant other to the car and took her home.

3

Agnes' house, or as she continually corrected me, our house, sat nestled halfway down the block between two new larger, more upscale homes. The small blue and white ranch with the carport and the Acacia out front welcomed us. Though I didn't say so out loud, I liked the place now that I'd made a few changes, such as making room for my things, and setting up the kitchen. Agnes said I could do whatever I wanted, so I did, unless it came to cooking. She was oddly conflicted about helping me cook. Sometimes she would, other times she would do her best to weasel out of it. This stood in stark contrast to our trips up north where she couldn't spend enough time with Meredith in the communal kitchen. She was proud of her accomplishments there, but rather nonchalant about applying those skills here.

Cook?

That was my job. Not that I minded, but I still felt the need to quarrel about it occasionally. "Why don't you take a turn with the fish tonight?"

"You know I like it better when you cook."

"Yes, but I think it's unhealthy for you to be so reliant on my taking care of your nutritional needs. Given your recent sessions with Meredith, I believe you're ready just unwilling."

She pulled up next to me, making sure I had a close-up view of her delightful breasts. "It's not that I'm unwilling, certainly when it comes to some things…" she said while unbuttoning the top buttons of my shirt and running her finger along the hairs on my chest. "I'm more than willing, if you know what I mean?"

"Really? Like what?" I knew exactly where she was taking this.

"Oh, I think you know what I mean…" Her hand continued towards my navel.

"So, essentially you're trading sexual favors for the domestic chores you would rather I do?"

"Essentially."

"I don't know that that's the best path morally or ethically."

She turned to me with a faux frown. "Are you saying you'd prefer to have me cook now rather than pleasure you?"

I returned the phony frown. "I didn't know they were mutually exclusive."

"Let's just say if I have to cook, I may be too tired later to provide you with the level of sexual satisfaction you're used to."

"I'll risk it," I said. At this point, we began lightly kissing each other. Her hand had found its favorite spot as had mine.

"How long does it take to cook the fish?"

I was losing my focus on the fish and the argument. "Um, about fifteen minutes."

"How about an appetizer?"

I have a fondness for appetizers. We adjourned to the couch.

After the appetizer, I gave up on the argument and got back to the fish. Agnes, all smiles, sat at the table and watched. Her bra in one hand, she brushed the hair out of her face with the other as I milled about the kitchen.

"You know I may not always fall for the appetizer ploy," I teased.

"I'll risk it." Now she was stealing my best lines.

We sat on the back patio enjoying the Cod and asparagus while shaded by the neighbor's tree. The house was situated such that the afternoon sun beat down on the front of the house, leaving the backyard a more hospitable place to spend a languid evening. Using some of the ill-gotten money I'd received from the Marshan affair, I had the yard xeriscaped for a numbers of reasons: water savings, being hip to new trends, and, most importantly, because I had no interest in dealing with a lawn. I'm lazy that way.

While admiring the solution to my vexation over the lawn, I could see Agnes staring at me. For a time, I was mildly alarmed by her affections, but figured there were worse things in life than being loved. Before these recent developments, I'd assumed that I would be on my own for the rest of my life. After Astral kicked me out and Joanie's infatuation waned, not a whole lot happened other than the occasional date. If I drank too much, I would fall into a fitful stupor imagining the pleasantries of having an actual girlfriend.

Now it was no longer a drunk's idle dream. I felt both perfectly at ease and deeply concerned while sitting on patio furniture as the sun made its graceful exit off to the west. I looked over at her. She was still staring at me. Maybe I *was* the best thing to happen to her!

Sounded like a lot of responsibility.

So, whenever she would make these grand statements, I assumed she was talking about someone else. No, she insisted, it was me, Monk Buttman, once known as Sunshine, so named when my freak parents were high on God knows what. The more disconcerting part was that maybe she was the best thing to happen to me. A part of me didn't like that; too much to lose if it fell apart. I didn't have the heart for that.

It's probably not a good thing to lie to yourself. "What's on your mind, beautiful?" I asked.

"You."

I rolled my eyes. "You'll get over it." I kept repeating this...

"Yeah, you keep saying that, but it's been more than six months and I still love you, and we're still happy together, so you're going to have to come up with something else, Sunshine."

...To no effect.

"Please don't call me that!"

A big grin covered her beautiful face. "Not going to happen."

Some things you never live down. "I got a call from my daughter today, right out of the blue, I said to change the subject."

Agnes leaned towards me. All she knew about my daughter was her name. I didn't talk about her much, and Agnes had never met her. At least I'd met Agnes' daughter, Anna.

"Rebekah?"

"Yeah, she wanted to talk to me about what she should do, something about Farrell, that's her idiot husband, wanting to move."

"What did you tell her?" Agnes moved closer as if I were about to impart some serious and important information.

"I didn't get the chance. Someone interrupted her, and she said she'd call back, but never did."

"Did you call her back?"

"A couple of times, but the line was busy. I don't quite know what to do now. She asked if I was coming out. She said her mother told her I was, but how would Astral know? I haven't spoken to her in years."

Agnes pondered this along with me. She also had an unnatural interest in what my former wife thought and did. Anytime I mentioned Astral, her interest in what I was saying picked right up. "Maybe she heard it from Moses. You did mention sort of wanting to go out there after he brought it up the last time we were there."

"Did I?"

"Pretty sure."

"Maybe. I guess we'll find out. Speaking of which, are we ready for our trip tomorrow?"

"We're all packed. Other than the food part, which is your responsibility, we're ready to go."

All ready to go. Damn!

. . . . .

After avoiding the place for twenty-eight years, not counting the two hours I spent there after I left Virginia, I was heading back for the fifth time in six months. Agnes loved the farm and more or less set the schedule while dragging me along in her wake. We had developed a pattern each time we went. We'd leave on a Thursday morning and return the following Monday. Unless we were in a hurry, we always went up on the coast highway and came back on the interstate.

One day or evening, depending on how busy they were, was spent with Agnes' daughter, Anna, her father, Simon, and his partner, Eric. In some ways, I found this part of our journey more interesting and more fun. Maybe fun isn't the right word. For me, the good was hanging out with Eric, but there were issues between Agnes, Simon, and Anna. The not so good came from the bad blood that had developed between them due to Simon's lying about his relationship with Eric, and Agnes' abusive relationship with an ex-boyfriend, Jordan, and the mental and physical damage he'd done to both Agnes and Anna.

Agnes desperately wanted to reconnect with Anna, but the dark shadow of Jordan made their time together difficult. Anna no longer trusted her mother or felt safe around her. Agnes was often childish and petulant when we were with Anna and Simon, which didn't help. Eric and I did what we could to keep the mood reasonably positive. Much as she wanted everything to work out with Anna on these trips, I knew Agnes preferred to be at the farm rather than here where she felt buried by the past. She loved the farm and the people there, and needed that to help heal the part of her that was so self-loathing, but Anna, and Agnes' problems with her weren't going away. Hiding at the farm wasn't the answer.

Enter Monk Buttman: go-between.

Somehow it was my responsibility to make everything work.

Agnes accepted this, sort of, but whined that Anna was more interested in me, at least in the short term. "You know, she spends more time with you than she does with me, her mother."

"I hadn't noticed." I tried not to roll my eyes as we fell again into this topic. "Like I told you before, she needs to know if she'll be safe around me; if she can trust me. So, she takes me to those places, like the restaurant, where she feels safe to make sure I'm an ok guy and that your choices in who you shack up with aren't a threat to her. If you really want her to come and visit, then she has to believe, truly believe, that I'm not like Jordan, that I pose no threat to her, or to you for that matter."

"Yes, you've told me that every time we've come up here."

"That's because you've complained every time we've come up here."

"You're a jerk, Buttman."

"Yes I am."

We hit our favorite stop along the coast for lunch; a place called Durocher's, and then motored into the bay area. As usual, we stayed at the same hotel just down the street from Simon and Eric's restaurant. It didn't matter that twice she'd had a breakdown at the place or that one of those ended with her being escorted out by the fuzz. No, we stayed here because it's where I told her we were ok; that her past wouldn't send me running, that I loved her all the same. That and we got a great price on the room.

It was also where I found the two dead guys in the alley, but that's another story.

The attractive young woman at the desk remembered us and had us shown to our room, the same room as all the times before. Agnes sat on the edge of the bed, lost in thought. I sat in the chair, glad to be off the road and out of the car.

"Do you think I'll ever have a normal relationship with Anna?" She looked tired.

"Depends on what you think normal is, but I believe that the two of you will one day find a place where neither of you is too weighed down by the past."

"That sounds nice, but it's been years since we had anything like that and each time we come up here, it never seems to change. She is always distant, always at arm's length. I want to be positive, Monk, I really do, but sometimes I feel like it's gone, like it's something I'll never have again."

I got out of the chair and had her lay back on the bed with me. We weren't expected at the restaurant for another hour or so.

"Sorry beautiful, but life doesn't always go the way you want it to. Remember what I told you the first time we came up here, that it would take time, a lot of time?" I kissed her forehead and tucked her under my arm. "I think you need to let go of the idea that this has to happen one way or another.

The ugly truth is it doesn't. That doesn't mean you quit or give up, but you need to re-think the process."

She put her arms around me, "And what does that even mean?"

"It means it's okay to be the same woman you are with me or Johnny or MaryAnn. Be the woman you are when you spend the day in the kitchen with Meredith. Just be Agnes, beautiful, wonderful Agnes. Be glad for the time you have with Anna, but don't make it a project or act like a child to make her like you again. Nobody wants to be someone else's agenda."

"You know I don't want to be a bore."

"Then don't be. Laugh once in a while. Forgive Simon and let go of whatever you thought he should be, because that's not who he is. He won't loosen up until you do." I could feel her body stiffen. Any mention of Simon caused her to tighten up.

"You've got this all figured out, don't you?"

"Absolutely, if there's one thing I know it's how to fix other people's problems."

"And your problems? Like with Rebekah or Astral?" She had to bring that up.

"I don't have a fucking clue. I'm as messed as you are."

She laughed. "That's not exactly reassuring."

"Except in this instance, you know I'm right."

She snuggled in closer and gave me a big squeeze. "It's possible."

I squeezed back, "That's better than *im*possible," I looked at the clock by the bed. "We have time for a quick nap, and then we'll head over. What do you say?"

"I love you, Sunshine."

"I love you, beautiful."

. . . . .

The San Francisco air, as is its wont, was both refreshing and bracing, nothing like the shimmering heat of LA. One of our acquired habits was walking from the hotel to the restaurant. We did this to avoid the misery of trying to find parking. Besides, it was only eight blocks, and walking is supposed to be good for you. It also came with the added benefit of allowing Agnes the time to get her act together before jostling with her ex and daughter. For whatever reason, she seemed more festive with a lighter step and kept up rather than pulling me back, complaining that my pace was too much for the shoes she had on.

She even entered before me as I opened the door.

"Monk, our man of sartorial splendor." Eric, Simon's partner and the happy face of Anna Barron's, their restaurant named after Simon and Agnes' kids, was there to greet us as we came in.

"Eric, you are, as always, dressed to the nines. How's life?"

Eric reached out and gave me a big hug. "Couldn't be better." He turned to Agnes. "Agnes, you look radiant tonight. I can tell Monk agrees with you."

Agnes came over and surprised Eric with a hug and a smile. "He certainly does. It's good to see you. How's business? Looks like a nice crowd for a Thursday."

"It's been good, even a little better than we had hoped. We've had good reviews, both in the paper and on social media. Simon's still ever vigilant, but I think it's going well. We have your table all prepared. May I get you a beverage perhaps?"

"You know it. It's a thirsty drive from LA," I said with a parched voice.

"The usual?" We slid into the circular booth not far from the entrance to the kitchen.

"That would be wonderful, Eric. Thanks again for having us." Agnes took his hand for a moment. He was, I think, shocked by her solicitude. In our previous visits, Agnes was always quiet and reserved towards Eric.

"Excellent, I'll let Anna and Simon know you're here." Eric headed off towards the bar, turning occasionally to make sure it was actually Agnes he'd been talking to.

I looked over at Agnes. "See, it's not so bad."

Agnes smirked. "Nobody likes a know-it-all, Sunshine."

I smirked back, "I'll risk it."

Occasionally, I hit the nail on the head. It doesn't happen often enough that I'm ready to write a book, but this time it was as if I knew what I was talking about. Agnes, surprisingly, took my advice and was more like the Agnes I knew than the unhappy nervous Agnes of our previous visits. She joined in the conversations when Simon and Anna came out to see us, she joked with Eric, she even good-naturedly ribbed Simon for being such a fussbudget in the kitchen.

"I know you two won't believe this," she said to Anna and Simon, "but I've learned quite a bit about cooking lately, haven't I, Monk."

"It's true. She's learning from Meredith on our trips to the farm. Not that she helps at home, but her biscuits and muffins are very good."

Agnes shook her head, "I don't help because, like Simon, you're too picky about stuff. Meredith is more generous than you two."

Simon laughed. "Some things never change, do they, Aggie."

We all laughed at that. Well, maybe not Agnes, who hated being called Aggie, but she let it slide. It was then that the sun came out for my beloved when Anna and Simon asked her if she'd like to join them in the kitchen for a while. It was the first time, in their company I saw that big beautiful smile.

"I'd love to," she enthused and off they went leaving Eric and me with our drinks. I sat back and took a long slow sip of my whiskey. Eric was still trying to sort out what had just happened.

"What did you slip into Agnes' drink?"

"Eric, I'm not that kind of guy. But if you must know, I asked her to just be herself, have some fun and laugh a little. I'm as shocked as you are that she listened."

Eric nodded. "It makes a big difference." He took a drink of water and then slid closer towards me. "Can you keep a secret?"

"Depends on the payoff. What's up?" I could tell something important was brewing, Eric had that twinkle in his eyes.

"Simon and I are getting married."

"That's great, but why the secret? Agnes?" I figured that had to be it even if technically Agnes had no say.

"Believe it or not, Simon is very sensitive to how our getting married would affect her. Given their history together, and the hard times lately, that's not surprising. We would like her to be on board with it even though I guess we don't need her to be. We've put off saying anything because she's been kind of, I don't know, gloomy when we see her, but I don't want to wait forever, and now I wonder if this is a good time or a bad time to say anything."

I thought about it. "Well, I don't believe what Agnes thinks should matter, it's your life, your relationship. I understand why you might be concerned, but I wouldn't put it off because of Agnes. She'll just have to come to terms with it. You realize if you do, this puts me on the hot seat," I said with a grave face.

I could tell he was amused by this, "Really? In what way?"

"Because then she'll want to get married."

"And that's a problem?" He was laughing at me.

"Well, no, but I don't want Agnes to know that. I'd never hear the end of it."

That got him laughing more. "You two are quite the pair."

"Thanks. Do you want me to grease the rails in anticipation of the announcement?"

"I might."

With that we tapped our glasses together in a toast. The others returned just in time to see this. Eric and I started laughing, and he then begged off claiming he needed to check the room. I played dumb just in case they asked what we were up to. Instead, Agnes went on about how much she enjoyed her tour of the kitchen and how maybe cooking wasn't so tough after all. Simon rolled his eyes while Anna stifled a grin. It was nice to have the evening be a light-hearted affair for once.

After Agnes sat down next to me, Simon spoke up. "We would like the two of you to join us for a little get together we're having at the house on Monday. I don't know what your schedule is, but if you can make it..."

I was watching Anna while he was speaking to gage her reaction. She kept a straight face, but I could tell she was in on it. Agnes looked at me for some reason, like I was the decider.

"It's ok with me. Agnes, do you want to go? You'd probably have to give Johnny a head's up since we'd be a day late."

Her eyes grew big for a moment, "I'd like that, Simon, I'd like that very much. Thank you," she said as she turned to him.

"Wonderful. Party starts at two with dinner at six." He motioned that he had to get back to the kitchen, and off he went.

"Anna, should I ask what's going on?" Agnes raised her eyebrows.

"You'll just have to wait and find out." Anna was beaming as she played it coy.

Agnes turned to me. I couldn't hide my smile. "You're in on this too, aren't you, Buttman?" I could feel her hand on my leg.

I pretended to be shocked. "I don't know what you're talking about." I winked at Anna, "Well, look at the time, we need to get going, beautiful."

"Uh-huh." Agnes narrowed her eyes.

We said our goodbyes to Anna and Eric, both of whom hugged Agnes and me. We promised to see them on Monday and wandered down the street towards the hotel. It was still relatively early, and the street was busy with the young and the restless. Agnes held my hand as we walked. The air from the breeze weaving in and around the buildings was neither too warm nor too cold. I didn't look to see if anyone was following us. The room was nice and quiet as we came in and got ready for bed. Agnes was oddly quiet, not the sad quiet that defined these visits, but a contented quiet. Once in bed, she tucked herself in next to me and kissed me goodnight.

I turned out the light.

"Simon and Eric are getting married, aren't they?" Agnes burrowed in next to me.

"I don't know what you're talking about."

"Sure." Agnes let the note ring through the room. "You know that means you and I can get married too."

"I don't know what you're talking about."

"We'll see."

I knew she was smiling, even though the lights were off.

4

It's said you should never mess up a good thing. I stupidly ignored that. It wasn't Eric's secret; I kept my mouth shut even though Agnes had guessed right. It wasn't Agnes' follow-up play for matrimony; I was ready for that. I'd rope-a-dope her just to see how worked up I could make her. I figured I was good for six months at least. Nor was it the impending weekend doing Emily's bidding; I already knew about that thanks to her mother's texts outlining everything Emily wanted to accomplish with my help in her garden at the farm. For reasons unknown, Emily had latched her eleven-year-old fingers onto me, and she wasn't letting go. I suppose it beats working in the kitchen. That was Agnes' thing.

No. It wasn't any of those.

It was that dickhead, Farrell. I probably should be more charitable towards him. There must be something admirable about him I don't see. I refuse to believe Rebekah married him and exiled herself to a life of misery just to get at her mother and me. Astral and I pulled the same stunt when we were teenagers, so there's that whole apple falling from the tree thing. I wouldn't have thought of it at all except I remembered Rebekah's call and impulsively called her number.

"Yes?" The man answering the phone wasn't Rebekah.

"I'd like to speak to Becky, this is her father."

The weasel let the line hum. "She isn't here right now."

"Just give her the phone, Farrell."

"I don't want you corrupting my wife. Good day."

And with that, he hung up, or whatever it's called when you end a call on these new touchscreen phones. Agnes heard me swear, "Goddamned little prick!"

"What's wrong?"

"It's just that..." I changed my mind about railing at her about Farrell, that goddamned little prick. "I tried calling Rebekah, that's all."

"You called your daughter a goddamned little prick?"

"No, just her idiot husband. Are we ready to go?" Agnes came over and put her arms around me.

"Yes, we can spend the time talking about the wedding."

"Yeah, no."

She laughed. "You can't win, Buttman, you know that."

So maybe six month's is a stretch.

• • • • •

The gang was there waiting for us: Moses, Meredith, Emily, and her mother, Calista, resplendent in their woodsy farming finery. Long gone was the flowing hair, at least for Moses, the muslin and gingham clothing evoking a nineteenth-century aesthetic that saturated my memory. Plausibly, nothing I remembered actually occurred. I spent so many years bound and determined to eliminate all traces of that time, that what I now think I remember could be a kind of projected history, one that sits well with how I thought it should be rather than what it was. I don't know how important that is. I remember reading once that memory is, in fact, fluid and polymorphous.

Whatever my memory, they seemed happy to see Agnes and me, though Emily was more reserved towards Agnes. She and her mother had joined the farm a few years before, after Calista's relationship with Emily's father ended. That's all I knew; that and the fact that Emily had an odd attachment to me. Maybe it was because all the other men of my approximate age at the farm already had kids, and Emily felt left out, or I was easy to boss around; either worked to my mind. I tried not to think about it too much, otherwise, my sad-assed relationship with Rebekah would begin to haunt me. I didn't need that.

After the obligatory hugs, Emily took my hand and led me to our room in the house where Moses and Meredith lived. The others followed behind content with their own conversations distinct from mine and Emily's. Emily loved her herb garden, and I was her helper. Together we planted, weeded, and harvested the herbs she carefully mothered. This weekend would be much the same.

"I like that we get to use the herbs in the kitchen. My mom says it's important to grow your own food, and that's what we do here, don't we, Mr. Sunshine?" There was that name again. At least Emily prefaced it with mister.

"Yes, it is."

With the bags safely ensconced in our room, we split up into smaller groups with Agnes and Meredith heading off to the large communal kitchen, while Calista and Moses stayed with Emily and me until we left the dining room. At that point, they headed off to the vineyards and Emily, and I went to her garden.

It was, as always, well cared for. She pointed out the varieties though I already knew, probably to make sure I was paying attention. They start early, don't they? The thyme and cilantro mixed easily with the basil and the rosemary. On the way I grabbed the box I kept by the shed so I could sit and watch as she worked her way around the garden. Emily was tall and lanky with thick, auburn hair. There was some of her mother in her face, but more of what I assumed was her father. She had big brown eyes that either shown in her enthusiasm or darkened when you didn't follow her instructions. In her eyes was her mother in all *her* glory. Calista struck me as being wound a little too tight. I occasionally teased Emily by acting like I didn't know what I was doing or purposely did it differently. We'd been at this long enough that she had caught on that I was a bit of a jerk.

She had a phrase for those times: "This is serious business, *Mr. Sunshine*!" She refused to call me Monk.

Having assured herself that no mischief had come to the garden since her last visit, she plopped herself on the corner of the wood planks that framed the garden closest to the man on the box.

"I think our garden looks pretty good, don't you?"

"I do, Emily. I think you've done a marvelous job."

"Thanks, Mr. Sunshine." Her eyes were shining. It was at these moments I wondered if this wasn't some kind of cosmic do over as penance for the poor way I treated Rebekah when she was that age. All those years hiding in the fields being more concerned with yields and soil content than the heart of my only child. I pulled out my phone and called, but no one answered.

Emily was watching. "Who are you calling?"

"My daughter, Rebekah, but she didn't answer."

Emily could see my disappointment. "Do you miss her?"

I smiled. "Yes. Do you miss your father?" All I knew about Emily's father is that he lived, or used to live, in Philadelphia.

"Sometimes. I have to go see him pretty soon." Her eyes had darkened.

"Isn't that a good thing?"

"He has other kids, and I don't like leaving my garden." She reached out and caressed the thyme leaves. "My mom worries I won't come back, but she says I have to go because the courts say so."

"I see. Does he live in the city?"

"He used to, but not anymore. I don't like it very much. I have to share a room with Abby; she's only six. I like having my own room."

"Yeah, I know how that is."

The dinner bell was ringing. It was time to join the others.

Communal meals at the farm are their own kind of affair, a kind I don't particularly like. I didn't mind all the people or all the interweaving conversations, unless they coalesced around me and what I was up to, which lately they often did. For whatever reason, I was fascinating to them. Maybe because I was Moses' eldest son and had been away for twenty-eight years; I lived in that cesspool known as LA; I used to be a farmer, but not anymore, or maybe it was the whispers about why I left in the first place: James and his ghost forever haunting me on that lonely dirt road. None of those things were remotely interesting to me. Agnes used the meals to impress me with the results of her newfound cooking skills. With the others, I tried to take in all the inquiries with my usual good humor while looking for the quickest way out. But with each successive trip, that was becoming more and more difficult.

After helping clean up the table following dinner, I wandered off to the barn hoping for a little alone time. I was being pulled back into a kind of life I had long given up. Truth be told, I enjoyed being a nobody lost in the miasma of greater Los Angeles. I had a nice, easy, inexpensive existence. I didn't mind the occasional visit to the farm or even the new living arrangements with Agnes, but I'd grown fond of my simple little bungalow, and with each passing day I was there less and less. Every trip to the farm pulled me further into the tussle of communal life, which I had no interest in. I'm not anti-social, at least I don't think I am, but it takes a certain temperament to navigate all the personalities and passions, to handle the pressure it takes to make it work. I'd rather be at the beach with my Panama hat, an ice chest full of cold beers, and my cheap folding chair. It was nice to just watch the waves, the surf bums, and the tourists.

I kept my box at one end of the shed next to the barn. It was a simple wooden box that had once been home to fresh-cut asparagus. Now it was my seat. At the corner of the barn, I set the box down and leaned back. From there, I could look down on the vineyards and the hills beyond. The sun was just behind some high clouds adding a luminous glow to them. A slight breeze was blowing. I closed my eyes to listen to the soft whistle and chirp of the birds. Someone must have sensed my contentment because it didn't last.

It was Moses who found me. He must have thought I was asleep. "It's a better view with your eyes open."

I opened one eye. "I imagine it is."

"The last time I found you here, you were sixteen, and your girlfriend was pregnant."

I opened the other eye. "Yeah, that sounds about right."

He was smiling. It wasn't a *it's good to see you smile*, it was a *I'm glad I'm not you* smile. "You have a visitor. Otherwise I would have left you to your solitude."

"It sounds like I should ask you to say you couldn't find me. Who would be here to visit me?"

"You'll see."

Reluctantly, I got up and put my box back by the shed.

She looked as beautiful as she did the first time I laid eyes on her all those thousands of years ago. I remember her smiling. It was down the road, a mile or so from here. She was walking with her friends when I noticed her looking my way. Somewhat out of character, I stopped and talked to her just long enough to know I wanted to see her again. Impulsively, I asked her out. She was Lisa then; she's Lilith now, but to me, she is, forever and always, Astral.

Moses' smile had changed now that the three of us were together for the first time since that terrible night when he shipped Astral, Rebekah, and me off to Virginia. Like mine, it was bittersweet. The woman I once considered the love of my life was standing in the living room looking at me. Her expression was stiff and anxious and I could tell she was uncomfortable being here.

Astral!

She and I picked that name when she moved to the farm after Rebekah was born. Lisa was the girl disowned by her parents, two people I hadn't spoken to or seen since the day Rebekah was born. They never came to Virginia. When Rebekah was a teenager, they relented, and she and Astral came back to visit. But not me. At that point, it didn't matter; I wouldn't have gone anyway. We chose Astral because I thought she was as beautiful as a star-filled summer's night. Sunshine and Astral: two sides of a perfect day. It all seemed so silly now that I looked into her worried face.

"Astral..."

"Sunshine." A tiny glimpse of a smile arose on her face as she said my name.

Moses interjected as we stood there, lost in the past. "Why don't we sit down?"

I wondered where Agnes was, probably off with Meredith, who no doubt got word from Moses that maybe it would be best if Agnes had other preoccupations rather than what I was up to with my former wife.

I couldn't stop looking at her. Had it really been eight years since I saw her last? My heart began to ache; another reason to stay away and never go back.

Her light brown hair was beginning its inevitable autumn turn with strands of white mingling within. I couldn't tell if she'd lost weight or if it even mattered. She wore a plain cotton dress so there was little clinging to those curves I tried so hard to forget. She rarely wore makeup or did up her hair, preferring to keep it shoulder length and pulled back. Now, though still the same length and still pulled back, she had bangs, which were neatly cropped, just above her eyebrows.

I found a chair and stated the obvious: "Moses tells me you're here to see me."

She sat across from me with Moses next to her on the couch. "As opposed to seeing him or Meredith, correct?" Eight years and she was still baiting me; some things never change.

"Something like that. I'm just surprised that's all, given how we mangled things at the end." I couldn't stop either; explains a lot.

Astral pursed her lips. She did this whenever I made a comment she felt was a bald-faced lie. Probably the "we" part. "We had a nice visit the other day," she said while tilting her head towards Moses. He supported this with his own nod. "But, yes, I wanted to talk to you."

"Well, that explains Becky's comment to me."

"You spoke with Becky?" They both seemed surprised by this. "What did she say?"

"Contrary to popular opinion, I do talk to my daughter every once in a while, and if you must know, she asked if I was coming out to Virginia. Apparently, you told her I would. Since you and I haven't spoken since you kicked me out of the house, I wondered how you would know this, but I can see now that my father is making plans which I haven't decided on."

Moses butted in. "What else do you have going on that you can't visit your daughter?"

"Nothing, but it's still my decision."

Astral became more animated, "What else did she say? It's important, *Monk*!"

Monk? Astral was as disdainful of Monk as I was of *Lilith*.

"I assume you'll explain why, but I only spoke to her for a moment or two. She said Farrell wanted to move, and she was worried about it, but we were interrupted. She said she'd call back, but never did, and when I called all I got was a brush off from that weasel Farrell."

"Are you coming out?" She said this almost pleadingly.

"I don't know."

Honesty, as they say, is a lonely word. Astral sat back, her face softened, and I thought for a moment she might be crying. It was completely disorienting. It was like a bad trip back to that night twenty-eight years ago, the three of us in the same place in the same room.

Rebekah was crying in the corner as I sat there battered and beaten after being thrashed by the Pronto brother's thugs. Astral was crying, Moses was a ball of controlled fury telling us we had to leave, and I was numb; bombarded by images of Miguel and me being forced at gunpoint to kill our friend, James. It was the reason I never wanted to come back here. I couldn't stand re-living it over and over.

"What's going on, Astral?"

She gave me half a smile. "No one calls me that anymore."

I smiled back. "I know. No one calls me Sunshine except my goofy girlfriend and Emily, who's eleven." I looked in her soft blue eyes. "What are you worried about? What's going on with Rebekah and Farrell?"

"I don't know. I haven't been able to talk to her. Farrell's left the church. When I went to their house, he became belligerent and accusatory saying all kinds of terrible things, that we were usurpers, that we were unclean, and he would no longer be part of a bankrupt Christianity."

I had no idea how to respond to that. She and I had argued about religion and faith many times; it was part of what pushed us apart, but whatever my feelings, I couldn't imagine her as unclean or a usurper or anyone, especially Farrell, using that language. "I don't understand, you guys were always pretty tight when it came to God and all that."

"Yes, you always were so sure about how well things were going, but you never really looked. Why do you think I was worried about her marrying him? Do you even remember that?"

"I remember thinking he was a putz..."

"Exactly, which meant nothing because you were off being unhappy." Tears were rolling down her cheeks.

"Yes, I'm familiar with my many shortcomings, but we're getting off track here. Why are *you* worried? Why do you think I can do anything given what you just said? What about Judah?"

She sat there wiping the tears away. "Judah tried to talk to them, but Farrell wouldn't let him in." Moses put his arm around her. I was, remarkably, simultaneously relieved and jealous by his doing that. "I don't know why I think you can help, but you are her father, and she is our daughter no matter how badly the two of us may have messed up." Finally, it was the two of us, not just me. "We were just kids ourselves, you know."

"Yes, I know." The room went quiet. I spied Agnes and Meredith by the front door. I sighed. My freeloading summer had come to a crashing halt. "I can come out. I'll need a few days to get organized, and it'll take a few days for me to drive out."

"I'm afraid for her, Monk." She blurted this out.

"Why?"

She hesitated to say. Meredith waved her hand, and they quickly moved past us towards the pavilion on the other side of the room. Agnes had big eyes as she looked at Astral and me. I raised an eyebrow. Astral was watching. She'd never seen me with anyone else.

After they passed through the door, she asked, "Is that the woman you're with now?"

"Yeah, her name is Agnes. We met about six months ago in LA. You're avoiding the question. Why are you afraid?"

I got the look again, the one I got so used to when she was vexed by my truculent behavior.

"I don't know exactly. I just feel there's something wrong and I'm not being crazy as you used to say." I tried not to look judgmental when she said that, even though that's what I thought. Astral twisted the ring on her finger; the one Judah had given her. "We both know that with Becky, we had our struggles, but for the last few years, I felt that she and I were finally finding some common ground together, that we could talk to one another. It wasn't confrontational all the time, and now she says they're leaving, but they won't say when, or where they're going, and I don't want to lose her."

I still didn't understand, but that could wait. "You have no idea where they might go?"

"I only know that Farrell has been following someone named DeBerry. He came to the church a while back to talk about getting back to God, renouncing possessions; things like that. I guess Farrell found something, but I don't really know anything more. You can ask Judah when you come out."

"Speaking of which, where is Judah?" I don't know why I asked since I didn't care.

"He's waiting in the car. I should probably go."

With that, she got up, and with Moses and me in tow, went to the front door. I could see Judah in the car out front. She turned one last time towards me, "You promise you'll come?"

"I promise."

Moses put his arm around me as we watched them drive away.

5

Perdition's flame leaping, hell and its labyrinths leading the accursed to that place where damnation awaits for the wicked to writhe and boil until the end of time; souls lost to the father and forgiveness, buried by afflictions and maledictions that led to their sorry fate.

It was probably a good thing I didn't believe in that stuff. It's all very quaint in this age of space travel, CGI monsters, and cellphones.

Astral had stirred up memories of the apocryphal screeds I'd pored over in those lonely hours out in the fields with her talk of usurpers. I smiled at the thought of Milton and Dante's epic poems of failed and wicked men. No doubt Farrell considered me one; lost to God, lost to the world.

Farrell.

She was right that I spent little time in any meaningful examination of his character or whether he was good for Rebekah. It was her life, her choice. Just as Astral and I had made our fateful decisions, so would she. I was not an exemplar in that respect, a man of gravitas, certainly not in those days. I was not rigid in my convictions or forthright in my demands for my daughter or her suitors.

I doubt they would have listened anyway.

The three of them watched as I ruminated about this: Moses, Meredith, and the acolyte, Agnes, sitting on the couch opposite me. Seeing Astral let too many ghosts out of the closet and I was having a hard time getting them back in. The sun had set, and the only light in the room was from a small lamp on a table near the couch where the gallery waited for my return.

"What?"

"Are you alright, dear?" Meredith drew first blood.

"I'm fine. I just wasn't expecting to see Astral, that's all," I said, in the hope they would disperse and leave me to my thoughts.

No such luck.

"I suppose I should have said something, but when she was here earlier, she didn't say she would stop by once I told her you'd be coming, so I held my tongue. To be honest, I didn't know how you'd react to seeing her." Moses, oddly, seemed uncomfortable.

"Why?" I knew why.

"I'm sure you remember your outburst the last time I tried to talk to you about Lilith."

"Astral!" I knew he didn't like that, but Lilith didn't belong to me, nor was she a part of my life. Astral was the woman I loved, and I refused to give that up.

"I'm not going to argue over what name you use."

"Neither am I, however, you needn't worry, as they say, time wounds all heels, and enough time has pass that I'm ok with where the two of us have ended up. It doesn't upset me anymore." True or not, I don't think they believed me.

Having salved worry number one, it was on to the next concern. "Are you going to go back to Virginia as you promised?" The old man wouldn't let up.

Geez, it was like being a kid again.

"Yes, just as I promised. I don't know what good it'll do, but, yes, I'll go." I kept waiting for Agnes to say something, but no, she just sat there watching me. "I don't know what everyone is so worried about. I mean is it any different from what you did all those years ago when you came out here to start this commune? Weren't your parents freaked out by it? Yet, in the end, it turned out ok—"

Moses interrupted me. "How did she sound when she talked to you?"

"I don't know, maybe a little troubled. Why?"

Meredith interrupted Moses. "We talked to Becky about a month ago. Sometimes she calls to say hello. She told me they were having problems conceiving, and Farrell believed it was God's doing; that they weren't being...how did she say it—"

"Righteous before the lord." It was my turn to interrupt.

"Yes, something like that," Meredith continued. "I guess Farrell's been on something of a spiritual journey, to find the right path, as they used to tell me, and he's become more dogmatic lately, especially in their home life. I got the impression Rebekah was torn between her concern for what he was doing and where he was taking her and her own beliefs like her promise to stay by his side."

"Then I'll find out when I get there." All this was wearing me out. Once again I'd forgotten to pack some whiskey, so I'd find no solace in the bottle. "I think I'll turn in. Emily's got big plans for me tomorrow."

"That little girl thinks the world of you," this from the oracle Moses.

"Yes, I'm aware of her attachment to me."

"We all are." He raised his eyebrows as he spoke.

I didn't know what to say to that.

Agnes followed me to our little room. She was unusually quiet. We got into bed and stared at the ceiling. I knew that sooner or later the questions would come. Agnes shuffled about before wrapping her arms around me.

"What are you thinking about?" she asked.

Finally, I could now go peacefully into that good night. "About when you were going to ask that question."

"I see." Her stirring continued, that meant more questions. "Are you really going to Virginia, like you said?"

"I kind of have to now, otherwise, we can never come back up here. I've made too many promises to too many people, I'm stuck."

"You don't want to go?"

It was my turn to stir. "I don't want to *have* to go."

"I don't understand?" She was running her fingers along my chest, gently tugging at the hair.

"It's a long way to go to a place I have no interest going back to for a situation over which I have no say and probably no business being involved in. It's like coming up here; it dredges up a lot of bad memories."

Her fingers were now slowly circling around my stomach. "It's not good to hide from the past." Sage advice from a woman who spent more than two years hiding in a bar because she couldn't face her own mistakes. "And I like it up here, so we can't stop visiting just because you have a habit of breaking promises."

"So this is really about you?" I kept my eye on her south wandering hand.

"That's how you like it, baby." She'd found what she was looking for. I could feel her hand moving up and down. "Maybe I can help take your mind of it for a while?"

"Maybe."

I didn't think I was in the mood for love, but magic fingers can do wonders for a flagging soul. I found that warm sensual spot between her legs, and our lips met. It was sweet and sticky, and when we were finished, I laid back, exhausted from my labors, and pass into a dreamless sleep.

It didn't last nearly long enough.

• • • • •

"Time to rise and shine, Buttman!"

"Already?" I put the pillow over my head.

There was a time when Agnes was loathe to rise from her slumbers before ten or eleven in the morning, but that was back in LA, back before the Kool-Aid served here worked itself into her brain and turned her into someone I didn't recognize. She stood there, tapping her foot with her arms crossed, willing me out of the bed, onward and upward to another glorious day of being bossed around by a eleven-year-old. I was certain a means of escape would come to me. Maybe I'd sneak off into town and get loaded. I wondered how far it was to Canada. Unfortunately, they'd come get me and drag me back. With that intellectual exercise out of the way, I got up, got dressed, and made my way to the kitchen to help with breakfast. Today, I was the pancake guy. After that, I helped clean up and found Emily, who was waiting just outside the kitchen door.

"Ready, Mr. Sunshine?"

"No."

Emily took this with her usual grimace, then grabbed my hand and pulled me off in the direction of the garden. I could, if I had wanted, said no, a real *no*, versus my usual, "I'm being a jerk" no. I had other things occupying my mind, but I don't know if an eleven-year-old would understand, and frankly, I needed something to occupy my mind so it wouldn't wander off in directions I wanted to avoid. With that, we followed the path to the garden, included the required stop at the shed for my box, and commenced with the daily rituals that Emily so prized.

We weeded, clipped, watered, and then made an inventory of where we were in the growing cycle. I perched upon my box and watched Emily take a second tour of the garden just to make sure. Having completed our chores, so far as the garden was concerned, it was time for our Sunday walk, something that had also become expected when I came to visit.

We decided we would go along the south road. It was quiet with only the occasional car or truck zipping by. In several places, wildflowers had been planted, back to the time when I was a kid running around these hills, and we would stoop down to see if they had any discernible scent. After a mile or so, we left the road and wandered up to a small embankment looking out over the valley. Neither of us said much. Normally, Emily liked to talk whether I paid attention or not, but today was different, she mostly held on to my hand. We sat in the grass and watched and listened to the birds. Ever since I was a child, I would listen for the sound of birds. I didn't know much in the realm of ornithology. I couldn't tell you what any particular bird was beyond the easy ones like eagles, blue jays, and peacocks, but I did love to hear them talk and sing. A number of smaller birds were flitting between trees, and the crows were squawking at one another.

The farm had its share of chickens, turkeys, and ducks. Emily preferred the ducks and was dismissive of my concerns that they were more sinister than they appeared.

"They're just ducks!" she would tell me.

"Hey, that doesn't mean they're not up to something. Just listen to those quacks! I can tell something's going to happen the minute we turn our backs. You'll see."

She looked at me like I was nuts, but I stuck to my guns.

From our vantage point, we could see the vineyards stretching along the valley and up the sides of the hills. At the crests were trees placed as though they were there specifically to be part of a pastoral setting.

Emily was picking at the grass under our feet. "I don't want to go."

"Go where? We just got here. I thought we'd have all day?"

She didn't get the joke.

"No," she said, "I don't want to leave and live with Abby. She pesters me whenever I'm there."

"Yeah, I know how you feel. I have to go back to Virginia; that's actually not that far from where you'll be. I know I have to go, but I'd rather stay here or go to the beach."

"Me too!" Emily turned to me as she threw some grass on my shoes. "Why do you have to go?"

"To see my daughter, Becky. Actually, it's a very beautiful place, tucked in the Shenandoah Valley by the Blue Ridge Mountains. It's a lot like here, lots of farms and vineyards." I threw some grass on her shoes.

Emily took stock of this. "If it was so nice, why did you leave?"

I thought about what to say. I could be truthful about why I had to leave, how I felt trapped, how my relationships had deteriorated. I could mention it was my second great failure after what happened with James and Miguel... maybe another time. "I was ready to do something else, and I wanted to come back to California."

"I wish I was going with you. I think I'd have more fun."

"I'm sure you'll have a good time in Philly with your dad, and who knows, maybe Abby will be more fun now that she's a little older."

Emily shook her head, no. "Why don't you want to go? Don't you like your daughter?"

"I do." I just don't really know the woman or where I fit in. "I'd just rather see her here than go all the way across the country. It's a long trip."

"Yeah." I think Emily got that last part.

We climbed down the embankment and back to the road. A mile further was a path that crisscrossed a fallow pasture on the west side of the farm. Lunch was over by the time we got back, so we made ourselves a sandwich and split an apple. When we were done, Calista reminded Emily she had chores to do, and Agnes, with her hands on her hips, proclaimed it was time for me to pay her some proper attention. Consequently, my afternoon was spent listening to, commenting on, and, finally, tasting the tarts she had learned to make under the tutelage of Meredith and the other women in the kitchen.

There were apple, cherry, and blueberry tarts, which I was obliged to sample. I did my best to appear reserved in my criticism while wiping the frosting off my chin.

"They're really good, aren't they?" Agnes sat right there beside me.

"Um, sure, they're pretty good." I tried to hide the smile.

"You can't fool me, Sunshine. I know you love them, just like you love me!"

"Then why'd you ask if you already knew?"

"A woman always likes to hear it!" The other women in the room were in agreement on this. For some reason, they were still fascinated by Agnes and me.

"Well then who am I to disagree?" I asked while reaching for another tart.

Agnes slapped my hand. "You'll spoil your supper."

"Nonsense," I replied. "You can't spoil something that hasn't yet been prepared, and even if its preparation was commencing, I fail to see how a tart, especially one described by you as "really good" could in the process of my digesting it, spoil that preparation. And, as you have seduced me with these bewitching pastries, I think it terrible that you then refuse me one more sample of your fine work." I followed this with a grin and a kiss.

"Fine, but only one, Buttman," she groused.

"Yes dear," I quickly grabbed two and ran for the door.

Agnes, shocked at my turpitude, ran after me. She chased me out to the courtyard where I grudgingly shared the sweets on one of the benches I helped build as a teen. The afternoon sun, filtered by the trees ringing the courtyard, kept us warm as we sat there. Monk and Agnes, still together were running around as if they were kids. Six months ago, I was hiding in my bungalow and Agnes in Johnny D's bar, both of us resigned to the fact that we were doomed to a kind of pervasive loneliness punctuated by foolish encounters with people who would never truly love us.

Agnes held my hand. "I love you, Sunshine."

"You mentioned that yesterday." I put my arm around her.

"And I'll mention it again tomorrow." She leaned in and kissed me. "And what do we say to that?"

"You're nuts?"

"And?" There on her beautiful face, with its beautiful reconstructed nose, was her beautiful smile.

"I love you too, beautiful."

She kissed me again. "See, that wasn't so hard."

I shrugged. I saw no reason to stop kissing; however, my pants pocket was buzzing. Goddamned phone! I didn't recognize the number.

"Yes?" I was understandably curt with the caller.

"It's Becky, I need to know if you're coming out." She was curt in return.

"I am, in a few days as a matter of fact. I just spoke to your mother, and she's worried—"

"When will you be here?" she demanded.

"I don't know, I'll need a couple of days to get ready, then it'll take probably four days to drive out—"

"We don't have that kind of time; just fly." Her voice was almost a whisper.

"I can barely hear you. I mean, what would I drive when I got there? I'll need to get around, but I don't want to rent some car..." I didn't want to fly. I didn't really want to go.

"You can drive the truck when you get here."

"The truck? You still have my old truck?"

I could hear her exasperation through the phone. "Yes, that stupid old truck! I need you here as soon as you can get here. I have to find him. I know something is wrong. I talked with Car; you can stay with him while you're here. Call this number when you get to the airport. I have to go."

And with that, she hung up.

"Rebekah?" I don't know why I said that; I knew the connection was broken.

I put the phone away. Agnes was waiting for me to say what's what. Strangely, given the situation, but perhaps not completely out of character, I started thinking about my truck, a 1968 Chevy custom camper, white and gold with a 386 V8. It was my other great automotive love besides the Falcon. I had given it to Rebekah when I left. I was positive she'd turn around and sell it the minute I crossed the horizon. My old truck! I kept that baby in pristine condition. The neighbors found that amusing; to them, trucks were for work and you wore them out. You didn't save them unless you were the guy with ten rotting by the barn. They weren't the status symbols they are in places like LA; they were just trucks.

Agnes tugged at my shirt. "What's up? Was that your daughter?"

"Yeah, she wants me to fly out as soon as I can." I was still trying to process the fact that she wanted *me* to come as soon as possible.

"So when are we going?"

"We?"

"Of course we! I'm going too." She said this with a grin.

"Wait, Johnny just left for Colombia, I thought you had to stay to keep the place running?" I could tell by the grin this was a setup.

"No, we decided to close up for a month. I wanted to spend some time with you this summer. Rey can take care of the bar. That's why I had to stay late those last few days, so we could get everything in order. I don't think you should have all the fun. Besides it'll keep you in my arms rather than someone else's."

Judith. I wondered what she was doing. Thinking of Judith brought back memories of that long graceful neck and the way she liked me to work my way from her ears to her breasts. Those soft hands guiding me as I...

"Buttman!" Agnes was pulling on my ear. Startled out of my reverie and mindful of my propensity to drift off at the most inappropriate times, I gave her my full attention. "Are you still here? You've got that look again like you're off in la-la land. We need to get our tickets if we have to go soon."

"True," I said without any enthusiasm.

"You don't want to go, do you?" I tried to fake a smile. She wasn't buying, "It's all over your face. Do we go or not?" I could see that anything other than yes would disappoint her.

"Yes, *we* have to go."

"Exactly." Agnes rose, pulled me up, and we were off, across the courtyard, to the schoolroom and the computer, to book our flight.

6

I watched as the baggage handlers tossed the luggage, boxes, and strollers onto the moving ramp. The treads patiently took everything flopped upon them and dutifully carried them into the aircraft. Agnes, who had thoughtfully given me the window seat from which I watched this carnival of thrills, sat in the middle seat and grasped my hand as if we were all going to die.

"You know they haven't even started the engines yet."

"Work with me here, Buttman, you know how I feel about flying."

I knew.

"Yet you still wanted to come along." I raised her hand to my lips and kissed it. "On the plus side, when we go down in a ball of flames, it'll be together arm in arm."

"You're a jerk, Buttman!"

I kissed her hand again.

"Yes, I am."

• • • •

It's amazing how quickly a few days can pass. One day we're sitting in a makeshift classroom, trying to figure out how to use a decrepit computer, Agnes mostly, and then with help from Calista; the next, or so it seems, we're mashed onto a plane, way too early in the morning, to fly to Charlotte and then to Richmond.

In the middle of these two days was the obligatory talk with the old man and the party at which Simon and Eric would announce their nuptials. I had no interest in the former, and despite her good cheer earlier; Agnes had no interest in the latter.

I could hear the waves crashing, the seagulls squawking...

Moses found me in the same spot where he had earlier informed me I had a visitor. I had once again come to this spot in search of a few minutes of solace. Apparently, in the future, I'd have to find a better spot. The old man thoughtfully had brought his own crate to enhance the moment. He sat down, and we both looked out over the valley. I had no idea what to say.

"What's up?" would have to do.

"What's up? I think the better question is, where are you going? Do you know?" Moses looked at me, the sun lightening his already white head of hair, "It's good to have you here, but I know you do it somewhat grudgingly."

"True, Agnes loves it up here, and I tag along."

He put his hand on my shoulder, "Why? What have we done? When you finally came back, you said we needed to talk, but other than that day out on the road, it's been nothing but pleasantries, not talk."

I did say that, didn't I? I tried to remember who I was as I looked into the face of Moses Bohrman, "True." I still didn't want to talk. I wanted it to all go away, all of it. "It's not anything or anyone, it's just me. I know that doesn't help since it's not really an answer, but it is what it is. I like coming up here even if I'm ambivalent about it. I'm not mad or angry with anyone. I'm not; I just don't care for the memories, that's all. Maybe by coming up with Agnes and spending time with you and Emily and everyone, those memories will fade."

"And what about Becky and Lilith; what about those memories, those times?"

"I don't know." I sat back and watched as a hawk sailed high above us, "I don't know. I guess, like everything I've done lately, I'll wing it."

Moses shook his head.

I turned to him. "And what about you, Moses the firebrand, Moses the voice of the people, the man railing against capitalists, militarists, the pigs, and all the other goddamned liars and perpetrators destroying the working man. What happened to you? I still remember all those sermons you gave at the table years ago. Where's that guy?"

His shoulders slumped, and his eyes watered. "He's still there, or I should say, in here." He touched his chest. "Turns out you can only harangue for so long. I felt I did what I could. Maybe I should have given up my life when I was younger and had the will, but then I would have lost all of this." He took my hand. "Maybe that's the point I want to make to you now, don't let go; don't give up, even if that seems like the way to go, be it good or bad. There are always opportunities, always. Becky wants to know who you are..." He looked at me. "You'll find those things are more important as you grow older. This is your opportunity to find your daughter. I believe that and I hope that you'll believe it too."

"We'll see."

"I imagine you will." He let go of my hand.

We said little else after that. The hawk was still gliding high above.

The party at Simon and Eric's was an eclectic affair. There were all kinds of people, and given Eric's background in performing and Simon's in the restaurant biz, most were not your garden-variety folks. I found it fascinating as it was the complete opposite of what I'd been conditioned to living in a small farming community. Other than Joanie, I knew few entertainers, whereas Eric, having done any number of gigs from straight crooning to gay theatrical camp, knew plenty. Most thought I was cute with my early sixties vibe. This was manifested, at least outwardly, by my choice of clothes; vintage suits will do that.

Agnes, as I expected, was a fish out of water and lost in this crowd of people. She was yesterday's news, a mistaken romance, an ex-wife. I understood why we were invited, but it was hard for Agnes. To her, it was one more repudiation of her failed marriage to Simon.

That's not to say the party was a complete bust, certainly not for me, but there were moments when enough familiarity, like an internet chat with Barron, and time with Anna, who sensed her mother's discomfort, kept the uglier aspects of Agnes' anger with Simon at bay.

"I don't know why we're here," she said as we stood in a corner watching the ebb and flow of the partygoers.

"You said you wanted to come, and you knew what it was about even if it wasn't explicitly stated out loud."

"It was explicitly stated out loud to you!"

"Yeah, but that's because I'm so delightful," I said with a wide grin.

Agnes elbowed me. "Are you saying I'm not delightful, Buttman?"

I kissed her cheek. "Sorry baby, but there can only be so much delightfulness in the world."

"You're lucky I love you, Buttman."

"Everyone in the room is, my love." She didn't get the joke at first, but a slow smile came to her.

"You're a jerk, Sunshine."

"I don't know what you're talking about."

It was at that point that two wonderful things happened: they served dinner, and we noticed Anna with a young man. The food was the reason I came since as an outsider there was no other reason for me to be there. I wasn't important in any substantive way except that I could keep Agnes under control, and, quite frankly, there was no reason for Agnes to be here except for the fact that Anna wanted her mother to be good with it so she could, one day, be good with her mother. And Agnes, accepting of her former husband's impending marriage to his lover; the man he left her for would have a significant impact on her rehabilitation in Anna's eyes. I knew this because Anna had confided it to me not long after we arrived. With the food out, I was in heaven. Every braised, sautéed, drizzled, crisp, tender, succulent, and seasoned delectable made the short trip to my plate and then quickly to my mouth.

Agnes was far more intrigued by the young man, introduced to us by Anna as Jeremy, than the food. Jeremy was tall, lanky, and reminded me of a beach bum. His hair was too long, he needed a shave, and his arms were covered with tattoos. I thought he slouched too much, but his soft-spoken demeanor and rather old-fashioned manners towards us, Agnes in particular, were somewhat endearing. He proffered that he was in culinary school with Anna and that he hoped to finish soon. Agnes asked him a lot of questions I didn't pay attention to. I was in full-blown eating mode, except where he and Anna pointed out their contributions to the soiree.

"Welcome to the family, dude," I said as I offered a fist-bump. He tentatively obliged as Agnes just shook her head.

"Monk has issues, so be careful,"

I shrugged, Anna laughed, Agnes sighed, Jeremy acted confused, and I returned to the buffet.

• • • • •

"What did you think of Jeremy?"

We were on the road heading back to LA. Agnes was wearing out and the toasts and formalities were over. We begged off after wishing the happy couple all the best. I had things to do before our cross-country adventure. I don't remember if we were invited to the wedding.

"He seemed ok, why?" I played dumb.

"I have to elaborate?"

"I think so." I was losing interest.

Agnes smacked me in the arm.

"Oww! Is he okay? How the hell would I know? I think he needs a haircut and a shave, but other than that, he struck me as a perfectly acceptable young man. Whether he's good for Anna or is husband or boyfriend material, I don't know. Does that answer your question?" I knew it didn't.

"I wonder why I even talk to you sometimes..."

"I wonder that too."

She struck another blow to my already injured arm. "Don't interrupt. Occasionally, it would be nice to get something out of you that isn't smart-alecky and actually helpful."

"I don't think smart-alecky is a word."

Her temper was coming to the surface. I had to be mindful of my idiotic comments if I wanted the rest of the drive to be pleasant or something akin to it.

"You know what I mean!"

"Yes beautiful."

Ah, as Moses had predicted, moments to treasure.

. . . . .

The flight was a long clinched jaw kind of affair. I'd never been on an airplane, so I didn't know what to expect. Agnes, on the other hand, having flown a number of times, mostly, she informed me, to Mexico where she and Simon failed to connect, held tight to all her irrational fears for the five hours the flight took to get to Charlotte. I figured the best way to approach this entire enterprise was as an amused observer. I noted the clots of people hustling from one point to another. First was waiting to deposit our luggage for its part of the journey, then being surveilled by the TSA for the purposes of being allowed to get to the gate where there was more waiting, before more standing, to then being seated in a cramped space next to a woman with an inexplicable fear of crashing into the Rockies. Joanie had advised me to stock up on water and to buy something for lunch because, as she put it, God only knows what they'll give you if they give you anything at all.

Duly informed, I purchased sandwiches, along with the other harried flyers packed in at the polyglot food court, on the way to the gate. Other than some flopping around over said Rockies, the flight was anticlimactic. There were no moments of terror, no crazed passengers acting out, no sinister plots afoot. Instead, it was a hundred or so of us bored and tired and longing for the flight to conclude. Once on the ground, we had to wait to deplane so we could then stretch our unhappy legs as we waited in another part of the airport for our delayed flight to Richmond. I called Rebekah to give her our new arrival time to which I got a terse "okay" and nothing more. Agnes, dazed and confused from the ordeal, and unhappy about having to repeat it in thirty minutes, continued to grasp my hand as if her life depended on it.

There's a reason I wanted to drive rather than fly.

"I should probably give you a head's up about a few things before we get to Richmond," I said as we waited.

"Like what?" Agnes moved closer, her eyes tightening. "More rich girlfriends?"

"No." I'm pretty sure I'm only allowed one of those. "Nothing like that."

"Then what?"

"No one calls me Monk here. They wouldn't recognize the name."

"I see. Then what do they call you, Sunshine?"

"They don't call me that either," I said rather emphatically.

"Then what *do* they call you out here?" I don't think she was interested in any of my little games.

"William, Will, and every once in a while I get called Willie."

She smiled at that. "Seems appropriate. Okay, so how many names do you have, Buttman?"

"The ones you know of are enough for any man."

Agnes pondered her boyfriend for a while. "Any other surprises I should be aware of, Willie?"

"Well, Aggie," I got a poke in the ribs for that, "it's possible, but nothing pressing comes to mind. The community where I used to live is fairly conservative and religious, and some of them think of California as Sodom and Gomorrah. I have no idea how I'll be received since I kind of fled in the middle of the night."

"Do we have to sleep in separate beds?"

"It's unlikely," I said.

"Then it'll be ok."

The plane to Richmond was smaller than the one we took from LA. It was also bouncier, which made Agnes all the more fearful as we rose and fell from Charlotte to Richmond. After we landed, I called Rebekah who informed me she'd be out front of baggage claim in five minutes. As a coda to our full day of airports and planes, we sat and watched the merry-go-round spit out luggage, but not ours, until the very last moment. Night was falling as my daughter pulled up to the curb to fetch us. Her weariness matched ours, so after an oddly impersonal hug, we quietly loaded the bags into the bed of the truck and sped off.

"This is Agnes," I said to Rebekah before turning to Agnes. "This is my daughter, Rebekah."

The three of us were nice and snug, side-by-side, across the length of the bench seat. I listened as the truck engine hummed. It sounded just as I remembered. Rebekah and Agnes waited for me to say something.

"Why don't we find a place to eat? I'm hungry, and I'm going to assume we have things to discuss."

Rebekah steered the truck into the parking lot of a family-style restaurant, a place called *Aunt Mable's*.

7

Aunt Mable's welcomed us with its own particular southern charm. It reminded me of a re-imagined Denny's with the same booths and tables, but the décor favored painted wood, off-white in this case, and the accents featured southern rural life. We were seated in a booth towards the back with a view of the highway just beyond the parking lot. I watched the stream of cars and big rigs as Monica handed us menus and assured Agnes that everything here was good. She was a stout woman with jet-black hair and wire-rimmed glasses. I ordered chicken fried steak; Agnes ordered fried chicken, and Rebekah reluctantly, after some cajoling, ordered bacon and eggs with toast.

"What's wrong?"

I saw no point in putting it off. The exhaustion was obvious. I don't think Agnes or I looked much better, but I could see the difference when I looked at Agnes and then at Rebekah. It was in her eyes, the worry, the fear; something was so bad that she felt compelled to ask me, someone she hadn't spent more than six hours with, combined in the last seven years, to help her. I'd only seen her twice since I'd left and both times it was during a stopover on her way back to Virginia after visiting the old man or Astral's parents. Being with her only heightened my sense of fraud. I wondered if I'd ever really been a true father to her.

"Is all of this about Farrell?"

"Something terrible has happened, and I think Farrell was a part of it." Her eyes were withdrawn, like her mother's when she was upset.

Rebekah was a mish-mash of her mother and me. Her figure veered more towards Astral in that she was curvy, but like me, her face was more angular; an odd combination, much like her mother and I. She was always popular with boys when she was young, which made her marriage to Farrell all the more perplexing to me. When I traced the shape of her face and eyes, I could see Astral and Sunshine in their youth before they fell apart.

I waited for her to say more, before asking, "What do you think he's done?"

"I…I don't know; I don't want to say something if it isn't true. I don't want to believe he's involved in this, but I don't know, and I don't know who to turn to."

"So you turned to me, the last guy on the list." Rebekah started to say something, but I cut her off. "I'm not blind to the situation, or to the way in which I may have failed to be a decent father, so I get why I'm at the bottom of the barrel, and much as I'd like to delve into that tar pit, it might be better for us to save that for another day and get to the basics of what's going on with Farrell first. What has happened that you think Farrell may be a part of?"

"A couple we know, who were part of the church Farrell wanted us to join, were found dead about a week ago. The police called it a double suicide, but I don't believe it. They were frightened when we spoke to them, but they were also worried about their decision to leave, and they were concerned that they might not be safe."

"Safe from what or whom?"

"The Angel," she said somewhat sheepishly.

"The Angel?" I didn't know what to say to that, but before I could blurt something out, Monica arrived with our dinner.

Agnes carefully picked at her chicken with a knife and fork, something she never did with fried chicken back in LA, all the while watching the two of us.

"Maybe you should tell me about this plan to move away; how it all started," I said between mouthfuls of potatoes.

Rebekah was playing with her eggs, something she did as a child. "We wanted, needed, a change in our lives. This is the only place either of us has ever lived, and in some ways, it felt stifling. We were having trouble getting pregnant, and Farrell believed he was being marginalized at church. He had some ideas and didn't think Pastor Davis was sincere in listening to them, and he was tired of working at the farm and feed with his father and brothers." She looked directly at me, alluding, I assumed, at my disinterest in the plow. "Anyway, one afternoon we went to hear a man named Lucian DeBerry talk at the church. He preached about returning to the kind of Christian communities that existed before the Romans took over, when being a Christian was a passionate act, when there was a greater sense of community and belonging that doesn't exist now because then it meant life or death to be Christian. It was, he said, a true calling, one where we would return to the kind of life that is more like the one found in the New Testament."

"And Farrell found this compelling?"

"It was all he could talk about," she said, rolling her eyes.

"And you? What did you think about it?"

Rebekah sighed. "It sounded really nice, but wasn't that what we were trying to do with the church we were already a part of?"

"You would think," I smirked, this from the apostate, Buttman.

She shook her head. "You don't even believe any of this, anyway, do you? Do you go to church anymore? How about you, Agnes? Do you go to church?"

Agnes looked at me wondering what she should say, or try to since at that moment she had a mouthful of chicken. I had my pat answer. "God is with you wherever you go, but you know as well as I that I haven't been to church since I left."

"I don't go to church, sorry. I did when I was little, but my parents lost interest and we stopped going." Agnes had finished her mouthful.

"Be that as it may," I interjected, "how does it tie in with the death of the couple you know?" My chicken fried steak was getting cold. I didn't know how I could eat it without looking like I didn't care, but I was hungry, so I reluctantly ate. It was so good. Maybe it was simple hunger or the fact that I used to eat this all the time when I lived here, but enjoying it only amped up the gnawing feeling that I shouldn't be here.

Rebekah noting my mouth full of food and the obvious joy on my face said, "It might be better if we finished eating first." Agnes merely continued watching us. "I have to say I didn't think you would actually come out here. I was certain that at some point you'd call or something and bail on me." It was her turn to smirk.

"Yeah, that's my M.O." I continued stuffing my face.

"So what changed? Why now?" Rebekah had her mother's eyes and her mother's condescension when addressing me. I kind of missed it.

"Because I didn't have any other choice!" There was no need to lie.

"Meaning?"

"Meaning that I foolishly got involved with this woman here," I nodded towards Agnes, "who then fell in love with the farm—"

"And you, Buttman!" Agnes said this with a smile.

"And me, so my usual pattern of wanting to, but ultimately failing to, wasn't an option anymore. When you run, you can't stop because if you do, you look back and then you're caught. I promised too many people I would, and I live with a woman whose nuts, so here I am."

"I feel so special..." Rebekah's smirk was gone.

"You know what I mean." I didn't know what I meant.

"No, I don't. I've never understood, and nobody would explain it to me. I've asked Mom, I've asked Grandpa Mo, and all they'd say is I have to ask you, and you never show up." She was angry now.

I should have kept running. Would Judith have forced me to come out here? I looked at Agnes; she too was waiting for an answer.

"Alright, what would you like to know?"

"For real, no runaround, no bullshit?" Rebekah did not normally swear.

"No B.S." I took a big gulp of the sugary swill they pass off as tea.

Rebekah sat there processing the thousand or so questions she wanted answers to, whether I had answers or not. Her face softened. "Why are you really here and why did you leave in the first place?"

"I left because I was broken because everything I thought I cared about was broken. Your mother detested me and threw me out for Judah. You and I barely spoke. I was angry and unhappy. I hated farming: I hated the life I had here. All I wanted to do was get away. Staying would have killed me. Leaving was the only thing I knew how to do. Besides, what was there to come back to anyway? It was easier to stay away, and the longer you do, the harder it is to return. I'm only here because of you. I do love you, I do miss you, even if I don't feel like I know you anymore, even if you don't feel like you know me, even if that's all we'll ever have. I'm not looking for redemption or forgiveness. I'm not here to mend fences or tell you I fucked everything up because you already believe that. I came back to help you find Farrell. That's why I'm here."

"I guess that's better than nothing..." Her expression hadn't changed.

"Sometimes it is." I waved to Monica for the check. "We should get going since we're still a ways from town."

Rebekah continued to sulk. I just wanted to get behind the wheel of my truck now that we were reunited.

"I'd like to drive if that's all right." I put out my hand for the keys. I almost said I'll drive, but it isn't technically my truck anymore, and I felt the need to be solicitous for the time being. Rebekah handed me the keys, and we piled in. Agnes, stuck in the middle, took my hand for a moment and kissed me on the cheek, which surprised me. Rebekah was already gone, her face turned towards the window.

It was quiet save for the sound of the motor and the tires riding the pavement. The city lights receded and we ventured along heading west. Agnes fell asleep with her head on my shoulder, Rebekah, too, was wearing out. She pulled an old blanket from behind the seat, placed it between her head and the window, and joined Agnes in a state of auto-induced slumber.

I couldn't help but fall back in time to the days when I used to ride this roadway when I was younger and so much angrier.

I watched for signs of the past, those memorials to a former life. They were everywhere. Houses, barns, and pastures called out to me as I drove by them, reminding me you never really leave and yet it's never the same. How long has this land been here? Through the valleys, fields, and towns I passed through, with nothing more than headlights and the faint glow of stars, I wondered. Fortunately, driving across Virginia isn't like driving across California; I would not be at this for hours on end. Before long we were on the outskirts of my former village, out amongst the farms, one of which used to be mine. Carleton's farm was coming up. I pulled into the driveway and honked. This woke up the two sleeping next to me. A voice in my head was asking about the dead and whether I should be more concerned. I pushed it away, time for that later.

Carleton came out of the house as we got out of the truck.

"Well, I'll be goddamned! Willie's back again at my house!" He had the same broad-faced smile.

Carleton was a big ol' country boy, six foot two, and at least two hundred and fifty pounds. His sandy blond hair had lost its crown and lines punctuated his eyes and mouth. He still wore jeans and tee shirts emblazoned with confederate pride.

"It's good—"

Carleton bear-hugged me before I could finish the sentence. He then hugged Rebekah while remarking that it'd been too long since he'd seen her last. Apparently, they had not talked in person. He took a long look at Agnes before giving her a big hug.

"My, my, Willie, who's this beautiful young woman you brought with you? My dear, I'm Carleton Hinsman." Agnes, by now used to these kinds of hugs, thanks to her time with Moses, gave Carleton a big squeeze back.

"My name's Agnes. I'm Monk's, I mean Willie's, future wife."

"Uh, that's yet to be decided," I declared.

He laughed. "Well, I hope he's gotten better behaved over the years, for your sakes, if you're planning on getting married."

"Hey, I wasn't that bad," I said as Carleton laughed harder and Rebekah snorted.

"Man, say what you want, but you were a sour sonofabitch back then. I just pray you've found some contentment since I seen you last. Come on in and take a load off."

We collected the suitcases out of the back of the truck and carried them inside.

Rebekah stood at the door. "I'm going to head out. I'll see you tomorrow." That distance, those miles between us, was there in her brilliant blue eyes.

"You sure you can't stay a few minutes, Becky?"

She smiled, but not at me. "Sorry, Car, but I'm really tired." She stared at me. Impulsively, I put my arms around her and held on for dear life. I could feel her arm slowly close around me. I softly kissed her cheek.

"Get some sleep." I gave her back the keys to the truck. This time she smiled at me. We watched as she drove away. Carleton left for a moment, and then returned with two beers. I took mine.

"Agnes, would you like a beer, or can I get you something else? I got some wine and some soda?"

"I'll have some wine, thank you." We followed Carleton into the kitchen. It took me a few minutes to realize that his house looked different. It was organized, clean.

"The place looks really nice; what happened?"

Carleton pondered this as he took a swig of beer. "Yeah, that's Leslie's doing. Ever since we got together, she's been cleaning up the house. Might as well, we decided to get married here soon. Hell, maybe the two of you could come on out for it."

Agnes lit up over that. "See, it's happening all around us. You're doomed, Buttman!"

"Buttman? She calls you Buttman?" He gave me the once over now that a new dynamic was in play.

"That's his name now: Buttman, Monk Buttman!" Agnes announced as Carleton handed her the glass of wine.

"We all make mistakes. So who is this Leslie?" I was desperate not to spend what was left of the evening discussing my name.

"You remember, Leslie Jorgensen..."

"I thought she was married to Duane?" I knew Duane through Carleton.

He lowered his head for a moment.

"Yeah. Duane died five years ago in a boating accident. Leslie and me starting going out about a year ago." Carleton acted as though that still surprised him. "You know, Leslie didn't really care for me back when we used to hang out with Duane, so I was kinda shocked when she asked me if I wanted to do something with her. Her kids didn't seem to mind, and it turns out we do pretty good together." He was rambling.

Carleton had been married before to a woman named Brenda. They had two boys and then split up, more or less amiably, when the youngest was ten. He'd been on his own since then with a girlfriend here and there.

I had to laugh. "Interesting where we find ourselves, isn't it?"

"It is, and you and Agnes, how long have you two been partners in crime?" He looked at Agnes for answers since he knew I could be evasive on occasion.

"The fabulous Mr. Buttman and I have been together for six months and a couple of days, right, Monk?"

Like I would know! "Sounds about right."

We sat down at the small table in the kitchen. Carleton was still looking me over. "There's the weekly potluck out at the grange tomorrow, you should go, bring Agnes, it'd be quite a show. Everyone would be mighty shocked at how much our long lost Willie has changed."

"What's different now?" Agnes had to ask.

Carleton laughed. "Well, for one thing, he shaved off his beard. Willie used to have one of those big mountain man type beards, and I don't remember you ever wearing a suit outside of church, and that was when you went to church. And, though it might be unkind to say out loud, they'd all be surprised you found a gal given how ornery you used to be."

"Yeah, I used to be quite a prize." There's a reason you never go back. "Do you think Pastor Davis will be there?"

My old friend couldn't resist. "You and the Pastor? My how you've changed. You're not god-fearing now are you?"

"Not in that sense, no. I wanted to talk to him about Farrell."

Carleton tapped the table with his beer.

"Yeah, there's been a lot of talk about Farrell lately. There was the blowup at church, and I know he ain't been happy working at the farm and feed for a while. Chess, that's his dad," he directed this to Agnes; I was well aware of who Chess was, "told me he was taking off with Becky to someplace in Oklahoma, but I see she's still here. She didn't say much when she called to ask if I could take you in, but I know Farrell left a week or so ago."

"I told her I'd help find him, so I assume he isn't in Oklahoma, at least not yet, or she wants me to go with her to see if he's there." I finished my beer. Agnes was nodding off; the wine was casting its hypnotic spell. Both Carleton and I took notice.

"Looks like I need to get you two to bed. I imagine you have a long day ahead of you. I know I sure do. Are you interested in the potluck, Willie?"

Not in a million years! "Why not, besides it might be fun," I didn't believe that.

"Terrific." I don't think he did either.

Our room was upstairs at the front of the house overlooking the yard and the fields to the north. Tobacco. Carleton still grew some just because, as he would say. He and his family had grown it for generations, and it still had a place in his heart. I could see the shadows of it as I stuck my head through the curtains. Carleton's house was at least a hundred years old and creaked and groaned from the weight of all that history.

A small bathroom was next to our room as was a room with a sewing table and bolts of cloth both on and beside another table. Leslie had indeed taken over. I tried to imagine Carleton's two boys, neither of whom had a religious bone in their bodies, alongside Duane's three daughters, who I remember as straight-laced young women. Pondering the beardless man in the mirror as I brushed my teeth, I figured it was possible they had all changed just as I had. Agnes was lying on the bed. It was humid, and while the temperature had come down, the California girl was sweaty even after washing her face.

"Is it always like this?"

"Like what?" I could tell she wasn't in the mood for my rapier wit.

"This miserable goddamned sticky heat, Willie!"

I laughed. "There's no need for that kind of language, and yes, this is the way it is here. It's a little better when you head up into the yonder mountains, but this part of the country is humid and just, so you know, buggy." I pulled her in close and kissed her. "You wanted to tag along," another kiss, "so I don't want to hear any bitching about the weather or the food or the disconcerting nature of the locals, understand?"

Agnes kissed me back.

"You're a jerk, Willie!"

"Yes, ma'am."

8

Agnes was running her hand along my face. The light of the morning was filling the room, and I realized I wasn't getting out of this; that I was here in Virginia, that it wasn't a bad dream. I turned to her as she pondered the deep and mysterious clod known as Sunshine-Willie-Monk. Her hair was all over the place except on her left side where it was matted down. She was resting on her elbow, seemingly fascinated by the stubble on my chinny-chin-chin.

"I don't know if I can picture you as a hayseed with a long beard. Did you sport overalls and a corncob pipe, Willie?"

"Sorry, no pipe."

"Hmmm..." In the midst of her inquiry came a knock on the door.

"You two decent?" boomed his voice.

"In what respect?" I couldn't help myself.

Carleton opened the door just enough to stick his head in, "I got to get to it. There's food in the kitchen, so help yourselves. I expect you got things to do, so I'll see you later at the grange. Remember, potluck starts at six."

"Do we need to bring anything, Carleton?" Agnes asked while holding the sheets above her breasts.

"Car works best, darlin' and since the word is out that our long lost Willie is back, you just need to make sure your ever-loving flight risk gets there." He winked at that. "No need to make anything, there's always plenty. Oh, and Leslie might come by, she's making a quilt for her granddaughter, Ramona."

"Thanks, Car, see you later," I said.

"Might could."

I laughed. I hadn't heard that in a while. He closed the door. We got ourselves together and headed downstairs. Sure enough, there was Leslie talking with Carleton out in the yard. He got in his truck, and she came in the back door.

"Well now, I don't believe it! Car was right! William is here, clean-shaven and dressed like a proper gentleman." Leslie was one of those women people used to call a live wire, a whirling ball of energy, someone who could never slow down. She wasn't very big, maybe five foot four, thin, with golden-brown hair that never went past her shoulders, and a strong aquiline face with soft grey eyes.

"Yes, I'm back. It's good to see you Leslie. I'm sorry to hear about Duane." I gave her a hug.

"Damn fool. I told him to be more careful, but he was so headstrong when it came to some things, like that damn boat!" She turned to Agnes. "I don't mean to be impolite, I'm Leslie."

"I'm Agnes."

"You responsible for cleaning up William here?"

This amused Agnes. "Unfortunately, no. Willie had already transformed by the time I met him."

Leslie sized up the two of us. "Car's right, you make a good looking couple. Can I make you anything? Get you some coffee?" I knew Leslie wouldn't accept any kind of no, or that she'd let me cook, so I said I'd have some eggs and toast and asked about her and Carleton. For a brief moment, her shoulders slumped, and she gazed out the window towards the fields.

"Losing Duane was awfully traumatic, Will. I didn't know what I was going to do. He was gone so quick. For the only time in my life, I felt lost. A week or so after we buried him, Car came over and asked if he could help. I didn't know what to say, but he told me not to worry, and he took over the fields, making sure the crops were worked. I don't know what I would have done without the help. I'd a had to sell, I expect." Leslie turned to me and smiled. "He never asked for any favors or anything like that, never made any advances, if you know what I mean. After a while I told him to come in for dinner, it was the least I could do. About a year ago, we decided to get together. I have to say, it's been interesting. You know I probably shouldn't say this, but I was never too fond of the two of you when you'd come over and hang out with Duane. I knew that with three girls, Duane would need to hang on to some of his men friends, but the three of you used to get under my skin. I was glad to see you go, bad as that sounds."

"I remember," all too well.

"It never occurred to me that maybe the three of you needed each other. You weren't what I'd call good churching men, although, believe it or not, Car goes to church with me now of his own free will, but I know it bothered them when you left and then Duane died…" Leslie put her hand on mine. "I think I understand better now."

"Well, we were a handful." That sounded better than jerks.

We sat down and had breakfast. Leslie asked Agnes the usual: Where'd you meet, have you got any kids. To me: Are you any happier than you were? I don't think I could have been any unhappier. Would it be awkward being around Lilith? I guess we'd find out.

Agnes talked about herself, as did Leslie, while I played dumb. I sat there listening, sort of, while wishing I was back in LA. I heard a knock on the front door and reflexively got up to see who it was. Leslie just waved me on; she was deep into her talk with Agnes. I got to the door to find Rebekah. She didn't look like she'd gotten any sleep at all. I opened the door and before I could say hello she had wrapped her arms around me and was crying as you would when you're worried and exhausted, and sure your life is coming to an end. I led her over to one of the couches in the front room and held on to her as she cried. Leslie and Agnes came in to find out what the hell I'd done. They sat down on either side of us with Agnes putting her hand on Rebekah's shoulder.

Leslie spoke first. "Oh baby, what's got you so sad on such a beautiful a day?"

She said nothing. All she seemed to want was someone to hold her.

"Did you sleep at all last night?" I asked. She just shook her head. "Whatever's happened isn't going to get better if you're not getting any rest. Why don't we find you a place to lay down?"

"Please don't leave me," was the last thing I wanted to hear from her.

"I'll be right here, but I need you to get some rest."

I picked her up and followed Leslie, who was directing me to a room off the kitchen with a daybed. We got her to lie down, and I stayed with her. An odd sense of melancholy found me as I held her hand. It didn't take her long to fall asleep. Leslie and Agnes were watching me at the door.

"What?" I asked as softly as I could.

Agnes smiled. "These are the times that remind me why I love you, you jerk."

"I suppose everyone has their moments." I found myself stroking Rebekah's hair, something I did when she was a child. Those days seemed like a thousand years ago. Leslie brought in a light blanket, and we retreated to the kitchen. As we sat there, Leslie asked Agnes if she sewed, Agnes said no, but she'd like to see how it worked. Then, without so much as a how do you do, they left me to my own devices.

I found a romance novel on the counter and spent the rest of the morning finding out if Rachel would discover love with Rodrigo in the sizzling Latin sun. I hoped Rebekah appreciated this sacrifice on my part. Later, Agnes and Leslie informed me they were going to the store as they decided to make pies for the potluck. I was tempted to say something to Agnes about how she was willing to cook for anyone but me, but held my tongue. Not long after that, I tired of Rachel and Rodrigo, and I fell asleep in the chair next to the daybed. It was the clattering in the kitchen that woke me. Rebekah was sitting up on the bed, staring at me.

"Did you get some sleep?" I asked. "Feel any better?"

"A little." She was clutching the pillow as if it were a stuffed toy.

"Something happened that got you all worked up, or is this just all of it piling up inside?"

A sad look came over her. "Why do you care?"

It was going to be a long trip.

"Because I do, because I know what it's like to be angry, and I can tell you're very angry, no doubt at me, but also at Farrell and your mother, and probably at life in general. Are you hungry? You need to eat." Leslie and Agnes had taken a break from the business of pie making and joined us.

"He's right, Becky, you need to eat something. Why don't I make us all a little lunch? What do you say?"

Rebekah hesitated before saying ok. I sat by her as we watched Leslie prepare lunch. Agnes did what she could to help, occasionally checking to make sure we were still here. Rebekah took my hand but didn't say anything; mostly, she just stared towards the kitchen. Car's house had a screened-in porch, so we had lunch out there, watching the squirrels run around the trees and listening to the birds sing. Leslie asked if Lilith was coming to the potluck, mostly to draw out Rebekah from her funk. Rebekah didn't know. Leslie asked if she was going, again Rebekah said she didn't know. I intimated with hand gestures that we'd take her with us regardless, and it was then that my delightful little phone refused to let me alone.

First Astral called. Yes, I was in town. She wasn't sure if she should believe the rumors. Yes, I had spoken to our daughter. As a matter of fact, she's right her. Could she speak to Rebekah? I held up the phone, but Rebekah said she didn't want to talk.

I wasn't enjoying this.

Astral said she was coming over and that I wasn't to let Rebekah leave. Astral hung up before I could say no.

"Your mother's coming over."

"I said I didn't want to talk to her!" A knot collected on her forehead.

Before I could respond to that, the phone began moaning again. It was *my* mother, Rebekah senior. She had just heard from Astral. We needed to deal with this, and as an aside, she said it was about time *I* came back, and had I planned to come see her? I lied and said I had. With the formalities out of the way, she hung up.

"Your grandmother is also coming over."

"I don't want to talk to her either!" Her exasperation with me was manifest.

"Welcome to the club, my dear, welcome to the club," I patted her hand. Leslie was doing her best to stifle a very large grin while Agnes' big eyes had returned. Leslie got up and tapped Agnes on the shoulder.

"Come on Ag, we'd better clean up and clear out before the fireworks."

"Ag?" I looked at her. "Really?"

Ag shrugged. "It's better than Aggie."

Leslie just laughed.

• • • •

To prepare for the one reunion, I absolutely had no interest in; that being with my mother, daughter, and ex-wife, I carefully thought through any and all of the asinine comments I might make which would only enhance their dislike for me. I blame my mother for this as I learned it from her in the last years of her misery on the farm with Moses. At the time I had an inkling of why she was so mad, that being Meredith and my three half-brothers, although at the time there was only one, but had no depth of experience from which to truly appreciate how much she came to loathe the man I called Moses. Naturally, as Moses' son, and given the less than noble reason I'd ended up in Virginia, my mother's verbal abuse, smart-ass remarks, and grave disappointment continued unabated through the years until Astral kicked me out and I bolted for California.

Rebekah remained in the kitchen as I manned the lookout for her mother and grandmother. This meant sitting on the front porch in eager anticipation of the many inquiries about my ongoing affairs. Then again, they might not have any interest in me, and were determined to focus on Rebekah's troubles with her idiot husband. I was half-tempted to bum one of Carleton's old moonshine jugs just to piss off them off since neither had a good opinion of drinkers. I knew the distances were not great from their houses to Car's and sure enough in short order, the two of them arrived ready to "get this all worked out" as my mother would say. I stepped down to greet them. My mother, the senior Rebekah, who, like Astral, dressed more modestly after giving up on being a hippie chick, surprised me with a smile and what appeared to be affection.

"My, you look rather dashing, William." She refused to call me Monk and thankfully gave up on calling me Sunshine. "It's good to see you. Your father said I should be ready to be amazed by your transformation, and as a general rule I take anything Moses says with a grain of salt, but you are indeed changed, at least on the outside." There's the mother I know.

"Thanks for noticing, and you, mother, are as radiant as ever." In a sense, she was. The usual somber tones that characterized her clothing were, today, replaced by a red and yellow flower-print dress and a scarf artfully draped around her neck. Her hair, as always, was pulled up in a bun atop her head. I gave her a hug and then turned to Astral, noting the worry on her face and in her eyes. "Rebekah's inside. She's not particularly happy the two of you are here, and she's had very little sleep, so you are hereby forewarned."

"Has she said anything to you? What's worrying her?" Astral asked in a strangely quiet voice.

"Nothing other than she's concerned about Farrell."

"Well," my mother intoned, "standing out here isn't going to answer any of our questions. Lead on, William, let's find out what we can."

Together we mounted the front steps, and I opened the door. There to greet us were Leslie and Agnes, wearing that unsure face I'd gotten used to when she found herself in unsure situations. Leslie knew both Astral and my mother and welcomed them to sit down. I pulled Agnes to my side for proper introductions.

"Mother, this is Agnes. Agnes, this is my mother, Rebekah. I don't think you were actually introduced to Lilith when she was in California so, Lilith, this is Agnes. Agnes, this is Lilith, who I call Astral, and yes, I will refrain from referring to you as that while I'm here."

Agnes tentatively stepped forward. "It's nice to meet you. Monk, sorry, Willie doesn't talk about you much so I'm glad to get this chance to meet you."

"Yes, *Willie* can be like that," my mother retorted. She then inquired, as everyone else had when I introduced Agnes, about our relationship, how long we'd been together, our plans; the usual. Agnes filled her in as only Agnes can while I went to retrieve my recalcitrant daughter. Rebekah had vacated the kitchen for a chair in the backyard.

"Are they here?" she asked this without looking at me.

"They are."

She turned to me, her eyes wet from tears and a lack of sleep. "Do I have to?"

I took her hand and helped her up, "Yes, you do. It's a family rite of passage. But believe it or not, they're worried about you, just as I am." I didn't sense she had a lot of faith in that.

Together we made that long trip toward the bosoms of the women who brought us into this world. Astral and my mother came to us, or more specifically Rebekah, and greeted her with hugs, kisses, and empathetic faces. I sat down and motioned to Leslie and Agnes they could go if they wanted. They stayed. Rebekah, uncomfortable amidst this gaggle of concern, stoically slumped onto the sofa. My heart went out to her. I remembered similar circumstances right after we'd arrived here. My mother, her husband, Donald, Astral, wanting to know what was going on that was so bad that the three of us had to be ushered out across the country in the middle of the night? I resolutely refused to say why, only that we had to, and I didn't know when we'd be able to return.

It was roughly twenty years.

I never did tell them about James and Miguel.

My mother spoke first, "Becky, dear, everyone's worried about you, and we can see that you're obviously upset, but we can't help you if you don't talk to us. Is what's going on so terrible that you won't even take your own family into your confidence?"

"It's not that. It's..." She twisted the wedding ring on her finger. "Farrell demanded I go with him to Oklahoma, that if I loved him and believed in him, I'd go, but after what happened to Molly and Jonathan I wasn't sure anymore. I didn't think that was the answer to our problems."

I assumed Molly and Jonathon were the suicide couple.

"You didn't answer when I asked why you thought Farrell might be involved with what happened to Molly and Jonathan." I thought that more important.

Rebekah sighed, "Because I don't know."

"Then what do you know that would make you think that?"

"I don't believe they killed themselves. We were there two days before and I didn't sense any desperation or sadness that would make them want to do that. If anything, they were defiant even if they were scared. And then later Farrell said he would meet this Angel and talk to them; something about convincing them that they were wrong about what they believed or had heard, and the next thing I know they're dead and Farrell is demanding we go right away and now he's gone."

No one had an answer for that.

My mother raised her eyebrows. "Who is this Angel?"

She continued to finger her ring. "I don't know, I didn't go when Farrell went to meet him. Molly said the Ghost had warned her about him, that he did the devil's work. She was confused by that."

I think we were all confused by that!

"The Ghost?" I had to ask.

"That's what she called him." She didn't elaborate on who he was.

"What did they say about this place that made you change your mind about going or worried you?" The women, certainly my mother and Astral, were uncomfortable with my questions.

"Is this really important, William?" My mother was asking.

"I think, as far as Farrell is concerned, yes, it's important."

"They didn't say what about it they didn't like other than they felt it wasn't for them. They said there were aspects of it they weren't comfortable with. I got the impression it had to do with Lucian, but they wouldn't say it directly. It was only when Molly pulled me aside that she said certain things were expected of the women there, although she didn't say exactly what, that she felt went against the sanctity of marriage. She also said it was something the Ghost had warned her of—"

"Of what, Dear?"

"Of what happened to a woman name Amy, something terrible that could happen to her too, and no, she didn't say what that was."

"She didn't say who the Ghost was?" Leslie asked.

"All she said was he was a strange man who approached her when she was working in the fields."

Our room of seasoned detectives took this in as the birds outside continued to sing.

Although it wasn't said out loud, and maybe that had something to do with me, Leslie and Agnes being in the room, I had the feeling that talk among them regarding Farrell had led to the rift Astral was worried about. I knew Rebekah had her fair share of talks about the responsibilities of marriage, and I assumed they did not want Rebekah making the mistakes they made whether with Moses or yours truly.

My mother leaned in. "What do you want to do, dear?"

I butted in before Rebekah could answer. "She needs to rest for a while. There's time, besides with the big to-do at the grange later she'll need her energy. We can talk about it when she's not so tired."

I could tell Rebekah didn't want to talk. We all got up and escorted her back to the room off of the kitchen where she laid down. I told her we'd be outside. Leslie and Agnes begged off and returned to the sewing room. My mother and ex-wife followed me to the chairs in the backyard.

9

The three of us sat beneath the white oak that spread easily over the table and chairs, shading us under its boughs, and moving softly with the northern breeze sliding along the distant mountains; they on the lounge chairs and me on the picnic bench. Astral and my mother held me in their gaze for a perplexing amount of time before speaking. Astral shared her daughter's exhaustion while my mother, oddly, seemed quite animated, but not in the churlish manner that defined the last few times we had together before I lit out for sanity's sake.

"William," she intoned, "What are we going to do about Becky?"

"She wants to find Farrell, so that's what we'll help her do. Whether that's a good thing or a bad thing, I don't know, but it's a start." I could see Astral flinch at that. "What?"

"Is that the best you can do?" She was nearly shouting. Her eyes were red, and the veins in her forehead stood out.

"It's the best I can do," I assured her.

"I'm tired of hearing that. I'm tired of going in circles with her, and now you!" I couldn't help but notice how both Rebekah and her mother shook in the same way when they were upset.

I sat up on the bench and directed myself to the woman I so dearly loved as a young man. "I know you're upset and you're probably not happy that it's come down to me being a part of this. I don't know, and I don't care. But, before we get back to foolishly bringing up the miseries of the past, I have a few rules that concern my visit here. One, I am not here to rehash the past, I am not here to seek forgiveness or make everything better, nor am I here to prostrate myself over my failures, mistakes, and shortcoming, of which there are many. Two, I'm not here because I want to be, although now that I am here, I'm going to have to rethink that because maybe I'm wrong, but that's how it is, so deal with it." I sat back and crossed my arms. "It's possible that maybe, just maybe, I can help. Anyway, I'm well aware that I was a lousy son, a lousy husband, and a lousy father, so there's no need to beat that dead horse. I'm not here to be angry or sullen, nor am I here for you two, or your respective spouses, to give me a lot of grief because you have issues. Do we understand each other?" I let those last words linger.

My mother scowled at me. "I don't think—"

"Sorry, there will be no discussion. I made plain the word, the word is out, and that's that." I watched them fume for a time. Astral slumped in her chair, and my mother waved her hand across the top of her head. "So, what's going on that's got you two so worked up about Becky? This high level of collusion is, I must say, rather surprising."

They considered each other before Astral spoke. "It's only surprising to you for all the reasons you put forth, and as you have made *plain* your disinterest in rehashing the past, I'll just put it this way: we're worried because they seemed to be doing so well, and then out of nowhere, and I'm willing to admit I don't know everything that was going on between them, there's all this unhappiness with church, with work, with us." Astral waved her hand towards my mother. "Even Moses is concerned that something serious is wrong. Becky has become so sullen and uncommunicative that it frightens me. It's like—"

"She's turning into me," I said.

Astral's eyes tightened, and her nostrils flared. "Yes, like you were, or are."

"Well, we can't have that." I took a moment to collect my thoughts.

"What happened to you, William?" For once, my mother had a kind of sadness in her eyes rather than the more distinct disapproval I was used to.

"I'm Monk now, Monk Buttman," I said with all the flair I could muster.

"That's a terrible name, William."

"Yes, it is, and I probably should have put more thought into it, but that's what I call myself now. Of the other people I used to be, well, Sunshine died on that dirt road when I was seventeen, and William was an angry fool I had to let go of because he loved a woman who wasn't right for him and because he felt trapped by expectations and a God who wouldn't listen. I'm free of that. I go with the flow now, content to be alive, and I do what I can where I can and forget the rest."

"Sounds like your usual copout." Thank you, Astral.

"God still loves you, William, he hasn't forsaken you."

"Perhaps, but my folly isn't the focus of this trip, it's Becky. And your worries about her, however well intentioned, wil not bring back Farrell, so we need to find out what we can do in that regard. Have either of you heard anything or have any thoughts on how we can locate him?"

"Jude heard he was with a group of men that are part of this church he wants to join or has joined," Astral said.

"Does the church have a name? I know a guy who's good at finding information on stuff like that."

She just shook her head. "I don't know, maybe Jude does; you can ask him."

Yeah, because if there's one thing, I want to do on this trip its talk to the guy who stole my wife. "All right. Mom, anything?"

She crossed her arms and sighed. "Are you happier now that you've moved away? I can see you've changed the way you look, and you've changed your name, which I have to repeat is terrible, but I wonder. You were so angry when you left, and no one knew what you were doing. You didn't even visit your father! And this Agnes, is it a serious relationship, or are you just sleeping around because you can these days?" She came over and sat next to me on the picnic bench.

This is why I run and hide!

"Mother," I leaned over and kissed her cheek, "I'm doing just fine. I don't particularly care for the term happy; I think that's for kids and idiots, but I am content. I live a simple life because that's what appeals to me. I'm not angry anymore, and I've accepted that this is who I am. As for Agnes, believe it or not, I'm not sleeping around just because I can, so yes, if there needs to be a term for what we have then serious is ok. I apologize for staying away so long, but I needed the time to let go of all the foolishness I was carrying inside me."

"And God? What about your faith, what about that? It's also important for God to be a part of your life, William."

God, what about God?

It was at times like these that I thought of the woman my mother was when I was a child, back during those hazy northern California nights when she'd see me off to bed. God then was a sprite who kept you safe when you slept. He kept you company in quiet moments, and there was no need for atonements for moral cowardice or obligatory demands for safe passage to the shores of Heaven. Jesus loved me and was a happening progressive dude. That woman vanished when she lit out for the east coast after her blowup with Moses. It was here, where her family was from, that she re-embraced the orthodoxy of her youth. Like Moses, she was raised in a conservative Christian home, but unlike Moses, she went back.

God, what about God?

When I arrived, with Astral and Rebekah in tow, it was my turn to embrace the faith. This was the price we paid to be allowed to stay. There would be no commune astride the Blue Mountains; I would not be the second coming of

Moses Bohrman. Astral took to it, changing her name to Lilith, codifying Rebekah's name, which I had been trying to convince her to change to something, anything, else. I invested what time I had to become the good conservative Christian that Lilith and my mother wanted me to be. There was *also* the time required to work the fields on the plot of land I had to pay for. I tried, but God never came to me, and Jesus never saved me. I sat in the classes, and I read the good book time and time again, but what I read wasn't what they read, and they tired of my questions and lack of faith in the face value of their words.

God, what about God?

And yet for years, I trod with my unhappy wife and my uncommunicative daughter to the church down the road to hear the words, the sermons, the homilies of the right Pastor Davis meant to fill me with the means to see my way along God's path to whatever he thought was important that Sunday. I spent the time grousing that there were better uses of my time, but on those occasions when I thought about whatever it was he was impressing upon us, I would look at the crucified Jesus above him and wonder if *he* found any of this remarkable? I suspected that once he made it back to the ethereal lands of his father, Jesus took off surfing the cosmos. After all, wasn't it Jesus who had said that our time here is insignificant compared to our time in the house of the lord? I'd probably be off surfing too.

That made me think of the beach.

My mother was waiting for my answer to her question concerning the lord, thy God.

"God loves us all, mother, you know that. I haven't given up on God, I just see him in a different light these days."

That look of disappointment I so remembered had returned. "You need to accept the Lord as your savior, William. It's important." She placed her hand on my chest. "In here."

I put my hand over hers. "I haven't forgotten."

Agnes and Leslie came out bearing cookies and lemonade and saved me from my mother's stifling proselytizing. We made nice with small talk about the weather and the bugs. This was, at least from my point of view, a reason to mention why California isn't so bad. There were the inevitable questions regarding our relationship status, which allowed Agnes to reiterate her desire for matrimonial bliss with one Monk Buttman; Monk remained non-committal. Talk of quilts and cooking, farming and small-town life, and children who don't turn out the way you thought they would, made up the rest of the conversation. I said little, preferring to spend the time wondering how

I continually found myself in these types of situations having to juggle present and former relationships.

There was a buzzing in my pants. It was Judith. Just what I needed, a hat trick!

I excused myself and went around the house to the front porch.

Judith Delashay was the beautiful rich woman with that long beautiful neck in her beautiful home in the hills of Beverly overlooking LA. I'd gotten involved with Judith during the search for her husband's girlfriend, and while I wasn't proud of myself for continuing to see her while living with Agnes, I'd done a wonderful job of convincing myself it was no big thing. Agnes, who I suspected was well aware of my occasional rendezvous with Judith, never spoke about it. Some of that was Agnes' fear that, if pressed, I'd take off for the good life with the rich woman, and some of it was that Judith and I didn't get together very often. I discovered that Judith had an interesting libido wherein the sex, while not frequent, was intense and committed. We had an unusual relationship that didn't interfere with the other aspects of our lives and allowed us to maintain a connection that we both found rewarding. As long as I came home Agnes kept quiet.

"Hello?" I noticed that my palms were sweaty.

"I hope you haven't forgotten me, Monk?"

"That I could ever forget you is, to me, unfathomable. Are you still in Michigan?"

"No, I'm back at home. I was hoping we'd have some time for one of your visits. I've missed you and your charms." As she spoke, I could feel her next to me, the two of us out by the pool where we spent most of our time together.

A strong ache crept into my stomach. "As delightful as that sounds, and you know how much I enjoy your company, I'm afraid I can't as I'm in Virginia trying to help my daughter with her runaway husband."

Judith started laughing. "What is it with you and runaway husbands?"

I was laughing too. "I don't know, it's my new thing now."

"I'm sorry to hear that." That urge to run away, this time to Judith, was beating in my chest.

"So am I." Out of the corner of my eye, I saw Agnes over by the side of the house.

"Let me know when you're back in town, and we'll make arrangements for a visit." I noted the disappointment in her voice.

"I will." I hoped she noted it in mine.

"Goodbye, Monk," she said in a purr she knew would make me crazy.

"Goodbye." I listened as the line went quiet. Agnes approached as I returned the phone to my pocket. She slid up next to me and put her arms around me. I reciprocated and put my arm around her.

"Is everything alright?"

"Yeah." I looked into her eyes, and she leaned in and kissed me.

"Good, cuz you're not going anywhere." She squeezed my waist as she said this.

"No? I thought we were going to the grange?"

Agnes smiled. "Nice try, Buttman, but you know what I mean."

I smiled back. "Yes, I do."

"That's an excellent line. I know just the place where you should repeat it."

"I'm sure you do."

• • • • •

Carleton found me in the living room nursing a beer, as the womenfolk were getting ready for our trip to the grange. Astral and my mother left to retrieve their own male appendages and their contributions to the food table. I reassured them I would be there. Man, you blow a few people off a couple of times, and all you get from then on is grief. Carleton grabbed a beer and joined me. After a few moments, Rebekah, who was both disheveled and refreshed, at least somewhat, sat down with us. She brushed her hair back with her hands. Carleton and I toasted her presence with a tap of our bottles, which signaled to Leslie to "come get this girl cleaned up".

Once Rebekah was made presentable, we piled into the two trucks and headed to the grange. Agnes rode with Leslie and Car, since he had a club cab. Rebekah rode with me in the old Chevy. We drove in silence. I knew she did not want to go, but there were people we needed to talk to.

The grange wasn't far away, and the adjacent dirt lot was filling up. I was dressed in my vintage sixties finery, which I knew would create a stir, as it was so different from what I wore the last time any of these folks laid eyes on me.

"I think maybe I'll stay in the truck for a while," Rebekah said with her head down.

"No, that'll only make the talk that much more tiresome, you know that as well as I. Stick with me and it'll deflect some of the questions about you and Farrell since I'm the main clown at this attraction and it'll give us a chance to talk to some people who might be able to help us." I put my hand on hers. "You have a lot of supporters here. It'll be alright."

I don't think she believed me. I didn't know if I did either.

As expected, the minute we were out of the truck folks started coming over, marveling at what's happened to Lilith's long lost Willie. There were lots of hellos, handshaking, and shocked faces. Could I really be the same guy who, when they last saw me, said little, fumed, and was voted most likely to run amuck? I utilized all my powers of concentration to present a more dignified front and answered, with as much positive sincerity as I could muster, as many questions as I could, most of which consisted of where do you live now, what do you do, and is that really you? Even Donald and Judah came over, with Astral and my mother in tow, to say hello and to confess their concern to Rebekah about whatever the hell Farrell was up to. There were questions for Agnes after she foolishly came over to see what was going on with her idiot boyfriend. The questions continued as we found our plates, helped ourselves to dinner and picked a place to sit.

Potlucks at the grange were loud, raucous affairs with people in constant motion. Eating and talking were the paramount activities and the main source of the din in the hall, to which an occasional amplified voice was added to apprise us of upcoming events, celebrations, or important community news. Everyone had their accustomed spots within the hall where they sat and communed week to week. Agnes and I sat near, but not too near, my mother and her husband Donald, at the end of one row of tables, which allowed the curious to stop by and chat.

Since I wasn't doing anything interesting other than being an object of curiosity, I omitted any talk of Desiree Marshan and that debacle. It might be a little too lurid for dinner, and I didn't think it would enhance my reputation any. The conversations inevitably turned to the usual suspects, farming, the weather, goddamned politicians, and did you hear about so and so? This, naturally, brought up the subject of Farrell, and I, reluctantly sought out Chess and the boys to find out what they thought. Rebekah unenthusiastically tagged along. They were over in their usual corner, not far from the pastry table. They were gluttons in that regard. That they were, or I should say the men were, rail-thin and still put away most of the desserts perplexed many of us who suffered the opposite effect when overeating pies, cakes, cookies, and the like.

Chester Jenkins was sitting with his two boys, Darrell and Carroll, his wife, Penelope, and their daughter, Melissa, who, as Chess always reminded us, was named after an Allman Brother's song. The two sons and the daughter brought along their respective spouses and kids. They were the biggest group in the grange. Rebekah and I squeezed in between Chess and Pell and inquired as to everyone's health. Pell and Melissa, who did not share the men's thin figures, complained about their assorted ailments before expressing their worry over the runt of the bunch, Farrell. I asked if they'd heard from him.

Pell, who often spoke for the family, filled us in. "We ain't heard from him, Darlin'." Pell called everyone darlin'. "I don't know what to think anymore. I always thought he was doing fine, but he was a little different, you know, the youngest are Momma's boys, but not Farr, he kinda kept to himself. He never really said anything about being unhappy till a few months ago, but like I said he didn't always confide in me about those things." She peered over at Rebekah, who was clearly ill at ease with the Jenkins. "You hear from him, Darlin'?"

"I haven't spoken to him in nearly a week." Rebekah was speaking to her hands.

"It's this whole new church thing, isn't it? That damned preacher who gave that talk a while back." Chess' mouth was full, but he was somehow able to pass on his dislike for Lucian DeBerry along with some spittle.

"Yeah, he was going on and on about it at the store just before he left," Carroll, who was working on two slices of pie, chimed in.

"We finally had to tell him enough already. I don't mind his looking for what he believes is a better way; it ain't my place to judge, but it got to be all he'd talk about, and we had to tell him to stop. He was annoying the customers," added Darrell, who had just returned with his own two slices.

Melissa apparently had no interest in her brother's problems. Chess, having finished one mouthful and preparing for the next, took in the two of us, Rebekah and me, with a queer kind of expression.

"I know you and Farr were having problems making babies and all," he cocked his head towards Rebekah, "and, pardon my saying this, but word around is that this is a family issue with ya'll." He lifted his hands and cocked his head towards me. "Of course, that's probably just talk, but I know that Farr had gotten it into his head that somehow this could be remedied by finding favor with the Lord." It was time for another mouthful. "Anyway, I think he blames you and your seed, Will, and even if it makes no sense, something in Farr believes he has to find some way around this. Unfortunately, he's done this on his own, so I don't where he is."

Moron!

"Well, I appreciate your time, Chess, Pell. We'll let you know if anything comes up. You all take care now." They nodded at this.

Willie, the hayseed, got up.

After freeing ourselves from the Jenkins clan, I dragged Rebekah over to where Pastor Davis was holding court with several ladies from the church. We said hello, and the ladies were quite taken with my more cosmopolitan appearance. I complimented them on their courtesy and asked for a minute of the pastor's time. They looked to the pastor first before leaving after he told them it was all right. Pastor Davis and I had many conversations over the years concerning God, Jesus, the Bible, and while most had been interesting, even pleasant, the last few were acrimonious due to my deteriorating home life. I was unsure how amenable he'd be to talking to me again.

Pastor Davis was a small affable man with soft brown eyes and the kind manner one finds in someone at peace with who he is and his purpose in life. This man of the church was, after thirty-plus years, someone the parishioners could turn to whenever they didn't know what to do or the shit hit the fan. He wore his faith on his sleeve and was proud of that. I admired him for being able to put up with the many yahoos in the community and his ability to look past the casual bigotries and stupidities that used to drive me nuts.

"Is this about Farrell?" he inquired.

"Yes," I said.

He noticed the sadness in Rebekah's eyes. "Then why don't we step outside." We followed as he led us to a courtyard just off the main hall. There we found a picnic table under a maple tree. "How can I help you?"

"We're looking for Farrell," Rebekah responded.

"I'm afraid I haven't seen Farrell in quite some time. I believe the last time was when he let me know that he meant to find a new church."

"Did he say where this church would be?" I was curious.

"Not in as many words, but it was my understanding it would be a part of Mr. DeBerry's fellowship." Pastor Davis was working hard to conceal his disdain for Mr. DeBerry.

"I don't suppose you have any information or know the location of his communities?"

"All I have is this." He reached in his pocket. "When I heard you would be here, I thought it best to bring it along." The pastor gave me the handbill. It was folded in thirds with printing on both sides.

"What did you think of Mr. DeBerry?" I asked.

The pastor put his hands together and pressed them to his lips. "I think he means well and believes what he preaches, and in that sense, I understand and agree with much of what he has to say, but the world today is not the first-century world of the early church. As wonderful as it may seem, to some, to want to return to those times and that perceived sense of community, I don't believe that's possible. The world is different, and our society is different. Is there work to do? There is always work to do, but it should be in concert with the times. To me, going back to an idealized image of the early church only makes the work to be done more difficult."

"Do you believe him to be an honest man of faith?" I looked into the pastor's expressive brown eyes.

"I do. I haven't heard any rumors or talk that he might be a confidence man or a fraud, but there's something about those who follow him..." he drifted off, his hand pulling from his pocket a crucifix.

"How do you mean? Have you met any of his followers recently?"

His demeanor changed, and the color of his face darkened. "I don't know that I should talk of this, as it came in the wake of the deaths of those two young people last week, but three men approached me and asked for a word. Only one of them spoke. He was a tall man with dark, deep-set eyes. He told me he was like the hand of God as concerns the prophet, Brother DeBerry. That's the word he used. He said I should be wary of those who speak idle thoughts and spread false rumors of Mr. DeBerry. I asked what rumors these might be so I might answer if I'd heard them, but he said such lies would not pass from his lips. While he did not threaten me, I got the distinct impression he was not averse to the use of violence. I reminded him I was a man of God and that he if his beliefs were as he intimated, should not be acting that way. All he did was smile and say he had the Lord's blessing in his work. I haven't heard from or seen him since."

"They call him the Angel," Rebekah added. "Molly called him that. They said the three had been to see them, to tell them not to repeat the stories they'd heard about Lucian DeBerry. She was frightened of him, this Angel. They had heard that people died if they didn't do what he told them."

I took her hand. "What stories?"

"Molly wouldn't say what they were, only that a man, at least she thought it was a man, approached them and told them that Lucian DeBerry was not what he appeared to be. She called that man the Ghost. He told them they should leave before what happened to the woman happened to her."

"What woman?" I tried not to sound overly disbelieving at tales of angels and ghosts.

"I don't know, she didn't say. I got the impression it happened out at this place in Oklahoma." Rebekah was trembling. "I don't want to believe Farrell is with these men."

"Maybe he's not, maybe he's on his way to this place in Oklahoma?" It was possible.

She turned to me. "Maybe, but maybe not." She was looking for something other than the fear that her idiot husband may have joined a self-appointed biblical avenger.

The Pastor took another piece of paper out of his pocket. He handed it to me. "Do you remember Art? Mr. Devaney?"

"Isn't he the guy who commuted to DC? Government man, as they used to say. Had that small place out by the Gilferries farm?" A vague image of a guy in glasses popped into my head.

"Sort of. As I understand it, he used to work at Langley for the CIA as an analyst. Maybe he can help you find out the whereabouts of Mr. DeBerry." He was clearly uncomfortable handing me this.

"Thanks."

The pastor stood up. "God be with you, William, and with you too, Rebekah."

10

We found Art as the party was beginning to thin. To my surprise, he was chatting with Carleton about a particular variety of tobacco. Agnes and Leslie were there too. Agnes was exhausted and overwhelmed by all the people and attention, and Leslie was bored and ready to go home. When he saw us approaching, Car gestured for us to join them. Arthur Devaney, physically, was much like the pastor in appearance: a small roundish man, except for a bald head in the place of the pastor's graying curls, and mischievous green eyes dancing behind black-rimmed glasses. Both were contemplative in their own way; one concerned with God's message, and the other with what we hid behind our smiling faces. Art held out his hand to shake, not only to me but to Rebekah as well. He had anticipated our desire to seek him out for information.

We said our hellos and sat down. The others gave us some room, though they did not leave. Art began the discussion, such as it was.

"What can I do for the two of you? I'm assuming an interest in the preacher, Mr. DeBerry, correct?" His eyes expressed merriment at knowing the subject of our interest.

"That's correct. Pastor Davis sent us to you," I said, as a matter of fact.

"Did he? The pastor is a curious man when it comes to the rumors and talk that afflict us in our interactions with one another; perhaps the fear of overt salaciousness, but I can't imagine his calling without all the innuendo and hearsay common in any community."

"People like to talk," I said.

He smiled at that. "Yes, they do, don't they?"

"I suppose he could be uncomfortable with that aspect of his ministry, the gossip and all?" I added.

"Oh, I think we both know he is, however, I see no point in humoring ourselves with the pastor's sensitivities," he paused long enough for me to wonder what I'd gotten myself into, "given that your concern is with what your husband, Farrell, is doing in the company of the associates of Mr. DeBerry." Devaney turned to Rebekah as he said this.

"I want to know what's going on, I want to know if Farrell's in danger from these people," she replied.

Devaney nodded. "Well, I can tell what I know, and perhaps that will help you determine the right path to take. I'm only an amateur tobacconist these days. You see, I've retired from my former profession, and merely moonlight when it comes to providing information, something I pointed out to Pastor Davis. Anyway," he turned to me, "I was asked to find what I could, as a favor to the pastor, after the reported suicide of the young couple off of Meridian Drive." He looked around before leaning in. "Turns out, Mr. DeBerry is both interesting and mundane, depending, I suppose, on how you perceive the man. He began life as Larry Bochner and had his misfortunes with the law, nothing particularly tiuntilating, mostly petty theft and fraud. After spending a few years in prison, he got out and became the preacher we now know as Lucian DeBerry. As to his recent activities, he seems to be exactly what he presents himself to be, a man preaching his personal epiphany and calling others to join him in Oklahoma."

"Just the one or are there more?" Rebekah wanted to know.

"As far as I could find there is only the one. Mr. DeBerry has no presence online and isn't on social media, so what's out there is slim, but there is chatter about him and some of his followers. Consequently, I've found that there are those beyond Oklahoma who are sympathetic to his cause and whom, I believe, he stays with as he travels. Also, his name comes up on church websites and calendars, which can provide another means of tracking him."

"So no simmering caldron of evil underneath the surface, no references to angels or ghosts?" I was already bored with Lucian DeBerry, with all of it.

Devaney smiled broadly. "You've heard about that too, have you? Yes, there are references to an angel and a ghost, most of which are cryptic in nature. It may be that they are related to the only incident of any kind I could find that is associated with Mr. DeBerry, or his community, and it is salacious, if you care for such things. It involves a murder-suicide that occurred there. I searched the local papers and a man named Justin Peterson killed his wife and then himself. She was found in a field and him in his home. If there was a motive, it wasn't reported. Mr. DeBerry wasn't there at the time and wasn't mentioned as having any part in it, probably just a local tragedy. That's about all there is out there."

"Anything to connect him to Molly and Jonathan?" Rebekah moved closer to me.

Devaney seemed oddly sympathetic to this. "Not that I could find. I talked to Bill Offry down at the police station about it. He told me they were found lying together in bed. The autopsy determined they'd poisoned themselves. There was no violence found on either body, and he said there was a note by the bed in which they apologized and asked for forgiveness."

"Forgiveness for what?" I was curious.

"It didn't say, it's assumed for killing themselves."

"And the references to the angel and ghost that you found?" Devaney seemed surprised I'd ask.

"Nothing specific, mostly stuff like beware the angel, and the ghost who was, or is, either a liar or a truth-teller. I don't know whether you ought to put much credence in it."

Rebekah stood up, tears rolling down her face. "So there's nothing for me to do; no way to find him?"

Devaney and I looked up in reaction to Rebekah's standing.

"What kind of phone does Farrell have? A smartphone, the kind with apps, that sort of thing?" Devaney reached out for her hand.

"Yes, he has one. Why?"

"Do you?" The merriment was back in Devaney's eyes. His hand was still outstretched.

"Yes, it's here..." She took out her phone and handed it to him. He looked it over.

"Excellent. Mind if I add a little something to it?" A sneaky little grin joined in the merriment.

"Like what?"

"Like an app to track his phone; how about that?"

"You can do that?" Rebekah was genuinely amazed.

"Yes, you can." Devaney began working the phone as the rest of us watched. It merely confirmed my suspicions that we were all being tracked all the time. As he was doing this, a thought popped into my head.

"You ever heard of a guy named Bernie Schoor? Lives out in LA?"

Devaney smiled. "About my height, sandy red hair, glasses, thin, looks much younger than he is?"

"Yeah." I was smiling back.

"Sorry, never heard of him." Devaney glanced up at me as he said this.

"Yeah, that's what I thought."

"It's a small world, Mr. Buttman, a small world." He handed the phone back to Rebekah. "Your husband is in Pennsylvania, outside of Morgantown." He pointed to an icon on the phone. "Use this app. Just enter his number, and it'll show you where he is or the last place he was when his phone was on." Art Devaney was quite proud of himself.

Rebekah wiped her eyes and closed them slightly as she looked at Devaney, "Is this legal?"

Devaney's eyes twinkled. "Are you planning on using it to commit a crime?"

"No."

"Then it shouldn't be a problem."

"Ok..." Rebekah was lost in thought, no doubt wondering what Farrell was up to in Pennsylvania.

The rest of us were tired and ready to go. I thanked Devaney, and he mentioned to Carleton that he wanted to continue their talk about tobacco at his convenience. We collected our stuff and almost made it to the trucks before being confronted by an equally tired mother and ex-wife. I had no interest in dealing with either of them and had no idea what we would do next other than maybe head out to the keystone state.

"Monk..." I was startled by Astral using my first name. I knew they didn't want to be excluded from whatever we were up to. The sound of the ocean was again calling to me. I checked to see how Rebekah was doing, but she was fading fast. They stood there waiting. Agnes shrugged her shoulders when I looked at her, so I made an executive decision.

"We'll come by tomorrow and talk. Go home, get some sleep, ok?"

"You promise?" Astral pleaded. Oh, brother.

"I promise." Reluctantly, they headed over to their husbands.

My extended clan piled into their cars and trucks, drifting off into the warm, humid evening.

. . . .

Carleton's house was quiet. Rebekah was in the guest room. Leslie gave her a little something to help her sleep after persuading her to stay here rather than try to go back to her place. I left Agnes in our room and settled into a chair on the porch. I had a strong desire to breathe free. The porch was screened in to keep the bugs away, and a cool breeze kept the humidity from becoming oppressive; I'd been away too long, I was no longer comfortable in my skin here. My skin belonged back in LA. Here I felt completely out of place. As much as I wanted to help Rebekah, I wanted to be as far away as possible. Even from here I could see that her relationship with Farrell was frayed and torn; it was like a replay of Astral and me. Did I really want to be a party to that? And what could I say if it is indeed coming apart?

Willie, the father nobody, cared for, including me. I was already a big enough failure in that regard. Did I need to be to adding to that sad-ass legacy?

I turned off the porch light and peered into the darkness. The sky is always alight in LA, but not so much here. When the clouds close in the dark can be suffocating, clinging to you as you try to orient whether you're up or down. On those evenings when the clouds part or the sky is clear, the cosmos sparkle with the fluorescence of the moon, distant planets, and the billions of stars stretching out into forever. In the past, when there was nothing at home that didn't involve yelling or brittle silence, I would wander out to an old tree planted along a ridge, probably as a marker when the land belonged to the men before me. There I would sit and stare into the starlight looking for God. I never found the God Astral or my mother or Pastor Davis had found, the one they were convinced I needed. Instead, I found God among the stars. I found the twinkle in his eyes.

• • • • •

Fortunately, or otherwise, the day's booze, food, and activities stunted my equivocating brain, and the next thing I knew the sun was shining and I was being roused by Carleton.

"Out here again? Man, it's time to get up. Ag's gonna think something's up with you."

I was trying to rub the knots out of my stiff neck and back. "She already knows that. It's the why is she's still hanging around that gets me."

He laughed. "Like I know. Anyway, it's time for breakfast. I'll give you ten minutes."

"I gotta have fifteen at least."

"Ten's all you get." He left me for the kitchen. With nothing better to do, I headed up to the bedroom to see if Ag was still asleep or even still here. I found it comforting to find her hiding under the covers trying to fend off the early light of the day. I sat by the bed, pushing on her hip to get her moving.

"Come on, Ag, time's a-wastin'. There's doings a transpiring."

She pulled the covers off her puzzled face. "What the fuck does that mean?"

"Now, now, there's no need to get all knotted up." I reached back for my best southern hick accent.

"Uh-huh. Where were you last night? We've got rules regarding where you're supposed to end up at night, Buttman, and its right here in bed with me." A laughable pout crossed her disheveled face.

"Sorry, I had some thinking to do, and I didn't want to disturb you. I inadvertently fell asleep on the porch." I leaned over and kissed her.

"Well, just don't let it happen again!"

"Yes dear." I gave a quick thought to joining her under the covers, but my ten minutes was running out. "Up and at 'em, beautiful, breakfast is on the table."

"Yeah, yeah, yeah."

The two of us grappled with each other in the small bathroom, trying to make ourselves as lifelike as we could and stumbled downstairs to the kitchen. Leslie and Carleton had the morning's fare spread out and waiting: biscuits and gravy, cinnamon rolls, and coffee filling the kitchen with their delightful aromas. Rebekah, looking nearly as lifelike as Agnes and me, took her spot in line as we filled our plates. We relegated talk of our day's plan to after breakfast so as not to harsh the good vibe we were getting from the comfort food in front of us. Leslie inquired into the quality of our sleep, at which point I had to confess that I'd fallen asleep on the porch. This brought out Carleton's stories about all the times he'd found me asleep on the porch during those bad old days when I'd need a place to crash after fighting with Astral. It was amusing to everyone but me. That's life, I suppose.

When breakfast was over, we helped clean up, and I called Astral to ask when it was convenient or prudent for us to come over. Rebekah protested, but not with any real emotion, and we were given an hour until we were to meet at my mother's house. Astral would call ahead. She also asked that I not bring Agnes along.

"Why? Won't Judah be there?" What did she care who tagged along as we took off after the runaway Farrell?

"I just think it would be better, that's all."

Agnes, for her part, had no interest in hanging out with my ex-wife. Leslie had offered to keep her occupied.

"Fine, it's not like I want to go either," I sniveled.

"Buck up, Gomer, you'll survive. If I have to deal with Simon and Eric, you can deal with Lilith and Judah. Just be yourself, that's what you told me to do," Agnes smirked.

"Yeah, like I know what I'm talking about," I smirked back.

"Exactly!" Agnes was loving every minute of this, as were Carleton and Leslie. Even Rebekah was stifling a smile.

"Well, you're all a bunch of jerks!"

Great, now they were laughing too.

Donald and Rebekah Altonberg lived in a quaint hundred and fifty-year-old home about twenty minutes from Car's. It was red with white trim, two stories, rustic in appearance and well maintained. I found it ironic that my mother would move from one rustic environment to another after complaining about the first one. But there's a difference, I suppose, between old Virginia rustic and hippie California rustic. It was set on two fairly bucolic acres that allowed my mother to have a garden and a grove of peach trees. I approached the place with trepidation. In the last few years before I left, I don't know that I came over more than once or twice. Anger does that. Every visit was a reminder of the things I was doing wrong and, naturally, all the things I needed to do to set my marriage right. At the top of which, as far as my mother was concerned, was becoming a more stand-up guy in the eyes of the Lord.

Bad vibes, man! That made me laugh. Rebekah looked up from her phone, but only for a moment.

Unlike just about everyone else in this part of the world, Donald Altonberg was not a farmer. No, he was a banker, and a reasonably fair one, all things considered. His reputation was more how can I help, versus, your behind on your loan; we're taking your property. Donald was a well-liked man. He helped set up the mortgage that allowed Astral and I to buy our plot of land. The mortgage was made through Astral's name, or I should say, Lilith Bohrman's. It took some work to get me a social security card given my background; apparently, it had slipped everyone's mind when I was young. Everything we earned was filed through joint returns with Lilith as the head of the family; it was just easier.

It was about this time that I set up the account in Philadelphia. It was where the money from my half of the land went after Judah bought me out. It's also where the bulk of the money from the Desiree Marshan caper ended up. James' money found its way there, but that's another story.

While a congenial man, Donald mirrored my disinterest in him with a disinterest in me. I had no problem with that, the plus side being he made no effort to back up his wife's entreaties that I get myself together. He blamed Moses for my failings because Moses was a cipher to him, a name with no face periodically ridiculed by my mother, and therefore an easy out. Because Donald and Rebekah had four children of their own, there was no need for me to be any part of their life, which, again, was just fine with me. I spent many years trying to decide if I liked my mother. I remembered her when I was a child in the hurly-burly days of the farm. As a child, I thought those times to be exciting and fun, but upon reflection, I now understand why she left, and if I were honest with myself, which I tend to resist, I would have too. But our years here in Virginia were sour and unhappy. I never found the woman who sang to me as a child and based on her constant chiding, she never found the man she thought I'd turn out to be.

Rebekah spent the majority of the drive looking at her phone.

"This app's kind of creepy. Look at the detail," she thrust the phone into my face, "it goes down to street level."

"Is he still in Pennsylvania?"

"Yeah, just north of Morgantown on highway 119." She put the phone in her lap. "Maybe he's staying with someone there."

"Maybe." It was possible there was more to that, but she didn't elaborate.

We pulled into the driveway of my mother's house. She and Astral stood there; no Donald or Judah, they were smart enough to bail. With little enthusiasm, Rebekah and I got out of the truck. Our greetings to Astral and my mother were fraught with ambiguity, and after a moment of acute discomfort, the four of us went inside. I didn't understand why they wanted to see us, or me to be precise; we'd had what I considered all the pointless catching up the day before. Once inside, Astral and my mother turned and asked me to give them a little time alone with Rebekah.

"Then why am I here?" I can't deny I was a bit defensive in the tone I used.

My mother took my hand and led me through the kitchen towards the back door. "We'll have some time to discuss things in a minute or two; be patient."

She closed the door, and I was by myself out on the back porch staring at her garden. Just beyond were the rows of peach trees and beyond that, the mountains easing their way into the sky. Further still was where I wanted to be, back in California, heading to Judith's for an afternoon of sensual pleasures. I foolishly promised myself I would forget about Judith once she left for Michigan. That would be it. All my attention would be with Agnes and wherever that went. That led me here where I was lost in thought over a woman I probably had no business fantasying about but about whom I couldn't stop.

My phone was buzzing.

I fished it out of my pocket, entered the code, touched the appropriate icons, and opened the text message from Agnes, who was passing along a text message from Carleton, who was passing along a message from Art Devaney. It was about the murder-suicide at DeBerry's compound in Oklahoma. He'd found a chat room, online thread, or something like that, where people associated with Lucian DeBerry's ministry, past and present, shared their thoughts. Apparently, there was a lot of buzz over the deaths of Molly and Jonathan and whether it had anything to do with Justin Peterson and his wife, Amy. At some point, a person using the hashtag, *#I Know the Truth about Lucian DeBerry*, left a comment, which Devaney thought would interest me.

"Do not believe the lies of the liar DeBerry. He knows what really happened to Justin and Amy... he knows who killed them. Justin did not murder his wife though it was made to look that way. I know the truth about DeBerry and Amy and you should too. Do not trust the liar DeBerry, do not believe his lies."

This was followed by comments from others warning them that to believe that Lucian was a liar would bring more scorn and derision to them and an unwanted visit from the angel.

"Do not believe these lies about Lucian," they said. "There will always be those who seek to disarm and discourage through false witness and hearsay."

It made me wonder what in the world Farrell had gotten himself, and Rebekah, into. Religious nuts, as Moses would say, fill their dreams and their heads with a utopian image of God and Man that has no relation to the real world. They live in insular communities where all you'll ever hear is a kind of pabulum force-fed, day in and day out, that only reinforces their isolation. Having lived in a semi-insular community, I thought that was a little harsh and somewhat hypocritical, given that the farm could be construed as the same. I wasn't worried about the teachings or beliefs so much, I'd heard most of them before. I was concerned about people dying unnaturally.

I'd had my fill of that and didn't need to be a part of anymore.

By the garden, I found a bench as I tried to figure out what I was supposed to do. It was a pleasant day, warm with a slight breeze and shade here and there if you needed it. The lands surrounding the house off in the distance were of the postcard pastoral variety; you could say it was quite beautiful and serene.

As I sat there admiring this panorama of rural life, the pit in my stomach continued to knot. Art Devaney would not have sent the message if it didn't mean anything.

11

His eyes were open, but they had dried out. The tongue in his partially open mouth was beginning to swell, protruding out of a grotesquerie that was once a man with a plan. I don't know why I wandered back into the church. I stood there; the wind blowing dust through the front doors, caking the silent pews along with the dead preacher.

He loved her.

That's what he confessed.

"We are never free of sin, Monk," he said just days before as we waited for Farrell to come out of hiding there among his fellowship of believers. The little prick never did come out; once again, he had run off. He was making me look bad. Me, and all the other failures who took off when the world buried them and their idiotic dreams. The preacher Lucian DeBerry, longing to be sympathetic and understanding of my exasperation with Farrell, spilled his own failures upon the floor where they mingled with the dirt and the filth.

I wasn't surprised. "That only works if you believe in the concept of sin to begin with."

"Sin is our stain, we cannot erase or wish it away." DeBerry held out his hands, turning them as if that signified something.

"But we can, just as we can let go of our presumptions about what or who God is."

"It's not good to let go of God, Monk, he is a part of you. Without God, where can you go? What will replace the void within you? It's not good. Loss, discontent, even evil, will take its place."

Evil, I could see it in the faces of the Pronto brothers and Todd Boyer.

DeBerry continued, "Embrace the savior, Monk. Let Jesus into your heart as I have. His forgiveness *is* the light and the promise of life everlasting." He had that soft, earnest tone in his voice. His eyes watered over as he implored me to accept Jesus as an alternative to my wishy-washy lay-a-bout religious philosophy.

The light. What light?

The light of salvation, the freedom from a world of sin and degradation would be mine if I simply uttered a few well-chosen words. I smiled. Somewhere in that utterance, there should be some belief, some feeling, shouldn't there?

Lucian DeBerry believed.

I don't know why I came back in to stare at his lifeless husk. Like before his hands were outstretched, open, but this time I noticed they were discolored by blood and dirt. I tried to relive our conversation, to remember the words that were spoken, but only three came to me.

He loved her.

The wind was carrying the distant sound of sirens.

12

Rebekah said little as we left her grandmother's house. Her eyes traced the hills, the farms, even the occasional tractor rumbling along the side of the road. Something was amiss in all this, something I didn't know. Whatever they talked about, they kept to themselves. My mother had interrupted my mental ramblings, telling me she loved me for no discernible reason and asked that I be understanding with Rebekah. What do you say to that? She looked at me for a long time without saying anything. Our distance remained. My inner Sunshine shed a tear, and there was that ache from when I was just a child, from the day she left.

Monk Buttman, however, took it in stride.

That's life.

Astral was next. She was tired, worn out by what I assumed was her fraying relationship with her daughter. Rebekah never looked at her as we were saying our goodbyes. Astral tugged at my sleeve and pulled me away from the others towards a large dogwood tree. It was odd to be alone with her. For the first time in that lost thousand years, she looked at me with an expression other than disgust or dismay.

"I'm sorry, Will."

I was shocked by the apology. "Sorry for what? If it's for the past, don't be." I tried to smile.

"For lying to you about the babies, about Judah; all of it. It wasn't fair or right."

It's amazing what a few words can do. I could feel the last of my resentments fall away as the words settled into me. It made me think that maybe someday I could really let her go.

"Maybe not," I answered, "but we weren't a good match and we were miserable together, we both know that. If I hadn't knocked you up at sixteen, we wouldn't have lasted another year. We were just kids. I'm just as sorry for wasting so many of our years together expecting us to be something different. I was distant and mean, and I know I hurt you. It's all right; it is. You're better off now."

Her eyes locked into mine and for the briefest of moments, I could see the woman I'd once loved. I cupped her face with my hands and kissed her. I don't know why, and I'm surprised she didn't pull away, but it was a better goodbye than the last one.

"Rebekah hates me."

"She's just angry. It'll pass, you'll see." I tried to be reassuring, hoping I was right, all the while knowing her relationship with Rebekah could end up just like my relationship with my mother.

"I hope so." A tear rolled down her cheek.

"So do I," I said to myself.

"Goodbye, Monk." She took my hand as we walked back to the truck.

"Goodbye, Lilith. Take care." I turned to my mother, who was standing off to the side of us. "Goodbye, mother." My mother nodded. With nothing left to say, Rebekah and I got in the truck and drove off.

Glum. The drive, the afternoon, the whole day wallowed in glumness. Rebekah wouldn't talk, and I didn't know what to say or do. We made it back to Carleton's where we all endured the awkwardness with stunted attempts at conversation until Rebekah announced she would lie down. Leslie and Car took the opportunity to run a few errands. This left Agnes and me with some actual time together. She was almost an afterthought through most of this and having just returned from Astral's unanticipated apology, I was ready for a few quiet moments with her. We made our way to the back of the house where Carleton had a picnic table.

"How are you holding up, Sunshine?" She leaned in and kissed me on the cheek. "You look like you don't know what you're doing."

I laughed. "What's your point, beautiful?"

"No point, it's just something I haven't seen in you before. Not that you *know* what you're doing most of the time, but normally you hide it better."

I put my arm around her. "That's very comforting."

"I'm a comfortable woman. You remember, don't you?" She shook her breasts and smiled in a way that made me want to commit any number of lascivious and carnal acts upon her delightful person.

I looked around quickly to make sure we weren't under surveillance and cupped one of her wonderful breasts in my hands. It was soft and so inviting. "I do indeed. Maybe we should head upstairs—"

"With your daughter in the house? Surely, there's someplace quiet and discreet out here for a tryst?" Agnes had that sparkle in her eyes.

I brushed my lips against hers as I held her close. "There's a barn just over that rise. We can go there." I point to the left between kisses.

"Ooo, I've always had the bad girl farmer's daughter fantasy." Her hand was caressing my hard-on.

"Then you should come with me, Daisy Mae."

"Promise not to tell?" she cooed.

"I promise." I took her hand and led her to the barn.

. . . . .

The late afternoon, early evening light peeked through the siding of the barn. It wasn't one of those big magnificent ones most people think of; this one was smaller, more a shed than a barn. Carleton didn't have animals in this barn, so the odor wasn't overpowering. We found enough hay and happily played out our erotic fantasy. Over the months, Agnes had become much more expressive in her sexual desires, and I was more than willing to assist as I had never been with a woman who wanted to do those kinds of things, another reason to hold on to her.

"Feel better?" Agnes was next to me, running her finger around my belly button. I felt oddly exposed since my pants were down by my ankles. She was similarly exposed with her dress above her waist, and her underwear bunched up in my hand.

"I do, thanks." I handed her back her underwear.

"I was hoping we'd have a moment to get a little crazy, but up until now things weren't looking too promising, so when the stars aligned I figured what the hell."

"I was wondering about the dress..." I was running my fingers around curve of her hips and breasts.

"Easy access, just in case." She smiled and grabbed hold of my erection. "I would think as an old farm hand, you'd have had many adventures like this."

"Yeah, you might think that, but no, this is the first time I've had carnal knowledge with a woman in a barn. Sadly, before you, my sex life wasn't all that adventurous."

"Minus the rich woman?" She squeezed as she said this. I'd forgotten about Judith.

"Yes." I squeezed her breast in response.

A nasty grin crossed her face. "You know I like that, don't you?"

A nasty grin crossed my face. "I pay attention."

Agnes leaned in and ran her tongue along the inside of my upper lip before kissing me. "Seconds?"

"Yes please." Who turns down vacation sex, even if this isn't quite a vacation?

I suppose it was possible that Carleton or Leslie, or maybe even Rebekah, might burst through the door, but it was highly unlikely we'd get another chance at barn sex, so I was willing to take the chance. We finished with a flurry and fell back onto the hay. The light was fading, meaning we couldn't stay too much longer or the others *would* come looking for us. Agnes must have been thinking the same thing.

"What's the plan, Sunshine?"

"I don't know about you, but I'm pulling up my pants."

"After that, smart guy." She reached over and lightly smacked me on the head.

"We should head back to the house." I zipped up my pants as she put her underwear back on and adjusted her dress.

"Do I appear sufficiently presentable?" She put her hands on her hips and tilted her head to one side. "I don't want to advertise our inability to keep our hands off one another."

I stood behind her and put my hands on hers. "No, we wouldn't want that," I kissed the back of her neck. "I suppose we should go..."

She leaned back into me. "I suppose..."

I carefully picked the straw out of her hair.

The kitchen light was on, and the aroma of good things to come greeted us as we returned to the house. Carleton was broiling steaks and Leslie was finishing up the potatoes and salad. My glum daughter sat at the table watching, her expression no different from the one she took into the bedroom for her nap. Car handed me a beer and Agnes a glass of wine.

"You two almost had us worried. I thought I'd have to come looking for you. I expect you enjoyed your walk?" he winked at me before taking a small strand of hay from Agnes' head.

"We did." I winked back.

"Well, I always like to say that no vacation is complete without a good walk." he slapped Leslie on the ass as he said this.

"Carleton! Behave yourself," Carleton just laughed. Leslie smiled and shook her head. Agnes and I sat down at the table with Rebekah.

"I'd like to go home now," she said.

"We'll go over after dinner." She was looking down at her phone.

"I'd like to go now."

"You need to eat something."

This time she turned on me. "I don't need you telling me what to do. Those days are over. You had your chance, all right! I want to go home." The good times were back, my daughter was yelling at me.

I almost snapped. Bad old Willie jumped back in my head, his words on the tip of my tongue ready to tell his daughter to shut the fuck up, that he didn't need any more of her crap, and if she thinks she knows it all then good fucking riddance. I could feel everyone's eyes burrowing in on me, like before, waiting and wondering what was next.

Monk had to take a moment.

"I'm not telling you what to do. Don't eat if you don't want to, but even anger needs fuel. I'm hungry, and Carleton and Leslie have made us a nice meal. The least we can do is have a pleasant dinner with them. I can take you home after that." I tried to say it in as calm a voice as I could. Rebekah looked at us. Maybe she, like me, didn't have the stomach to return to the bad old days. The four of us were across from her; as she started to rise, Leslie came over, and carefully put her hand on Rebekah's shoulder.

"We know you're upset, and it's been a trying time for you. It'll be all right. Have a little something to eat. You'll feel better, huh, baby?"

Rebekah started crying. I handed her a napkin, and we waited for her to get it out of her system. Car quietly got up and retrieved the steaks while Leslie brought over the potatoes au gratin and the salad. She poured herself and Rebekah a glass of wine. Rebekah wiped her eyes and took a drink.

"I'm sorry," she said in a small defeated voice.

"It's all right, baby, it's all right." Leslie put her arms around Rebekah and kissed her forehead. "I know just how you feel." She sat down and held out her hands. The rest of us held hands as Leslie said grace.

"Lord, may you bless us and our friends here tonight as we enjoy this good meal you've given us. And may you look kindly on our dear Rebekah who needs you and to help us guide her through this trying time, Amen."

"Amen," we chorused. With that we pass around the food, and I filled my plate. Even Rebekah made herself something to eat. Leslie made small talk about what they, she and Carleton, were planning for their wedding, which would be next spring and we, Agnes and I, should think about attending, which Agnes thought would be fun. I just smiled between mouthfuls. Inevitably, the talk turned to what was next for Rebekah as far as Farrell was concerned.

"I need to find him," was all she would say.

I didn't want to say it, but I figured there was no other option, minus my not going. "We can head out tomorrow, no point in waiting. Pennsylvania is closer than Oklahoma."

"I guess..." The phone was back in her hand. I noticed her watching me. She put the phone down and grabbed my hand. "What did mom mean when she said she was sorry about the babies and Judah?"

The pins were dropping for all to hear. I struggled to get the food down my throat.

"I'd like to know," she said.

I turned her hand over and place my other hand upon it.

"It doesn't mean anything now. What she was referring to is that she lied about not being able to have any more children with me and that she was seeing Judah behind my back, but I already knew all that. Still, it was almost comforting to hear her own up."

"I don't understand?" The tears were back, cascading down along the contours of her beautiful face. This was breaking my heart. The last thing I wanted to deal with was the last years of my life with Astral. It was bitter, hateful, and angry. This is why I had no interest in coming back here or reliving any of it. There was nothing here but misery and sadness. I lifted her hand and kissed it.

"I'm sorry, Becky, I don't know what to say, but the truth is your mother didn't love me and didn't want to have any more children with me. We didn't plan on having you; you were a happy accident. We were very young, only sixteen; we had no business being parents, so your mother lied to me when we tried to have more kids, saying there must be something wrong with me, or that God didn't think it was the right time, but all the while she was on birth control. I found out about it years later."

I wiped the tears from her cheeks.

"As for Judah, well, much as I hate to admit it, and as much as I don't like the guy, he's been a better husband to your mother than I ever was. I'm sorry to say that because I truly loved your mother, but I didn't know how to love her the way she needed to be loved, the way that Judah loves her. I knew they were seeing each other; I knew they wanted to be together even when she lied to me about it. That's what she meant. It's in the past. I don't think it's good to hold on to your resentments. A part of me still loves your mother, but a bigger part has let her go. I left because I had to, because it was the only way I could let go. I needed the distance and the separation. I'm sorry I left you. I'm sorry I wasn't a better father. I don't know what else to say."

I let go of her hand, and she pulled it back. A crooked half-smile, half grimace crossed her face. "So it's all true," she whispered, her eyes looking up.

"Yes."

She sat up and wiped her eyes one more time. Leslie brought out the lemon meringue pie and the crème de menthe. For no other reason than it couldn't hurt, we toasted each other and discussed the best way to head north. I offered to help with the dishes but was told to take care of Rebekah, so as the three of them cleaned up, Rebekah, and I left for her place.

The ghost was waiting for us.

13

"There's no need for the weapon," he said.

I turned to see Rebekah with a shotgun in her hands. I didn't recognize it at first, but then remembered it being behind the seat of the truck. I put it there years ago after hearing reports of vagrants hiding in our fields. A pair of vagabonds had surprised old man Filtsner, who farmed about five miles down the road and had a heart attack. Word got out, and I was advised to carry some protection, so I reluctantly put the shotgun, which, in thinking about it, I bought from Carleton, in the truck. Apparently, it remained there.

The man on the porch of Farrell and Rebekah's small house, partially hidden by the cloak he was wearing, hardly seemed ghostlike. Thin and wiry with sharp eyes behind a pair of round wire-rimmed glasses; he stood in the shadows of the halide lamp illuminating the driveway. The lamp was precariously attached to a post to the left of the house, and it swayed with the wind causing the light to wax and wane as we approached. The man put up his hands to assure us his intentions were peaceful. Rebekah responded by pulling the hammers back on both shotgun barrels. I wondered if the shells were even any good after all this time.

"It might not be a bad idea to explain your presence here, buddy." It seemed the thing to ask.

"Where's Farrell?" Rebekah shouted.

"Your husband is at the home of Breck Sindalar. He and members of Lucian DeBerry's cult live there. They use the house as a way station for people being indoctrinated into their cult before they leave for his *community*, as he calls it, in Oklahoma. Your husband is with them, in the company of one Ashton Cox, who most people refer to as the angel," he said.

"And who are you in all this?" It was my turn.

"I don't want people to be fooled by this charlatan and his cult." His eyes kept floating between me and the angry woman with the shotgun.

"YOUR NAME?" Rebekah drew closer, the shotgun leveled at the man's chest.

"I'd be happy to share what I know, but I'd prefer that you lower the weapon first."

She looked at me like I had the answer. I didn't but thought it better to keep the possibility of violence to a minimum and motioned with my hand for her to lower the shotgun. She slowly released one of the hammers and moved the gun so it rested across her arms.

"Who are you?" she asked again.

"My name isn't important. What is important is that you know what your husband is getting himself into and perhaps you as well." He stood his ground on the porch while Rebekah and I stood ours about ten feet away.

"Alright, say what you came to say. It's late, it's dark, and I'm not a big fan of creepy. My daughter is tired and angry and armed, so get on with it. I'd apologize for being short with you, but this isn't how people normally conduct their business."

The ghost, with his hands out, pass on his litany of evils perpetrated by Lucian DeBerry, fraud and abuser. "I came to warn you that your husband is in danger, that despite the homey tones and sweet preaching the fraud DeBerry spreads, his group is nothing more than a personality cult that isolates and brainwashes its adherents. I know of sexual abuse being engaged in at his so-called community, and I know personally of lives destroyed by this man. Whatever your husband is looking for, he won't find it with this cult, and if he draws you into it, then be prepared to abandon your vows, and God knows what else. The man is evil, his cult is evil, and he will destroy your marriage; of this, I'm sure. That's what I have to say."

We stood there, the melodrama hanging in the air, wondering what to do next. Rebekah glared at the man while I wanted nothing more than to be in bed with Agnes.

"Anything else?" Rebekah raised the shotgun.

The Ghost offered a slight grin, "No. I've said what I came to say." He quietly slipped to the side of the porch, out of the shifting light, and into the darkness. Rebekah traced his movements with the shotgun until time and distance assured her that he was gone. In the dark, we heard the sound of a car starting and driving off.

I looked over at her. "Well, that was weird."

We walked, under the sway of halide lamp to the front door. There we stood. "Maybe we should go inside," I suggested.

Rebekah opened the door, and we went in. My eyes adjusted as the lights came on; they were too bright. The place was a mess. "Yeah," was all she said.

After releasing the other hammer on the shotgun, she placed it by the door. I watched as she picked at this and that among the detritus littering what I assumed was the living room before sitting on the couch. I carefully followed and sat at the other end of the couch after moving the bag of loose clothes out of the way. The house, or what remained of it, was a small manufactured home that had seen much better days. I thought for sure that Rebekah was much more organized than this, but really, what did I know. I'd only been here once before, and that was at the door to let her know I was leaving. I never actually stepped inside. I think she just stared at me before closing the door.

I got up to leave.

"I'd like you to stay." She was as uncomfortable as I was, which made the request just that much more awkward. We were having a lot of those moments lately, but that's common with strangers, even those related to one another.

"Why?"

"Because I'm afraid." She was rubbing her hands.

"Then let's go back to Car's."

"No." She looked up at me as I stood there. "Why is it so hard for you to stay here with me?"

"If that's what you'd like, all right." I sat back down and phoned Agnes to give her the good news. I was hoping she could save me, but no such luck.

"Be nice," was what she told me.

"What does that mean?" I knew what it meant.

"It means don't be a jerk, Buttman." I was tempted to make one of my patented clever remarks but held my tongue. "I'll see you tomorrow. Goodnight, Sunshine." I could hear the concern in her voice.

"Goodnight, beautiful." I put the phone away.

There was a fly in the room, buzzing back and forth, circling around my head. Other than the sound of Rebekah breathing and the fly, it was unnervingly quiet.

"Did you believe him? What he said? Do you think he's right, that Farrell's in trouble?" she was speaking to the room more than me.

"Maybe, but he said danger not trouble. Frankly, I thought it was all a little too contrived. If in fact, there's fraud and abuse, you'd think that it'd be out there, but I don't remember Art bringing that up, so I'm not convinced. Something may be rotten in the state of Oklahoma, but it might also be that this guy simply has an ax to grind."

"I think he's the guy that spoke to Molly and Jonathan," she said again more to herself than to me.

"You're tired, and we've got traveling to do, so you need some rest. Where am I sleeping; here?" I motioned towards the couch.

"Yeah, the place is a mess, and *yes*, this is the only other place to sleep besides my room. I assume you don't want to sleep with me?"

We got up only to stand there. Rebekah was looking around the room, to my mind, an apt metaphor for her messed up life, then turned to me and before I could do or say anything, she came and put her arms around me. Instinctively I put my arms around her, her grip around me tightening, and she began to break down. First came the tears, then the sobs, and finally, the shaking and the loss of strength to even stand. I lowered us back down to the couch and let her get it all out. I didn't quite understand what she said; something about not being loved, or being stupid, or why was I here. It could have been any of that or none of it. Other than an occasional five-second hug, I couldn't remember the last time I'd held her so long. I ran my hand along her hair, pulling it out of her face, and holding on for dear life. I could feel the tears running down my face. It was deeply embarrassing, but there was no one there to notice, not even the sad young woman we named Rebekah. The sobs subsided, and she grew quiet and then fell asleep in my arms. The couch was a large matted gray thing with a matching gray ottoman. I pulled it closer with my foot, let my head settle on the bulky couch, and before long, I too fell asleep. I figured she wake up in a little while and head off to her room; instead the morning light found us still on the couch.

I had to pee.

I eased her off me and found the bathroom. After relieving myself, I washed my face and tried not to dwell on the clutter all around. I rummaged through the kitchen for something to eat and drink, finding little. There was coffee, although the pot was dirty, and some milk that didn't smell too bad. I cleaned the pot and brewed the coffee. While waiting, I picked at the papers and trash on the table adjacent to the kitchen. I sat down to read three religious tracts extolling the virtues of Christian life before empire and the corruptions of power and wealth. I couldn't think of a better life than being part of a despised and persecuted minority. I understood the allure, but it was borne out of illusion, like living on the early American frontier. It was, in truth, a hard brutal life, full of privation, terror, and death.

Naturally, none of that unpleasantness would intrude because, together, as the tracts explained, they would forge anew the testament of Jesus Christ here on the Earth, plus there was the not so insignificant fact that this was not ancient Rome, or even the roiling Middle East. I was feeling smug as I worked through the cheaply produced flyers, so much so that my sense of fair play began nagging at me. The product, I suppose, of too many years among good Christians, too much indoctrination of my own. All that church and bible study in the years before I left, so maybe I shouldn't be making fun of these earnest efforts to find a more meaningful life. Who was I to judge?

I chided myself for all the equivocation.

Rebekah had risen from the couch, shuffled off to the bathroom, and returned to sit across from me at the table.

"Coffee?" I had retrieved two cups just in case.

"Thanks."

I filled her cup and watched as she took a tentative sip. "Feel any better?"

She picked up one of the tracts, looked at it momentarily, and set it back on the table. "You don't believe any of this stuff, do you?"

"Why would you think that?" I could hear her mother and grandmother in her voice.

"I don't remember you being very religious, and I remember you and mom arguing about it all the time, that's why," she said in a rather derisive tone.

"Yes, your mother and I argued about religion and faith quite a bit. That doesn't, in and of itself, imply I have no faith or belief. It simply means I don't toe any particular line of Christian faith. Your mother, and your grandmother, and I suppose you as well, subscribe to that faith, and it bothers them that I did not."

"They're worried about your soul." A mischievous smile came to my conservative daughter.

I smiled back. "Perhaps, but they have no control over that any more than I have control over what happens to theirs. As far as these are concerned," I held up on one the tracts, "it's not that I don't *believe*, it's that I don't think you can create, or recreate, something for which you have no firsthand knowledge or which is based on conditions and circumstances that no longer exist."

Rebekah smirked. "So you don't think people should try to live their lives in peace with one another in a community of support and faith in the teachings of Jesus?"

I wondered if she was buying it.

"I'm not saying that," I said. "I think all Christians should, and maybe are trying to do just that, but this strikes me as a fantasy, a way to bypass the hard facts of trying to practice first century Christianity in twenty-first-century America, simply to avoid dealing with people like me." I put the last of the flyers back on the table.

"So you say." Her eyes were dancing under the messy pile of hair on her head.

"So I say. You seem to be a little more with it this morning. Did you get some sleep?"

She actually smiled. "Yeah. I guess sleeping with you isn't so bad."

"I guess. What's the plan? Stay? Go? What?"

"I need to get cleaned up, and we need to put the canopy on the truck. Then we can load up and go." She looked around the place. "I'm already packed, and there's no reason to stay."

"What about the house?" I didn't care about the house, but I wanted her to confirm my suspicions; she was moving on, but where?

"It belongs to the Jenkins, they're welcome to it. Place is a piece of shit, and I'm tired of living here."

I was about to ask more, but my phone buzzed. It was my beloved. "Butt Monkman, at your service."

Agnes laughed. "Serious, Monk, are you ever going to grow up?"

"Doubtful, what's up?"

"I'm calling on behalf of Leslie, inviting you to breakfast, assuming you haven't already eaten." She sounded wonderful and inviting.

I looked at Rebekah and mouthed, "Do you want to eat breakfast at Car's?" She shook her head yes. "No, we haven't eaten yet, and yes, we'd like to come over for breakfast, but we'll need a little time, say an hour." Rebekah intimated this was good for her as Agnes asked Leslie if that was ok.

"Ok, see you then, Sunshine."

"See you beautiful." I was smiling. This amused my daughter.

"You and Agnes seem pretty happy together."

"We have our moments," I said.

She smiled without saying anything.

The canopy was resting on the side of the house. As Rebekah was cleaning up, I swept out the bed and manhandled the canopy onto the truck and fastened the clamps. Her bags were just inside the bedroom door. After confirming they were ready to go, I lugged them to the truck. I put the shotgun back behind the seat. I checked the shells and discovered they were new. I called Carleton and asked for Art Devaney's number. I wanted to know if he could find anything on one Ashton Cox, the angel. His response was, why not? Rebekah wandered through the house one last time for reasons unknown before closing the door.

"Are we ready, Becks?" I said that without thinking. It was the nickname I used when she was little.

"Yes, Mr. Sunshine, I am." I'd forgotten she used to call me that.

Another reason to never go back.

• • • • •

There's a saying I have, and it's possible I picked it up somewhere in my running from place to place that goes like this: If you're running away, never look back, because if you do, you're screwed. I ran from the Pronto brother's because I was an idiot teenager who was sure if I returned, they'd kill Astral, Rebekah, and me. I ran from Virginia because there was nothing to keep me there, not family, not work, and certainly not love.

I was a miserable, unhappy prick whose wife had left him, whose mother disowned him, and whose daughter wouldn't talk to him. I found solace in big anonymous smoggy traffic clogged LA. I resorted to a joke name I made up as a kid, cut my hair, lost the beard, and became the dressy nobody I was destined to be. I had a little money and maybe if I was lucky, half a life left to live. I was lonely, but at least I was actually alone rather than lonely with a miserable disinterested wife who wanted nothing to do with me and preferred a chump named Judah Martindale.

My beautiful beach was calling me, and I was yearning to heed its call.

But I had to look back, and when I did, there was no more running.

My daughter spent the short drive to Car's staring at me. After collecting what little she wanted from the decaying home she had shared with her runaway husband, she came over and kissed me on the cheek and said thank you. Now she was freaking me out by looking at me as if I had somehow become interesting.

"What?"

"I don't know. I've always thought of you in a certain way, and now I don't know what to think." She was leaning against the truck door, her eyes continuing to give me the once over.

"That's good, right?" I raised my eyebrows, like that would help.

"I don't know."

I shrugged my shoulders. "If you come to an epiphany, you let me know."

Leslie made pancakes for breakfast with eggs and sausage on the side. After breakfast, Agnes and I gathered our belongings, the assumption being that we were done with our cavorting in this little corner of Virginia. I pushed away the odd feelings of nostalgia and the idea that I would miss these people, the same people, not long ago, I couldn't wait to get away from. Agnes, as she had on the old man's commune, found the rural life fascinating and grumbled about having to leave just as she was getting to know everyone, which to my mind meant Leslie, with whom she had bonded over quilts and an affinity for men with suspect histories who seemed to be a little more mature in their later years.

"So, we're not coming back here?" She was standing in our little room in Car's house, the disappointment in her voice.

"Probably not," I was getting the doe-eyed treatment. It was her go-to move when she wanted something but wasn't ready to blurt it outright. "If we have to follow Farrell all the way to Oklahoma, I don't think it makes sense to come back here just to then fly back to LA."

"Doesn't Rebekah have to come back?"

"I don't think she's coming back. I think she's done with living here, with or without Farrell."

She sat down on the bed. "Really?"

"Really. Something bigger is at play between the two of them, although what that is she hasn't said, but it can't be good given how upset she been lately." I sat down next to Agnes.

"Do you think he has something to do with the death of that couple she was talking about?" She put her arms around me.

"It might, but I hope not. Farrell's got his problems, but if they didn't kill themselves, then what did kill them, and who's responsible for that? Farrell? This Ashton Cox guy? I'd rather not go there." Agnes pulled my arms around her and looked into my eyes, "What?"

"I missed you, and I need my morning kisses."

"Didn't I kiss you already?" It's possible I hadn't.

"Come on, Buttman, there are some things I keep track of, and kisses are one. So kiss me, or I may become difficult."

I kissed her. "Really?"

She kissed me. "Really."

"I don't remember agreeing to this." I kissed her again.

"Not my problem." Probably not.

Once the mandatory kissing was concluded, the group assembled by the truck. Leslie presented us with a lunch basket so we wouldn't have to suffer through a fast food meal, and reiterated our invitation to their upcoming nuptials. Agnes assured her we would be there with bells on. Carleton simply smiled before pulling me aside.

"How are you set for protection? It's never a bad idea to be safe." Carleton had the habit of keeping a firearm close, if unseen to those around him. He and I argued many times about it in the past, but since I knew he was also keenly aware of how quickly a gun could kill, I didn't consider him a wacko.

"There's the shotgun behind the seat," I assured him.

He smiled. "That old double-barrel I sold you?"

"Yeah, Rebekah held on to it."

He rubbed his chin. "Well, that's no good if you're out and about, lugging around that shotgun. Here," he reached in his pocket and handed me a snub-nosed 38 and a six-inch switchblade, "this should help."

"Um, I don't think I'm going to need to be armed like this."

He just shook his head, "This ain't California," as if California, or specifically LA, is any safer than southwest Pennsylvania, "and it's better to be safe than sorry. Considerate it a loaner."

"I'll get them back to you as soon as I can." I put them in my pocket, along with a box of shells. Sufficiently armed, we said goodbye, exchanged hugs and best wishes and were on our way to wherever the hell Farrell Jenkins might be holed up.

We didn't make it thirty miles.

14

The three of us were mashed together on the bench seat, motoring along when my phone began buzzing. I squirmed and elbowed Agnes trying to pull the thing out of my pants pocket.

"Wouldn't it be smarter to keep it in your jacket, so it's easier to reach?" she said.

"Sorry." I thought about offering to kiss it and make it better, but concluded that might be inappropriate, even though, I thought since we were all adults, inappropriate how? "Yeah?" I blurted into the phone.

"I hate to call you like this, but ya'll need to come back." It was Carleton.

"Why, is Farrell there?"

"No, he ain't here, but there's a little girl named Emily, who came directly to see you, Mr. Sunshine." He was laughing. I was not! I passed the news on to Agnes and Rebekah as I slowed to turn the truck around.

"All right, we're on our way back," I grumbled. I put the phone in my jacket to Agnes' evident approval.

The women wanted answers.

"Who's Emily?" asked Rebekah.

"She a little girl who lives with her mother on your grandfather's farm," I told her.

"How'd she get out here from California?" asked Agnes.

"I don't think she came from California, I think she was in Philadelphia with her father. Looks like she took off." This I assumed.

"How'd she know to come here?" asked Rebekah.

"I told her we would be down here." The two looked at me like I had planned this. "I merely mentioned it in passing while we were talking about having to leave her garden. I didn't tell her to come on down if that's what you think."

"Then, why?" Agnes was suspicious.

"I don't know. She did say she didn't like being there, didn't like having to share a room with her stepsister, and would miss her garden. I sorta mentioned I used to have a farm out here. Take your pick."

"Doesn't she know how dangerous it is for a ten-year-old to be out on her own? Good Lord, imagine all the terrible things that could have happened to her, all the perverts?" Agnes was aghast at the thought of a ten-year-old running off on her own.

"Well, Carleton didn't say she was hurt, so it appears she made it there safely. Besides, she's eleven." I merged into the southbound traffic and headed back.

• • • • •

Emily was sitting, quite erect, on the plastic seat clutching her oversized backpack. Luck and providence guided her to the town of Bedford, Virginia, where she appeared resolute in her search for Mr. Sunshine. The how's and whys, at the moment, were immaterial to the fundamental question of what to do now that she had successfully made her way to the county seat. The sheriff was contacted only after it was determined that no Mr. Sunshine lived in the county, but small towns are places where everyone is known and once the name Buttman came up, Carleton was called and then I was.

Emily had no interest in sharing any information besides the peculiar names she gave. As she was expected to do, she thanked Rex for giving her the ride down from Richmond. That she found Rex, or that Rex noticed her, or that they were both headed to the same part of the state, and that Rex was a nice understanding man, was serendipitous to the point where I briefly considered that maybe, sometimes, there might actually be someone up there watching out for us. I wasn't willing to entertain that as a true, purposeful intellectual inquiry, but the fact that she was here, in good shape, and for the most part in good spirits, made me wonder.

When I trooped through the door, and she saw me, the backpack hit the floor, and the confident little eleven-year old ran and wrapped her arms around my waist, her face buried in my stomach. Vance Thomas, the sheriff, was both relieved that she knew me and perplexed at why these things kept happening to him. I didn't ask what that meant. After assurances that we were not a threat to the girl's safety, we sat down to figure out what to do next. Calling her father seemed to top the list. Emily disagreed.

"I don't want to go back. Ever!" she blurted out.

"I get that, but he still needs to know that you're safe and where you are, plus we should call your mom, so she isn't worried," I said in my most soothing fatherly voice.

"I don't want to go back. I want to see your garden here, remember?"

"I remember, but first things first. Sorry, but that's the way we have to do it."

"I won't go." Her eyes were red, and the tears were coming, but she refused to want to cry. She was definitely her mother's daughter.

"I know how you feel." Agnes smacked me after I said this.

"Good God, Monk, don't say things like that."

"Sorry, beautiful." I made a mental note that Agnes was getting bossy.

I called the old man, or more specifically, the farm, and asked for Calista. She was out in the vineyards. I said it was important, she needs to call me back: it's about Emily. Little was said in the five minutes it took for a worried Calista to call back.

"What about Emily?" she asked.

"She decided to take a side trip to Virginia while I was here to visit family and friends. Were you aware that she'd skipped town?"

"No. I haven't heard anything. Is she alright?" The alarm sounded through the phone.

"Yes. Would you like to talk to her?" As if she wouldn't.

I handed the phone to Emily, who knew she was in big trouble. Quietly, with her jaw clenched, she listened to her mother, stated her case, apologized, and promised not to do it again. Emily reiterated her unwillingness to go back to her father, but her mother was unmoved. The tears were running down her face as she gave me back the phone. My heart sank. Few things eat at me more than sad children even if I know they fucked up.

"She needs to go back to her father. I don't need him hounding me about this." Calista was crying too.

"Let me have his number," I said, "and I'll arrange to get her back. As a matter of fact, I was going that way with Agnes and my daughter, Rebekah, so we can take her back. That might give her some time to come to terms with this."

"Just a minute..." she gave me the number for her ex-husband, Thomas. "Please call me when you get there, ok?"

"Not to worry, I'll let you know how it's going and when we get there."

She wanted to talk to Emily again. Emily wiped her eyes and took the phone, listening intently, shaking her head, and quietly crying. When she was done, she returned the phone. I sat next to her.

"We have to let your father know where you are," I told her.

Emily nodded but said nothing.

Thomas answered on the third ring, or rather, his wife did. I filled her in and asked to speak to her husband. She thanked me for calling, and after a few seconds, Thomas came on the line. I explained the situation, assured him his daughter was in good shape and in good hands and that, if he was all right with it, we would bring her back to Philadelphia. He seemed neither angry nor unconcerned, mostly resigned. I got the distinct impression that this wasn't the first time something like this had occurred. I asked if he wanted to talk to Emily and then handed Emily the phone for the third time in ten minutes.

She did not want to talk to him and was tight and monosyllabic throughout their short conversation. She gave me the phone, and I got the address and promised to keep him and Alisha, his wife, informed of our movements concerning Emily's return. I handed the phone to Vance so he could hear from Emily's father that it was ok for us to return the runaway. He was happy to be relieved of any further responsibility. Having managed to work through our interactions with the police, we headed back to Carleton's house.

It was lunchtime.

Through much negotiation, mainly between Leslie and Agnes, it was decided that it was best to stay another day and head out after church. Agnes wanted to see what it was like, and it gave her a few more hours with her new friends. Rebekah wanted to find Farrell first, so it was also decided we would go to Philadelphia by way of southern Pennsylvania. If we were staying, Emily asked if we could go see my old farm. I explained that it didn't belong to me anymore. Rebekah said she'd take care of it. Taking out her phone, she called her mother and explained the situation. During her talk, Rebekah must have rolled her eyes a dozen times but continued to say yes to whatever it was that Astral was asking for.

"Then we'll be over in a little bit." She turned to Emily, "Are you ready to go, Emily?"

"Yes, Rebekah."

Rebekah smiled at her. "Call me Becks." Emily smiled back.

"I didn't think you'd want to go?" I was surprised.

"Who knows when I'll be back?" was her answer.

"You and I are going to have to have a little talk here soon about what's going on with you." I tried to be stern.

She gave me a half-smile and took Emily's hand, "Come on Emmy, let's go." I watched as they headed out towards the truck.

Agnes stayed with her new fast friend rather than trudge through my not so distant past. It was Saturday, and that meant fried chicken, mashed potatoes with country gravy, corn on the cob, and peach cobbler. She and Leslie had work to do. Car had some things to take care of in one of their fields, which left me no choice but to get in the truck and head over to my ex-wife's house, which used to be mine, and wander the farm that also used to be mine.

Good times.

"What did you agree to with your mother that I should know about?" I asked.

Rebekah grinned. "I promised that we'd be nice to Judah, that we'd be nice to her since it's possible she may tag along, and that we're not to say anything about how Judah had to use your journals to get the farm back on solid ground."

"My journals?" I'd forgotten about those.

"Yep. Judah didn't have much success the first few years after he bought the farm and he was tired of hearing about how much better the old crank, Mad Willie, was at farming. I had your journals, and mom begged me to let him see them. After he started following what you did, things picked up, but they would both be mortified if you were to gloat about it, and it's not a very Christian thing to gloat over your rival." I felt a perverse sense of accomplishment that my daughter took some pride in my farming practices. "Are you going to behave, Mad Willie?"

Emily thought that was cute. "Can I call you Mad Willie, Mr. Sunshine?"

Rebekah burst out laughing. "Yeah, what about it, Mr. Sunshine?"

I tried to be serious. "I would prefer it if neither of you ever called me Mad Willie since I already have to endure Mr. Sunshine."

"But Sunshine is your name?" Emily wasn't having it, and I could tell it was bad news letting her hang out with Rebekah.

"Yes, we've discussed this, Emily. As for you, Becks, I hope you give me the same courtesy you agreed to give Judah and your mother."

Rebekah looked at Emily. "What do you think, Emmy? Should we be nice?"

Emily gave this some thought. "My mom says we should be nice to people, and I like Mr. Sunshine, so we should be nice to him."

Rebekah put her arm around Emily. "All right, we agree to be nice to you while we're there."

"Thanks," I said dryly.

We pulled up to the house. My stomach hurt. Lilith and Judah came out, and we made nice with pat introductions for Emily's sake and small talk about life in general and farming in particular. Judah did his best to hide his contempt and saved us all a lot of forced niceties by having other things to do. He drove off leaving me with the ex and my real and, for now, faux daughters.

Astral had the same disconcerting tones she had when she apologized the day before. I found I kind of missed her being perpetually pissed at me.

The rise, a kind of berm, beyond which were the fields, was just north of the house. The house itself still looked as quaint as it did when I left. It was a two-story farmhouse with a large front porch. There were no additions or different paint schemes. It didn't appear any more worn, nor did it appear to have been improved upon. The boys, we were informed, were with their grandfather, so they wouldn't be bothering us. Seemed like a setup to me.

We wandered up to the rise, which allowed Emily to look out over the length of the farm. There were checkerboard squares of different plants laid out across the fields. It wasn't a particularly large farm, about fifteen acres. To the right of the house just below the rise was the barn. It was the stock faded red people expect, but that told me it hadn't been painted since I did it prior to leaving. We followed Emily as she carefully walked the rows of the fields, taking time to examine the plants and ask questions.

"Is this how it was when you were here?" she asked me.

"For the most part, yes." Actually, it was eerily the same.

Years ago I built a covered Cabana between the house and the barn at the top of the rise where the view of the fields and the mountains convey a measure of serenity. It gave us a place to have meals in the evening or sit on quiet Sunday afternoons when we were finished with church. In the last few years, before I left, it was where I spent my time lost and alone waiting for miracles to save me and my fractured family. I sat down with Astral at the cabana as Rebekah took Emily through the patchwork of crops, stopping here and there, talking and laughing. It was the happiest Rebekah had been since I arrived, and it must have been longer than that because Astral made the same observation.

"It's good to see her smile again. I worry about her, Will. She's unhappy with everything these days; Farrell; her family; church, everything. When I asked her to pray with me, she told me prayer didn't work, that God wasn't listening to her anymore. I try to help, but she doesn't want it. She doesn't sleep, she doesn't eat, and she doesn't laugh. Anytime I try to do something she yells at me...." Her voice trailed off. Rebekah sounded just like her father during the last days of Mad Willie before he ran off. She was ready to do the same thing. Astral put her hand on my sleeve, "She's not coming back is she?"

"I don't think so. She's said very little to me other than she wants to find Farrell and that she's not coming back, at least not to the place where they lived. Whatever it is, and maybe it's tied to Farrell's decision to go off with these people from Oklahoma, it's hit her hard and she struggling with it."

Astral kept her hand on my arm. I found it disconcerting.

"Maybe she does need to get away like you did. You seem so different now. It makes me think that maybe the problem between us was me after all. You left, and now you're remade and happy. I guess that's what's going on with Becky, she needs to be remade like you."

It was odd to hear her say that, even if I thought she was right, maybe not so much about us, but about Rebekah.

"I don't believe it's your fault or something you've done wrong, and as someone who's spent far too much time kicking himself about those kinds of things, all I can say is doing so is bad for your heart and bad for your love life. Becky has to figure this out for herself. That's just the way it is. I'm not saying everything was wonderful for her when she was growing up, it wasn't, but it wasn't terrible either. At some point, you have to let go of that and focus on what you can do today, not kick yourself for what you can't do. That's what happened with me. I had to let go. I had to move on." I put my hand on hers. "Are you and Judah happy together? Honestly?" I looked her straight in the eyes.

There on her face was a sweet smile as she thought of that doofus Judah. "Yes, we are. It's been a wonderful eight years. I guess I want Becky to share in that. Maybe that's what hurts so much, that I'm happy and she's not, like I failed her when my fortunes turned around and hers did not. And you, what happened to you? How'd you turn into easy going, let it go, Monk Buttman?" Her eyebrows scrunched as she said the name. "It's a terrible name, you know."

"I go with quirky." I could see the girls walking by the stalks of corn out of the corner of my eye. Rebekah picked up Emily so she could reach the top of the corn. "I was so angry when I left that I don't really remember leaving, and I don't remember the drive across the country. I know I found myself at the gates of the farm, and I remember the memories of James' death flooding over me to the point where I couldn't breathe. Apparently, I had a big fight with Moses. I don't remember that either, though I'm sure it happened. What I do remember is finding myself on the Pacific Coast Highway ready to drive off the cliff and crash into the rocks below. I was lonely and angry and certain that I'd not only wasted my life but yours and Becky's as well. If I went over the side it'd be quick, and I'd be forgotten, probably for the better."

I looked at Emily and Rebekah.

"Instead, for hours I sat there, on the hood of the car, watching as people came and went, looking across the ocean to the edge of the world. After a while the sun began to set, and I started crying at the beauty of it, overwhelmed by sadness, and I thought it will always be here but that I won't. This is all I get. When I'm gone, that's it. I had a pair of scissors in the car, and I took them and, standing up against the guardrail, I cut off the beard, threw that ratty old farmers hat I had into the sea, and let William Bohrman go. I watched as he sank to the bottom along with his foolish dreams. Once the sun was down and the stars began appearing in the sky, I felt I was ready to move on. I made my way to LA, found an old couple that had a place to rent, threw out every last piece of clothing I had, cut my hair, bought all new, or used, clothes; however you choose to look at it, and became Monk Buttman: a happy anonymous nobody in a sea of humanity."

"And what about Agnes?" Astral was looking into my eyes.

What about Agnes?

"Agnes and I are good for one another and we get along. I love the woman, and she loves me. It's all I can ask for, and that's enough." It was strange to proclaim my love for Agnes to Astral, a woman I had loved so dearly.

"Are you going to marry her, Monk Buttman?" Her soft smile to this question carried the mischievousness of our own odd matrimonial connection.

"Who knows, but I wouldn't bet against it."

Astral kissed me, which surprised me. "That's makes me feel better, and I'm happy for you, I really am."

I didn't know what to say to that. "Thanks."

I called to Rebekah and Emily that it was time to come back otherwise we'd be here for days. The four of us sat together at the table under the cabana. The last time I could remember Rebekah, Astral, and me sitting here without arguing had to have been more than fifteen years ago when Rebekah was fourteen. All that wasted time! Emily watched the three of us in our unease. She knew what it was even if she couldn't articulate it, so she tried to help.

"I like it here," she said. "It must have been fun to grow up here." This was directed at Rebekah.

She turned to her mother and father sitting across from her, her eyes taking us in, trying to remember, trying to say something her heart would let her. That angry smile animated her features. "I'm sure it's just like the fun you have now at Grandpa Mo's farm."

Emily didn't get the joke, but I did. Emily kept going, "You should come out and see our garden, shouldn't she, Mr. Sunshine?"

This brought a smile to Astral's face. "Becky used to call her father that, Emily." Astral had to say that. Damn!

"Yeah?" She looked up to her new pal.

"Yeah, he used to be Mr. Sunshine to me too." No joke there. Rebekah continued to eye her mother and I. "Now that the two of you have finally found your happy place, maybe we can start taking care of my problems for a change." That angry fire roared back to life.

Astral, stung by the insult, was ready, and unfortunately willing, to get sucked into another of Rebekah's emotional traps; some pennies never stop turning up. I wasn't, so I butted in. "We're here to do whatever your heart desires," I mused.

"I don't need your sarcasm…" Rebekah's face tightened.

"I'm not being sarcastic. Speak your mind. Let it out. Just remember there's an impressionable eleven-year-old next to you, so all I ask is you take care with your language. What would you like us to do?" I put out my hands for effect. She hesitated. "I know you're angry; you have been for a long time. I also know that you blame your mother and me for a lot of what's gone wrong in your life. I appreciate that, but we all make mistakes. I have, your mother has, and you have. Life never turns out the way you think it will. It's smarter to focus on what we can do now, not on wasting more time beating each other up for our inadequacies and failures. We've come to the end of that road. We're willing to help; we want to help, but that means you have to do more than just being uncommunicative and angry. I can accept the angry, but you're going to have to articulate your peeves cuz I'm not interested in guessing." I was willing to push my luck due to the natural high I was riding from Astral's unexpected kindness towards me.

"Mom?" Astral looked at me, but I was no help.

"I'm going to go along with your father on this, and yes, I know how shocking that sounds, but I can't continue this hostility between us. If you have to go, then I guess you have to go. I just hope it's the answer you're looking for."

Rebekah wasn't having it. "And grandma? What about her? When we talked yesterday, she could barely contain herself. All you two could talk about was how I needed to be a better wife and more understanding, that I was the reason Farrell was unhappy and wanted to leave, and that I shouldn't listen to, as your mother put it," she pointed at me, "to a man who hasn't been a factor in my life for years, who just shows up and thinks he knows what to do."

Emily, without saying a word, got up and ran out into the fields until she was far enough away that she couldn't hear us. Rebekah, realizing that maybe this wasn't the best time or place to be harping at us, got up to follow her.

"Sit down," I said.

"I should go—"

Rebekah, sit down!" I was almost shouting. She sat back down.

"I'm sorry about yesterday, Becky." Astral had tears in her eyes.

I just wanted this to end. I was tired of the crying.

"Your grandmother can be overpowering sometimes, and it's true I have a hard time standing up to her, but I shouldn't have let her talk to you like that. I'm sorry. I don't know anymore what I can do for you. I just want you to be happy even if that means you have to leave us, or Farrell, or whatever. I love you, and I worry about you, but you have to do what you have to. I won't try to stop you or say it's the wrong thing to do. All I ask is that you come back more often than Mr. Sunshine here."

"Hey?"

"It is what it is, Buttman." Now Astral was ganging up on me, tears be damned.

"I had my reasons," I protested.

"Sure." Rebekah gave me the bullshit face; like mother like daughter.

"Ok, now that you two have had your laughs at my expense, what's your beef, Becks? What do you want from us?"

She looked at Emily, who was moving further from us. "You can't give me what I want. It's too late for that. I'm sorry for making a scene. I should go get Emily."

"Maybe you should," I said. Rebekah got up and headed in Emily's direction.

"What did she mean? It's too late for that?" Astral asked.

"She meant you and me. Going back. Second chances. The things we can't give her."

"Then what do we do?"

I smiled and held her hand. "We get on with our lives."

We got up and went to take Emily and Rebekah back to the truck.

15

He loved her.

He continued to repeat this, ad infinitum. I got that part. Let's get on with the confession. If I had to bear the burden of absolving his personal tragedy through the rite of confession, fine, but enough of the pronouncements of love, it wasn't helping.

The confession took place not far from a small church much like the one we were in, something Lucian DeBerry preferred. No large amphitheater churches for this prophet. No sweet love sung to the rock and roll beat, no pounding the pulpit through microphones and sound systems. No, his comfort zone was found in small cloisters and community halls. I thought this dusty mausoleum of a church would have been a better place than where he did confess since it would have allowed a deathbed confession, and who knows, it's possible he recited the same lines before the killer drove the blade into his chest.

He loved her.

Life confounds us all.

Only after finding his calling did he find love. He was both torn and fulfilled by his desire for her and, apparently, in her desire for him. Her husband was a repressed and fumbling lover, inarticulate and moody, unable to satisfy her wants both carnal and spiritual. Into this unhappy match, strode Lucian DeBerry. He mused at how quickly they came to an understanding of the nature of their love, and lust, for one another. As if it were explanation enough, he proffered a photo of her, feeling it a sufficient answer to why he would fornicate with her against God's laws.

She was young, certainly in the photo, no more than twenty-five with bright green eyes, blond hair, and a pleasant round face. The glint of the eyes and the nasty smile revealed her to be more Magdalene than Mary. I wasn't surprised by his adultery. I knew far too many adulterers to be wagging my finger. That made me think of Judith and her long beautiful neck. The prophet brought me back to his tale of woe with the need to explain himself.

He was not, he lamented, a man with a long history concerning love. He wasn't confident as a teen, and during his years in prison, he alluded to being the object of affection to the older man with whom he shared a cell. In exchange for sex, he was watched over by this veteran of the prison system and educated in its ways. Whether he enjoyed the sex or reciprocated, he didn't say. Orgasm is orgasm, I suppose.

Once out, he told me, he was determined to find his calling, which came to him as he prayed one day in a small church. There he had been given a pamphlet on the early suffering of the church and its being a means to understanding Christ's love, which led him to read about the early years of the church, and from there he decided he was meant to reinvent the spirit and soul of those early believers in the here and now.

I gently prodded him to get on with it.

As he grew more confident in his calling, he happened upon the man and his wife. They too were searching for community as an answer to their difficulties, and for a while his ministries to them were just that, but soon she came to him alone, confused she said, by her growing fondness for the preacher, and her continuing lack of interest in her husband.

Naturally, they prayed for guidance. And naturally, I suppose, they fell into each other's arms. He expressed his surprise at her sexual appetites and nearly described them to me in lurid detail. I got the picture, I said; best to leave some images hidden within. He was trembling at the thought of her, of his love for her, many times confessed. Tears fell from his eyes as he tried without success to justify his actions. He wanted her. She wanted him. They were like so many couples before them, some biblical, some not, trapped by circumstance or bad luck.

We're only human, fallible sinners struggling with our inner lusts and desires, I told him. Pray for forgiveness, commit acts of kindness for those in need, and God will claim you as he has before. He wiped the tears away and thanked me for listening.

I said *sure*.

Those eyes were lifeless now. No more time with which to seek forgiveness. No more heartbeats longing for the woman in the picture. The police were turning off the main road, sending more dust into the sky, their sirens wailing.

He loved her.

16

The second try worked better than the first. Unlike the day before, we were actually on our way to the various parts of Pennsylvania calling our name. Unfortunately, to my mind, it took longer to get the hell out of town. The previous evening was pleasant enough. The food was wonderful, the mood light. Even Rebekah couldn't keep up the churlishness with Emily happily by her side. Rebekah was her new big sister, just as I was her new stand-in father. Emily's spirit and drive did a splendid job of hiding her loneliness, her insecurity, but all of us who got to know her recognized it after a time. Rebekah was no different, and in some ways, Emily was like Rebekah as a child. At first, she claimed ignorance when I mentioned this, but as someone who was there, however competent I may or may not have been, I saw the same small child in both of them.

Emily, as ever, had many questions and observations, which she directed to Rebekah and me. I thought it was cute; Rebekah not so much, but the little girl would not yield in her curiosity. Her questions centered on what we were like, what the farm was like, what we did, was it fun, and on and on. This required us to think more intimately of that time and, reluctantly, we agreed it wasn't so bad. We did do things together; we did have a relationship that had its moments, whether it was riding the tractor, carving pumpkins, or playing hide-and-seek. There were even bedtime stories, and kisses before the lights were turned out. The memories were, as expected, bittersweet. When the evening drew to a close, I came to see them to bed at the express request of our eleven-year-old runaway. We shared a story, and I kissed her goodnight. Rebekah promised to be right back, as they would be sleeping in the same room. I thought she was going to say something, but no, just another chagrined smile and a quick hug.

The next morning we got up, had a small breakfast, and trooped to the church for morning services. The point of the sermon was the elasticity of our ability to cope, to love, to forgive. To embrace the words of the Lord and make them the foundation of our interactions with each other; that our common humanity was far more important than possessions or station. Preoccupation with ourselves removes us from our humanity, so put the phones down, Pastor Davis implored, if only for a moment so we may gain the gift of a shared personal connection. It wasn't exactly boilerplate, and Emily asked several questions as she always did; some I even had answers for. Agnes sat with Leslie on one side and me on the other. She continued her infatuation with rural life much to my dismay.

Once the service was over and the glad-handing concluded, we headed back to Leslie and Car's for Sunday brunch, and then, after a replay of our goodbyes from the day before, we hit the road with not three, but four people uncomfortably mashed into the old Chevy truck. Emily sat on Rebekah's lap. Agnes, sandwiched in the middle, took advantage of our proximity to rest her hand on my thigh.

"I hope you put your phone in your jacket, so we don't have a repeat of the incident from yesterday?" She pinched my thigh as she said this.

I tapped the breast pocket of my jacket, "Yes, I did, and no more pinching."

"Now don't be a grump, Sunshine," she purred.

"Anything for you, Aggie." That got me another pinch from the bossy woman. This time I flinched. Rebekah was amused, and Emily didn't understand.

Next to the phone in my pocket was a note, a receipt, from Carleton for the .38 revolver.

"Just in case you get asked about the pistol. That way your ass is covered," he said.

Great.

Adding to my personal discontent, the weather was baleful as we headed out. Gone were the soft blue skies and the exquisite light. The sun had disappeared behind ever-darkening clouds bringing down the temperature and our spirits. None of us wanted to be on the road. I longed for the warm dry California climate, Agnes wanted to stay in Virginia, Emily didn't want to return to her father, and Rebekah willed us to find her missing spouse. The rains followed us along the eastern ridge of the Blue Ridge Mountains and again as we crossed into West Virginia before turning north towards Morgantown. Reluctantly, we had to stop. The truck's windows would not clear on the inside from all the moisture the four of us were exuding, and the wipers on the outside were failing, leaving little more than smudgy streaks to see through. I parked at a lookout and we waited for the rains to abate.

"Can I have something to eat?" Emily was hungry and bored. The basket Leslie had prepared was back in the bed of the truck under the canopy. Someone was chided into getting the basket, rain, or no rain.

"I don't want to get soaked. We can wait a minute or two," I whined.

Rebekah checked the weather on her phone and the whereabouts of Farrell Jenkins. "The rain is supposed to last a while, maybe another hour."

"Man up, Buttman, your loved ones need you." Agnes was all smiles.

"This whole loved ones thing is vastly overblown," I said, not wanting to go.

"Tough. Get the food." She nudged me towards the door.

"You're a jerk, Duquesne!"

Agnes laughed. "Yes I am."

With exquisite movement and skill in play, the plan was to absorb the least amount of rain by taking the shortest amount of time possible to retrieve the basket. I had the canopy key ready, had the entire enterprise worked out mentally, and I executed it flawlessly. I still got soaked. The women tried to be supportive while suppressing their glee at the man drenched behind the wheel.

"Thank you, Monk," Agnes said after giving me a peck on the cheek.

"Thanks, Mr. Sunshine." Emily was rummaging through the basket before finding the grapes, which she reluctantly shared. Rebekah just nodded, her face buried in her phone.

"Is he still there?" I said as I wiped the water off my head.

"I don't know. It shows the same location, but the time and date haven't changed. It still shows three days ago."

"Maybe his phone is off," I offered.

"I guess." She was withdrawing again.

"It's not that far, maybe another couple of hours. Now that I'm soaked the rain should stop. Hopefully, whoever is at this place can help us." I couldn't stop whining.

She looked at me with nothing resembling hope in her eyes.

As I predicted, the rains slowed to a drizzle now that I was all wet. Agnes and I shared a ham sandwich, while Emily and Rebekah split one with turkey. We divided an apple and finished the grapes. I turned us back onto the highway. The occasional shower continued to oppress us on what should have been a pleasant drive. Normally the canopy of oak, maple, and pines eased whatever nonsense was bugging me and, dappled by sunlight, made living more palatable. Our afternoon and evening instead became increasingly claustrophobic with dread-laden clouds hovering just above the tree line.

Maybe it was just me, and I was, to be honest, both bored and anxious.

Perhaps sensing the anxiety among the adults in the truck, Emily took it upon herself to entertain us by reading aloud from the young reader's book she pulled from her backpack. I groaned, Agnes elbowed me, and Rebekah said nothing. Soon we were all deep within the psyche of Mandy, a lonely young girl trying to cope with moving to another state with her father after her mother's death. Meeting her father's creepy aunt with whom she spent her days while her father is at work, and the spunky neighbor girl, Rosie, who helped Mandy out of her shell as they investigated the case of the disappearing dog. This kept us from fixating too much on the next slowdown caused by an overturned delivery truck that took a turn too sharply in the rain or the missing idiot husband.

As Mandy and Rosie continued their search for Roscoe, the disappearing dog, the clouds began to lift, and by seven we were in front of the house with the address of the last known whereabouts of the disappearing husband. Our arrival nicely meshed with the end of the book: Roscoe, it turns out, had been abducted by Cyrus, the creepy aunt's accomplice, due to the dog's barking, which infuriated her. Mandy and Rosie promised to be best friends forever, and Mandy's father promised that she would no longer have to stay with the creepy aunt.

I congratulated myself for not making any snarky or inappropriate comments during Emily's reading of the book. Agnes, sensing my smugness, pinched me. Once again, this made me flinch.

The house was one of five nestled along the road. All were small single-story homes of varying colors: blue, green, dark red, light red, and a dirty white. The houses were backed up against a hill covered by brush and trees, lending an ominous note to the already ominous fog and drizzle surrounding us. We were in front of the blue house at the south end. Two cars were in the driveway, but no lights were on, unlike the houses to the north. Rebekah looked out but seemed unwilling to approach the house.

"Would you like me to go check?" I asked, not wanting to.

"No," she said after a moment or two. She opened the door of the truck, slid out from under Emily, and very slowly went to the front door.

Agnes had a hold of my hand, "She'll be aright, won't she? Maybe you should go?"

"Maybe..." I opened my door and stepped out. I felt for the 38 under the seat, putting it to my pocket. I got out of the truck and moved over by the hood and watched. The house stayed dark. Rebekah rang the bell and knocked a couple of times. Nothing. She looked back at me and I told her to come back. I went around and met her as she reached the truck.

"No answer?" Duh! If they had answered, we wouldn't be having this conversation.

"No." Rebekah turned back to the house.

"Maybe they're out. We can stay at the hotel we saw down the road. We'll come back tomorrow. How's that?" The rain was picking up again, and I was still damp.

"Ok."

I wasn't sensing much faith that this was going where she wanted it to.

The Riverbed Motor Lodge was a mile down the road from the blue house and, all in all, not a bad place. It was an older two-story motel with a pool on one side and a small park with benches on the other. We took two adjoining rooms, both with queen-sized beds, and for dinner, we finished the fried chicken, potatoes, and corn from the night before. Leslie insisted that we take them otherwise it'd just go to Car's waist. Car didn't deny it.

I changed out of my wet clothes, hanging them up in the bathroom, and joined the others in our room. Rebekah and Emily sat on the couch while I sat on the bed with Agnes. Emily had her cards out and was arranging them on the coffee table in front of the couch. I called both of Emily's parents to inform them of our whereabouts and that, God willing, she'd be back with her father by tomorrow night. Both thanked me, said a few words to Emily, and conveyed no positive emotion one way or another. Weighed down, exhausted, resigned seemed to sum up their reactions.

Rebekah was watching Emily lay out her cards.

"Any idea what you want to do if Farrell isn't there, or if they don't know where he is?" I asked her.

"Do you know how to play hearts, Becks?" asked Emily.

A contemporary eleven-year-old wanting to play hearts, I didn't get it.

"No," was Rebekah's answer to us both.

"Would you like me to show you?" Emily turned to Agnes and me, "It's better with four."

That was our evening for the next hour. Emily explained the rules, which all the women understood, and which, unfortunately, took me a few hands to get leading to my inability to win a single game. I don't know *why*, it's just a fucking card game! My inexplicable failure to grasp the game was highly amusing to the women.

"Geez, Monk, you're terrible at this!" Agnes wasn't helping.

"Really, Dad!" Neither was my daughter.

"It's not that hard, Mr. Sunshine." Not even Emily!

"Yeah, yeah, yeah, card games aren't my thing," I huffed!

After far too much abuse and too many losing hands, I offered to go across the street, where there was a gas station/convenience store for ice cream. Noting that the rain had stopped, they decided to take a break as well and join me. The rain had taken its leave, but the night air was heavy with moisture and residual heat. It was a hot muggy evening. Perfect.

The store, an aging relic from the distant past, was basically a small gas station that pushed out the repair shop for a convenience store. Outside were two dual-sided pumps, and inside the store, a large reach-in cooler with pop and beer on one end and three rows of shelves filled with nothing of any nutritional value on the other. The ice cream cooler was across from the cash register by the front of the store, although now that I think of it, it's probably not considered a register anymore.

A twenty-something woman with blue hair, a nose ring, and tattoos up and down her arms seemed happy to have someone come into the store. Agnes and Rebekah helped Emily pick something from the rather mesmerizing selection of frozen treats. Watching her trying to choose reminded me of the exhilaration of those days long ago when Miguel, James, and I would gorge ourselves on pizza and burgers, the stuff the old man dismissed as crap and unfit for human consumption.

"It'll take years off your life eating that junk," he'd bellow.

I didn't care. Hey, at least I never acquired a taste for the dope we were peddling, but that was also Miguel's doing. He wouldn't work with dopeheads, or, more specifically, his cousins who supplied us wouldn't. That and Astral didn't like it and I wasn't about to give her up for a joint.

After much deliberation, and a soliloquy from Michele, the woman with the blue hair concerning life behind the counter out here in Nowheresville, Emily went for a rocket pop, Rebekah a drumstick, Agnes picked a big ice cream cookie, and I settled on a plain old ice cream sandwich. We thanked Michele for her help and nearly made it out the door before Rebekah went back to the counter.

"Have you seen this man?" She showed Michele a picture of Farrell on her phone.

Michele looked at it for a moment. "Yeah, he came in a few times with two or three other guys. I haven't seen him for a while though, maybe three days. Are you looking for him?"

"Yeah." Rebekah pondered this. "Thanks."

"Well, good luck," were Michele's parting words to us.

Back at the motel, I turned on the boobtube, so I had something to do besides lose at hearts. I found a Pirates game and watched that without the sound. Emily put away her cards and came and sat down next to me. Agnes sat down with Rebekah.

"Don't you want to hear what they say, Mr. Sunshine."

"Nah, after a while, it's all the same. I've watched enough baseball to where I don't need to be told what's going on, and quite frankly, I get tired of the gibberish that passes for analysis. I mean its baseball for chrissakes."

"Monk, watch your language around Emily." Agnes made a face.

"What? Chrissakes is a bad word?" I got more of the face. "Fine! Emily, I apologize for saying chrissakes in front of you." Emily laughed. "Happy?" I said this to Agnes.

"As a matter of fact, I am." Agnes turned in triumph. The woman was way too bossy.

"How did you two meet?" Apparently, Rebekah was interested.

"Your father had a meeting with my boss," answered Agnes. "I thought he was cute and asked him if he was attached. When he said no, I asked if he was interested in having a drink. He's been hanging around ever since." She smiled at me in that goofy I love you way that I found deeply endearing, "Isn't that right, Monk?"

"Oh, I don't remember it that way at all." I smiled back.

"Uh-huh..." She blew me a kiss. "You're not getting out of this, you know."

"I can't imagine even trying, beautiful." The minute I said that I worried it might upset Rebekah, but oddly she smiled.

"I'm glad you're happy together." Tears started running down her face. Agnes put her arm around Rebekah.

"It's ok to be sad. I know how you feel. You're father does too. We've been there. That's why we're here because it's too hard to have to do it alone. You don't have to keep it inside, and you don't have to be ashamed either." Agnes kissed her and held her close.

"I don't want to do this anymore," she cried.

"Do what?" I asked. I'd moved to the end of the bed, closer to the couch.

"I don't want to pretend anymore, I just want to..." She sat up and wiped her eyes.

"Move on?" I said, finishing her sentence.

She looked at me. "Yes."

"Then why go after him?"

She thought about that. "Because I have to, because I have to make sure. You don't like Farrell, do you? He's not your kind of guy?"

"It's not that exactly. For the record, it's true; I don't have a particularly high opinion of Farrell. I thought you married him just to get out of the house so you could get away from your mother and me. I felt you could have found someone better, someone more in tune with who you are, someone more interesting. Maybe I shouldn't say this, but I always thought you were more like me than you wanted to admit and I worried you were trying to get with the program, as your grandmother would say, instead of doing your own thing." I handed her a tissue.

"Your mother doesn't seem to like you much, does she?" Agnes was asking.

"Not really."

"She says it's because you've forsaken God like Moses did." Rebekah wiped her eyes with the tissue. "She said you ran away like he did and that you were trouble the minute you got here." She looked at me like a child wanting answers, wanting to know the truth. "Why did we leave California? No one would tell me, not mom, not grandma, not even Moses when I was out to see them for their gathering, the one you said you'd go to but didn't. They all said I should ask you, so I'm asking."

In the past, I'd have blown her off, but with Agnes there, and her knowing, I saw no reason to hide the truth. "I left because my friends and I ran into big trouble with the local gangsters after they found out we were selling weed on their turf. It was, as they used to say, a bad scene. They said they would kill you, me, and your mother, so Moses sent us out here to stay with your grandmother. She wasn't happy about it. We disrupted her perfect little life, which I thought was ironic since she ran away years earlier. We fought because neither of us was what the other wanted or expected. I even left for a while, but I loved you and your mother too much to stay away and I was responsible for us being out here so I tried really hard to adjust and adapt, but it wasn't me, and once your mother lost interest in me, I...well, you know that part of the story." I saw no reason to add that I left for other reasons not related to them or that I very nearly meant to never come back.

"So it's all true?" A rueful smile from a grown child repeating herself.

"From their perspective, sure, but it's not like I was anything special to begin with."

"I think you're special." Agnes, my beautiful Agnes.

"Yeah, but you're nuts." We laughed at that. "Rebekah, I'm not ashamed of who I am or where I've been, or of the things I've done... well mostly. I've had good times and bad times just like everybody else. And yeah, there are a lot of mistakes I wish I hadn't made, but that's life. What you think of me is what you think of me. I love you, and I care about you. If I didn't, I wouldn't be here."

I didn't expect anything from her by saying that and I wasn't disappointed when she said nothing, but I did notice a little light in her eyes so maybe it wasn't a complete loss.

"Don't worry about Monk, Becky, I'll keep him in line, right, Monk?" My Agnes, always being helpful.

"I don't see why not."

Rebekah hugged Agnes and signaled to Emily that it was time for bed.

"Goodnight, Mr. Sunshine; goodnight Agnes," she said.

Agnes, delighted to be included by the usually reserved Emily, wished them both a good night as did I. They went into their room and closed the door. Agnes gave me a hug for no apparent reason and demanded a kiss. I demanded one in return. Once our demands were met, we went to bed where we delighted each other as quietly as we could.

. . . . .

In hindsight, we should have left for California the next day. Three days, four tops, and we'd be back to the sun and the surf. Emily's father wouldn't miss her, and she could hang with us for a few days before we took her back up to her beloved garden. Rebekah could start her life anew, away from her failing marriage, but no, we had to find him.

She had to make sure.

17

"What do you believe in, Monk, in your heart?" Lucian tapped his chest for dramatic effect. "Is there no place for God, for our savior, Jesus Christ, in here?" Another tap: That's how his confession began with the ever-present need to proselytize.

I had to laugh.

"Why is what I believe so important? And, why is the supposition always that what I do believe is not what I should; that instead, it should be overwritten by other interpretations of the same story," I said.

Lucian DeBerry wasn't a big man. Slender, with a youthful face, deep-set soulful eyes, and a crooked smile set atop a black suit, he radiated that knowing belief that no matter what, I would be a better man simply by hearing his words. He had a head of dark brown hair combed straight back, and he kept his face clean-shaven; no scruffy beard or five o'clock shadow covered the lines of his jaw or his Adam's apple.

"The gospels and letters need no modern interpretation to be relevant. They are, in their original intent, all they need to be. I'm not seeking to overwrite what you believe, only to clear the clutter of too many other interpretations, to reunite your heart with the Lord's words. And they are gifts, Monk, for they give us the means to be as God intended us to be, to ourselves and to one another." A bible by his side came into his hands. "Would you pray with me, Monk? Would you share these words with me?"

The deep-set eyes were imploring. In return, I smiled and let him speak.

What a difference a week makes!

The sockets were still deep-set, but now dark and empty. I reached over and pushed his eyelids down over the desiccating orbs. He was wearing the same suit, now crumpled and caked. He longed to be loved, to be a messenger of hope and salvation, of a new harmony blessed upon this dusty patch of the Great Plains.

I prayed with him. I saw no harm in that. He prayed for the usual: my soul, my finding God once again, my coming together with him for a more joyous contemplation, but I had seen the Lord's work in others, and while in some it was indeed righteous, for too many it was not. Jesus did not lead my mother to find forgiveness in any of us. He did not lead Moses to understand the untimely death of his younger brother. He did not stop my unhappy wife from fornicating with a man she met at church. He did not stop the man praying with me from doing the very same thing with the young wife of a recently converted couple. But then why was it Jesus' responsibility in the first place? Hadn't he given his all as an example, a sacrifice, for these very people so they might not suffer as he did? Shouldn't they, we, know better?

The corpse didn't have any answers.

I thought about the man before me. Was he sincere? Was it all a terrible tragedy of love wronged or longed for, or was it more animalistic, a baser need for control and corruption? Was she, the woman in the picture, willing and knowing, or was she a manipulation, a conquest?

He loved her, he said. Did he truly believe that?

Did I believe that?

18

We woke to the sound of work trucks rumbling down the road outside the motel. The sun was out, sort of, drifting between the laggard clouds trailing yesterday's storm. Like the sun, we drifted from room to room collecting our belonging, preparing ourselves for the day's adventures, and wondering what to do for breakfast. The decider among us, Emily, wanted waffles and stated that a waffle house was just up the road so we should eat there. There were no dissenters. I turned in our keys, which had surprised Agnes in this day and age of card access, loaded up the truck, and drove the five minutes to the restaurant.

Like most of these places, they didn't skimp on the portions, so the bacon, eggs, pancakes, and hash browns supplied all the calories I would need for the day. Much as they tried, Agnes, Rebekah, and Emily could not finish what they started, but if nothing else, they were not hungry, and would not be for some time. The table talk centered on what-ifs. What if Farrell isn't at the quiet blue house? What if no one is at Emily's father's house when we get there? This was Emily's way of trying to get out of going back. I told her it was unlikely as they were expecting us, and if Farrell wasn't there, then after dropping off Emily, we'd have to decide whether to head towards Oklahoma, something I was not keen to do, or head back to Virginia, something Rebekah was not keen to do. Agnes was just along for the ride.

The blue house appeared as it had the night before. We pulled up in front. Once again, Rebekah went to the door as I watched from the truck. Once again, there was no answer. Rebekah put up her hands in frustration. I joined her on the front porch. The two windows at the front of the house had their curtains drawn. The house was longer than wide. I wandered to one side to see if any of the other windows had their curtains open. Rebekah checked the other side. I was along the fence line when a man approached from the house next door. He was portly with little hair on his head and what looked like two days of beard on his round face.

"Whatcha looking for?" He seemed friendly enough.

"Seeing if anyone's home. We came by last night, but no one answered, and since there are cars in the driveway, we came back this morning. My daughter is looking for her husband, and we were told he was here." I saw no reason to be cagey.

"Well sir, there've been quite a few people coming and going for quite some time, but I didn't pay too much attention. They were always polite and nowhere near as rowdy as the boys who were renting the place before. Then about three days ago the place got quiet and, to be honest, I haven't heard anything coming from the house since." He put his hands on the top of the fence. "My name's Oscar, by the way, Oscar Sklarsen."

"Monk, Monk Buttman."

He smiled at that. They all do. "That's quite a name."

I smiled back. "Yes, it is. I was going to see if I could look in one of the windows. You don't mind, do you?"

"Not at all, as a matter of fact, I may join you, if you don't mind?"

"The more, the merrier."

Oscar came around his fence and we walked along the side of the house. All the windows were closed with their curtains drawn. In the back was a small porch with a door to the kitchen. It was there I saw the leg stretched out just past a wall through the window in the door. Oscar saw it too. Something was moving out of the corner of my eye. I looked over to see Rebekah picking something up. I checked the door. It was unlocked. I knocked several times. The leg didn't move.

"What do you think, Monk?" Oscar seemed unsure.

I think we should get the hell out of here.

"Maybe we should see what's going on." It was all I could think of. Rebekah joined us on the porch. I slowly opened the door. "Anyone home? Hello?" I bellowed, making sure anyone in the house could hear me.

Nothing.

We went in slowly. The kitchen was clean, no dishes or utensils on the counter, just a toaster. We eased up to the wall where the leg was.

He was a young man, maybe late twenties with that awful blank stare on his face. The gun was by his side. There was a hole in his head at the temple, a line of blood running down the side of his face and discoloring his white shirt, with more splattered on the wall. Rebekah screamed, and Oscar nearly fainted. Breakfast wanted to make a return engagement on the floor. We stepped back.

"How many people lived here, Oscar, do you know?"

His hands were shaking. "Five. Two couples and a brother." He pointed at the dead man when he said brother.

"Ok. I'm going to check the other rooms. Maybe it would be better if you two stay here."

Neither said anything. I carefully moved past the dead man and checked the other rooms. The house had three bedrooms, one was empty, but the other two had a man and a woman lying on the bed in what was a rather serene pose. They were next to each other, arms across their chests. They were, of course, dead. I saw no signs of violence on any of them, but they were ripe and getting riper. The house was clean and organized as if on display. I went back to the kitchen. Oscar and Rebekah were out on the porch.

"Better call the cops," I said to Oscar, "we'll be out front."

"Yeah," was all he could say as he went back to his house.

"Is Farrell in there?" Rebekah asked, her eyes big and moist, no doubt fearing the worst.

"No." I thought she'd be relieved, but instead, she swore.

"Goddammit." More profanity!

"What?"

"I found his fucking phone!" She showed it to me. Other than being wet, it wasn't damaged.

"I wonder if it still works?"

"The battery's dead. I guess we can see if it'll take a charge." She looked at me; the sadness was gone replaced by anger and frustration. "What do we do now?"

"We have to wait for the fuzz." My hands and legs were shaking. I needed to sit down.

"The fuzz?" she asked quizzically.

"Sorry, the cops. They'll be swarming the place soon. Tell them the truth that we were looking for Farrell, but don't mention the phone. It's a good thing we had a big breakfast, we might be here a while." We walked back over to the truck.

"Is he there?" asked Agnes. She had come out of the truck to the front porch. Emily, still in the truck, looked up from her book.

"No, but it's bad..." I turned her away from Emily. "There are five dead people in the house."

"Oh my God, Monk!"

My thoughts exactly. "Let's go back to the truck. I wouldn't say too much about this to Emily."

It didn't take long for the constable and his men to arrive. Oscar came out to join us and we told them our tale of discovery. The police went in while we waited. One of them stayed back with us. The constable came back and asked the usual: who are you, why are you here, did you know the victims, what did you touch, please follow us to the constable's office. There we were asked the same things. The five of us were sequestered, and after a long morning and early afternoon, they let us go. I called Emily's father and told him we'd had some trouble, although I wasn't specific, and said we'd be there as soon as traffic allowed. Only three hundred more miles to go; how long could it take? A slow-burning headache was tightening around my skull.

"They wanted to know about Farrell," Rebekah said with a hard edge in her voice. "Why he might be there…I said I didn't know, that we hadn't talked in a while. I told them we were having problems. I wonder if that was a mistake."

"It's the truth, which means it keeps you out of trouble. If Farrell had a part in what happened at the house, I guess we cross that bridge when we get there. We don't know. All we know is that his phone was there, which means it's possible he was there, but he could have left before those people were killed. Besides, maybe what we saw was what happened: a murder-suicide, some kind of disagreement or something. Maybe Farrell had nothing to do with it."

"Yeah, maybe." She wasn't any more convinced than I was.

"Did you tell them about the phone?" I had to ask.

"No, I still have it. It's here," she took it out of her pocket. "There's a charger in my purse that works in the truck's cigarette lighter."

Agnes handed her the purse, and Rebekah fished out the charger. I was surprised the lighter still worked. New cars don't even come with cigarette lighters anymore, now they're power outlets for all our electronic baggage. Then there was whether the phone would even work having been left out in the rain. Rebekah plugged it in, and it chimed, notifying us that it needed to be charged. She then placed it on the dash and put her arms around Emily.

Emily snuggled into Rebekah and announced she was hungry.

At a truck stop off I-76, we went in to eat more greasy food, but were amazed to find the food very good. It was one of those odd places where expectations are turned upside down. They had the usual fare you'd expect, burgers, fried chicken, more waffles, but whoever was in the kitchen spiced them up. I had an excellent Rueben sandwich with sweet potatoes fries, crisp and flavorful. Rebekah and Emily shared a grilled cheese sandwich that was made of real cheese with onion rings that were sweet and light. Agnes, sated her pizza addiction with one made of prosciutto, Portobello mushrooms, and red onions, on a thin crust and a basil tomato sauce. The food lightened the mood which, given the day's earlier event, was somber.

"What were they like?" Agnes, who hadn't entered the house, wanted to know.

"They were young, no more than thirty at the most, lying on their beds, primly dressed. The women had on long dresses, the men had on shirts with collars buttoned to the neck. Their faces showed no distress. They were laid out as if on display." I could see the two women, their hair pulled back behind their heads, their faces free of makeup.

"Were they poisoned? I know you said the man you found had been shot, but the others?"

"Like Molly and Jonathan," Rebekah said, as a matter of fact.

"I assume so. The police didn't say."

"Seems like such a shame," Agnes was trying to make sense of it.

"It does." What else was there to say?

To the west, beyond the picture windows of the truck stop, beyond the rise of the Appalachian Mountains, the sun was fading, finding its way to California and the Pacific. We were outside Harrisburg with another hundred miles to go. Emily was beginning to fidget the closer we got to her father's home.

"Why can't I stay with you? I like being with Becks, she's more fun than Abby."

"That may be, but we have no choice but to take you back, sorry," I said.

Emily frowned.

On the way out to the truck, my phone chimed. It was a message from Judith, a picture of her in all her naked glory, just what I needed. Then it chimed again, this time from Joanie. California wanted me back and, oh, how I wanted to go! Agnes gave me the eye.

"It's from Joanie." That didn't placate her.

"What does *she* want?"

I shook my head. "She wants me to call." Agnes and the girls piled into the truck, and I moved it fifty feet to the section of the truck stop reserved for cars. As I filled up the tank, I called Joanie.

On the third ring, she answered. "Monk?"

"What's up?" I asked.

"Bennie died yesterday." There was anxiety in her voice.

"I'm sorry to hear that. Bennie was a fun guy. I enjoyed talking with him, hearing about the—"

She cut me off. "Ardis moved out two days ago and gave me her keys. Once again she told me I should talk to you, and when I asked why, she said it was because you own the place. Is that true?"

"Yeah, it's true," I admitted.

Silence.

"How long have you owned this place, and why didn't you say anything?" She was pissed, and I didn't have the time or energy to banter with her.

"About five years and I didn't see any reason to bring it up."

"What?" I pictured her standing over me with her arms crossed. It made me smile.

"Listen, I know you're angry or confused, probably with me, but unfortunately, I don't have time to explain everything right now. I'll do that when I get back—"

"And when will that be?"

"I don't know, a week, maybe two. Anyway, call Taylor Lagenfelder at Aeschylus and Associates. She can help you take care of any contracts or legal questions. Go ahead and move into Ardis' old bungalow if you like, it'll be ok." I gave her Taylor's number. It was a perk they gave me for keeping my mouth shut after the Boyer affair; legal services at an affordable price. Not bad for a nobody.

"I don't understand any of this, Buttman."

"Neither do I, but it'll have to wait. I got more than my hands full where I am now—"

"Where are you?" For whatever reason, her voice had calmed.

"Pennsylvania, on our way to Philly. I'll talk to you later. It'll be all right."

"Sure, whatever, Monk," and with that, she hung up.

I sighed.

The women were watching me.

"Problems?" Agnes was smirking.

"Naturally."

Nobody laughed.

I got in the truck. "Hold on, we still have a ways to go."

The road to Philly was paved with lots of cars and the ill-humored drivers within. After two and a half hours, we finally made it to the burb of Darby and the comely colonial of Emily's father, Thomas. Thomas and Alisha were at the door waiting. I had called as we hit the outskirts of Philadelphia. Emily clung to Rebekah and began to cry. Rebekah and Agnes did what they could to console her and assure her it would be okay. What else could they say? That she would be miserable and lonely, longing for her garden and her freedom? She had her entire adulthood to be disappointed, no need to start just yet.

Thomas was of average height, maybe five-ten, slender with hair the same auburn color as Emily. Alisha was shorter than Thomas by a few inches, and she was not slender but shapely with a pleasant face. She had a sweet smile and a small two-year-old boy in her arms who was introduced to us as Michael. Abby stood just behind her mother; she looked to be about five. Thomas kneeled down and gave Emily a hug which she returned, she was still crying but more softly now. Alisha invited us in, and the coterie of mothers and daughters took Emily into the kitchen.

Thomas and I stood there watching. I found it amusing, though I doubt Thomas did. He had that worn outlook so many have who spend too much time chasing dreams with dollar signs. They used to be called company men; maybe they still are. Having never been one, I couldn't say. The old man considered them lemmings and fools.

"Thanks for bringing her back," he said quietly.

"No problem." Well, a few...

"Drink?" he gestured towards a cabinet just off the pantry.

"Whiskey, if you have it."

The house was a nice size and still compartmentalized, as it had been when it was built rather than opened up as so many older homes were nowadays. Thomas filled two glasses, and we retired to the living room, which was to the left of the small foyer at the entrance to the house. I thought of Calista, Emily's mother, and pictured the two of them together. Too similar, I thought; too tightly wound. We sat down listening to the distant talk the women were giving Emily, assuring her that everything would be okay.

Everything will be okay.

I wondered if the people I had found this morning had been told that as they drank whatever killed them. They weren't that much younger than Thomas and Alisha. I noticed my hands were shaking.

"I'm sorry you had to be dragged into this. I had no idea she was so upset, although you have to give her credit for knowing how to get around. With everything being available online all you need is a credit card and a little ingenuity..." he drifted off.

"Your card?"

"Yeah, I must have left it out, or she grabbed it when I wasn't looking. She's always been bright, like her mother." He pondered his drink. "She gave me an earful yesterday…and maybe I deserve it. Emily hasn't been happy here. She always seems angry with me, again, like her mother." He was fishing for sympathy.

"No, she's just lonely, and she misses her garden. I get the impression you don't have much time for her when she's here." Sometimes, I'm not a particularly sympathetic guy.

I must have struck a chord because Thomas' demeanor changed.

"I have a very demanding job, which means I don't have the time I'd like to spend with her. I'm trying, Mr. Buttman, I am. I don't want you to think I don't care. I do, it's just that I find it difficult to connect with Emily sometimes. She's not the only child here wanting my attention, there's Abby and Michael too." He said this with what I thought was too much defensiveness.

"I get that. I don't agree with it, but I get it. Here's an idea. Take some time off from your demanding job and spend it with your daughter. She loves to garden. Let her show you how it goes, she's good at that. But don't forget she's here to see you, not your wife or your kids. Is that fair? Probably not, but it doesn't matter. She's already eleven. Take it from someone's who's been there."

I took a long drink of bourbon and looked at my trembling hands.

"My daughter barely tolerates me," I continued, "and we haven't had a meaningful conversation in more than a decade because I always had other things on my mind and because we like different things I couldn't take the time to let her share those with me. Emily knows you're a busy guy. She's well aware that because of your domestic situation and your relationship to her mother, she'll never have the relationship with you that you'll have with Abby or Michael. That's life."

I took a last swallow of the whiskey. Thomas fingered his glass.

"Calista tells me she's very fond of you…"

Sheesh!

"I suppose. I think she likes having someone to boss around. I don't mind, it gives me a chance to learn again how important life and family are, and she's a character, and I have a thing for characters, but you're still her father, not me and she misses you. She won't be young forever and hearts harden. That's life too." Thomas seemed to be listening, or maybe he was thinking about work, who knows? It made me feel better about my time with Rebekah when she was eleven, fifteen, not so much. "That's just my opinion."

"I appreciate that."

I don't think he did.

The others came into the room. It was late. Abby and Michael were nodding off, and Emily looked exhausted. Then again so did Agnes and Rebekah and Alisha for that matter. It was time to go. They already had their talk with Emily. We walked to the door and onto the porch. Emily wrapped her arms around me.

"Goodbye Mr. Sunshine. Thanks for showing me your old farm and bringing me back." She looked up at me, the sadness filling her eyes. I felt a terrible ache at having to leave her. All I wanted to do was pick her up and run, run to the other side of the world, back to our garden. "You'll check the garden when you get back, won't you?"

"You know I will, and after you get back, we'll get it ready for fall."

"You promise, Mr. Sunshine?"

I wish she'd call me something else.

"I promise if you promise to try to have a good time while you're here?"

She grimaced. "I promise."

We left them standing on the front porch waving as we drove off.

19

The Comfort Inn availed itself to us and into another hotel we went. The two queen-sized beds were comfortable enough, and I was thankful Agnes, and I had taken advantage of some quality time the night before as it appeared unlikely we'd have much of it in the near future. I sat up in one bed and found a west coast game on the boobtube. The Dodgers were hosting, of all teams, the Phillies. As I listened to the national broadcasters, I longed for the lone voice of Vin Scully, longtime play-by-play man of the Dodgers. I turned the sound off. Agnes, who had no interest in baseball, went into the bathroom to wash her face. I noticed Rebekah standing by the bed.

"Mind if I watch with you?"

"Not at all, have a seat." I moved over to give her more room as she got on to the bed. For the first ten minutes we just watched saying little. "Do you want the sound on?" I asked.

"No, I like the quiet." She then did something completely unexpected: she put my arm around her and laid her head on my shoulder. Agnes came out of the bathroom, looked at the two of us on the bed.

I laughed when her mouth dropped open.

"Do you need me to give you two some time alone?" she asked.

"No, there's room." Rebekah patted the bed. She and I moved yet again to give Agnes room on my other side. Agnes, taking her cue from Rebekah, put my right arm around her and laid her head on my other shoulder. I shrugged my shoulders, and they slid down enough, so it was comfortable. The Dodgers were up by two in the third.

"I heard you talking to Emily's dad..." Rebekah's hair was irritating my nose while she said this. Agnes smiled and brushed it out of my face. My arms were useless at this point.

"Eavesdropping?" I asked.

"Yeah. Did you mean what you said about Emily and you, about starting over?"

"I suppose, but I don't consider it starting over or a second chance, just an opportunity to help. Emily reminds me of you, so maybe it's a chance to regain a little insight into being a father again."

"I also heard you say we don't talk, but when would we? I mean... I don't know. I guess I don't know anything anymore." She let out a long sigh.

"I don't know about that. I think you know what you want. As for us, these things happen, and the two times we've been together since I left there just wasn't any time to talk." She sat up, letting my arm fall down around her waist.

"Alright, we have some time, let's talk. I want to know what happened to you, really."

"Talk?" I faked a bit of amazement and tried to think of something to say. "Well, the simple answer is I had to figure out who I was, corny as that sounds. The truth is I was completely unprepared for being a grownup and when the shit hit the fan I didn't know what to do, so I did what I was told, by Moses, by my mother, by Astral—"

"You know she hates that name," Rebekah noted this triumphantly.

"I don't care, that's who she is to me. Anyway, after years of trying to be the person everyone else wanted me to be, I left to be what I am now, a nobody."

"A nobody?" Rebekah looked at me as if I were insane. "Did he tell you this, Agnes?' She peered over at Agnes, who was happily ensconced next to me.

"Oh yeah, I know the story," Agnes replied.

"A little support would be nice," I mused, mostly to myself.

"I'm sure it would, now get on with your tale of discovery. Hey, your words, Buttman," she said after I shot her a disapproving face.

"Discovery indeed," I snorted.

"So if you've discovered who you are, why did you blow off the gathering at the farm? I was there, you know? Everyone was there, even your mother."

I looked up at her. She had her mother's deep blue eyes.

"Because I had no interest in it, that's why. No interest in answering a lot of questions about what happened to me, why I left, all that! Just the thought of going up there, of reliving a failed past, made me want to be anywhere but there."

Rebekah frowned. "So what changed? I hear you go up all the time now?" Her deep blue eyes tightened.

"Agnes happened," I said as if it were no big deal.

"Agnes? I'm going to need more than that, Dad."

I shrugged my shoulders and looked at Agnes, who smiled.

"It's because we were two big chickens," Agnes chimed in. "I wanted to see my daughter but was too frightened to go alone. We'd had a bad falling out. Monk here wouldn't go to see his dad by himself, so he held me up, and I held him up. After that, it wasn't so bad." Agnes pulled on my shirt. "And, just so you know, I'm not going to Simon's wedding and I don't want you going. I don't care how well you and Eric get along."

I looked at her shaking my head. "First, why would they invite us? They are well aware of your ambivalence about it, and generally, you don't invite your ex-spouse to your wedding. I wasn't invited to Astral's wedding to Judah—"

"That's because no one knew where you were," Rebekah interjected.

"She wouldn't have invited me anyway. I'm sure we'll get an announcement, and maybe we'll send a little something, but I don't see us going."

"I still don't like it." Agnes made another face.

"Tough, besides your stuck with me, remember?"

"Simon's your ex-husband?" Rebekah looked past me to Agnes.

"Yes. Fifteen years, then he decides he wants to be with Eric."

"Oh..." I don't think she knew how to respond to that. "So why are you stuck with this guy?" Rebekah poked me in the stomach.

This is why guys hang around with guys, to avoid this kind of talk.

"Well, he's kinda cute, and he dresses nice. You don't see many regular guys wearing suits anymore. He's good in the sack—"

"I probably don't need to know that," Rebekah said, smiling.

Agnes laughed. "Probably not. He's handy around the house, decent cook, and most of all he loves me just the way I am, warts and all. After Simon, I made a lot of bad choices when it came to men and Buttman here not only was good to me, but he didn't care about that, and that meant a lot to me."

"I see." Rebekah looked at me. "What about you, old man?"

"What about me?"

"Why are you with Ag?" Aggie and I smiled at that.

"Do I have to be serious?" they both nodded. "I guess if I must be serious, I'd have to say that besides being attractive and fun, and I can't believe I'm saying this out loud, the two of us are, in a way, kindred spirits. We understand one another, we accept one another, and most of all, as Johnny D puts it, Ag here has a good heart, and she's good for me."

"Plus I have great boobs," Agnes said, laughing.

"And she has great boobs." I had to be honest!

Rebekah grimaced. "Good to know. Are you getting married? I heard a reference or two about it."

"It's possible," I said.

"It's going to happen, Buttman, you know that." Agnes gently poked me.

"You don't want to, Dad?"

"I didn't say that, I—"

Agnes interrupted, "It's his rich girlfriend. He doesn't want to give her up, and he knows that once we're married, he has to stop."

"She's not my girlfriend, and I don't want to talk about this." As I said that, Judith's text and picture flashed before my duplicitous eyes.

"You let him have a girlfriend? I don't understand?" None of us did.

Agnes looked at me. "I know how it sounds, and I don't know all the details because it's the one thing Monk here is very tight-lipped about it, but like I said we have an understanding about who he loves and where his home is, and at the end of the day he always comes home to me, and he knows I'll never let him go. So, for now, he has a grace period to get it sorted out. Right, Sunshine?" Another pinch.

"If you say so, beautiful." I pinched her back.

Rebekah considered this, but I don't think she got it. Of course, I didn't get it either, but Agnes was right, it was my problem to resolve.

"Is this some kind of California thing?" she asked.

"No," I whined, although I guess it could be?

The game was still on the flickering television, which was a comforting old indistinct cathode ray model. The Dodgers were still in the lead. Now it was my turn.

"And you, Rebekah Jenkins, what about you?"

Her countenance changed. Talking about Agnes and me was more fun than what was troubling her. She sunk back down next to me on the bed. She played with the wedding ring on her left hand.

"I don't know. No, I do know… it's just this anger. I've been so angry lately, and I don't know why I can't control it?"

"You think it's more than just what's going on with Farrell? Or is this more about where you are now, as a person or being older?" I was clutching at straws.

She continued to play with the ring, "I'm tired of Farrell. I know that's a terrible thing to say, and mom and grandma told me it's a part of marriage, but it doesn't feel that way this time. We've been married for ten years, and I never felt like it was finished like I do now, and it makes me angry because this isn't what I wanted. It isn't what I expected it to be."

"What did you expect?" Agnes was holding my hand as she asked; something I found disconcerting.

"The usual, I guess. A better life, maybe somewhere different, a better house than that run down piece of crap we've been living in, and kids, I wanted kids; lots of them. The more we tried, the worse things seemed to get. Farrell would just get agitated when I'd ask him to go with me to the doctor. He didn't need doctors to tell him he was the problem. I don't know that he even was the problem. It might be me. He didn't want me to go, so instead, we prayed and hoped that God would someday give us children. And we need to be better Christians, and now there's this whole thing with this preacher, which I don't understand, and I don't know where he is or what he's doing, and now I'm here in this motel room trying to explain this to my father, who's nothing like he used to be, and his girlfriend, not his rich girlfriend, but the one with the great boobs." She pointed at Agnes.

Agnes and I couldn't help but laugh at that; even Rebekah joined in. It was good to hear her laugh.

"So I'm tired of all of this. I'm almost thirty now. Is this what my life will be like for the next thirty years?" Her exasperation was evident.

"That's up to you," I said.

"But it's not just me! Isn't marriage supposed to be a joint venture? Aren't we supposed to work through this together? Isn't that what gives marriage its validity, its vitality, the reason for its existence? That's what I signed up for, that's what I want, not chasing him around the country while he looks for some perfect Church."

"I don't know if it helps," Agnes said, "But I know exactly how you feel. I was with Simon for fifteen years, and I too expected it to be a partnership and fulfilling, and it wasn't that at all. Maybe a partnership when it came to raising the kids, although with his working evenings, I did most of the heavy lifting, but it was lonely and frustrating, and I foolishly thought he come around some day. Now he's getting ready to marry his *boyfriend*. How depressing is that!" Agnes squeezed my hand tighter, "I'm sorry, Rebekah, I didn't mean to start with my problems."

"It's ok. I don't know what I'd do if Farrell told me he was gay. I hate to say it, but in some ways, it would be a relief."

"Trust me it's not. All it does is make you wonder why you squandered away so many precious years in a dead-end marriage." I could feel the tears on my shirt as Agnes nestled in.

"Yeah, I can see that. And it's okay to call me Becky, Rebekah is Grandma." Becky nestled in too. Monk Buttman, human pillow. "What do you think old man? Both mom and grandma were certain you'd give me bad ideas, and I'd ruin my life and do something stupid like run off to California?"

"I'm shocked? However, it's interesting that they say that given that your mother ran off with Judah, and my mother ran off when I was ten, and I'm the bad influence," I huffed.

"Let it go, Buttman." Agnes was smiling at me with her teary eyes. "Hey, that's what you tell me."

"Again, thanks for the support."

"That's what I'm here for." She wiped her eyes.

"I would have never known! Anyway, I think life's too short to waste on trying to live fairy tale dreams. If it works, great, if it's fixable, absolutely do what you can, but if it's wearing you down and there's no light at the end of the tunnel, I can't see why you'd want to continue to make yourself miserable. That's what I think."

"Sounds like something out of a self-help book," Rebekah moaned.

"What's your point?"

"I have to spell it out?"

"It worked for me, so that's what I go with." I impulsively kissed her head. "Like I mumbled before, I don't want you to be unhappy. You've always been bull-headed, so you'll do what you want, but self-help or not, I think it's good advice."

"Thanks."

We watched the rest of the game in relative silence. Rebekah and Agnes seemed content where they were so I obliged. The Dodgers held on to win the game. Agnes fell asleep and snored through the last two innings. After the game, I gently extricated myself from them, and we went to bed.

The next morning I woke to find Rebekah already up and sitting in one of the chairs examining Farrell's phone. After taking a shower and dressing, I sat down in the chair next to her. Agnes, as usual, was still asleep.

"The snoring didn't bother you?" I arched my brows towards the noisy woman in bed.

"Huh?" She looked at me. "Oh no, Farrell's worse than that. It was kind of comforting to be honest." She was going through what appeared to be pictures on the phone.

"Anything interesting?" I asked.

She smirked, "Depends on what you find interesting."

I was game. I'd had a good night's sleep even after the previous day's events. I thought about that. A small voice wondered if I should be concerned that I wasn't bothered more by what I'd witnessed, but I chose to ignore it. "All right, what do *you* find interesting?"

She showed me the picture on the phone. I recognized the people standing in front of the camera; they were dead now, but the picture, which was taken just three days before we found them, was of five smiling faces.

"There's more," she said, handing me the phone.

I looked through the photos of the couples, of the brother, and of three other men who didn't belong with the soon to be dead, but whose presence was there at the house. Two of them were more menacing looking with scowls on their faces wearing drab tee shirts and jeans, but the third one stood out. He was middle-aged, handsome with a soft smile, and appeared to be a rather dapper man. He wore a well-tailored suit and tie, had short hair, and a clean-shaven angular face. He was the tallest of the three, though not by much, and the only one seemingly at ease in front of the camera.

I gave the phone back to Rebekah. "You think he's traveling with these three?"

"You would think." She fiddled with the icons on the small screen, "There's more, in the memo section. It's like he was keeping a diary." She played the comments of her husband.

He *was* up to something.

"I have decided to join Ashton and the two other men, Teddy and Guy, as they visit Brother Lucian's community houses. I'm told this is where people who are interested in going to Brother Lucian's community come first. I guess to see if they're really into it or if they're just killing time. At least that's what Ashton says. He knows I met the ghost, but seems to understand my desire to accept Brother Lucian's word is stronger." This was the first entry recorded a week ago. The next few were nothing more than been here, did that, arrived at the house. But the final two were more interesting, as Rebekah put it.

The first: *"I met the ghost by the convenience store. Once again he warned me to beware of Ashton and Lucian. I didn't really know what I would do next. I assured him I knew what I was doing and that it was possible he was wrong. He said I'd learn the truth. I decided not to say anything about this to Ashton."*

The last was recorded two days before we arrived. I don't think he knew he had the recorder on...

They were talking, murmuring, a collection of indistinct voices. The first voice we could hear clearly was somber. *"This ghost, this fearmonger, no doubt is intent on destroying us, in destroying everything Brother Lucian has spent so many years building, and it is our duty, our calling, from God almighty, to prevent it."*

A distant voice, a woman's, asks if what the ghost says is true.

"It is, as these things always are, immaterial whether it is, by his words, true; although I know it to be a malicious falsehood and that they are lies spread for no other reason than to destroy us. We cannot allow this to continue, and I will not accept that you would believe such words. We are the foundation of this church, and I will not allow cracks to form in that foundation."

Another voice seemed troubled by the idea that they shouldn't question the veracity of the ghost's accusations.

The somber voice became more agitated. *"I have known Brother Lucian from the start, and I am well aware of the situation that this man, who acts as if he can go from place to place without regard for time, has used to vilify Brother Lucian. You must not believe it, and you must not allow it to spread. We cannot doubt; we cannot wonder. We are the foundation, the clay on which this new church will reclaim the true gospel, the right gospel of our Lord, Jesus Christ."*

A second female voice asks about Molly and Jonathan.

The somber voice becomes more reflective. *"The Lord has called them to their place by his side. I believe whatever happened was to the Lord's benefit, and we must accept that. I don't want to discuss this any...Farrell, what are you doing?"*

"I was going to take some pictures..." Farrell stammered.

"I told you I don't like those things. I allowed you to take a few pictures the other day, and that was enough. Give me that thing."

"But I need it..." A rustling is heard along with unintelligible voices. Evidently, Ashton is relieving Farrell of his phone.

"No, you do not." This was followed by what sounded like footsteps and a door opening and closing. That answered the question about why the phone was where Rebekah found it.

Agnes had roused from her sleep, "What?"

We looked over at her. I spoke. "We were checking out Farrell's phone."

"Anything interesting?" Agnes was surprised by our laughter. "What?"

I told her what we'd found, or more specifically what Rebekah found. There were also a few phone numbers Rebekah didn't recognize. I suggested we call them after breakfast. I was hungry. Agnes trooped off to the bathroom to clean and anoint herself. Rebekah continued to ponder the phone and its ramifications.

"What do you think he's up to?" I asked.

"Same old stupid shit, getting into places he can't get out of. What do you think?" I think she was hoping I had some answers beyond stupid shit.

"I don't know, but I do think you're right that he's mixing it up with this Ashton Cox, and possibly this ghost character as well. Personally, I don't know how smart that is considering the recent rash of murder-suicides. I guess we'll find out."

Rebekah sank into her chair.

"How far is it to California?" she mused.

"Three days," I said. I drifted off to beaches and to a certain woman in a house on a hill.

20

After proclaiming herself presentable, Agnes inquired about our plans for breakfast, of which we had none, and in exasperation decided the restaurant here at the Comfort Inn, a place called *Connie's* would be good enough.

"How hard is it to pick a place to eat?" she asked with another poke to my already overly poked arm as we were seated in a booth by the window.

"It's not hard, but if we had, then we would have missed out on your fine performance just minutes ago."

Agnes smiled and shook her head. "You're a jerk, Buttman."

"I believe it's in poor taste to vilify a man in front of his progeny."

"Un-huh." She leaned in and kissed me, "I apologize for my comment, Becky, but your father is a jerk."

"I had no idea! But now that you mention it, I can see that now! Thanks for allowing Agnes to open my eyes, father dear."

I should have asked to be seated in a separate booth.

The glop at Connie's was mostly edible. The eggs were a bit rubbery, but I preferred that to undercooked and sliming across the plate. Agnes' dry French toast was made palatable by a gallon of syrup, and Rebekah was saved by having cold cereal and fruit. The weather was to be gray and pointless, as Rebekah's enlightened us after consulting her phone. Agnes shrugged her shoulders and asked what the plan was.

Cuz if there's one thing we've got going for us, it's a plan.

"I don't know that plan accurately describes our venture to this point," I said.

Agnes glared at me. "Isn't that how you got into that whole Desiree Marshan mess? By not having a plan?"

"Hey, I had a plan, and it went more or less how I thought it would..." More or less.

"Really?" she huffed. "Did that plan include ending up in the hospital?"

Rebekah chimed in, "You ended up in the hospital? What happened?"

"A couple of guys jumped me."

"You should have seen him. He looked terrible. Fortunately, it was mostly bumps and bruises, but you scared the shit out of me. I'm thinking I finally meet a nice straight guy and he gets all beaten up." Agnes was being overly melodramatic.

"Are you finished?" I asked bemused.

She smiled. "Maybe..."

"What's the Desiree Marshan mess?" Rebekah raised her eyebrows. I gave Agnes the face, but she simply continued to smile.

"It's what happens when fools think they can pull a fast one on the powerful in this world. It didn't turn out like they planned. It was a scam, a setup to find a long-hidden killer, and Desiree and her man, Martin," I began.

"He's the husband of Monk's rich girlfriend," Agnes unhelpfully added.

"She kicked him out. Anyway, Desiree and six others ended up dead trying to steal something that wasn't there. It was my job to find her, which I did, thank you very much, but, if nothing else, it was instructive in the ways of the world."

"I don't understand? There's got to be more to it than that? What long lost killer, what powerful people?" Rebekah wanted more.

"What's to understand? The story, if you like, is this: A powerful man with ties to the drug cartels is killed in the late eighties after transferring his wealth out of the country. That money supposedly disappears. People hear about this missing money, think they know where it is and how to get it. So they try to scam the banks that supposedly have the money. But they were the ones being scammed. They were being set up to lure the killers of the powerful man out of hiding, because they also wanted the money. Unfortunately, for those going after the money, including Desiree Marshan, it cost them their lives." That was the story.

"Who are these people?" Rebekah, like those before her, wanted to know.

"I don't know. They didn't tell me, and I didn't push it. I survived and got paid, that was enough for me." I waved to the waitress for our check.

"So you're an old hand at this finding people thing?" Sarcasm was writ large upon my Daughter's face.

"We'll see, won't we?" I was ready to snap off another snarky comment when my phone began its miserable bleating. Reluctantly, I answered it. It was the retired intelligence analyst, Mr. Devaney.

"Mr. Buttman, how are you? Any success?" he said in a cheery manner.

"Success, no, but we've made a small amount of progress and now have no idea what to do." I recounted to him our visit to the house, its contents, and finding the phone and what it held. I spared him the details of Emily's travails. "What have you been able to find, Mr. Devaney?"

"Just call me Art." Art was being glib.

"*Art*, why are you calling?"

He laughed. "Now, now, Monk, no need for that. I blame myself. For some reason I thought being a gentleman farmer cultivating tobacco strains would be more involved, more interesting, but no, and as I have time to kill and, quite frankly, I'm a little bored these days, this adventure of yours keeps me moving." I had no response to that. "To answer your question, I have some information that may help you."

"Concerning Ashton Cox?"

"That is the name you gave me. Now there are a number of Ashton Coxes out there, so it took a while to narrow it down, but when cross-referenced with our preacher, Mr. DeBerry, I was able to refine my search as it were. First, let me send you a photo..." I motioned to Rebekah if I could both talk and receive the photo. She shook her head as if I were some kind of moron and took the phone, placing it on speaker and telling Art to send away. The photo showed a younger version of the dapper man in the suit.

"That's the guy," I confirmed as my condescending daughter looked on.

"Excellent. Then we've come across a very interesting character in this man." Art Devaney drew a breath before proceeding. "Your Ashton Cox is approximately fifty-five years old, a scion of an old New England family, well-educated and troubled. Mr. Cox has had a lifelong infatuation with religion, both good and bad, and he is a, how shall I say this, a conflicted homosexual." Devaney paused. "I don't say that to be dismissive or prejudicial, merely that it plays a part in his upbringing. When he was seventeen, he was admitted to a private hospital by his family for deviant behavior. Apparently, he was communing with a neighbor boy, and this offended his mother's sensibilities. He was in and out of hospitals and therapy for a number of years before going to seminary, primarily to sublimate his sexual yearning."

"How do you know all this? Aren't medical records private?" Rebekah asked.

"You would think, but this was the Seventies, and to certain individuals, the only thing worse than being a communist was being a homosexual, and Ashton Cox, to those concerned with his sexual behavior, was a bit of an enthusiast in his youth. After hospitals and therapy, he dove into religion. That's how he ended up meeting Lucian DeBerry. He was radicalized at the seminary and took part, as an accessory, to the bombing of an abortion clinic. That landed him at the same prison which later incarcerated Mr. DeBerry. His extremist position put him on an FBI watch list, and I imagine that's how they were able to obtain these records. Mr. Cox attached himself to Mr. DeBerry's ministry after he was released from prison, and they have been associated ever since."

"And since his release, any other information out there?" I felt the need to ask.

"No, as I said before, whatever their earlier escapades, both Cox and DeBerry have kept themselves out of the crosshairs of law enforcement since their incarceration. The only notable event was the murder-suicide at this community they have in Oklahoma, and that didn't involve either of them directly based on the police records and information I could find. Now if they are somehow tied in with what happened there and to what happened at this house you just visited, then matters become more problematic."

I got the impression it would thrill him for this little adventure to become more problematic.

"Yes, they may be." I looked at Agnes and Rebekah. They were not as thrilled as Art Devaney with the idea of foul play in the air. Both had an expression of incomprehension. "And what of this guy running around calling himself a ghost? What's his game?" I was thinking out loud, which was probably a mistake.

"Right now, I think that's the million-dollar question. What little social media comes up about our merry band of first-century zealots generally involves this dispute between the ghost and his evisceration of Mr. DeBerry and those who contend that what he says is nonsense and slander. What lies at the heart of this dispute is where we'll find our answers. That's my take on it. It would help if we could get a real name versus this nom de guerre he uses or was given to him."

The waitress set down the bill, gave the three of us huddled around my phone an odd look, and walked off. Art fell silent; I assumed he was finished.

"Well, thanks, Art. I guess we'll have to head out for Oklahoma."

"That reminds me, where are you?"

"Outside Philly," I said.

"Then you're in luck. I found a message board that states Mr. DeBerry is scheduled to appear tomorrow evening at a church in Kentucky. He may have some answers, assuming you have an interest in speaking to him."

I had no interest in DeBerry. "Great, maybe we will." I took the information on the church in Elizabethtown, Kentucky. "Thanks again."

"Let me know if there's anything else I can do."

I assured him we would before I hung up. I put the phone away and turned to my confederates. Their looks of incomprehension had not changed.

"I say we head west and don't stop until we reach the Pacific." I was being honest.

"That's your answer for everything, Sunshine," Agnes said, smiling.

"Only because it applies so nicely to a vast number of questions and answers. I did give it due consideration before I took off, you know." I smiled back. "And who knows who you'd be with," I let that linger, "if I hadn't?"

"Uh-huh." She wasn't taking the bait. "How far is it to Elizabethtown? Any idea?" Something was cooking inside Agnes' cute little head.

"I don't know..."

"It's 730 miles." Rebekah held up her phone. Agnes seemed disappointed.

"Why?" I asked.

"Oh, I thought if we had time maybe we could do a little sightseeing since we're here, but I guess we don't have time." That did sound a lot more interesting than chasing down either Farrell or Brother DeBerry.

"Probably not."

"I feel like I'm wasting your vacation having you help me find Farrell." Rebekah put her phone on the table. Agnes looked at me. Evidently, this was my problem to resolve, which I *had* in my proposal to drive back to California.

"No, we came here to help you and that's what we'll do. Since we're, apparently, coming back for Car's wedding, we can add a little time to go sightseeing then." Problem solved. Oddly, none of us seemed happy with that resolution. "We're burning daylight, people, let's motor."

"Let's motor?" Agnes snarked.

I rolled my eyes. "Just go with it, Aggie."

Aggie poked me yet again. I made a mental note to put a stop to that in any prenup I might need to sign.

Vita est absurdum: life is absurd. I find that to be both logical and comforting at times like these. It came to me years before while I was driving, just as I am now. Then I was running away, lost, angry, and filled with a deep abiding hatred for life and dreams. I wondered if Rebekah was going through her own version of that. Whatever dreams she had when she married Farrell, it seemed plain to me they were gone, drowned in the black water of foolish adolescent expectations. Love and desire were replaced with the determined need for resolution and closure. I wished her well, but resolution and closure are never permanent *until death do us part*. We are all absurdists in search of something more permanent than our finite existence.

My revelation hit me just outside of Denver, where the Rockies begin their long climb into the sky. This while I lurched westward in the Falcon. Like the truck, it was in need as well. I thought Bernie would love to get this old dog into his shop, and I meant to do that, but the truck itself seemed unsure California would ever become reality.

The motor, while functioning, was losing its grip on power; its rings were worn, and its exhaustion was manifest in the oil it burned and the odor it shared with the three of us in the cab. Fortunately, the truck ran well enough that I was willing to talk myself into the notion that it would make it all the way to LA. There it would be reborn as the Falcon had been, as I was, from the ashes of a dead life. I wavered on whether I would give the truck as asinine a name as I gave myself.

Agnes and Rebekah were staring out, dead-eyed, at the layered sky. Darker clouds from the south walked along the tops of the mountains while blocking out the lighter ones above. An occasional shimmer of sunlight would brighten the moment only to be curtained with another set of cumulus filters. At the edge of the western sky, there was light. This became more promising as we finished our passage through the eastern Appalachian Mountains of Pennsylvania. I could feel both the truck and my companions sigh as we descended towards the Great Plains and the sunlight to the west.

"Can I ask you something?" Rebekah was staring at me.

"Sure."

"Do you still believe in God? I mean really? Did you ever?"

Maybe I should think first before I say sure to any question, particularly one about God?

"Why the interest?" I countered.

"Why not answer, yes or no?" she weaved.

Funny, I was just musing about this. "Do I believe in God? Like you do? Your question being, assuming you still do, is do I believe God to be what you believe him to be?"

"Yes, do you?" She persisted, no matter how I evaded the question.

"And if I don't?"

"Alright, don't answer. I was just curious..." She turned to the window and the dreary road ahead.

It was my turn to sigh, and not in a good way. "You know I don't believe in God the way you do, or your mother does or like my mother does. That's no secret."

"Then what do you believe, assuming you believe anything?" She had the same manner as her mother in being both curious and dismissive when questioning my motives or beliefs. I found it to be an inexplicable talent, one that dug under my skin.

"Yeah, Buttman, what do you believe?" Agnes felt the need to pile on.

"I believe that if everyone lived their lives as Jesus preached, we'd have peace on Earth. However, knowing people the way I do, I don't think it's within them to live that life in the numbers it would take to make peace on Earth a reality. As for the rest, having read the stories and inquired both empirically and spiritually, I find I don't believe in virgin births, miracles, or resurrections. I don't believe in a mercurial or capricious God who favors some but not others and who will judge us at some indeterminate point in the future. I believe that what others believe to be God is really a magnificent engineer who created a universe based on laws and logic and then sat back and let the energy fly."

"So you think what I believe is wrong?" I knew Rebekah was baiting me just as her grandmother had.

"I didn't say that. You can believe what you like. That's the beauty of faith. I'm not saying you're wrong, only that I don't believe everything you do. The thing that does irk me is that conservatives always assume a different belief or a disagreement automatically means you don't believe or that it means you're saying they're wrong," I harrumphed.

"I see," Rebekah harrumphed back.

"Then explain how it matters?" I already knew the rebuttal, having heard many times.

"It matters because without God in your heart, you will never know true love and you'll be forsaken when death comes, that's why. The church wouldn't have lasted this long or be so important to so many people if it was all make-believe. I don't think it's right to disparage what people know and feel inside or to denigrate their connection to God," she implored, although in a disingenuous tone.

"Then amen to the people who believe, and I'm not disparaging them. They'll be just fine if I don't share their beliefs. Whether I do or do not believe shouldn't have any impact on how or why they do or do not believe. And again, just because I don't believe as you believe, you assume I don't have God in my heart." I felt as if the universe or God was laughing at me.

"Uh-huh." More disdain.

"Then may God strike me dead as we speak!" I waited a second or two. "See?"

"That means nothing, and it's the same argument you used to piss off your mother."

"Is it?" I did regularly invite the Lord to strike me down in order to anger my mother during our long dark nights together.

"God did not strike you dead because your mother prayed that he would not," she said with great authority.

"Really? I think my mother would enjoy seeing the Lord strike me dead in righteous anger. It would save her the trouble. So, does that mean you prayed for me just now?" That made me smile. I could see my mother with her fatuous smirk as I lay smoldering from God's wrath. Rebekah must have had the same thought because she was smiling too. "Alright, we've had some fun at my mother's expense, but something made you bring this up, and I doubt it's concern for the dispensation of my soul in the afterlife."

"I'm shocked that you think so little of our regard for your life after death..." Her smile faded a little. "Alright, maybe there is more..." She was once again spinning her wedding ring around her finger.

"If it involves questioning your faith or belief, you know, we all do; even the most devout as they say...right, Agnes?" We both turned to our erstwhile companion who was completely caught off guard.

"Huh? Yeah, I guess..." We started laughing, which prompted Agnes to elbow me in the ribs.

"Careful," I said, "I'm driving here."

"Then pay attention to that, Mr. Philosopher."

"Yes dear." It was good to fill the truck with laughter.

We still had a ways to go.

21

We were arguing about faith, about the need to be a part of something greater than ourselves, or our particular moment in time, when he brought up the need for confession.

"Confession as release or absolution?" I was hoping to keep the conversation from veering into the personal.

"In this case, it would be for a sense of release. I can't imagine you believing you have the power of absolution in God's name," he mused.

"Neither can I."

The distant sirens were growing more shrill as they got closer to us, reverberating along the inside of my skull.

Here we were, my dead companion and I, communing together in this relic of a church.

At the time I thought he was about to confess to an illicit relationship with Ashton Cox, instead, it was more like an elegy to lost love. Lucian DeBerry longed for the essence of things, the promise of something old yet unspoiled; of purity, which he believed was to be found in the early stages of any profound movement or moment. Thus his fascination with first-century Christianity, of Paul and his church before it was corrupted by state power and wealth. He clung to the notion it was this early church, a church he believed to be united rather than scattered, that shared his unified vision of a returned Christ soon to bless their devotion to his ministry. He wanted to return to or recreate that comity, that devotion, that clarity, but love was unraveling his dream.

"I don't understand this conflict, Monk," He said while looking off into the distance. "I can't get away from it. I look for answers in the good book, for examples to draw from, to help me, but I continue to return to David, to his love for Bathsheba. That if he could be forgiven..."

I hesitated to bring up all the other issues concerning the house of David and the great King's tumultuous reign. It didn't seem to be on par with a small-time preacher and his small band of followers, although both king and preacher were riven with conflict.

"Have you sought forgiveness from those you know you have wronged?" It was all I had.

"I can only pray for them now," was his answer.

"And their families?"

He looked at me as if I knew the truth. "None have come forward, not a word. I thought for sure someone would whether in grief or anger, but no…"

Was that why he ended up here in this dusty church? Praying to the dead for absolution? Praying for someone to forgive him for loving her?

Was death his absolution?

I sat in the pew directly across from the altar watching the dead man and listening to the sound of the tires tugging at the gravel out beyond the worn wooden doors.

I walked out to greet them.

22

We rolled into Elizabethtown at dusk. The clouds stayed on their eastern trajectory leaving us with a pleasant evening of shaded western light after a long drive. Rebekah had her phone out and was directing me towards the location of the church where Brother DeBerry would be speaking the next day. To our mild surprise, he was there sitting just outside the front door as we drove by.

"That's him?" I think Agnes expected him to be more statuesque.

"Yep," was all Rebekah said.

"Should we barge on up to him?" Agnes asked just as another man approached DeBerry, and they entered the church.

"Why don't we find a place to stay first, and then we'll come back," was my suggestion.

Agnes murmured something and a mile down the road we found a hotel. It was another Comfort Inn. Like the night before, we got a room with two queen beds on which we piled our belongings. Rebekah was weary and seemed ambivalent about rushing back to confront Brother DeBerry.

"I'm tired," she complained as she covered her face with a pillow. Agnes, ever sympathetic, added that she too was tired and would like to lie down for a while.

"Then I'll head down there and have a word or two with DeBerry, and when I get back, we'll figure something out."

There was more mumbling as I left the room.

Given the sky's thin red hues, and the warmth of the evening air, I walked to the Bethany Church of Christ both to exercise my legs and to ponder my options. Should I be confrontational or informational or inquisitive? Confrontation wasn't my style, and what information could I pass on aside from the incidents of death by suicide? I concluded that I would be of an inquiring mind, whatever that meant.

Elizabethtown struck me as just another small American town, much like the one I grew up in, or to be precise, near: quiet and convivial. A few people passed me, and we exchanged hellos. The church had a small lawn in front with a reader-board announcing the week's events including tomorrow's guest speaker, Lucian DeBerry. The parking lot was to the right of the building. Light was glowing through the column of stained glass on the right side of the building now that the sun had reached its western horizon, and darkness was taking its place. I slowly opened the door and encountered an older man seated in the lobby of the church.

"Yes sir, how may I help you?" He had a head of white hair and an easy smile.

"If it's all right, I'd like to have a word or two with Mr. DeBerry, assuming he's still here. My name is Monk."

"Well, Monk, let me see if he's still here. Please have a seat." The man offered his hand, which I shook, smiled again, and left me sitting in the lobby.

I wondered if lobby was the right word. Churches have their own names for all the different spaces like nave and sanctum. I decided not to let it bother me.

The church appeared to be of mid-century vintage with a soaring peak at the center, which carried into the nave. To the left of the lobby was the entrance to the nave and to the right was a hall that led to offices and rooms for bible study and gatherings. Several wooden crosses adorned various walls above bulletin boards with children's decorations of various psalms and the teachings of Jesus. It seemed much like the church I haunted for years in Virginia.

The older gentleman returned with Lucian DeBerry and another man, who wore a pastor's collar and, to me, appeared to be as old as the man who greeted me. I got up as they drew closer.

"I apologize for interrupting," I said, "but I was hoping for a few words with Brother DeBerry." DeBerry raised his eyebrows at my use of the term *brother*.

"Not at all, Mr.?" asked the pastor.

"Buttman, Monk Buttman." The three of them looked at me with the same expression of disbelief. DeBerry smiled and offered his hand.

"That's quite a name, Monk."

I offered him mine. "It has its good days and bad."

The three of them were headed out the door and carried me along for good measure. The pastor asked if I would join them for the service tomorrow to hear Brother DeBerry talk and I replied that my companions and I were looking forward to it. He seemed pleased to hear this and wished us a good evening. The two older men returned to the church and closed the door.

"What can I do for you, Monk?" The timbre of DeBerry's voice changed just enough to let me know he had more than one face he presented to the world.

"My daughter and I are looking for her husband, Farrell Jenkins. We believe he is with three of your associates, Mr. Cox and two men named Teddy and Guy. We were hoping you might know where we could find them."

Lucian DeBerry held back for a moment. "I haven't heard from Ashton in some time, I'm afraid. Neither of us is partial to mobile devices, so our meetings often are infrequent. What makes you think your son in law is with Ashton?"

"We found his mobile device at the home of some of your supporters in Pennsylvania, north of Morgantown. On it were pictures of Mr. Cox and the others. Farrell had commented that they were stopping at halfway houses to rally the troops concerning allegations made about you and your ministry," I said with a half-smile. "Have you eaten yet?"

"No, I haven't." Lucian DeBerry replied a little more haltingly than a moment before. I looked him up and down. He was about my height, six-foot, maybe a little under that; thin, wearing a black suit and black shirt with no tie. His eyes were the aspect of his face that made him attractive, a bright grey, giving him a kind of spectral gravitas.

"Neither have we, why don't you join us? We're staying just down the road. A short walk," I offered.

"That would be nice. Often, on these stops, I have the good fortune to be taken in by one of the parishioners who are kind enough to feed me, but the family I was to stay with were unavoidably detained, as the Pastor just told me. So providence has given me you and yours as companions."

Indeed the ways of providence.

"Excellent, I'm sure Rebekah and Agnes are looking forward to it. This way."

While the idea of surprising my companions had a certain allure, I instead used my mobile device to warn them of our impeding arrival. More grumbling. A petty pang of envy overtook me as I thought back to the not so long ago when I had no phone and was none the worse for it. Whatever DeBerry and Cox were up to, their lack of an intimate cellular connection worked, I thought, to their benefit. No conversations or movements to track. I didn't know if that extended to Teddy and Guy, but given Cox's reaction to Farrell and his phone, it wouldn't be shocking to find them phoneless. DeBerry asked for some biographical information, so I gave him the sanitized version: I'm just a guy from California helping his daughter, with his girlfriend by his side.

"Are you a Christian, Monk?"

"Not in the strictest sense," I added to the biography my church history and my feelings on the subject of the teachings of Jesus and resurrection.

"Then perhaps I can bring you into the light," He smiled when he said this.

"Perhaps," I said, but probably not.

. . . . .

A nice little diner was found down the road, and we were soon ensconced in our booth, ready, if not completely willing, for an evening of informed repartee. Rebekah and Agnes were up and mostly coherent when Lucian and I knocked on the door. I assumed it to be better than barging on in even though they knew we were coming. The introductions, such as they were, pointed to Rebekah's unease with our man of the Lord, but we marshaled on anyway.

The place, aptly named the Elizabethtown Diner, was, as Rebekah informed us, rated on one of her food apps as quite good. The décor was right out of diner 101, faux fifties version with bright lights, white tables, red cushioned seats, and American iconography on the walls. A series of large plate glass windows looked over the parking lot and the main drag illuminated with ornamental streetlights. A pleasant enough place to discuss Jesus, suicides, and wayward husbands as we perused the menu. Agnes wanted to try the massive all American burger with onion rings but knew it was too much for so delicate a creature as herself, and summarily decided we should split it. Rebekah had once again lost her appetite and consoled herself with a salad. The wildcard among us, Brother DeBerry asked if the catfish was any good, as if the waitress would impugn its quality, and went with that. An uncomfortable silence followed the ordering after which Lucian DeBerry excused himself to use the restroom.

"Why did you invite him to dinner?" Rebekah snarled.

"Why not? It can't hurt to talk, although for now let's not bring up the dead. I'd prefer to save that for tomorrow." I'd changed my mind on the suicides.

"And Farrell?"

"He claims he doesn't know; that he doesn't keep in touch with Cox or the others, only that they meet from time to time. He doesn't carry a phone."

"Must take you back, huh?" Agnes was enjoying my discomfort with electronic surveillance.

"Yes, it does."

"But then you wouldn't hear from your rich girlfriend—"

"Goddammit, I'm not going to talk about that! Do you understand? She's not here! I don't want to hear another goddamned word about it!" I shouted with instant regret. Agnes shrunk from me, and I was surprised by the ferocity, but I was tired of hearing about Judith. I lowered my voice. "Time and place. We'll talk about this another time, but not now."

"Sure, we'll do that..." She looked away.

I looked at Rebekah, she wasn't happy either. "Now that we're all upset maybe Brother DeBerry can find the appropriate words to salve our discomforts."

"That's not funny, Dad"

"Maybe not, but here he comes..."

And he was smiling, which always makes things better.

Once our guest had positioned himself comfortably on the Naugahyde seat, we were asked about ourselves, and our place in the world. I let Agnes and Rebekah go first. Agnes was quick: what little church she went to happened early in life before her parents lost interest or were too busy or simply tuned out. She didn't know why they stopped going. What she knew of Jesus mostly came from Christmas and Easter movies. When pressed whether she needed to find Christ, she shrugged her shoulders and said she hadn't given it much thought.

"Then I'm doubly glad you'll be coming to the church tomorrow." This was news I hadn't yet shared with her.

"I look forward to it, Lucian," she said. We were to call him Lucian now that we were breaking bread together. Agnes pinched me under the table. I flinched which got a rise out of Rebekah.

Having been raised in the church and having attended both regular Sunday services as well as bible school and prayer groups, Rebekah was conversant in the ways and teachings of our brand of American conservative Christianity. As far as I knew, she had always believed what they taught her and hewed the line when it came to what was expected of her. I could still see her at the door with her mother before they left for church, her eyes imploring me to get dressed and come along as if it were that simple. With DeBerry, she was reserved, like her grandmother when she felt her faith being threatened. Lucian must have been used to this because he simply danced around her objections and focused on the common ground they shared.

I was next.

"What about you, Monk? Surely the words you heard in church still resonate within you? Jesus never leaves us even when we leave him." This he intoned with its due solemnity.

"Of that, I have no doubt," I assured him.

"Why did you quit the church? And if you didn't believe, why did you go in the first place?" Rebekah was in a mood. My snapping at Agnes over Judith had triggered a return of the angry woman I so remembered.

"I quit the church because your mother stopped sleeping with me, and as that was the only reason I had for stayed that long, I saw no point in continuing to go." I held up my hands as I said this.

"So it was just about sex?" she smirked.

"No, it was about the end of our relationship, which was signaled by your mother's disinterest in sharing a marital bed with me."

No one had a reply to that. I knew Rebekah wanted to understand what had happened to us beyond the obvious miseries she had witnessed growing up. The only problem was I had no easy answers for her, yet went on anyway.

"If you must know, I went to church because it was a precondition for being allowed to stay when we came out from California. I had no real understanding of Jesus other than what passes for common cultural knowledge. While Moses and your grandmother both came from deeply conservative families, there was little talk of religion when I was a kid. Moses never went back and never forgave God. But your grandmother grew tired of Moses' open relationships and went back home to Virginia and re-embraced God."

Our food arrived. Once we assured the waitress the food was just fine, I finished my tale.

"For all my time in or at church, it never really clicked for me. Maybe that's because I didn't grow up with it like you did and I wasn't longing for spiritual answers. But I put my time in and studied and I did my best to understand, and on a certain level I do, so I try not to be too judgy or condescending." I tried to give my next little comment as much gravitas as I could. "I went because I loved your mother and I wanted her to love me, and she wanted me to be her idea of a good Christian man. I tried to be that, but it wasn't enough. I don't blame God, and I no longer blame your mother. I'm as sorry as you are that it didn't work out with Astral—"

"Lilith," she corrected with a sad smile.

"Sorry, Lilith. After that, as far as I was concerned, there was no reason to continue going."

Rebekah nodded that she understood, and went back to playing with her food.

Agnes, alarmed at the tenor the conversation had taken, asked Brother DeBerry what his story was. This perked up our guest.

"I'm glad you asked, Agnes," he said leaning back.

I pinched Agnes and smiled when she flinched.

Lucian put his hands together. "To be honest, I don't find my story to be that remarkable, although it does follow a common trajectory. I was, for the most part, a bored disinterested child in a family that was neither good nor bad. I didn't feel particularly close to my parents, and I don't think they felt particularly close to me. I hung out with the wrong people, but really they were no different than I was, and when you're young and stupid, you do stupid things. Mine was to feel no compunction in taking other people's money by lying and being a cheat. And like most stupid people I got caught, got a second chance, and blew that which landed me in prison." He spoke with an even cadence and paused so we could do a little pre-epiphany judging.

"Naturally, I thought prison would be no big thing, but I was wrong. For the first time in my life, I felt the full weight of my foolishness because it *was* a big thing and I was completely unprepared for it. Prison isn't the same as jail. Yet, the Lord works his magic in interesting ways, and after some rather unpleasant experiences, I ended up meeting Ashton Cox, and from him, I found this path to sharing the Lord's promise." With that, he returned to his catfish.

I think Rebekah and Agnes were expecting more, but I was fine with the break. The All American burger was bigger than either Agnes or I had imagined and required that I give it as much attention as possible. This necessitated giving DeBerry less. I ate what I could, delighted in watching Agnes struggle with her portion and gave up about halfway through.

"I'm not the man I once was," I explained.

Agnes just smiled and said, "Good to know." This from a woman who was doing no better with her half. She gave up about two bites after I did.

"No more gut-busters, beautiful," I admonished.

"I might have to agree with you on that."

I believe she was more relieved of this burden than I was. The rest of the meal was quiet. The food, having sated our hunger, left us in a peaceful stupor. We passed on dessert and parted ways at the church. The pastor was letting Lucian stay in the small adjoining house. The three of us ambled back to the Comfort Inn and with what little strength we had left cleaned up and went to bed.

• • • • •

It was the phone that woke me up. I was surprised at how late it was, after eleven. Both Agnes and Rebekah were still asleep. That didn't surprise me. I picked up the phone and answered without thinking.

"Yes?"

"I miss you, Monk." It was the enchantress with the beautiful neck.

"Give me one minute..." I fell out of bed, threw on a shirt and a pair of pants, and fled for the front door. Once I was safely on a bench by the pool, I wondered why she would miss me. "What's up? Isn't it like eight in the morning there?"

"Yes, and I know that's early for me, but it's been a bad couple of days, and I needed to hear a friendly voice. How are you, Monk? Do you miss me?"

Oh, man!

"You know I do. I almost thought you'd finished up with me, but after your last text I can see that's not true..." Her picture was there on the phone. She was lounging by the pool with nothing on but a delightful smile. Just looking at it gave me a painful erection. All I wanted to do at that moment was race to her beautiful house and that beautiful neck and make myself needlessly crazy.

"Do you want me to be done with you?" She let that hang in the air. Judith Delashay was no fool when it came to Monk Buttman. She was well aware of the answer to her question.

"No, and you know that."

"Still it's nice to hear," I could feel her breath on me; smell her perfume. "Where are you?" I told her of my travels, the ones that were keeping me away. "When do you think you'll be back? I'd like to think you wouldn't make me wait too much longer?"

"Maybe a week or so..." I would have preferred five minutes.

"That's too bad. I had a few things I wanted you to take care of..." She then went into a level of detail that I was sure would cause my heart to explode. My hard-on certainly thought it would.

"You know you're making me crazy with that kind of talk."

"Then you've made my day. I expect you'll get in touch with me as soon as you can," her voice a sweet whisper. "Goodbye, Monk."

"Bye." I set the phone down and took a minute to remind myself that this bench was not the place to furiously relieve myself of unexpected sexual frustration. Fortunately, I was important enough for yet another call from southern California. That dispelled the erotic euphoria Judith had cast.

It was Joanie.

"Buttman here." I knew she would hate my saying that.

"Very funny. I called to let you know that I'm now your employee and that means I have some questions for you."

"Me?" I feigned ignorance.

"It's early, and I'm not in the mood!" I nearly uttered a smartass remark, but I held my tongue. "Ardis went over everything she could think of, and she collected the last of her things today. I already have a number of people calling about my bungalow, or the one I'm moving out of, so is there anything I need to know from you before I rent it out? I mean the rent here is pretty cheap... did you want to raise it any? I don't know. When are you going to be back?"

I was kind of surprised by Joanie's uncertainty. Normally, I'm the one who doesn't know what to do.

"I'm hoping within a week or two. Right now I'm in Kentucky and will probably end up in Oklahoma before too long. Hang in there; you'll be fine. I have all the faith in the world in your many, many talents. Whatever you think will work is fine with me."

"That's not much of a pep talk, Buttman."

"Sorry; it's all I got. We'll talk when I get back." After, of course, I satisfy Judith's requests. "I'm sure Ardis knows more than I do."

"Of that, I have no doubt. Alright, I'll see you when I see you."

"Ok. Bye." I tried to say that with as much brio as I could. She left me with a distinctly underwhelming goodbye. My erection was long gone. I sighed long enough to elicit a smile from Agnes, who was standing behind me.

"Troubles, Sunshine?"

"Yeah. California called to say I'm sorry, all is forgiven, and please come back." She sat down beside me.

"So I heard." Her hand was slowly moving along my leg.

"You know it's not nice to eavesdrop." God only knows how long she'd been standing there.

"I heard that too." Agnes leaned in and kissed me. It was a nice sweet kiss, which only made me feel like a bigger ass. "I'm sorry about last night. I shouldn't have said anything."

"I shouldn't have snapped at you. It was uncalled for," I said between kisses.

"I promise I won't say anything more," my erection was back, "but that doesn't mean our understanding has changed." Her hand was still on my thigh, and mine was brushing the underside of her breast.

"I don't expect it to."

"It's too bad we don't have our own room. I could use a little attention if you know what I mean?" Her hand was on my erection.

Maybe we should sneak off and find a secluded spot somewhere..."

"Like where?"

I looked around knowing I couldn't be seen fondling her out here in the open. There was a path just behind the building. "Maybe up there..." I pointed to the hill behind us.

"Ok." That's my Agnes.

The path zigzagged this way and that, out of the view of anyone below. I quickly unbuttoned her blouse as she unzipped my pants. She thoughtfully wasn't wearing a bra. Our kissing, like our breathing, was frenetic, as if we couldn't stop ourselves. Our hands were busy doing what the other longed for those hands to do. I knew I wouldn't last long, and I didn't think Agnes would either. She must have thought the same thing as she pushed her underwear to her knees and turned around.

"You know what I like."

I did as I entered her from behind. My hands found her breasts as she leaned against a tree, and I tried to be as controlled as I could. It didn't take long for us to orgasm. As we were slowing down, the obvious vulnerability of the situation caused us to quickly cover ourselves and head back to the bench. I was still panting.

"We should do this more often." She ran her finger along my lips.

"I can't think of a reason not to other than getting arrested for public indecency." I put her finger in my mouth, something I knew she liked.

"I'm not suggesting we do it in the town square, Monk."

"That's good cuz it's possible I'd suffer from stage fright."

"And we certainly don't want that do we?" I don't think she believed me.

"Rebekah must be wondering where we are..." I was trying not to picture myself screwing Agnes in front of a gaggle of gawkers.

"She's probably still asleep." Agnes was once again running her hand along my pants leg.

"Asleep?" I was missing something.

"Didn't you hear her crying last night?" she asked incredulously.

"No, I was zonked last night. Must have been that burger you talked me into." I tried to use humor to mask my poor parenting skills.

"Poor girl is struggling with this mess. I got up and held her for a while. She's sad and lonely, Monk. I gave her a few of my sleeping pills, which knocked her out. We should probably go wake her up."

"Probably." We got up and headed back to the room. "Thanks for going up into the bushes with me."

"My pleasure, Sunshine."

Yeah, I need to get my shit together.

23

My daughter was still out of it. It was almost noon, and now that our animal urges had been satisfied, Agnes and I were hungry. As a means of hunger sublimation, I suggested we take a shower together.

"It's a good thing we think alike, Buttman."

"I'm not complaining, Beautiful." I put my arm around her waist.

"Just remember that when the time comes..." I knew what she meant but let it slide.

Rebekah was sitting up in bed when we reemerged from the bathroom squeaky-clean. She was rumpled, and a bit dazed from the medication, but she was smiling at us. I can't imagine why.

"I assume its ok for me to use the bathroom now that the two of you are finished with whatever it was you were up to?"

"I believe it is." I returned her smile. "Did you get some sleep? Ag said you had a tough night."

"I did. Her pills put me down for the count, but I feel a lot better now." She looked over at the clock: it was twelve-thirty. "I should get cleaned up; it's already lunchtime."

"True. I was thinking it might be time to get something to eat," I said.

Rebekah grabbed her stuff and shuffled to the bathroom. Agnes and I sat on the couch doing our best to behave. Sometimes I think I don't have a clue about life. I love this woman, have no reason whatsoever to be involved with anyone else, and she tolerates it which I don't get and occasionally abuse. Still, here we are, in Kentucky of all places, together, and as I sit here I hear the same words running through my head as if a loop: I'll never let you go, you belong to me, and a big part of me is deeply content with that, and yet...

"What're you thinking about?" She had to ask.

I started laughing; what else could I do? "I was thinking about us, you and me."

"And that's funny?" She was trying hard not to laugh too.

"Yes, sometimes it is, Beautiful, sometimes it is." I put my arm around her and continued to wonder what was wrong with me.

• • • • •

Lunch was at a little sandwich shop Rebekah found on her phone. Makes you wonder how anyone survived before the ubiquity of smartphones? The sandwiches were good as were the salads that went with them. I desperately wanted a beer, but going to church with beer breath didn't strike me as the best plan. We stopped at the church to make sure we had the time right and discovered it was a potluck, which given that it was Wednesday made sense. It was a good way to get people to come over. Agnes abruptly decided we should bring something and wandered into the church. We found a nice middle-aged woman named Lillian who consulted with two other women of the same approximate age and said that it would be kind of us if we could bring some deserts, pies preferably as Lisa, who normally bakes pies for their potlucks, was sick. As we did not have the means to bake pies, Lillian suggested The Tasty Treat two blocks down.

"They have the most wonderful pies, especially the pecan, but any kind is fine."

"Then we'll do that. Thanks, Lillian," Agnes said, solicitous as always.

"See you soon," they chorused, and we were on our way to The Tasty Treat.

Lillian was not misinformed, and after much debate we settled on pecan, cherry, and chocolate cream. Having thusly sated Agnes' desire not to be a thoughtless outlier at the evening love fest, we returned to the church where a very delighted Lillian put the pies in the fridge.

We still had three hours to kill before Brother DeBerry's shindig at the Bethany Church of Christ. Since neither Agnes nor Rebekah had a swimsuit, the pool was not an option. Rebekah once again went to the magic phone and found a community park not far from us, and it was agreed we would waste our time there.

The weather cooperated by providing a light breeze to compliment the sunshine and the soft clouds strolling along quietly above us. The park had play areas for dogs, kids, and for the adults, barbeques. We ended up by the kid's area, which didn't surprise me, but I was surprised by flashbacks of the park in South Laguna with Jones and that woman Dahlia including the fear that we were being watched.

The kid's area had the requisite jungle gyms and swings, a big lawn to run around on, and a wading pool. We found a table not far from the pool and watched the kids run around, splash, and scream. A guy in an ice cream truck was selling frozen treats, so much like the day before we were soon comforting ourselves with sugary delights.

"This detective business isn't what they make it out to be," Rebekah surmised.

"I spose," I said while nursing a creamsicle.

"Shouldn't we be doing something?" She was bored.

"You can call the numbers you found on Farrell's phone." That's all I had. I didn't know if DeBerry could help us.

"Alright, I will." She pulled Farrell's phone out of her pocket.

Agnes seemed completely uninterested. She was watching the kids. "Do you ever think about having more kids, Monk?" Both Rebekah and I turned towards her.

"Yeah, Dad, have you?" Rebekah had that nasty grin on her face.

"Shouldn't you be working the phone?" I muttered.

"I have a few minutes to spare." She was far more intrigued by Agnes and I having children.

"I don't know that I want to have any more kids. I'd be in my sixties before they were out of high school. Besides, you're no spring chicken. You might not enjoy being pregnant at your age."

"I know, but I liked having kids around, and I'm not that old!"

"I don't know if I can do diapers and formula again," I reasoned.

"I don't think breast milk will be a problem," she continued.

I took in her wonderful breasts, "Maybe not, but still..."

"Then what about adopting an older kid?"

I had the feeling I was being set up. "I don't know; maybe..." Agnes was smiling at me. "...We can talk about it later." She wrapped her arms around me. It *was* a setup.

Rebekah returned to Farrell's phone. There was no answer from the first number. She sighed. But the second number brought an answer. She put the phone on speaker.

"Yes?" a man's voice spoke.

"I'd like to talk to Farrell." Silence. "Hello?"

"Who is this? How did you get this number?"

"I'm his wife. I found his phone at the house where those people died." There were muffled voices in the background.

"I'm sorry, but Farrell isn't here." It was a different male voice, older, I thought.

"The ghost said he was with you!" Rebekah was playing a hunch.

"The ghost is a liar. Goodbye!" They hung up.

I looked at my daughter. "What do you think?"

She put the phone back in her pocket. "It sounded like that Ashton Cox character." She took the phone back out and called the number again. No answer this time. Back in her pocket it went. We returned our attention to the kids enjoying the park. That brought me back to Agnes wanting children. It had never come up before. I assumed a life of just the two of us. It hadn't occurred to me there might be more, and we were at that age where it was now or never.

"Why the interest in kids all of a sudden?" I asked.

She put her hand on mine. "I don't know, probably because I like the idea of our having a stronger bond and what's stronger than having a family?"

"We already have three kids between us."

"I know, but they're grown, and they're not *ours*." I'd forgotten the woman was nuts. "It was just an idea, that's all." She squeezed my hand and laid her head on my shoulder.

"I think Agnes is right! What you need is your own love child." Rebekah had to chime in.

"Yeah," Agnes thoughtfully added.

"I said we'd talk about it..." I was sorry I brought it up.

Two little boys raced by with water pistols blasting everything in sight. A minute later, they were back and gave us a few blasts before laughing and running off.

"Oh yeah, what we need is some of that twenty-four hours a day," I said as we wiped the water off our faces.

"Our kids would be angels, Sunshine," she cooed.

"Uh-huh. Well, best evidence doesn't support that hypothesis." I pointed at Rebekah, who shook her head.

"Hey, don't put this on me."

We watched as the two boys made themselves nuisances to a number of other onlookers. It was hard not to fall into the past with all the kids and parents around, although mostly it was moms. There were babies and toddlers, some bored teenagers, and the two punks with the squirt guns. I wondered what having more kids would have been like. Maybe I could get both Agnes and Judith pregnant; now there's an adventure for the bold. I doubted whether I could talk Judith into it, but you never know. It would certainly make life with Agnes far more interesting, although probably not in a good way.

Idle thoughts.

Out of the cacophony of the park, we heard a whisper of music emanating from Rebekah's pocket, Farrell's phone. It was the first number.

"Yes?" Rebekah answered.

It was Farrell! She put it on speaker.

"Where are you? Are you still with those guys? They said you weren't there!" Rebekah was angry.

"I can't tell you where I am. Yes, I'm sorta with Ashton, but there's more to it. I can't really talk right now..." His voice was faint, a quiet whisper. We got the impression he had sneaked out on that Ashton Cox character.

"What about those dead people, Farrell? What about them?" Her anger was rising.

Silence.

"Farrell!"

A few of the moms around us looked over.

"I don't know anything about any dead people."

"At the house where we found your phone. They're all dead, Farrell, dead! What have you guys done?" I put my hand on Rebekah's arm so she'd look at me, and when she did, I put my finger to my lips. She pursed her lips in response.

"I don't know anything about that!" We could hear him breathing. His anger was rising.

"Farrell, don't lie to me."

"Go home, Rebekah, go home. I know what I'm doing," there were voices in the background and not from the park, "and I know what you've been doing, so don't pretend to be all worried about poor stupid Farrell."

And just as he sprang forth, he disappeared.

Rebekah continued to stare at the phone, lost to her thoughts. Agnes put her arms around her and Rebekah put the phone on the table and wrapped her arms around Agnes, tears running down her face. I felt like the odd man out. We sat there among the happy and the harried, the playful and the played upon, while the sun drifted across the sky. I reached for Rebekah's hand, and as a salve to my discomfort, she held on to it as she cried. A little girl wandered by and put her hand on Rebekah's knee.

"Are you sad?" she asked.

The three of us turned to her. She had sandy blond hair and bright blue eyes set in a sweet round face. She looked to be about six.

"Yes," Rebekah answered.

"I'm sorry." Her mother called her name, and she turned towards her. "I have to go. I hope you feel better. Bye." She sped off.

Rebekah let go of Agnes and me and wiped her face with her sleeves. "We should go."

I didn't ask where.

It was to the motel. Rebekah wanted to lie down. We still had an hour before we had to go to the church and I was regretting this whole miserable affair.

"I think we should just go home," I whined.

Agnes was sitting with me on the chairs just outside our door overlooking the pool. We left Rebekah in the room. "Maybe, but she needs to find Farrell."

"Why? The guy's a fuckup, and God only knows what he's up to. We can take her with us. There are a million things to do in LA. Why chase after someone who just wants you to go home, which is a dump."

Agnes looked at me like I was a moron and patted me on the leg. "I'm pretty sure she's pregnant, Monk. That's why we're doing this. Even if she's planning on leaving him, it's important for her to do it in person, not on the phone or text or whatever."

"Pregnant?" Monk Buttman, hard-boiled private dick.

"I think so. Does it make sense to you now, mister detective?" She was wearing that smile she knew irritated me because she knew better than I did, not that it didn't happen often, but you never admit it.

"Yeah, but the snarky crack was unnecessary," I huffed.

"Oh, I think it was." She pulled her chair over and put her arms around me. I had no other choice but to put my arm around her and give her a kiss. The pool had attracted a number of guests, so we listened as they flopped and splashed away. Rebekah came out a little later and borrowed a chair from the empty room next door.

"How're you feeling?" Agnes inquired.

She smiled and rubbed her eyes. "I'm ok. Is it time to go?"

I wasn't convinced. "We have a few more minutes. We don't have to go if you don't want to, or I can go if you'd rather stay back..."

She shook her head. "No, I should go."

The following minutes were spent in anticipation of her next move. Agnes and I were just along for the ride and to provide support. If she was pregnant and ready for splitsville with Farrell, it explained all the intrigue with her mother and grandmother and why Astral was so worked up about this. Babies change everything. I ought to know. I also know the environment she was raised in, and you don't just run off. Suspect husbands do, so you can be with the right man, but I don't think Rebekah had a Judah to take up the slack like her mother did, and Astral wasn't pregnant... at least I don't think she was. That ugly thought never occurred to me. There are reasons for that dumbass! If she was pregnant it was Judah's not yours, conjugal visits weren't happening, remember?

I remember.

"Do you think I should just go home?" She was playing with her ring again. "Maybe this is all a terrible mistake, and I should just wait it out."

"I think you know the answer to that." I knew Rebekah liked to bounce possibilities off people even when she'd already made up her mind.

Agnes had the answer. "Sometimes, the truth is painful. We know it all too well." Agnes gestured at me. "Your father's never said it out loud, but I know there was a time, long before he left your mother when he knew it would never be what he wanted, but he kept holding out just like I did. I knew for a long time that Simon wouldn't be who I needed him to be. We were never going to have what we wanted. That's why your father and I get along so well because we're what we both need. Only you know how you truly feel, and we'll do whatever we can to help, whether that's going back to Virginia or continuing to look for your husband, but I think you know already, you're just not ready to say it out loud."

"Yeah..." A half-smile to go with the spinning ring.

24

I counted about forty of us sitting mostly towards the front, but some scattered back among the pews. Not a bad crowd since I figured the church could seat a couple hundred. There was a decent mix of ages rather than mostly older faces. It was a comfortable church, and as always, I could feel the love-hate relationship within me rise to the surface. I couldn't deny that I enjoyed the people and company I found at services even as I couldn't deny that I didn't buy a lot of the teachings. I wasn't worried for my soul or my place in the universe, and I was at peace with my beliefs. Still, there was a part of me that missed the community you find in churches even if that community sometimes didn't extend much beyond the outer doors. Common desire for a place of peace and communion, I thought.

The pastor said a few words and a prayer before turning over the pulpit to Brother DeBerry. I don't know what I was expecting, but it was nothing more than a paean to core Christian values, the kind that are hard to not want, like love and compassion, treating others as you would want them to treat you, forgiveness, and the power of community to enrich the lives of everyone. It was, to my mind, why people go to church. Some fear death, or maybe most do, but beyond that, it's the belief that the vicissitudes and happenstance of life can be mitigated or soothed by a common belief in a caring and participatory God. I listened as DeBerry spoke in a singsong cadence, which rose and fell in volume, pulling the audience in and I watched Agnes and Rebekah's responses to it. I found that more fascinating than what was spoken. I'd heard that many times before.

As expected much of the talk revolved around first-century Christians.

"I often hear that faith is fading, dying on the vine, that it is receding from our lives, so I ask myself what can we do today to bring the glory of God's message back?" DeBerry paused and looked at the cross above him. "I believe the first thing we need to do is clear away the clutter of modern life with its emphasis on wealth and material gain. Like the early Christians, we must embrace the joy we feel and express that to those around us. We need to focus on the lesser of us and support them, and we should lead by showing the power of our community as Christians did so long ago. Possessions and wealth are a fool's gold. We don't need politicians from Caesar's realm pretending to understand God's work; we have all we need in our hearts and in the ministry of Jesus Christ."

He began pacing behind the pulpit. "People will know us not by our possessions, but by our word because we act upon that word and through God's grace, we share it with those around us." DeBerry spread out his hands and looked upon us with beneficence. "We are blessed in this church because we wish to spread that good word and benefit from it. And like those before us, we will encounter those who mock and vilify us for our devotion, but we also know that God walks with us and that God looks after us as he did those so long ago first bringing the gospels to the pagans and the godless of the ancient world. They suffered, but still, they believed and profited by God's love and his promise of eternal life."

Brother Lucian put his hand on the good book and raised it from the pulpit.

"I'm not asking you to be martyrs or to give up what you have. I understand the modern world, though I must confess that I don't care for it much, only that it not keep you from the life Jesus promised. That it not sidetrack you from being fully in the embrace of the Lord. I'm often asked about the fellowship, the community we've created in Oklahoma that we've patterned after early Christians, and my answer always come back to a sense of shared belief, of shared commitment, of a shared bond to one another. Sharing God's love, sharing the joy of God's calling, and being thankful for Jesus Christ and all he gives us. I so very much want that for all mankind; for all the people of the world, but if nothing else, I want to invigorate our Christian community and remind it of this awesome gift we've been given. I believe our community is a beacon to others so they may see and live as God commands; that we are with you, and that there is joy in our being here today."

DeBerry went on for little longer, thanking the pastor and the members of the church for their hospitality and for giving him the opportunity to speak. We prayed and clapped. As they led us to where the food was the pastor and DeBerry shook our hands and thanked us for being there.

"I understand you were kind enough to bring us some of these wonderful deserts tonight?" The pastor, whose name was Brookfort, thanked us.

"We just wanted to do our part," Agnes responded. "I hear they're very tasty."

"They are indeed."

The three of us grabbed a plate, food, and found a table towards the back of the room. I preferred that so I could watch the crowd. The fare was tasty. I could hear the snobby Californian in me, and it was a little more caloric than I was normally used to, but this trip had blown a big hole in my diet. When in Rome, I said to myself, which made me laugh given DeBerry's sermon. I contented myself with fried chicken, a soft roll, salad, and a slice of chocolate cream pie. I raised my eyebrow at Agnes, who had a slice of all three pies in addition to a full plate.

"What?"

"Nothing," I said. She noted the different in our plates.

"I'm being polite. I think it's good form to try a little of everything, Mr. Smart Guy."

"Yes, it obviously isn't your sweet tooth, my dear."

"Obviously," she pouted. "I was going to share, but now I don't think I will."

"Not share? And this after Brother DeBerry's admonition to do just that and in a church no less. For shame."

Agnes shrugged her shoulders. "I don't think he was referring to pie."

"Oh, I believe he was."

"Then go get your own," she huffed.

"Too late. Lillian and her lady friends have already divvied up the pies."

She smiled and patted my leg. "Then you'd better be a lot nicer to me, Monk Buttman."

I decided to ignore that particular suggestion by engaging my silent daughter. She had said little in the last hour and was picking at her plate. If she were pregnant, you'd think she'd be eating more, but something was eating at her.

"Is this what he said the last time you heard him speak?"

"Yeah."

"Then why would Pastor Davis be leery of him? It didn't strike me as being anything more than what you usually hear?"

She thought about it while contemplating a fork full of mashed potatoes. "If you remember, it wasn't DeBerry so much as the wash that followed him."

"The ghost and the angel?" I asked.

"Yes." She put the fork back down. "Where do you think the names came from? I mean, did they pick them for themselves; did someone make them up? They seem rather clichéd, don't you think?"

"I think it makes for good theater and it evokes particular images for people. It's possible the names came from comments or references..." I looked over at DeBerry. He saw me watching and made his way over to us. "Why don't we ask the man himself? Perhaps he knows."

There was an open chair next to me, and the man took his place. Agnes spoke first.

"I enjoyed your talk." While she said this, I reached for a slice of pie, but she slapped my hand. "You had your chance."

"A woman should honor her man," I reminded her. "That means sharing her pie."

"A man should know better." She smiled as she moved the pie beyond my reach.

"I'm glad you enjoyed what I had to say, Agnes." DeBerry thoughtfully interrupted our domestic spat. "I find that people are quite receptive to the message I've been asked by God to share and I believe there's a longing in society for what God has to offer, but too often it's lost in all the noise we hear around us." He turned to me. "And you Monk, did I rekindle the fire of your faith in any way?"

"I don't know about that, but it's hard to find fault with the belief that we should care, respect, and love one another. Within these walls, such sentiments are welcome and safe, but it's outside where our selfishness resides, and those sentiments are harder to live by, especially when someone stomps on your foot." I had no interest in modifying my beliefs.

"True. We're asked to take extraordinary steps in our faith, and they're not always on an orderly path, but with the right resolve and the Lord's support we can get there."

He didn't notice my daughter gathering steam.

"Then what about the waters swirling around you? What about this ghost and this angel, and what's become of my husband, and what of the people who have died? What of Molly and Jonathan and the people in Pennsylvania? Where is the Lord's support in all of that?" Rebekah's empathy was not with our guest. Lucian DeBerry winced at the word ghost and angel.

"I appreciate everyone's concerns for your husband's welfare, I do, and I wish I had more to tell, but unfortunately, I don't. If he was traveling with Mr. Cox and is no longer with them, then I can only assume two things: that he went on to Oklahoma, which is what commonly happens to those who start out with Mr. Cox, or he has decided to go his own way. I know that there has been," DeBerry began waving his hand in the air, "distractions because of what this person has been saying about us and me in particular."

"Who is this ghost?" I asked.

"I assumed he was the father of Justin Peterson. He accosted me some time after Justin killed himself saying I was to blame—"

"Were you?"

The eyes of our man of God filled with tears. DeBerry looked at the cross above the door to the dining room. I followed his eyes to the cross.

"I had no reason to harm Justin. I only wanted what was best for him and his wife. I," he paused, wiping away the tears. "Sometimes, it can be difficult to understand the ways of the Lord when it comes to tragedy. I know that, like Job, we are tested in our faith, that we must persevere in our love for God and his plans for us, even if, at times, they seem inexplicable. I don't know what happened to the people you mentioned, Rebekah. I feel a great sadness at their passing, and I wish there was more I could tell you, but I do know that God has a plan for us, wherever it takes us, and all we can do is keep our faith and know that we will find our place beside him in the next life." Brother DeBerry took a moment to compose himself, evidently, he wasn't expecting to talk about this and I felt there was more to it whether it was spoken of or not.

"Maybe you can tell us about these names, ghost, and angel. They seem like something out of a comic book." Rebekah hadn't softened.

"I guess they do. I don't really know about the ghost. Ashton seems to think it's because there was a rumor that Justin's father had killed himself or died and was now somhow haunting us, but that seems absurd. The name angel is quite simple. As I told you yesterday, I met Ashton in prison, and he took me under his wing. Another prisoner called him my guardian angel, and it kind of stuck over the years. I never thought of it as having any spiritual or mystical significance."

DeBerry put his hands together as if praying. "I try not to let whoever this ghost person is affect my ministry. If he is associated with Justin or his family, I understand their grief and I pray for them. I know what they say about me and accept that it is my cross to bear." He took in a deep breath, closed his eyes, and mouthed a prayer to himself.

The three of us watched. I thought about making a move on the last slice of pie Agnes had, but figured it might reflect poorly on my character. Agnes must have sensed this because she moved the plate further away while pinching my leg. Damn woman!

DeBerry opened his eyes and did his best to smile and bring back the man we'd seen at the pulpit. "God watches over us, Rebekah; I truly believe that, and I know with patience, the answers to your questions will be found." He rose from his chair.

"So you think Farrell is in Oklahoma?" Rebekah asked in a softer tone.

"I do. God be with you."

We watched him head over to Pastor Brookfort and other members of the church. Agnes, my beautiful Agnes, set the last small pieces of pie in front of me.

"Thanks."

"You're welcome." She pinched me again. "Just don't expect it every time, Sunshine."

"You're a jerk, Aggie." I rubbed my leg.

"Yes, I am." She made a kissy face. I could see Rebekah curling her nose.

We didn't stay much longer. Rebekah was tired, and there was only so much chitchat I was up for. Even Agnes, who seemed in her element and enamored with small-town life, ran out of questions and interests after a while. We thanked Lillian and the ladies for their kindness, assured the pastor that the evening was both enjoyable and enlightening, and headed back to the Comfort Inn. We didn't see Brother DeBerry on the way out.

I assumed he had things to do.

Back in our room, we cleaned up, and I found a game on the boobtube. Rebekah asked for a few more sleeping pills from Agnes and crashed. I turned down the sound, and we watched the flickering images to the sound of Rebekah's breathing. Agnes put her arms around me and rested her head on my chest.

"Do you think Farrell is the father of this child you think she's carrying?" I was curious.

"It makes you wonder, doesn't it?" That was her answer just as it was mine.

"Should we inquire or let it slide?"

She tightened her grip. "I have a feeling the truth, whatever it is, is simmering just below the surface, so to answer your question, I think we'll find out sooner rather than later."

"So, you think she'll own up?"

"Maybe."

"Yeah, maybe..." We could always hope, as DeBerry would say.

The game wasn't particularly interesting or competitive. I flipped through the channels for no reason other than boredom, finally settling on a show about people looking at houses. Agnes fell asleep. With cat-like stealth, I carefully wriggled free and covered her up. I rose for one last trip to the bathroom when the knock came upon my door. I looked through the curtains to see Brother DeBerry standing there with his head down. I opened the door.

"I apologize for coming by so late, but I was hoping to speak to you."

"Me?"

He seemed surprised by that. "Yes, I'd like a few words with you if you can spare them, Monk."

"Ah, sure, but we'll have to talk outside, the girls are asleep." He nodded. I grabbed the card key, and we went down by the pool.

Confessions are an odd thing.

The buoyant character Larry Bochner created, our Lucian DeBerry, had his dark side or sad side or misunderstood side that was kept under wraps as he traveled the country looking for kindred souls or those longing for something to believe in. Despite DeBerry's declarations to the contrary, this ghost of his was wearing on him, at least that's what I believed in the beginning. Now a competing ghost was dogging him and his carefully conceived vision of God's plan.

In the pale of the moonlight reflecting off the surface of the pool, Lucian DeBerry shrank, and his shoulders slumped. He cried a number of times as he spilled the contents of his broken heart and of his trials and tribulations. Perhaps, I thought, as he continued to lament, I'm being unkind towards him, uncharitable and uncaring. We all ferry down the same river, whether we control the paddle or not. It took him a while to come to the reason for picking me to be his confessor.

"Why are you telling me this?" I wanted to know.

"Confession is good for the soul," he confided.

"Perhaps, but why me instead of someone else, say Ashton Cox or Pastor Brookfort for instance?"

"They are too close to me, to who I have become. Ashton wouldn't understand, and Pastor Brookfort would struggle with the discomfort it would cause him. You are a stranger, we have no intimate connection, and yet I feel you are an empathetic soul. I believe that even if you choose to judge me, it will not be vindictive or hateful."

I considered his choice of words. "And if you're mistaken, if I'm none of those things, then what?"

He stood and wipes his eyes. The moon, now full and bright, illuminated the hope on his face. "A man has to have faith in those around him. He has to." He turned to me and smiled, "May God be with you, Monk."

"May God be with you, Lucian." I watched as he disappeared in the direction of the church.

I spent the night staring at the popcorn ceiling there in the dark. At some point, I fell asleep. A poke in the ribs woke me at about ten in the morning.

"Time to rise and shine, Sunshine." Agnes thought that was funny. I didn't. "What's the plan?" was what I wanted to know.

"Oklahoma is the plan," Rebekah said as if a matter of fact.

I was afraid of that.

25

I let Rebekah drive as we worked our way across Kentucky into Missouri. Her spirits were better from having gotten some sleep, and she was eating, which was important to Agnes, concerned as she was with a possible baby on the way. I stared off into the distance. Lucian DeBerry continued to singsong his confession in my head. Oklahoma, where the wind comes sweeping down the plain. The question was where we'd be swept to? I was tired of thinking about it, about where we were going and why. I didn't care about Farrell, and I didn't care about DeBerry or his problems even as they continued to swim around in my head. I just wanted to go home.

"What are you thinking about?" Agnes had her hand on my arm.

"Going home."

Agnes moved her hand to my shoulder. "What's wrong?"

"What do you mean?" I knew what she meant.

"I mean you've been unusually quiet."

"I talk too much as it is." It was something to say.

"Yeah, I'm not buying it. Someone was at the door last night. Is it that? Who was it?"

"It was DeBerry. He wanted to talk."

"About what?" she asked.

I thought about that. What did he want to talk about? I don't remember saying much, just listening. "He wanted to confess."

"Confess to what? Monk, what's going on?" Her hand was back on my arm; the things you notice.

Rebekah, who had said little as we weaved through the south of Missouri felt compelled to join in. "Was it about Farrell?"

"No, it had nothing to do with Farrell."

"Then what?" They were tired of my evasions. So was I, time to move on.

"Rebekah, are you pregnant?" I wanted to know, and I wanted to care.

She didn't answer right away, and I returned to the rolling hills and farms coming in and out of my view from the passenger side of the truck. It was all starting to look the same. The only sound was the whine of the tires tearing at the pavement.

Rebekah cleared her throat. "Yes, I'm pregnant."

"Is Farrell the father?" My bad mood was coming through.

"I don't want to talk about it!" So was hers.

Agnes was stuck in the middle. "What does that have to do with Lucian DeBerry coming to see you last night?"

I looked at Agnes and took her hand. "I don't know, I just know I want to go home." I didn't think that would satisfy her for long, but she sat back and sighed. No more questions.

• • • • •

Lucian DeBerry's community lay in the panhandle of Oklahoma, outside the small town of Goodwell, nearly a thousand miles from Elizabethtown. The truck didn't have it in it to go that far. The road noise from the tires began morphing into something more troubling, something I'd worried about from the moment we'd left Virginia. There had been no time to have the truck serviced, as was my compulsion before road trips, and that bad vibe was back. We made it into Missouri but only to Springfield. The water pump was dying; you could hear it failing; the temperature of the engine rising on its way to failure from exhaustion. We pulled over just outside of town, and Rebekah looked up repair shops, hoping to find one that specialized in older vehicles. I called Bernie.

"You're where?" Once again, he found merriment in my predicaments.

"Outside Springfield, Missouri," I said.

"Really?"

"Yes." I could hear the smug in his voice.

"Sorry, Monk, I don't tow that far away." Always the wise guy.

"Yeah, I figured that. Know anyone out here who works on older cars that we can trust?"

"Wow, give me a minute." Agnes and Rebekah were standing with me next to the truck, as the traffic zipped past. It was early afternoon, and I was tired, and they were hungry. Bernie returned to the phone. "Found a place called Jimbo's Kustoms, with a 'K', in Springfield. What did you do to the Falcon?"

"It's not the Falcon; it's a sixty-eight Chevy truck."

Bernie started laughing. "And you're driving it from where?"

"Virginia, with stops in-between." More laughter.

"You know how to live, Monk; I'll give you that. Anyway, if I were you I'd call them." He passed along the address and phone number, which Rebekah dutifully recorded on her phone.

"I'll call," she said.

"Thanks, Bernie," I said.

"No, thank you, Monk; you made my day. Take care." Yeah, good times. I ended my call as Rebekah began hers. Jimbo's wasn't far away, and they were willing to help. The tow truck took thirty minutes to arrive, and the four of us packed into the cab. An affable fellow name Barney met us at the shop and grinned as the truck was brought in.

"Boy, look at this." Barney wandered around the truck. "Not in bad shape, not in bad shape at all. You know, most of the time when we get these old Chevys they're nothing but rust buckets; way too much time out in the weather, but yours looks pretty dang good. No body rot, not even any real dents, nice." The hood was popped, and after looking and tugging, he announced that yes, it appeared the water pump was giving up the ghost.

"Well, what do you think?" I asked our interested shop manager.

"Fixing it shouldn't be a problem other than we might have to order the pump, which means you might be here for a day or so." The trip was already taking too long. I think Barney could see the weary on our faces. "Tell you what, let me go check and see what we can do for ya. How's that?" We all murmured something before I spoke up.

"That'd be great. Is there someplace to eat around here?"

"There's a diner down at the corner, it's good regular cooking."

"And a place to stay if we need it?" Barney nodded in sympathy.

"There's a Comfort Inn about a mile from here. We can give you a lift if need be."

"Thanks for your help." Great, another Comfort Inn, our home away from home.

The diner welcomed us with its regular food. The hour of the day, it being mid-afternoon, gave us a reprieve from the lunch crowd and the noise. Other than ordering, there was little conversation. Agnes went from me to Rebekah trying to lighten the mood, but she gave up when the food arrived. Rebekah stared at her plate, and I fixated on the traffic rumbling by, imagining how many, like me, would rather be at the beach instead of in the middle of nowhere. I pushed the plate away after a few bites. I wasn't hungry.

"You need to eat." Agnes had that look in her eyes I remembered from when she first saw me after I was beaten up by Artie and Gordy.

"I thought I was hungry, but it doesn't taste good. I'll eat later." Agnes took a bite of my sandwich. The food was fine. I had lied.

"Tell me what's wrong, Monk, please."

"This is about me, isn't it?" Rebekah looked up from her plate. "It's about me being pregnant and running away, isn't it? Whether I'm doing that or not!" She wiped her eyes with her napkin, "I don't like everybody judging me, especially you."

"What does that mean?"

"It means I'm not like *you*."

I shook my head. "Oh, baby, you're just like me, you always have been, stubborn and thoughtless and selfish. Like me, you hide your foolishness behind your practicality thinking you can somehow organize a chaotic world full of chaotic people so that they'll do what you want. Blaming me is a waste of time because it doesn't make any of this any better or easier." That just made her cry more. "Does Farrell know you're pregnant? Does your mother or grandmother?"

"I haven't told anybody."

"Not even the father? Shouldn't he know?" I was being an ass.

"I don't want to talk about it!"

"Suit yourself."

"Fuck you!" Oddly, it stung more than I thought.

And with that salutation, she ran off to the bathroom. Agnes wasn't happy with me either. The anger in her eyes was rare enough that I immediately felt bad. It was hard for me to truly piss off Agnes, but I had.

"What's the matter with you? You've been moody and mean all day. What good can it do to be like that? She's lonely and scared, and she needs you to be at least a little supportive."

Now I was pissed off.

"I've always been supportive, goddammit! I don't need you to tell me how to behave. You weren't there; you don't know."

Agnes smacked me on the arm. "Don't give me that crap, Monk Buttman. You know better!" Damn! Agnes was tearing up. Two crying women, just what I didn't want to deal with.

I sat back in the booth, trying to collect myself. I handed her a clean napkin so she could wipe her eyes. Being an ass wasn't providing the payoff I thought it would.

"Alright, alright, I'm sorry I yelled at you..." I reached out and put my arms around her. She hesitated a minute before wrapping her arms around me.

"You're a jerk, Buttman!"

"Yeah..." It wasn't funny anymore.

Rebekah returned after about fifteen minutes. I had to keep Agnes from going in after her.

"She'll be out when she's ready," I said.

She sat down and finished her lunch. She didn't say a word. Agnes elbowed me in the ribs a few times thinking this would elicit an apology from me, but I wasn't in the mood. She didn't like me arguing with Rebekah; too much like her and Anna, but I can be a stubborn prick sometimes and this was one of those times when that's what I wanted to be. To placate my equally stubborn girlfriend, I choked down as much of my now cold sandwich as I could stand. With the meal finished and our argument taking a break, I paid the cashier and we wandered back to Jimbo's Kustoms.

The ghost had other ideas.

Out from between two buildings he came, standing there before us. In the light, I could better make out his features. I had that odd feeling that he was the same but not the same. He wore the same jacket and hood, was almost spectrally pale, the wireframes of his glasses glinted as the sun passed in and out of the meandering clouds. A sneer best described his expression, and he meant to keep us from moving around him.

"Where's Farrell?" Rebekah demanded.

"Farrell is where he should be," he said snidely.

"And where is that?"

The ghost's sneer grew into that of a Cheshire cat. "He's exactly where you think he's is, Rebekah." It was evident that he was delighted by Rebekah's anguish.

I just wanted to get moving. "What do you want? Otherwise, get out of our way," I told him.

"I'm here to warn you, Mr. Bohrman—"

I raised my hand to keep Agnes and Rebekah from responding to that name. "Of what?"

"I think you know."

It was my turn to sneer. "That you'll kill us like the others?"

"It's not me that's responsible for the loss of those lives. Ask the men who were there, the *angel* and his goons. Interesting how people continue to die wherever they go." The ghost kept his hands in his pockets, making me wonder if he was armed. Unfortunately for me, the shotgun and 38 were back with the truck. "Interesting that the religion of peace is forever bathed in the blood of innocents, isn't it, Mr. Bohrman? Inquisitors and guardians of the faith hastening the journey to the afterlife of the unbelieving in order to perpetuate the illusion of purity."

"I'm shocked you don't care for Brother DeBerry's vision for humanity."

"That claptrap about early Christians?" he chided. "Christianity has been fractious from the start, and they've been parading nonsense to the ignorant while killing one other for just as long. No, Mr. Bohrman, I do not care for Brother DeBerry's song and dance."

"And Justin and Amy, what's your connection to them? *Are* you his father?" I asked.

The ghost's demeanor changed. Gone was the sneer; in its place was straight up hate. "No, Mr. Bohrman, I am not Justin's father. Justin's murder, like all the others, are on the head of Lucian DeBerry and all who praise his lies. Talk to the *angel*, assuming he doesn't kill you too."

"Like Larry Bochner?" I asked.

"Like all of them!" he screamed.

Something snapped in the ghost. Sweat was caressing his features. He stepped back and turned around to survey the street and the cars passing by before returning his gaze to us. He took his hands out of his pockets. The sneer was back.

"What about Farrell?" Rebekah yelled.

He said nothing before taking off between the buildings from whence he came. We stood there for a few moments wondering what to do, what to make of this idiotic turn of events.

I looked at my companions. They had the same uncomprehending expression I assumed was on my face.

"I say we load up and get to California as fast as we can."

Agnes appeared ready to go, but Rebekah just said, "No."

Barney informed us that the truck would not be finished until the next day. They could pick up the part in the morning, but today it was too late. Since the truck would be in the shop I asked him to do some regular maintenance; oil change, tune-up, check the brakes; change the fluids, whatever it would take to get the thing to LA. Not a problem he said. We collected our luggage. I put the 38 in my pocket, and I put the shotgun in the back. Barney noticed and asked if he could see it.

"Boy, look at that, an old double-barreled shotgun!" He released the latch exposing the barrel where the shells were loaded. The shotgun was, assuming I remembered correctly, about eighty years old, a relic. But like most of the junk I'd purchased over the years, it was in good condition and worked. "Look at the engraving on this!" Barney was quite enthused. "Any interest in selling it? Trade it for services?"

"Let me think about it," I said as he handed it back.

"I collect antique firearms, and I wouldn't mind having that one." I got that the first time.

"I'll give it some thought."

As promised, one of the assistant mechanics drove us down to the Comfort Inn

26

The room looked much like the other two. The only real difference was we were on the second floor here in Springfield. I went across the street to the 7-11 and bought a six-pack. I sat on the bed nursing the second bottle after downing the first. Agnes and Rebekah had gone for a walk, probably for the best. Agnes was right; I was in a foul mood. Nothing about this miserable trek to find that miserable bastard Farrell was doing any of us any good. I didn't like being angry with Rebekah or snapping at Agnes, but what was I going to do with an unhappy pregnant daughter who wouldn't talk and had this pointless obsession of finding her idiot husband? Then there was all this crap with Lucian DeBerry. I didn't need any of it.

On top of that, the dead were beginning to creep back into my dreams.

After the second beer, the pity party was in full swing. All that was left was someone to bitch at. The girls arrived just in time. I got up to vent, but before I could open my mouth, Rebekah began crying and wrapped her arms around me. She was trying to say something, but I couldn't make it out. Agnes put her hand on Rebekah's shoulder and gently the three of us sat down on the edge of the bed. I looked over at Agnes who smiled and mouthed, "deal with it." She then took the beer and put it in the mini-fridge. Rebekah cried on and off for almost ten minutes. She let go long enough to blow her nose and realize there was snot on my shirt. She made a half-hearted attempt to wipe it off.

"Sorry."

"It cleans up." She let her head rest on my chest, ignoring the goo, "ready to talk?"

"No!"

Great, just what I wanted to hear. Agnes shrugged her shoulders which I assumed meant we'd talk later or there was nothing to tell.

Rebekah held on for a long time. This surprised me. Mostly these attempts at bonding lasted a few awkward moments before we returned to our corners until the next round. This round was uncomfortably long. Finally, I confessed to needing to use the bathroom, all that beer. Reluctantly, Rebekah let go of me and retreated to her bed. Agnes kept her eye on me as I passed her. I sat in the bathroom, wondering what to do. I was much better at doing nothing and running to the beach than solving people's problems. I did okay with Agnes, but I considered that a one off and not necessarily applicable to my relations, especially those that were still morose and unhappy. Realizing I couldn't spend all night in the bathroom, and actually being hungry, I gave up the ghost and returned to my daughter and girlfriend.

"Everything alright, you were in there quite a while?" Agnes knew I was hiding.

"I didn't notice. Anyone else interested in getting something to eat?" I gestured at Rebekah. "Maybe your magic app can find us something reasonable around here."

"I'm hungry too." Agnes was trying to help. We both looked at Rebekah.

"Yes, we should eat." I sat down and listened to the air conditioner whine as Rebekah stared at her phone. Ta-da! There was a place not too far away, somewhat hip, and the food wasn't bad either, or so it said.

"I doubt we'll find a more ringing endorsement than that," I quipped.

"Then we should go," added Agnes.

We collected my weepy pregnant daughter and walked the ten blocks to *A Modern Affair*, with its former warehouse turned hip establishment vibe, and it being a Thursday, room for three travel-weary strangers. I ordered a bottle of wine and seriously thought about not sharing, but the handsome young sommelier brought three glasses, and I was forced to be a decent companion. Agnes was concerned.

"I don't know if it's good for Rebekah to have any wine."

I poo-poohed that. "It's just a glass, besides Jesus imbibed, so it's all right."

"Jesus wasn't pregnant!"

I smiled. "So?"

"You're a jerk, Buttman!" Agnes was once again unhappy with me.

"Always have been, isn't that right, Becks?"

"Yeah, I'm told it runs in the family." It was nice to see her smile even if it was only half of one.

Rebekah ordered a salad with bacon, Agnes wanted chicken, and I desired a steak preferably with mashed potatoes. With that out of the way, there was little left to do, besides waiting for our food, than to stare blankly at one another. An apparent side-benefit to endlessly searching for someone you have no interest in.

"Who's Larry Bochner?" My dear Agnes had forgotten.

"Lucian DeBerry," I reminded her.

"Then why did you tell that ghost guy he was dead?"

"I simply threw his name out there."

Agnes didn't like me beating around the bush. "Just answer the question please!"

Yeah, Mr. Bohrman, just answer the question." Rebekah got it.

"I was merely ascertaining the limits of the individual's knowledge of recent events," I replied.

"How did he know you were once called Mr. Bohrman?" Agnes had a frown on her face.

"I assume he asked someone or did some digging, but either way it's clear he only did his digging or asking in Virginia since that's the only place where I'm known as Mr. Bohrman."

Agnes was still confused. "I don't understand?"

"What's to understand? He's been following us or DeBerry or maybe Ashton Cox. Perhaps they're all heading to Oklahoma, on a collision course, so to speak."

"Is that what DeBerry told you last night? That he's being followed?"

"No."

This only exasperated Agnes more. "Why won't you tell us what he said? Why all this mystery?" She was not amused.

The dinner was here; my answer would have to wait. Agnes wasn't happy about that either. We patiently waited for our waitress, Sherilynn, to distribute the plates, thanked her, and I dug in. Agnes glared at me.

"Your food's getting cold," I helpfully informed her.

"I'm aware of that. Why won't you tell us what he said?" I could feel a pinch coming on.

"Because it was told to me in confidence. Would you prefer I blurted out everything I know or that I'm told? That includes our personal conversations, my love." She reached out, but I ducked and weaved. Thank you, Mr. Jones.

"Do you two fight a lot?" Rebekah was taking a break from wolfing down her salad.

"No, we rarely ever argue," I said, "however this trip has tested us in more ways than one, so there may be more on the horizon." Agnes didn't like that either but held her tongue. "I'd like to spill the beans, but I don't feel that I can. You'll just have to accept that for now. I mean I haven't pestered you with questions about what the two of you talked about while you were out, now have I?"

"Who says we talked about anything?" Rebekah was being coy.

"Exactly." I raised my eyebrow in Agnes' direction, "Eat your dinner before it gets cold."

"I don't care for you much right now, Mr. Sunshine."

I blew her a kiss. "I love you too, beautiful." She reached for me, but once again I masterfully avoided those pinching fingers.

Rebekah saw them first as we left the restaurant. I was more interested in other things than to notice the two men loitering in the corner of the parking lot. I also didn't see Rebekah fumbling with whatever was in her pocket. Instead, I was wondering if I should sell the shotgun. It was probably worth some money. The engravings ran from the stock to the barrel. Waterfowl flying across...

"I know those faces!" Rebekah went off in their direction.

I looked over. I knew their faces too: Teddy and Guy. What were they doing here? Were they following us? How would they know we were here in Springfield? Neither was particularly striking either in stature or size. They were two middling young men in Jesus T-shirts and jeans. One was a couple of inches taller than the other with an unkempt beard. The shorter one had a baby face and more hair on his head. Rebekah approached the taller one. They came out from behind a Buick.

"Where's Farrell?" she shouted.

"Who are you?" the tall one responded.

"I'm his wife, the one you blew off on the phone."

"I don't know what you're talking about." He seemed unsure, hesitant.

I followed Rebekah, worried that her temper would get the better of her. Neither Teddy nor Guy acted like bodyguards or appeared to be highly trained in taking people down, which only led me to visions of Rebekah beating on them or the two of them ganging up on a vulnerable pregnant woman. The one with the baby face saw me and came towards me. Rebekah continued to shout at the taller one about Farrell. Soon we were all face to face, agitated.

"Why are you following us? How did you know we were here? Did DeBerry tell you?" I demanded. It seemed like the right thing to demand.

Babyface was more in your face than the taller one. "We don't have to tell you anything."

"WE KNOW WHO YOU ARE," screamed Rebekah.

"Yeah?" The taller one spoke!

"Yeah, your pictures are on his phone," which she pulled out of her pocket. I assumed this was what she was fidgeting with. I shook my head as the three of them took a time-out while she turned on and scrolled through Farrell's phone for the pictures we'd found earlier. She shoved the phone in the taller one's face. "See!" Her thrusting the phone caused him to step back. I stepped towards them, which apparently provoked Babyface, who shoved me. I thought it was funny, but Agnes did not.

Agnes had been in the bathroom when Rebekah and I went outside, and I'd forgotten about her. As I moved back after Babyface shoved me, Agnes, out of nowhere, rushed up and kicked him in the nuts. A painful groan came out as he hit the pavement.

"*You leave him alone!*" she shouted at the prostrate Babyface.

"Agnes, what are you doing?" I was genuinely shocked!

Rebekah and the taller one stopped in their tracks, surprised by Babyface and his sore nuts.

Agnes surprised by my reaction became flustered and sheepishly looked at me. "I thought he was going to hurt you and I got scared, so I ..."

That made me laugh.

"For God's sakes, nothing was going to happen, he..." I looked at the taller one. "Is he Teddy or Guy?"

"He's Guy," said Teddy.

"Sorry, dude, she's kind of protective of me." I reached down and helped him sit up. Agnes stood back as Guy continued to groan. "Now that someone's been hurt, maybe we can start over with a little less dumb-assery. Are you guys watching us?"

"Don't answer that!" We turned to see Ashton Cox approaching us. He cut a more striking figure in person than on a phone. Tall, slim, and well-groomed, wearing a grey sport coat over a black turtleneck with grey slacks, he looked as out of place as I did. His face showed no expression. He surveyed the five of us before saying anything.

"Where's Farrell?" Rebekah demanded.

This brought a faint grin to Cox. "Ah, the dutiful wife, come for her errant husband. Too bad he wants nothing to do with you."

"Just tell me where his is." Her hand was back in her pocket.

"Why the interest, Rebekah Jenkins? Wasn't cheating on him enough? Now it's important to rub his nose in it? You disdain the teachings you claim to be important, you disobey the man who loves you, and then chase him across the country. Why?"

Rebekah pulled the 38 out of her pocket. "Tell me!"

"Or you'll shoot me?" Cox was mocking her. "I have no fear of the afterlife. I have no fear of your threats or your violence."

I reached over and took the gun from Rebekah's trembling hand. "There's no need for any of that." I put the 38 in my pocket. "Are you following us, Mr. Cox?"

"No, Mr. Buttman, we are not."

"Then the ghost?" The Angel lost his smile. "He warned us about you and your merry band."

"Did he?"

"Yes."

Ashton Cox reached down to help the beleaguered Guy to his feet. Guy and Teddy retreated to the side of Cox while Agnes and Rebekah parked themselves behind me.

Cox stared at us for a time before speaking. "Lucian believes you to be a good man, Mr. Buttman, but I am more circumspect of those I don't know. Perhaps the two of us should speak in private."

"Perhaps..." I said.

Rebekah didn't like that. "You can talk to all of us."

"I will not be told what to do by a deceiving woman. If you wish to discuss the situation, you may do so later on your own, but I will not be a part of it."

"It'll be alright..." I put my arm out to dissuade her from encroaching any further on Cox.

"*Dad*!" Rebekah was not a happy camper.

I gestured to Agnes. "You two go back to the hotel. I assume Teddy and Guy will go back to... wherever, yes?"

"Yes," was their very reluctant reply after glaring at me for an uncomfortable period of time.

"The bar?" I pointed to the restaurant.

"I don't drink, Mr. Buttman," Cox tersely replied.

"Fortunately, I do."

We watched as the four of them reluctantly left us with each pair going in opposite directions. Once our companions were off in the distance, we went to the bar situated in the far corner of the restaurant. We found a booth in the back where it was quiet. I ordered a beer and Ashton Cox a bottle of sparkling water.

"Since you know of my conversation with Lucian DeBerry, I assume the two of you talked recently. From your rant on Farrell's phone, I got the impression you didn't care for our modern obsession with connectivity."

The reserved Cox took in my comment and then a drink from his glass. "Whether or not I care for the amenities of these times is irrelevant to this discussion, Mr. Buttman, or is it Bohrman?"

"It's Buttman. Bohrman is historically accurate, but like Larry Bochner, archaic."

"I see. And this meeting with Lucian, did you seek it out?" Cox was very deliberate in his mannerisms and movements. I found him to be very careful, very observant.

"Not directly. We were on our way to Oklahoma when we were alerted to the fact that Lucian would be speaking in Elizabethtown. As all of this craziness revolves around him, I thought it might be a good idea to speak to the man himself."

"And who alerted you, if I may ask?" He leaned onto the table, resting on his forearms.

"Just a man I know who's conversant in information retrieval. He has no connection to anyone in this business if that's your concern." I leaned forward onto my forearms.

"My concern is for Lucian and his ministry..."

"Not love?" I saw no reason to avoid the obvious as I knew of their liaison, if that's the right word, in prison.

Cox didn't bite, "I'm not ashamed of my feelings for Lucian, Mr. Buttman. I've made my peace with who I am and I am at peace with its imposed limitations. God challenges us all in this life. I'm no different. My love manifests itself in other ways, and I have no reason to hide that." He sat back. "So to answer your question, my concern for his work is more important than the love I have for him."

"And the woman he loved?"

Cox looked away for a moment. "Very unfortunate, Mr. Buttman; very unfortunate. I cautioned him many times to be careful, to be prudent..." He returned his eyes to mine. "I told him it was wrong, that he should focus his passions elsewhere, much as I have, but emotions are powerful things and this love he had he couldn't deny. It has caused a lot of dissention within our community, and I have had to be strong to keep it from destroying his work."

"And this man calling himself a ghost..."

Cox's jaw tightened. "The man is a liar and a sower of discord. He follows Lucian, preaching falsehoods and poisoning minds like your Pastor Davis."

"He says you killed them all, from Justin Peterson to the five in Pennsylvania."

Surprisingly, this brought a smile to Ashton Cox. "I won't respond to something like that. It is just another example of the filth this man spreads.

It amazes me that people would even begin to believe it." He continued to look right at me.

"Perhaps, but you can't deny the pattern, and you can't deny the dead," I said, returning his gaze.

"The dead go into the arms of the Lord. My hope is they found grace in the eyes of God and are saved. It is why I don't fear death or its agents." His eyes glassed over.

"Then what do you fear, Mr. Cox?" I was tiring of our conversation and was hoping that somehow I could talk my daughter into giving up on this idiotic quest and head west. Cox took a drink and thought of what to say.

"I fear the dissolution of the word of God, of the order and precepts that give a life given to God its meaning. Too often we go off on our own, thinking we know better simply because we disagree or feel constrained by the laws of the church, which are the laws of God. But that dissolution robs us of the majesty of God's message, of God's love. It sends us out into a world of momentary pleasure but no real love, no eternal light."

"Yet the word of God is a human creation, the product of councils and competing visions. It was never a single unified word." I wasn't a disciple, and I wasn't new to any of this.

"Lucian told me you were not charmed by the ideal of the early Christian myth. Neither am I, but I know the value of ritual and creed no matter its origin. Nor am I am ignorant of biblical and church history, but to me that is incidental to the mission and the ministry because it is that mission and ministry that brings light and love to humanity, and I recognize that authority needs to be exercised in maintaining the word, less it become diluted and rendered meaningless. Lucian has no desire or talent for authority, so it falls to me. For all of his gifts at spreading the word, he needs a steady hand, and that hand is mine. I won't let malicious lies destroy what is good and beautiful, Mr. Buttman."

"No matter what?" I wondered if he was capable of murder, multiples murders, all in the name of God.

"What matters is what we leave behind, that which is solid and permanent. Faith is not a team or a sport to be rooted for and forgotten. It is intrinsic to our being and our relationship to the all mighty. It is not to be disregarded lightly or thoughtlessly as so much of modern life is. It is not a commodity to be used and then thrown away again and again. My work is the Lord's work, no matter what, Mr. Buttman. My purpose is to safeguard the vitality of our religious life for all of our lives through its rituals and beliefs for they are sacred and meaningful and I won't allow anyone, whatever they call themselves to destroy that, no matter what."

He rose to leave.

"And Farrell?" I asked. He looked out towards the door.

"Farrell is where he wants to be, and is where you expect him to be." Ashton Cox pulled a small crucifix from his pocket and placed it on the table, "Lucian's believes you to be an honorable man, Mr. Buttman..."

I think he meant to say more but changed his mind. I watched him leave, then went back to my beer. I put the crucifix in my pocket.

27

The action in the bar picked up as I drank my beer, and a woman named Natalie asked if I was waiting for someone. I said no. She then asked if she could join me. I figured why not and offered her a seat. Natalie was a pleasant woman with a pleasant face, a little too much makeup, and her hair done up in long curls. She had a nice figure and was chatty. Normally, I didn't care too much for that, but after a long day and given recent events I found it oddly comforting.

Natalie was an office coordinator for a paper products company not far from here. She was divorced with two kids who were spending the week with their father. I bought her a few drinks and listened as she talked about this and that. She moved closer when the second drink arrived and asked what I did for a living. I told her I was doing some investigative work looking for an errant husband named Farrell.

"Wow, that sounds so interesting!" she gushed. Ah, the effects of alcohol.

I assured her it was not. After more talk of errant husbands, her former being one and the struggles of raising kids in this day and age, something that never goes out of fashion, I decided it was probably best to head back to the hotel. I didn't know exactly that Natalie had any designs beyond someone to talk to, but her proximity to me, and her hand on my arm gave me ideas. Fortunately, a pair of her friends found us and I used it as an excuse to bid her farewell. I noticed the look she gave her friends and the phone number she pressed into my hand, which she held for longer than was necessary. If there was one thing this little trip of ours didn't need, it was me sleeping around with strange women. Natalie was rather friendly, if not lonely, but not strange. I said goodbye and hit the street.

There were more people out and impulsively, I made sure the 38 was in my pocket if I needed it, but no one I passed seemed even remotely threatening. Agnes was sitting up in bed watching a cooking show where the participants were dressed like chickens. I didn't ask. Rebekah was fast asleep. More assistance, no doubt, from Agnes' pharmacological stash.

"Must have been some talk?" Agnes patted the spot next to her.

"Which one?' I decided to be provocative as I took off my coat and shoes and sat down beside her. She smelled really good. I leaned in and kissed her.

"What do you mean which one?" she asked.

"Cox or Natalie?" I replied.

"Natalie." I believe she was suspicious.

"Oh, just a woman I met. I needed a moment to think, and she stopped by so we had a drink." I smiled.

"I see. And who is this Natalie you had a drink with?" She smiled.

"Like I said, just a woman I met."

"Uh-huh." Agnes leaned in. "I'm going to need a little more than that."

"Okay. About five-five, attractive, divorced, two kids, curly hair, nice face; said she was an office manager or something like that..."

"You seem to have a thing for office managers, don't you?"

"I do." I played it coy, all the while keeping an eye on her fingers; can't be too careful.

"Did she have nice boobs?" Agnes made sure I got an eyeful of hers.

"You know you've ruined me for all other women when it comes to great boobs, although from what I can remember her boobs were all right." I ran my finger between her wonderful breasts.

"And what did you and Natalie talk about?" Agnes's hand had found my leg.

"She did most of the talking; about herself, the kids, work, She asked what I did. I told I was looking for an errant husband, which allowed her to sorta vent about Dennis, *her* former errant husband..." I brushed the hair away from her neck and kissed her below her ear. It was nice to feel her respond to it.

"Uh huh..." I don't think she was listening anymore.

"Then her friends showed up, and I left..."

She started unbuttoning my shirt. "Anything else?" This between kisses.

"No, once I got her number I took off..." My hand was caressing those wonderful breasts.

"Does that mean you're planning on seeing her again?" She pulled back to look at me.

"Well, since it's highly unlikely I'll ever return to Springfield, Missouri, I'd have to say I have no plans to see her again." We went back to kissing. Agnes put my hand between her legs.

"If I wasn't here, would you have slept with her?" Her hand was between my legs.

"That depends on what you mean by you're not here..."

Her mouth moved down to my neck. "Again, I'm going to need a little more than that..."

I wasn't interested in Natalie anymore, even as a topic of conversation. I was more interested in what her hands and mouth were doing.

"If you're not here, but we're still a couple then no, but if you're not here and we're not a couple then maybe..." My finger pressure had grown between her legs, and her hips were slowly moving in response to that.

"And what would you be doing to her, lover boy?" Her hand was on my erection, which desperately wanted out of my pants. We both looked at my sleeping daughter.

"I don't think I can violate you with Rebekah snoring in the bed next to us," I sighed.

"Yeah, and now that you've got me all hot and bothered I really don't want to stop..." She looked in the direction of the bathroom.

"How powerful are those pills? Will we wake her?"

Agnes thought about it just long enough. "I doubt it, not if we're quiet." She looked at me, wanting me to say out loud what she'd already decided. I took her hand, and we pleasured each other in the erotic glow of the bathroom nightlight. Another vacation memory, the two of us humping each other while watching in the bathroom mirror. Good times.

"I guess we can scratch that off the places to have sex list," I said as we washed ourselves.

"It wasn't on my list."

"You didn't like it? Could a fooled me."

She smiled at that. "The sex was just fine. You've obviously been paying attention—"

"I do what I can." I patted her ass. "So what didn't you like?" She put my hand on the counter. It was hard and cold. "If it bothered you, you should have turned me around. I doubt I'd have noticed it," I said in my know-it-all voice.

"Oh, I think you would have..." She pushed me forward, causing my genitalia to come in contact with the counter. I reflexively jumped back. "See?"

"All right, I get your point, but you have to admit, the sex has been interesting on this trip. I mean, how often have we even had sex in a bed?" She rubbed up next to me and took my cock in her hand.

"True. Any more thoughts about Natalie?" She added a not so subtle tug for emphasis.

"Who?" I squeezed her breasts.

"Good. Seconds?" The tugs were more tempting now.

After cleaning up a second time and getting mostly dressed, we sat on the edge of the bed and watched my allegedly unfaithful and pregnant daughter sleep. She hadn't moved.

"How powerful are those pills?" I wondered.

"They'll knock you out if you're not careful. I only gave her half a pill." Agnes said this almost clinically.

"Where'd you get them?"

Agnes' face darkened. "I got them after my…fiasco with Jordan. I had a hard time sleeping, and the doctor prescribed them. I was on them for quite a while…"

"And now?" I worried about her taking such powerful drugs.

"I have you now. I only use them if you're away and I get anxious." She put her hand on my thigh and took my arm, which she wrapped around her shoulder. "You're my wonder drug, Sunshine."

I just shook my head.

We went back to watching Rebekah. "Do you think Farrell is really in Oklahoma at this community place Lucian talked about?" she asked.

"I think so. I have a nasty feeling that's where all this will play out, and I'm pretty sure that idiot Farrell has managed to land himself right in the middle of this war of words between Cox and whoever the ghost guy is."

She looked up at me. "Do you think they had anything to do with all these people who have died? I mean I guess they could have killed themselves or each other, but that seems kind of ritualistic, doesn't it?"

"Unfortunately, I think they're tied to the deaths of these people, although I don't know exactly how. Anger and fanaticism are a bad combination. I'd be a lot happier if this was just Rebekah wanting to end things with Farrell because she's sleeping around or bad feelings or whatever, but I don't like all this religious stuff thrown in the mix. It gets people worked up; makes them angry and defensive." I was thinking of DeBerry and Cox fending off that ghost of theirs.

"What did you and that Cox guy talk about? Assuming it wasn't a privileged conversation." She stuck her finger in my ribs.

"There's no need for that…" I pushed her hand away. "Mostly he talked about defending his faith. That whatever its origins, its creeds, and practices were more important that some obscure historical artifact that had no bearing on its day to day practices, or the malicious lies being spread by our friend the ghost. The foundation and the firmament must be protected at all costs you know."

"Do you believe that?" She yawned as she asked.

"Doesn't matter what I believe." I was tired too. "Time for bed, beautiful." We pulled up the sheets after discarding our pants, and I fell into dreams of dead men and churches.

• • • • •

The truck wasn't finished until well into the afternoon. The question was head out now or wait until the next day. Rebekah wanted to go. We could take shifts driving if need be, but the sooner we got there and got this over with, the better. Agnes and I just sighed, and we packed up the truck. Barney still wanted the shotgun. I told him I was tempted but needed to do a little research first. We exchanged personal numbers, and soon we were on the road to the Oklahoma panhandle and hopefully Farrell and the end of our journey. California, and the drive there loomed in the distance.

"They did a nice job! The truck sounds good, even has some pep," I enthused.

Agnes and Rebekah weren't listening. I doubt they cared. Rebekah said little, and I didn't particularly care whether the baby was Farrell's or somebody else's or who that somebody else might be. As we meandered across the south of Missouri and into Oklahoma with five hundred miles to go and darkness right on our ass, I made an executive decision to find a place to stay. Tulsa was on the horizon, and though it wasn't late and we hadn't been driving that long, I was tired and ready to take a break.

"We're stopping for the night in Tulsa," I said in a most authoritative tone.

"Why don't we keep going? I can drive..." Rebekah objected.

"And stay where? We'd get there in the middle of the night. We'll stay here then head out bright and early."

"But—"

"I'm not going to argue with you." I raised my voice just enough to let her know I was serious. It had been a long day of sitting, at the hotel, at the repair shop, in the truck. I needed to get out, walk; something we should have done earlier in the day while waiting for them to finish. "This isn't a forced march, and Farrell isn't going anywhere either—"

"How do you know that?" she demanded.

"Because he's in cahoots with Ashton Cox, that's why, and that's where Cox sent him, all right?" I shot back.

"Fine." She slumped back against the seat.

"Look for a Comfort Inn," I said.

"Seriously?"

Like I was anything else at the moment. "Yeah, I have a rewards card now. Tut-tut." Both were looking at me in a whole new light. I could see that by the expression on their faces.

Only fifty more miles to go.

There is something about miles and miles of the same crop, be it wheat or corn. The vastness of the Great Plains and the undulating of the hills covered by the same thing, broken up only by silos and barns or small towns that come and go before you know it. Along with a sallow and grey sky, the drive left me longing for the edge of the world, the waters of the Pacific and home.

I was hurtling towards the one place on earth where I had no desire to be. The closer we got, the more the five of them continued to haunt me. They were young, just beginning their lives. They were also sallow and grey like the sky, their skin collapsing around their faces, their eyes falling in. I struggled to forget them just as I had struggled to forget the four at the house in South Laguna. They too haunted me with their expressions of incomprehension that their idiot plans would end with a killer's bullet blown through their idiot heads. I didn't want to find Farrell, much as I considered him an idiot, in the same condition with Rebekah by my side.

The Comfort Inn was on East Archer off the interstate. Rebekah made the reservation on her phone without having to talk to anyone, but she was still unhappy about stopping for the night.

"You know there's one of these places in Goodwell!" she muttered.

"Then you know where we're staying tomorrow!" I harrumphed.

"Why can't we just keep going?"

"Because I need a little time to figure out what to do after we get there, that's why."

I pulled into the parking lot and sat there. Rebekah and Agnes waited and wondered what I was doing. It was simple, I was still in Pennsylvania contemplating a young man with a hole in his head and a finished life. He was with God now. That's what they told me. That was their answer to why he was gone. For a caring God, I found it incredibly cavalier, but I knew better, God didn't kill him any more than I did.

"Are we getting out?"

"Yeah..." It was my turn to mutter.

With grim determination we once again took our belonging out of the back of the truck, trudged up the stairs; actually, we took the elevator, entered the room, and noted that it was exactly like the one we had been in the night before and the night before that. A sandwich shop across the street provided dinner and the television what passed for entertainment. Once more we were watching people cook in goofy outfits. Rebekah was staring at Farrell's phone.

"Anything interesting?" I inquired.

"Just looking at the pictures..." She gave me the phone. She figured prominently in the few that were there. I thought there would be more of the Jenkins clan, but no, other than the ones of Cox, Teddy, and Guy, the pictures were of Rebekah when they were first together, happy and smiling. I handed the phone back. She put the phone away. "Do you think Farrell had anything to do with the deaths of those people we found?"

"It's possible..."

"We make quite a pair, don't we?" I thought for a moment she might start crying, but she merely sighed instead.

"If everything I know or assume is true, then yeah, I'd have to say the two of you do. How much of this does your mother know or suspect? I take it that neither she or your grandmother knows you're pregnant by someone other than Farrell, because if they did, I'm sure I would have caught a lot more hell because, obviously, you're following in my godless footsteps."

She laughed.

"Your godless footsteps? I already told you I didn't tell them, besides, maybe they're right..." She was back to rolling the ring on her finger.

"I'll need a little more than that," I could see Agnes shaking her head. I was stealing her material. Rebekah laugh-sighed again.

"I don't believe in God anymore. I've guess I've lost my faith... I've lost it all, Farrell, my family, church, work... all of it." She stated this in a slow funereal tone.

I didn't know what to say. "Should I ask?"

She bowed her head for a moment and then turned to face me. "I wanted my babies, and I was tired of waiting for God to give me his blessing." There was anger in her voice. "And I was tired of fighting with Farrell about it. I tried everything they asked of me and I prayed and prayed waiting to hear from God, to let me know he heard me, but I knew in my heart that it was plain old biology at work, so I snuck off and got tested. When the doctor told me there wasn't anything preventing me from getting pregnant I begged Farrell to get tested, I told him there were things they could do to help.

"But he wouldn't listen to me and instead began throwing himself into crazier religious arguments about how we were on the wrong path and making God mad and we needed a period of separation to purify ourselves. I asked God why he was doing this to me. I'm not Sarah. I'm not Job. I haven't done anything wrong. I've been faithful and supportive." She was tugging at the ring, "I continued to pray hoping for something, anything, but all I felt was trapped, and no matter what I did, I was never getting out. God wasn't going to save me. No one was. I..." she turned back towards the television, "... I was tired of waiting. I knew a man at work who liked me, so I went out with him a couple of times or so and now..."

"Does he know you're pregnant?"

She furrowed her brows. "Not really..."

"Not really? What does that mean, not really? Jesus Christ, Rebekah, this is a big deal! Babies are a big deal. He should know! I know you want kids and...I mean... Rebekah! Have you thought about any of that?" I wanted to shake her stupid ass.

"Did you think about any of that when you had me?" she smirked.

"No, and you know that, *I'm* the cautionary tale, remember? *I'm* the person you don't want to emulate. Rebekah is not supposed to be like her idiot father who never thought past the end of his nose until *he* was trapped in a life he didn't want—"

"So you didn't want me?"

Well, Sunshine? "Of course I wanted you, but in *California*, not Virginia, but did I consider any of that? No! And do you know why?" I blurted out.

"Because you were an idiot, Mr. Sunshine?" It still hurt to hear that!

"Yes, because I was an idiot." Agnes started laughing, which caused Rebekah to start laughing. It was not happy laughter. "That's not funny. Agnes, you're not helping."

"Sorry, Mr. Sunshine." Now they were laughing harder.

"All right, show's over. Come on, we need to be serious here... seriously." More laughter. It was beginning to affect me. "Don't make me laugh, goddammit!"

"Then what's the answer, Mr. Serious, hmmm?" asked Rebekah.

"I don't know. I need a drink." I took a step towards the fridge. "Goddammit!" I shouted.

"Now what?" Agnes tried to feign interest.

"I forgot my beer at the other Comfort Inn."

Agnes nearly rolled off the bed laughing.

I just shook my head.

28

I still didn't think it was funny. Once the laughter died down, Rebekah left for the bathroom and Agnes grinned and motioned that I come join her on the bed. I thought about making a beer run, but my darling companion nixed that saying she needed my company.

"You know this isn't a laughing matter?" I insisted.

"I know, but we'll cross those bridges when we get there. Isn't that what you tell me when these kinds of things get dropped at our door?" She was rubbing my thigh again, knowing it distracted me.

"I don't remember it that way at all..."

"I'm sure you don't," she said with a self-satisfied smile.

"So how much of this did you already know?" I demanded.

"Most of it. I didn't pry into every last detail..."

"Don't you think you should have said something to me?"

"This from mister 'I can't divulge what was confessed to me, but the rest of you have to tell me whatever you know'," she said with a fair amount of self-righteousness.

"That's different. DeBerry's a stranger, I'm Rebekah's father; I should be told." I tried to sound indignant. "So who's the father? Please tell me it's not someone I know..."

"I doubt it."

"Don't you think she should tell him? He's responsible too!"

Agnes patted my leg. "Maybe, but she doesn't love him, lied to him about being on birth control, and he's already married with his own kids. So I'm thinking while it might be right to tell him, as a practical matter, I can't imagine how it would help the situation." Once again, she said this as if it were no big deal.

"So, she fucked this guy because she wanted a baby and he wanted some action on the side." I couldn't believe I was saying this.

"Pretty much."

Yeah, it happens every day. "Doesn't that bother you?" I asked before instantly regretting doing so.

"Yes, but I used to drink too much and fuck strangers in their cars, and you're fucking another woman while you fuck me. I don't think either of us should be touting ourselves as virtuous role models for your daughter." She pinched me as an exclamation.

"Please don't do that!" I grumbled.

"Sorry."

"And I'm well aware that I shouldn't be," I really didn't want to talk about Judith, "fucking someone else. I should just decide and do that. Do you want me to leave?" I already knew the answer, and I knew it would bother Agnes.

"I don't want you to leave, you know that." Her voice softened as it always did when this came up. "You know how I feel about this. I don't like it, and I want you to only be with me, and I know I should demand you decide once and for all..." Agnes took my arm and held on tight. She didn't finish the sentence, but I already knew the rest of that too: I'm afraid you'd leave me for the beautiful rich woman.

Six months ago, when this whole thing started, I would have laughed at that. And while I didn't spend a lot of time with Judith, I knew it was no longer just occasional sex between consenting adults. No laughing it off anymore. I didn't know what Judith wanted, and I tried not to think about it. It was simple. I made time for her when she wanted me. Call me weak, call me stupid, call me a jerk; call me what you want. There was something about her, beyond the obvious, that appealed to me, and I was determined not to give it up. I know it's foolish and hurtful, and I know what it says about my supposed character.

I don't care.

It's times like these when I think Agnes should kick me to the curb. The key is not to think about it.

"You belong to me, Monk Buttman. Don't you ever forget that!" She was holding on tight.

"My love, I know that better than anyone, believe me, I do."

Fortunately, in moments like this, I have a crazy pregnant daughter and *her* problems to distract me from *my* problems with the woman next to me, who is also crazy, and the fact that I'm not a very good person.

Rebekah emerged from the bathroom.

"Anything else we should say about this?" I asked.

"I know, I'm selfish and irresponsible, and a bad wife..." she said, mostly to herself.

"That's not where I was going with this. I mean what's the plan now?"

"The plan is to have my baby and do what I have to do." She sat on her bed, facing the two of us.

"And Farrell?"

"I'll figure that out when we find him." That didn't answer my question, but I was tired and ready for something else even if my only option was trying to sleep.

I sighed, more of the same.

• • • •

Agnes proclaimed herself tired of sitting and demanded her turn to drive. I looked at Rebekah who wasn't listening and gave the keys to Agnes. We still had three hundred miles to go, and if she wanted to drive, so be it. The weather was lovely and for the most part we sat back and watched the world go by. I was half tempted to opine about the virtues of California and LA, but that was mostly because I wanted to go home, so I kept my mouth shut. Rebekah said little. I got the impression that having owned up to being a not so very good person she too was ready to move on.

We made reservations at the Comfort Inn in Goodwell, although we argued about how long to stay. I was aiming for a quick in and out but she wanted to make sure she had enough time for whatever it was she had in mind but did not share. Agnes was happily motoring along having found a radio station playing contemporary country music or what passed for country music. I didn't care for it, but no one else was interested in what I thought.

Rather than stop, we did drive through for lunch and pleasantly elbowed each other while trying to consume it. By mid-afternoon, we had arrived in Goodwell and the next Comfort Inn in our cross-country tour of Comfort Inns, unpacked our belongings yet again, and inquired at the desk about where we might find Brother DeBerry's community. The woman behind the desk had no idea. Neither did the manager. They thoughtfully pointed us in the direction of the chamber of commerce. It's possible they might know. Having the directions to the chamber of commerce, we headed out.

There was some discussion at the chamber as to what we were talking about until I brought up the deaths of Justin and Amy Peterson, which brought out a collective "oh" from the three people assisting us. We were then directed to drive about forty miles that-a-way to a place called Basker's farm. They weren't sure if there was a sign, although the gentleman among the three suggested that the feed store might know. After all, if they're farming and have livestock, they're going to need feed. We agreed that was probably true.

We were then directed to the feed store. We thanked them for their time and patience, assured them we were not related to the dead couple, took in a few deep cleansing breaths, and moved on. I mentioned my butt was tired, but no one cared.

Marlon, the dude at the feed store, wondered what we were up to, but we assured him we had no malicious intent. We were simply looking for my daughter's husband. Apparently, the murder-suicide of Justin and Amy Peterson had tongues wagging, especially after that stranger went around telling everyone it was a conspiracy perpetrated by the people at Basker's farm to cover their asses. I hadn't forgotten how small towns could be hard places to hide your business.

"I can tell you," Marlon said with authority, "that the people at Basker's farm are good people. I've had no trouble with them or heard anything bad about them. I don't know what happened out there when that man killed his wife, but I can't believe they're all up to something. They've always been friendly and polite and helpful if you need it. There's been no weird kind of cult activity that I know about," he said, as if weird cult-like activity was common elsewhere.

"I'm sure they are and I've spoken to Mr. DeBerry and Mr. Cox, and they were helpful as well. They told us that Farrell would be down here, we just didn't know exactly where." I wanted to assure Marlon that we could be trusted with directions to Basker's farm. My head began to ache.

"I understand, mister…?" his voice rising in pitch.

"Buttman, Monk Buttman," I said.

"Sounds like a joke name." This caused Agnes and Rebekah to snicker. "Ladies?" Marlon raised his eyebrows at their laughter.

"Sorry," answered Agnes, "but we agree it's a goofy name." Rebekah shook her head in agreement. "However, it is his name, believe it or not."

"You know, you can change your name," Marlon said with all due solemnity.

"I've been told that. Thanks again for your help."

"Sure. If you meet a man named Alan, tell him I got his order ready." He followed us out the door.

"We'll do that. Thanks again." We got in the truck and waved as we left. Marlon watched us drive off. I was back in the middle, as I had been for most of the day. I laid my head back hoping the road noise would lull me to sleep. Then I could dream of warm beaches with cold beers and beautiful rich women with necks that longed to be kissed by guys named Monk. I closed my eyes for a while.

But only for a while…

We found him sitting by the side of the road.

Farrell Jenkins.

Agnes nearly drove past him. Rebekah looked back at the last second and screamed we had to turn around. It was him, the man we'd been looking for, the man we'd been chasing for the last week. He was sitting by his car, staring into space. His car sat precariously at the edge of the road that fell off into a culvert I assumed was there to capture runoff. We parked on the other side of him and got out.

"Farrell!" Rebekah got to him first.

He looked up at her. Anger and revulsion was what I saw. I don't know if he saw Agnes and me standing next to Rebekah; his eyes were fixed on his wife, the pregnant adulterer.

"Farrell?" She said it softer the second time, perhaps beginning to see that this wasn't a good idea whatever the reason. He was dirty and needed a bath. His hair flopped down along the sides of his head, and the mop on top was here and there; wherever his hand had pushed it.

I looked away and saw the man down in the culvert. He was on his back. He didn't move.

It was the ghost.

Farrell noticed me looking at the man, got up, and brushed off his hands. Rebekah moved closer to him, and he slapped her as hard as he could. She fell back into me without uttering a sound, her hand on her reddening face. Farrell turned around, got in his car and drove off, the front wheels spinning as he pulled back onto the road. I asked Agnes to take Rebekah back to the truck.

She didn't cry or say a word. Then again, what would she say? I eased myself down the embankment to the dead man. I had the same odd feeling I had the last time I'd seen him, familiar but not quite the same. His throat was badly bruised, and his tongue was partially out of his mouth. I looked up at the embankment and could see that he had fallen to where he now lay. I got close enough to make sure he wasn't still with us and then gingerly climbed back up to the road. Agnes was standing by the truck door on the passenger side. Rebekah was sitting in the truck.

"What's down there?" She didn't want to look.

"A dead man, the ghost, or whoever he was." I brushed off my pants and wiped off the bottoms of my shoes on the grass at the edge of the road.

"Oh, my God," she slowly moved away from the truck to look. "Was he killed?"

"Well, that usually leaves you dead," I said.

"You know what I mean." She returned to the side of the truck where I was. "Should we stay? What about Farrell?"

The road we were standing on stretched to the horizon, inviting us to head to California, just like all those Okies from days past. I was sorely tempted to just go, but that wasn't an option. It was time to bring in some real authority. "Fuck Farrell, I'm calling the cops."

I explained the situation to the 911 operator, promised we'd stay where we were and did my best to tell them where we were. "Out on the county road from Goodwell heading towards Basker's farm," I told her; how many miles I didn't know. I leaned against the hood of the truck and surveyed the farmland around us, looking for homes or barns, storage sheds, something. What I saw was a lot of nothing.

"Aren't you hot in that suit?" Rebekah was asking. Her head was back against the top of the bench seat; the side of her face was bright red.

"I don't mind. It looks heavier than it is. It's not the heat that bothers me, just the humidity, but you get used to it. How's your cheek?"

"It hurts, but..." She lifted her head back up and touched her cheek. "Did you ever want to smack mom for running off with Judah?"

"No, but I thought about burning down the house and the barn and the sheds, everything. Leave 'em with nothing, but I needed the money. At some point you push it away."

I had no interest in thinking of Lilith and Judah.

"It must have worked. I still think you look so different now. All you wear are suits and ties. You look like someone from a different era and you shave every day. I don't think I ever saw you shave when I was a kid. You had that big, redneck beard."

I had no interest in talking about myself, but it kept our minds off the dead man thirty feet from us. "I decided to be someone else. I always admired the look. It appealed to me, and in LA I found a lot of places where I could get the clothes for a good price. I was tired of the beard." I turned to Agnes who was staring off into space, "Agnes, which do you prefer? This look or me in a pair of overalls and a mountain man beard?"

My better half was standing there smiling. "I could say that I'd love you no matter what you looked like, and that's true, but I prefer the dressed-up

Mr. Buttman to the dour Mr. Bohrman. Assuming what I heard about your Virginia days is true." She nodded to Rebekah.

"He had his moments, but he wasn't as terrible a father as he sometimes makes himself out to be." She stared at me. "After all, you're still here. I don't know that I would be if I were in your shoes."

"Oh, I think you'd surprise yourself. Children change you." I could hear the sirens in the distance. So could Agnes and Rebekah.

"What do we say about Farrell and the man in the ditch?" Agnes pointed towards the dead man. And there was Farrell, what about him? I wandered over to the edge.

"He was here, that's what we know. Whether he had anything to do with it is their problem." I returned to the truck, to Rebekah. "Are we still going after him? Is there more to this?"

She stared out into space. "I still want to talk to him."

Yeah, that was just what I wanted to hear.

29

The officer in the car was young, maybe mid-twenties, tall with blue eyes and brown hair. We pointed to the dead man. He tried to act like it was no big deal, but I doubt they find many dead guys in trench coats out in the middle of farm country. As I had, the officer carefully descended to where the dead man lay and then came back up out of the culvert. He returned to his car and called for the sheriff. The county coroner was already on his way. We gave the officer our names, explained why we were on the road, where we were going, and why we stopped here. Farrell's name came up at that point.

"Where was he?" the officer asked.

"Sitting by the side of the road," I replied.

"Did he say anything to you about the man down there?"

"He didn't say anything. He got up and drove away." I refrained from mentioning Farrell's slapping Rebekah for the time being. If need be we'd have time to discuss that later.

"Can you describe him?"

"He's my son-in-law, Farrell Jenkins. I'll show you his picture." Rebekah handed me her phone, and I found a suitable picture for the officer.

"Do you have any idea where he went?"

"No. We thought he'd be at Basker's farm, but whether that's where he went I can't say." The officer wrote this down.

"I'll need you to wait until the sheriff gets here," he said.

"We figured that."

The officer returned to his car. He was speaking to someone on the radio, either the dispatcher or the sheriff. Agnes got in the truck and closed the door. I stood outside by her window, which she had rolled down. It was evening, and the light was heading west, followed by streaks of red, blue, and gold. Dinner would not happen anytime soon. Nothing was said. Agnes and Rebekah sat in the car listening to the radio. Agnes had found her country station and was absent-mindedly humming along to the songs of drinking, dancing, and loving. Rebekah stared off into space, the right side of her face swollen by Farrell's slap. God only knows what was going through her head.

I wondered about the dead man. Was he the same guy we'd met at Rebekah's home, who surprised us in Springfield? Was he following Ashton and his boys? He'd been there in Pennsylvania. Was he following DeBerry? Was he following us? Why would he do that? We were bit players, nothing more. What was Farrell's part in this? Did he kill the man? Did he kill the people we found at the Blue house? Too many questions and I was tired of the dead. So what if I was certain something didn't add up with the dead man. Let the cops figure it out. One thing was for certain: he was a ghost now.

The sheriff arrived twenty minutes after being called by the officer. He was my age or close to it, stocky, maybe five-ten, with thinning hair. He wore black-rimmed glasses that obscured a hard face. He went directly to the officer and ignored us. The coroner was right behind him. Together the three of them went back down to the dead man. Two other officers arrived. There was a lot of hushed talk between them as they examined the corpse. The two late-arriving officers made sure we didn't venture too far from the truck. Agnes asked how long we would have to stay. I didn't know. Unlike the last time we stumbled upon the dead, it was late in the day versus early and we were tired and uninterested in what happened to the man in the ditch.

Colin MacAfee introduced himself after coming back up from the culvert. He too asked us about Farrell and what we saw, and I reiterated what we'd told the officer now working with the coroner. The sheriff noted the swelling on Rebekah's face.

"He slapped her," I said, explaining the bruise.

"Do you know why?"

"Because she's pregnant." It was the simplest answer.

"Did any of you know the man down there?" was his next question.

"We'd come across him twice, once in Virginia and once in Missouri, two days ago. Don't know his name; he never gave it, others referred to him as the ghost." I was disinclined at this point to say more, besides I had the feeling the sheriff was already aware of references to *the ghost*. "I realize there are things about this we'll have to discuss with you, whether they're relevant or not, but we're tired, and it's been a long day. We're staying in town if you want to get a hold of us, and if we take off, you know our faces, our vehicle, and the number on the license plate. We don't know where my son-in-law is, and if we had anything to do with the death of this guy I doubt we'd have called you out here, so maybe we can continue this tomorrow?"

Sheriff MacAfee considered this. He went back to the first officer, we spoke to and after a few words with him returned to us.

"All right, you can return to town. We'll be in touch."

I got in the truck, and we made our way back to the Comfort Inn.

Neither Rebekah nor Agnes was hungry, but I was so we picked up a little something at a supermarket just down from the Motel. I grabbed some beer and wine. Agnes bought some cream for the bruise on Rebekah's face. Rebekah had returned to her shell, saying little and merely mumbling whenever we asked her anything. Whether she had considered any of this when she set off on her quest for motherhood was anyone's guess. It is what it is, and I'd given up on the idea that she was ready to bale on settling her differences with Farrell. I bought stuff for sandwiches, some fruit, and offered to make whatever they wanted, but the dead man had done his work on their psyches, whether Farrell had murdered him or not.

Rebekah curled up in bed, Agnes had a glass of wine, and I was thinkless, a condition where the less I thought about anything, the better. I had a sandwich and a beer; that was enough. I closed my eyes and pictured the beach off Malaga Cove near Torrance. I used to walk the trail there and sit and listen to the ocean's endless repetition of waves striking the sand. With the breeze cascading around me, I was in beach-bum heaven. There was no better way to waste a day. I could smell the water, feel the sand between my toes, and never leave. Seagulls were squawking when an unpleasant thought entered my head. That's the problem with being thinkless; troublemakers rush in.

I took the phone out of my pocket and sent a text to Art Devaney. He wanted to be a part of this dunce's parade, and I was happy to give him a plum role. Maybe he could answer the troubling questions rattling around in my pea brain. I put the phone on the table by the bed and went to Rebekah. I picked up some Kleenex. I sat on the bed next to her. I don't think she'd moved since we got back to the room. She rested her head on my lap; didn't say a word, but the tears flowed along the contours of her swollen and darkening cheek. I handed her the Kleenex. I looked over at Agnes, who offered a sad half-smile in return. I assumed there were better days down the road for Rebekah once this was finished, but until then I wondered if she'd thought at all about what she was doing when she dropped her pants for the guy at work and blew her well-known world to pieces. I ran my hand across her head, pushing the hair out of her wet eyes, remembering her holding on to me when the storms outside her room frightened her.

None of that seemed real anymore. Another fabrication, like the memories of my childhood on the farm. I was a stand-in for whoever had a better handle on all of this.

Agnes asked Rebekah if she needed any help getting to sleep. Rebekah shook her head no. I let her up to go to the bathroom, and when she came back she crawled into bed and turned away. I kissed her cheek as softly as I could, told her I loved her, grabbed a beer, and went outside. It was still warm out. I found a bench by the pool, much as I had the day before (Or was it the day before that?) and looked up at the stars. God was supposed to be up there somewhere watching over his errant flock. If he was, he was either incompetent, or we weren't worth the trouble. I never believed he watched over us, anyway. We had a place to live and basic instructions on how to behave. If life was fucked up, it was because we fucked it up, plain and simple. And if God was watching, he was shaking his head in disappointment.

Agnes was standing next to me. I hadn't noticed her following me.

"May I join you, or is Natalie coming over?"

"No, apparently she found a nicer guy at the bar. Have a seat."

Agnes sat down beside me. "Oh, I don't know, you seem reasonably likable for a guy in a suit." She ran her hand along the sleeve of my jacket.

"I don't think I could ask for a more apt appraisal of my peculiar charms." I took her hand in mine. I was profoundly thankful she had invited herself on this thankless journey. It would have been pure misery to do it on my own. I leaned in and kissed her. She kissed me back, and we spent the next five minutes necking by the pool. Hopefully, no one would call the sheriff.

"If nothing else, you're a good kisser, Sunshine." She was smiling at me with that goofy grin that came over her at times like these.

"Well, when you have lips such as yours to kiss, it's easy to be good, beautiful." There was more kissing. A light wind kept the humidity from clinging too dearly to us. I put my arm around her. We both looked up again for something other than distant stars.

"Were you surprised when he slapped her?" She was still holding my hand, tight.

"No, I was thankful he didn't do more."

"Do you think that's why he left without her because he knew she'd been with someone else?" Agnes put her head on my shoulder.

"I don't know what he was thinking, but yeah, I think finding out that Rebekah was sleeping around really messed him up." I'd been there. I remembered how badly it hurt. It didn't matter that I knew there was nothing left; that Astral was sick of me. I couldn't wait to leave, yet it still fucked me up. Even now I can feel it, though it's more like a breeze than the hurricane I remember.

"Do you think he killed that man?"

Did I? "I don't want to think about it. It just gives me a headache."

"Then where do we go from here?"

I wondered about that too. "I figured we go to Basker's farm and see what the fuss is about. Besides, I have some questions for Brother DeBerry and Mr. Cox. I assume everyone's back home."

"Maybe we should just go home. I miss our house and our bed."

I kissed her forehead. "So do I, beautiful. So do I."

. . . .

The sun rose bright and early, bringing me up with it. Between too many beers, worries about Rebekah, and an overactive imagination, sleep kept its distance and by the time the sun rose, I saw no reason to stay in bed. I showered and waited for the others to roust themselves, or, I would. The phone rang. The sheriff gets up early or never went to bed, perhaps that's the way it is when a dead man is found out on a county road.

"Monk Buttman," I monotoned.

"This is Sheriff MacAfee, Mr. Buttman. I'm calling in regard to the event last night." His voice was as steady as a train rolling across the wheat fields just beyond the hotel window.

"I'm all ears." I don't know if he found that amusing or not.

"I'm asking that you remain in town for another day or so. I have some questions to ask you and your daughter, but it's doubtful I'll be able to find time today." He had the same steady treble.

"That's all right. We're going out to Basker's farm today, tie up some loose ends. Can I ask if you've found Farrell?"

"Yes, we're talking to Mr. Jenkins now. I'm looking at talking with you tomorrow, Mr. Buttman. I assume that's doable?"

"It is," though I'd rather finish up today. I decided not to ask if Farrell was being charged with any crime.

"Good. I'd hate to have to send a car after you." I believe he was serious.

"So would I."

"Why are you going out to Basker's farm?"

"Since I'm here, and having heard Brother DeBerry talk about it, I wanted to check it out for myself." That sounded plausible.

"Thanks for your time, Mr. Buttman; I'll be in touch."

I'm sure you will be.

I turned on the boobtube at nine to get Agnes and Rebekah out of bed. The local news recounted the story of the mystery man found on county road thirteen. How appropriate, unlucky thirteen. Sheriff MacAfee had little to say other than it was under investigation and that the man had met a violent death. The sheriff said they had a person of interest with whom they were interviewing. That got Agnes up. Rebekah merely looked at the two of us, attempted to speak, failed, and left for the bathroom.

"Does that mean they found Farrell?"

I looked over at my rumpled companion. "Yes, it does."

She adjusted her nightgown. More than a little of her bosom was in plain view. "Hungry?"

I smiled as she covered herself up. "Yeah, I guess so..."

She brushed the hair out of her face while noting my smile at her semi-nakedness. "And what are you hungry for, Sunshine?"

"Bacon and eggs, beautiful, and maybe a bagel." The smile remained.

"Nothing else?" Agnes made a point of shaking those delightful breasts. She too was smiling.

"A few things, but I don't think it advisable at the moment," I said as we heard Rebekah stirring in the bathroom.

"Then bacon and eggs it'll have to be." She flounced once more for effect.

I sat on the bed, watching her getting dressed. There's very little privacy on the road. Agnes, though, didn't seem to mind. A non-verbal nod let her know that I liked the particular pair of panties she was putting on. After the bra, top and slacks were slipped into, the delightful Agnes Duquesne rejoined me on the bed. Once Rebekah came out of the bathroom, in went Agnes. With her hair pulled back, Rebekah's bruised cheek was in full bloom, a dark purple with a splotch of black and a halo of streaked ochre surrounding it. An ugly swollen mark to her infidelity. She saw me looking at her.

"How are you doing?" was my question.

"Does it matter?" was her answer.

"It's a little early for a pity party, don't ya think?" I wasn't in the mood for adolescent drollery. She touched the bruise.

"I'm fine, I guess. My face hurts, and I don't feel well. Is that better?" Her eyes were staring directly into mine.

"It's a start. How far along are you in your pregnancy, if you don't mind my asking?"

"About four months, give or take a week." She kept up the eye contact. Agnes came in and sat down beside me. "You don't approve of my situation, do you? You think I've screwed this up big time..." She smirked at that. "I remember you using that phrase when I was having trouble at school."

"This isn't high school anymore, is it?" It was my turn to smirk.

"No, although there was a lot of things that went on during that time that you didn't know anything about—"

"Like you're sneaking into the shed with whatshisname, the drinking? Yeah, I didn't know anything about that." I wasn't a complete idiot.

Rebekah frowned. "John Milner. It was John Milner. And we had a few drinks too..."

"So that's your excuse for what's going on now? I had my moments as a teen, and I'm damaged-goods so whatever I do is because of that? Save it for your mother or grandmother, assuming you ever tell them the truth, but not me. I understand you were unhappy and you felt trapped, and I know you want to have kids and all that, but why this way, why not just divorce Farrell and meet someone new? I don't get it. I mean, did you think about any of this while you were fucking around with this married guy? And you lied to him? What the fuck's wrong with you? It's like you deliberately meant to blow everything up. Kapow! Boom! It's all rubble. Nothing to go back to, nothing to put back together because there's nothing left to put together." Her head was down now; maybe she was crying again, but I didn't care, "And what's the plan? Have Farrell slap you around some more? We came all this way for that? And then what? Where are you going to live? How are you going to support yourself and this baby? What about that?"

"I'll figure something out," she whispered. "Maybe I'll go live with Grandpa—"

"Moses?" Yeah, let's all go live with Moses.

"What was your big plan when you left California? You ended up with your *mother*." My how condescending!

"I was running for my life on top of being an idiot, remember?"

"So I can't be an idiot too?"

Oh brother. "No, you can't be an idiot too!"

She tried to scrunch her sore face. "How is that fair?"

Another stupid question! "Fair?"

Agnes butted in. "I can ask Johnny about finding you something to do and we can figure something out about where you can live." She turned to me. "Like your bungalow." My bungalow? I love that place. It's my sanctuary!

Agnes knew how I felt about it. She didn't like me having a place to hide away in. "Right, Grandpa to be?"

"Moses, huh?" Yeah, she could go live with Moses.

I wondered if I could afford Hawaii.

30

Why do people live out here when there are greener pastures elsewhere? Why stay? Why bother? The cynical answer was that most didn't. They departed for California during the dust bowl. The rest? Who knows? The road we were bouncing along cut through a whole lot of nothing. Beyond the wheat fields lay scrub and cattle with the bluffs rising in the distance. This is where the southwest begins and stretches all the way to the California deserts before falling into the sea. It was also hot and dry and inhospitable.

After coming together with a half-ass plan for the future of my idiot daughter, we had breakfast at the local pancake house and were soon on the road to nowhere here in the expanse of the Oklahoma panhandle. As a change of pace, I left the tie at the hotel and opted for a nice light polo and a seersucker suit I'd found long ago, but had never worn. It screamed city dude but was light and cool.

We zipped past the spot where we'd found Farrell and the ghost. Further along was Basker's farm and the idyll of Brother DeBerry's Promised Land. A small sign off a dirt road indicated the way to Basker's farm.

The farm was in an oasis that allowed enough irrigation to feed the people occupying the dozen forlorn wooden structures settled between the bluffs of this Christian hideaway. It reminded me of the sets they used to build for old Hollywood westerns: unusually clean and organized along a main street. The wood had weathered to gray for every structure, be they homes or barns or storehouses. I didn't see a church. Off on the other side of the farm, beyond the buildings, were the fields and there we could see the members of the community working. We parked the truck and made our way to where we could impose on someone for information. Agnes and Rebekah followed behind me as we approached a young man in overalls. A wide-brimmed hat covered his head.

"Can I help you?"

"Yes," I said, "we met Brother DeBerry a while back in Kentucky, and at his urging came to see for ourselves this community he spoke of. My name is

Monk. This is Agnes, and my daughter, Rebekah. Perhaps you could tell us if he's here, or if Mr. Cox is?"

The man slid his hat back and smiled, "I know they both have come back, but I haven't seen them today. I believe Ashton went into town to speak to the sheriff—"

"About Farrell Jenkins?" I asked. "Farrell is my son-in-law." I wanted to see his reaction to that bit of news.

"I think so, but I really don't know anything about it..." The man noticed the bruise on Rebekah's face.

"Where, if I may, might we find Brother DeBerry, mister...?"

My name is Nathan. I'm the manager. I take care of the more mundane tasks around here," he said with a smile. "If I know Lucian, he's probably at the sanctuary. It's atop that plateau." He pointed past the fields to a bluff. "He likes to spend some time there when he returns to us." Nathan continued to look at Rebekah. "It's early though, and it's possible Lucian needs his privacy. He likes to rise a little later after he comes back from a long trip. Perhaps I can show you around until he's ready, if as you say you'd like to observe our community?"

"We'd like that, Nathan. We can talk with Lucian later." I was leery of being too pushy in regards to Brother DeBerry.

As Nathan showed us around, a wave of nostalgia hit me. Basker's farm was just a more religious, more conservative version of the old man's farm. Here, like there, the homes were organized towards the communal hall where Nathan explained, they all gathered for their meals and where they held their services and said their prayers. The hall contained a large kitchen to one side and two long tables, one for the women and children, and one for the men.

"You don't eat together?" Agnes asked.

Nathan smiled. Agnes wasn't the first outsider to be amazed by this. "No, we believe it builds a greater bond between the members of the community. I know it can seem strange, but those of us here find comfort in the traditional roles associated with men and women. We know who we are and what we are and what is expected of us. As for the families, once supper is over, we return to our homes for what you would call quality time together."

"Well, as long as you have some quality time, eh Monk?" Agnes grabbed my arm.

"Yes dear."

Nathan smiled at that too.

Next, we visited the school. There were about sixteen children of various ages, the oldest looked to be about fourteen. The teacher had the kids turn around as we said hello; again, much as it was when I was a kid. Next, we ventured out into the fields. A variety of crops had been planted, certainly enough to feed the people here and quite a few more. Nathan said it was to pay for whatever they might need from the feed store. I mentioned our talk with Marlon. Another smile. Nathan smiled a lot. We were also shown the well and the new septic system they put in to support the growth in the community, there were three new families this year. I was tempted to ask about Justin and Amy Peterson, I wondered what he had to say about them. I had a lot of questions that were probably inappropriate.

Maybe later.

It was lunchtime, and they invited us to join them. Rebekah continued to hide behind me, and Agnes wasn't thrilled with having to sit at the women's table, but I accepted their offer on the women's behalf and asked what we could do to help. Nathan led us back to the hall where a young woman named Daphne took Agnes and Rebekah to the kitchen. Nathan introduced me to the rest of the men. Most were younger with a few close to my age. They all seemed friendly and asked what I thought of what they'd built here.

"Well," I began, "to be honest, this place reminds me of where I grew up. Not so much in location or climate, because, let's be honest, the panhandle is not like northern California, which is where I'm from, but I grew up on a commune where everybody had a job to do and worked for the benefit of all. I had to help with the animals when I was little and then helped with building and farming when I got older. It's what I did for twenty years before I decided to do other things, so I find this all very familiar. We had a small schoolhouse, and the kids had their own bunkhouse. We didn't have separate tables for the men and women and we weren't particularly religious, although Moses, (A number of them raised their eyebrows at the name.) my father, insisted we follow a number of Christian virtues like caring for others, practicing forgiveness, and not allowing ourselves to be consumed by malice and greed."

The men seemed humored by this. I knew the look, having witnessed it time and again from my days in Virginia. If you practice some Christian virtues, then why not embrace the whole of Christianity? I returned their good humor and we sat down.

The girls from the school brought over our meals then went to the other table. The conversation centered on farming and my thoughts on agribusiness versus communal farming. I tried to be sympathetic and understanding, but I'd long lost interest in such things, so I mumbled on about need versus cost and labor, using or not using industrial fertilizers, harvesting seeds, and nurturing interesting but difficult crops. Mostly though, I listened and bullshitted when I had to. It was their life, not mine. I was only interested in getting Rebekah past her Farrell problem and lighting out for LA.

After thanking God for his providence and helping to clear the table, we hooked up again with Nathan. It was time to journey up the plateau where we would find Lucian DeBerry. Agnes, forever curious, wanted to know why the church was so far away.

Nathan agreed it seemed odd at first, but, "Originally, there were two compounds or groups of houses. The men lived up on the plateau, where the church is, and the women lived down here. After they abandoned the farm, the houses on the plateau fell into disrepair and began to collapse, so the people who later bought the land saved the church and moved the houses that were salvageable down here and tore the others down. As I understand it, for a long time, this place was used as a refuge, where you would live down here and then go to the church to commune with God. There's a small room in the back of the church with a bed, that's where Lucian likes to stay. You'll find him there. Just follow the path."

Nathan thoughtfully made sure we knew where we were going, but it was a wide road, I couldn't imagine getting lost.

"Thanks for your help," I said.

"My pleasure. Please ask Lucian to come see me when he has a chance."

"I will."

Nathan watched as we ascended the hill before returning to whatever else he had to take care of.

The hike up the hill was pleasant. The day was warm rather than hot, as it had been the previous week, and a nice crosswind met us at the crest of the plateau. It was easy to see why the church was here and not below. The plateau looked to the west towards a series of ravines and hills in the distance that snaked north and south. The trees they planted all those years ago had thrived, much like the ones down by the houses, which surprised me since they didn't have the natural protection the trees below had. I imagined the sunsets and the faint hope that on a clear day a hint of the Rockies could be seen.

The path to the church was bordered by the remnants of the foundations where the other set of houses had stood. A testament to the lives that preceded ours. Between the fallen foundations were the trees, now well over a hundred years old. They swayed in the breeze, indifferent to us as they were to all the drifters who had come and gone.

The church beckoned at the end of the path. Gray and weathered, just as the other buildings were, it stood straight and square under the filtered sunlight. It was a sturdy rectangular box with a steeple in the front above the double doors and the porch. While the siding was world-weary, the roof was recent and the windows and steps sturdy. The doors were closed, so we knocked and waited.

Nothing.

After a second knock and calling out, I pushed on the door. It wasn't locked, and there we found the murdered Lucian DeBerry. It's possible Agnes, or Rebekah or both of them screamed when we found Lucian. If they did, I don't remember. It's also possible they did not. Again, I don't remember. What we found was at such odds with what we expected or had earlier experienced that we just stood there in a state of shook. I looked at Jesus up on the cross, and then at the second dead man we'd stumbled upon in two days. Agnes and Rebekah stayed back while I drew closer to him. He'd been stabbed multiple times in the chest and abdomen then laid out Christ-like against the pulpit.

Agnes inched in and pulled up behind me. "What a terrible thing..."

"Yes," was all I could think to say.

"What should we do?" she asked.

"Call the sheriff. He's not going to be happy. All we bring is bad news..."

Agnes nodded. I tried my phone, as did Agnes and Rebekah, but there was no signal.

Nothing.

"Now what?" Rebekah wondered out loud.

"The two of you go down to the others. We need to get the sheriff out here. I don't know what you should say, but they need to know. I'll stay here."

"You sure?" Agnes asked.

"It'll be all right."

"Here, take this..." Rebekah had the 38 in her hand.

"What are you doing with that thing?" I took the gun from her.

She acted hurt that I would even ask. "You never know..." She touched her swollen cheek as she said this. Was she going to shoot Farrell if he struck her again?

"All right, you two get going."

Agnes kissed me for no reason, and the two of them headed back to Nathan and the people we had just met.

Maybe we were bad news.

The church began to wither and withdraw from me as I wandered over to the window, looking at the sage and the prairie grasses, watching Agnes and Rebekah disappear down the road. The pews were covered in dust, as was the floor. Now it looked its age, old and tired, spent. I sat down in the front pew and looked upon the late Lucian DeBerry, the man of God, the man who needed a confessor.

"Do you believe in forgiveness, Monk?" That was his question once we got beyond my approbation for certain elements of the Christian faith, but not the more miraculous presumptions that I didn't buy into like resurrection and virgin birth.

"I suppose. Why do you ask?"

"To use a much-repeated phrase, I've sinned, I...broke God's laws..." He was studying his hands, waiting, I assumed, for me to ask the nature of his sins.

"Is this about Ashton Cox?"

DeBerry turned to me and tried to smile. "No, Ashton is much stronger about such things than I am. He made a commitment years ago and has stuck to it, no matter what he may desire. I wish I had that strength. No, my transgressions are more profound." He returned to his hands. It reminded me of Rebekah and her obsession with spinning her wedding ring. "I... I don't normally go on such extended... retreats from our community. My preference is to spend my time there. These trips to speak to congregations are usually short, three or four days at the most, but I've been away for nearly three weeks, I'm almost afraid to go back. I've had to summon my courage and face the part of me that wants to run away, to flee, if you will, from the damage I've done. The members of our community have been very supportive and have tried very hard to move beyond what happened and to not let the words of this ghost prejudice their feelings and beliefs, but there is some truth to what he says." Lucian took a small crucifix from his pocket. "I haven't been completely honest with them about my part in what happened..."

"What did happen?" I asked.

His eyes glazed over. "I only wanted to help, to be supportive. They were struggling, trying to work out their problems. I'd heard from the others of shouting and the sounds of violence. He was abusive at times, but also quite effusive in his sorrow at how he treated her when I spoke to him of our concerns for their welfare. This went on for some time and at one point he left so he could think things through."

"Justin and Amy Peterson?"

He nodded, "You knew them?"

"No. I heard of them. He murdered her then killed himself. Is that correct?"

"Yes," he murmured.

His confession was swimming around in my head as I sat on the dusty pew. I could see the trail on the floor where his body had been dragged from the back room. I took the 38 out of my pocket and slowly made my way to the half-opened door. I took care not to step in the blood. I pulled the hammer back on the pistol.

The room was empty.

Someone had stabbed him on the bed. Quite a bit of blood had soaked into the sheets. The back door out of the room was open. The sunlight filled the room, drying the blood splattered within it. It was a small room with a dresser, a chair, and a table with a water basin on it. A washcloth rested on the lip of the basin. Next to the basin was a bible. I put the 38 back in my pocket and returned for a moment to the pulpit and the murdered man.

He was speaking of her as I walked past.

"She was only twenty-three, sweet, caring... I sensed a desire in her to find a better path in life, a deeper understanding of God's will. I also found we were drawn to one another—"

"So you slept with her?"

He didn't want to answer. After a minute or two, he nodded. "Yes." Lucian DeBerry shook as he admitted this. "I loved her, Monk. I know how that sounds, and I understand if you don't believe me, but it wasn't my intention for this to happen. I only wanted to help, truly, I swear to God I had no other motive."

We sat there, I remembered, in the glow of the motel lights and my eyes wandered to the darkness in the woods behind us. At the time I wondered if the ghost was right, that all was not golden in DeBerry's Oklahoma Eden. Rot exists; always has.

"I want you to know that I loved her and that she loved me. I know that doesn't excuse what I did and I know I must come clean to those who I care for and who care for me; that I have to accept their judgment of me..."

"Yet you long to be forgiven, don't you?"

He looked at me, tears running down along his cheeks. "Yes."

I put my hand on his shoulder. "We all do, my friend, we all do."

I stood up. I'd heard all I wanted to. I seemed awash in infidelity, between my own, Rebekah's, and now DeBerry's; it was too much. I had no desire to judge. I simply wanted to go home. I left him sitting on that bench just as I left him rotting against the pulpit.

The sirens grew close.

31

Sheriff MacAfee was not happy to see me.

"He's in there," I gestured in the direction of the door. The sheriff said nothing and went into the church. Nathan, Agnes, Rebekah, and many of the community members were standing at the edge of a quick cordon the sheriff's men had put up. Having directed Colin MacAfee to his latest headache, I got up and went over to where my freaked out girlfriend and daughter were. Nathan was no longer smiling; sad, amazed disbelief had taken its place.

"Is it true?" he asked.

"I'm afraid it is." I assumed Agnes told them what we'd found. I put my hand on his shoulder. "I'm sorry, Nathan." I left the others to mill around. I knew it wouldn't help. "If Sheriff MacAfee wants me, I'll be down at my truck. Come on girls, let's go." I said this to no one in particular.

The walk down wasn't as pleasant as the walk up even though the weather hadn't changed. Agnes held one hand as Rebekah held the other. We sat in the truck and waited. No one had anything to say. We watched in silence as the rest of the community made their way to the church. Ashton Cox, Teddy, and Guy, back from their trip to town, joined them. Cox looked our way for a moment, but only for a moment. He face was a stoic shade of white, and his shoulders slumped as he followed the others to the place of their pastor's murder.

"What do we do now?" Agnes, like Rebekah, was fiddling with the jewelry on her hands and wrists.

"We're here until the end, beautiful."

"What does that mean?"

"I don't know." I was lying.

Perceptively, my phone began to chime. It was Art Devaney's reply to my text from the day before.

You have a knack for this, Monk; am I right? However, the answer is not two, but three. How bad is it, bad as we feared?

Bad as we feared I texted back. I asked for names and whether they were still alive. He already had the answer.

And so did I.

The parade of officials pertinent to the pursuance of justice in the case of a man stabbed to death continued unabated. Soon the dirt road leading to the small grouping of houses was filled with members of the sheriff's office, the coroner's office, and men I would later learn belonged to the Oklahoma state police and their agencies. The sheriff came to greet them and pointed them in the direction of the mayhem that required their expertise. After jawing with a stout middle-aged man in sunglasses, the sheriff came our way.

"What's your story, Mr. Buttman?"

"No story. We stopped by to visit. Nathan gave us the tour and we went up to the church to say hello to DeBerry. That's where we found him. Nobody touched him. I had Agnes and Rebekah go down to alert you because we had no signal on the hill and I waited for you to arrive. That's all there is."

"Why don't I believe that, Mr. Buttman?" I couldn't tell if he wanted to be angry or not.

"Because this kinda shit doesn't happen in a nice place like Goodwell, that's why." I don't know why I said that other than to piss him off.

His eyes grew tight and his face hardened. "Careful, Mr.—"

"Sheriff!" One of his deputies was calling him to come over.

"Just a minute," he gestured to the officer before turning back to me. "I want to see you all bright and early tomorrow morning in my office, eight AM. I'm going to get to the bottom of this Mr. Buttman. Count on it!" He left us with that.

"Smooth." Agnes jabbed me in the ribs.

"I thought so."

"So, where to now, Sunshine?" I think she was pissed off too.

"Back to the Comfort Inn, beautiful; back to our home away from home."

"I'm going to stay here," Rebekah said out of the blue.

"What?" Agnes and I said this together as she got out of the truck.

"I want to talk to Farrell."

"Why?"

"Because it's important to me. Let me have the gun if you're worried. He won't hurt me, I promise." She put her hand out. I hesitated.

"You're not going to shoot him, are you?" I had to ask.

"No," she said. "This is something I need to do. Well?" her hand was still out. Agnes gave me another shot to the ribs.

"Please stop doing that!" I reached into my pocket.

"Then give her the gun!" Agnes was shaking.

Goddammit Agnes—"

"Dad!" Rebekah reached further into the cab.

"Fine, I just hope you know what the fuck you're doing. This isn't a goddamned game."

"Really?"

I put the 38 in her hand. *"Really."*

She put it in her pocket, slammed the door and walked off towards the bluff.

Agnes moved away from me to sit on the other side of the cab. *Fine; do what you want!* I started the truck and slowly maneuvered around all the other vehicles. A deputy held us up before getting the ok from the sheriff to let us go. I turned the radio on and let the twang settle us down.

"You said you didn't like this crap?"

I looked over at her and shook my head. "It'll do for now."

She crossed her arms and turned to the sights outside her window. An hour later, we were back in our home away from home. I took a beer out of the fridge.

"Thirsty?"

"You know I don't like beer," she growled.

"What? Still pissed off? That's too bad. We do have some wine, you know. I'd be happy to pour you a glass..." I winked at her, wanting desperately to break the tension.

"If you stop bugging me, I'll have some of that."

Fortunately, she was starting to crack. She had a tough time being angry with me even if I deserved it, probably my puppy dog eyes. I found a plastic cup and uncorked the bottle of chardonnay. With alcohol in hand, I sat next to her on the bed. She took her glass and then a sip.

"Better?" I asked.

"Maybe..." She tried mightily to maintain her unhappiness.

"Good, because I don't think I can do two crazy women at the same time."

"Oh, poor baby." There was that smile.

"You got that right." I leaned over and kissed her. "So what's got you so worked up, a couple of dead guys?"

"That's not funny." She put my arm around her shoulder.

"You're right, it's anything but funny." I put the bottle to my mouth. The beer was nice and cold. Agnes squirmed a bit before settling in with her head against my chest.

"All these dead people and when Farrell hit her...maybe that was it. After he hit her I thought of Jordan, and I...I'm sorry, Monk."

"No need to be sorry."

We sat in the quiet of the room, nursing our drinks. My mind was racing between Art's news and Rebekah's obsession with her idiot husband. "I don't think she realizes what's going on with that idiot Farrell or God help us if she does. Either way, it isn't going to be pretty," I said just to get it in the air.

"Do *you* know what's going on with that idiot Farrell?" She was mocking me.

"And if I do?" I closed my eyes to the room only to find myself back at the church with Lucian.

"Is this going to be like the confession of the dead man where you know, but you won't tell, making me want to grab you until you cry uncle? Cuz if it is I won't be responsible for my actions, Sunshine." She wasn't smiling anymore.

"Christ, two crazy women at the same time," I kissed her head.

"So spill, Buttman! What's going on?"

I waited a moment or two to say anything, to add to the excitement. "Well, you know, I'm kinda hungry. You?"

"BUTTMAN!" I flinched as she pinched me.

"What? You're not hungry?" She pulled away and smacked me in the chest. I feigned shock. I guess I'd be pissed too. "All right, all right, there's been enough violence for one day, but I am hungry..."

She made a face that said one more smart-ass remark, and it would be an even longer night. I don't know why I thought it would be fun to play on her frayed nerves, maybe to sooth my own frayed nerves.

"Monk, please..." She was shaking again. I'd forgotten how terrifying it was to find someone murdered. I had become better at internalizing that shaking, but having it in front of me in Agnes' eyes I notice my hands were shaking too.

"Sorry." I pulled her back in.

"You're a jerk, Buttman!" Oddly, this made us both laugh.

"Yes I am." It was good to laugh a little, "And I am hungry, so let's get something to eat, and I'll confess what I know."

"I'm not hungry." She snuggled in closer to me.

"Then humor me."

Agnes groaned, "Fine, but you're still a jerk, Buttman!"

Some things never change.

Down the block was a local mom and pop restaurant. I choose to believe the folks in there enjoyed seeing me in my seersucker suit. If not, it was their loss. The room was filled with voices talking. What conversations we could make out, were about what in God's name was going on out there at that farm, with the crazies, who can't just go to church regular, like the rest of us.

They have my sympathies.

I had to nag Agnes to eat something. Other than dessert, she wasn't interested. I ordered a salad that we could share and promised if she had a few bites, we'd share a slice of pie.

"So talk to me. What's going on?" she was imploring me to get on with it.

"I don't really know, but I have a few ideas..." I started.

"Meaning?"

"Meaning we'll see." I took a deep breath. I was surprised at my reticence to share what DeBerry had told me. I mean the guy's dead! "It's obvious that we're stuck in the middle of a feud that's turned ugly—"

"*Really?* I hadn't noticed. Did he kill them, Monk? Is that what he told you?" she interrupted.

"As far as I know DeBerry didn't kill anyone. His mistake was who he slept with—"

"The gay guy? I thought he liked him?" she harrumphed.

"Do you want me to talk or not?" Our food had arrived, and I found I had no real interest in talking about this. The waitress put the plate in front of me and smiled, just at me, glanced at Agnes, then left. I looked at Agnes, "I wonder what that was about."

Agnes shrugged. "Since I won't let you fuck her, it doesn't matter."

"Really, Agnes, such language!"

"Uh-huh. Keep talking," Agnes took some salad from the plate.

"It's not about his relationship with Cox. He alluded to it when we talked, saying it helped him survive prison, and I know it was mostly one-sided—"

"So he's doing what with Cox?" She wasn't getting the disjointed picture I was painting.

"Nothing. Cox loves DeBerry, but once this ministry thing started taking off, they no longer engaged in amorous activities. DeBerry said this was because Cox believed it would be bad for business. As you know, personally, a lot of people are still deeply uncomfortable with homosexuality." I raised my eyebrows towards Agnes.

"I have my reasons." She didn't like me pointing out her aversion to certain gay men.

"So I've noticed. Anyway, they felt if it came up, they could show that they were not giving in to their throbbing biological urges."

"Ok, so if they weren't blowing each other then who was he sleeping with?"

I shook my head. "Nice. No, Lucian DeBerry was having an affair with Amy Peterson."

Agnes' eyes widened. "I should know that name, right?" The wheels were spinning.

"I don't know that you should. They lived at DeBerry's community for a while, Justin and Amy. Apparently, theirs was not a happy marriage and Justin left for a time during which DeBerry started counseling her."

"Counseling, huh? I guess that's one way to put it," she smirked.

"He said it was not his intention to seek out a physical relationship, she was, after all, a married woman. But however it started, it turned into a sexual relationship, and when Justin returned and found out, he killed her and then himself."

"Oh my God!" Lights were going off in my beloved's head. "That's what that ghost guy was talking about, wasn't it?"

"Yep. I don't exactly know his relationship to Justin; he denied being his father, but it was the murder-suicide that started all this."

Agnes pondered that. "Did DeBerry say anything about what happened? I mean the murder of his girlfriend?" His girlfriend? No sympathy in death for Lucian.

"He wasn't here when it happened. Makes you wonder if Justin would have killed him too. I know it haunted him."

Agnes thought about that. "Wait a minute," an odd expression crossed her face, "who is killing who here?"

"Doesn't make sense does it. You could assume that maybe Cox and his goons, if you can call them that, killed the ghost, but then who killed DeBerry. Cox wouldn't. If anyone was going to kill DeBerry over this, you would assume it would be the ghost, but that can't be because he was killed the day before."

"Or was he?" Agnes' eyes grew bigger. "Maybe DeBerry was killed before the ghost. It's just that we didn't find him until now?"

"Maybe, but my impression is that Nathan talked to him yesterday, late enough in the day for it to be after we found the ghost."

Agnes slumped back into her chair. "I don't understand."

I smiled at her. "Neither did I, but an idea came to me that Art corroborated."

"Which is what?" I just kept smiling. "Monk!" Agnes was frowning again.

"Yes?"

She let out an audible groan. "Who killed DeBerry?"

"The ghost," I said.

"The ghost? The *dead guy* from yesterday? How?" she asked incredulously.

"No, he was dead." I could tell she wanted very much to pinch or smack me, but, fortunately for me, she was on the other side of the table.

"I still don't understand, and you're being a jerk. Why don't you just tell me?"

"Because, for now, it's only a presumption. I'll know better when we talk to the sheriff tomorrow."

She wasn't mollified. "Was it Farrell?" She needed something.

"I don't think so. I think Farrell is in this up to his eyeballs, but I don't believe he killed anyone. If I thought that I wouldn't have let Rebekah stay there."

"Wow. Do you think he's back at the community?" she asked.

"I think so. And I don't think Rebekah's been honest about her communications with Farrell, certainly not with us. I know she's been on his phone a lot and she tells me it's because of the pictures, but I'm not buying it. I think he told her he was there and for her to meet him."

"I guess that explains why you said what you said."

"We'll see. I say a lot of things."

"Yeah, you do don't you?" At least she was eating.

We finished the salad and shared a slice of apple pie a la mode. As we were leaving, a hick made a smart-assed remark about my suit and I complimented him on his keen sense of taste and style. Agnes kept pushing me towards the door, mumbling something about having had enough of that for a lifetime. Once again, we were back in our cozy home away from home. Agnes lay down on the bed, and impulsively I seductively flopped on top of her.

"You look really good, baby. Come here often?"

Agnes smiled in that lovely way that made me realize how lucky I was to have her around. Maybe it was the beer?

"You tell me lover…"

I brushed the hair from her neck and kissed her just below her ear. "It appears that for the first time in a while, the two of us have the room to ourselves…" I continued to slowly work my way down her neck to her collarbone.

"Monk," she put her hand on mine as I tried to undo her blouse, "maybe this isn't a good time?"

"No? I was thinking as an antidote to this less than stellar day we could spend a little quality time pleasuring one another…"

"I know, but..." Her hand let go of mine as she tried to smile.

I knew the look. I rolled off of her.

"Are you mad?" She reached out and began running her hand along my arm.

"No." I lifted my arm, and she reflexively tucked herself under it.

"Sorry."

It had been a long day. Not everything lends itself to amorous activity.

I kissed her forehead. "Don't be."

"Still love me?"

I thought about it. "I wonder what Natalie is doing?"

I got a goodnight pinch for that!

32

"The sheriff will be out in a few minutes, please take a seat." The deputy directed us to the chairs against the wall. We sat down. Agnes was unusually nervous, playing with her jewelry, crossing and uncrossing her legs.

"You all right?" I asked.

"Bad memories. The last time I was in a police station it was after I got out of the hospital and they were pushing me to answer questions about Jordan." She paused, "I just wanted to run away and hide, which, I guess, is what I did."

I took her hand. "It'll be okay. I don't think they're after us, just trying to figure this out."

"Gee, I'd have never guessed that!" Lovely.

"It's a little early for sarcasm, isn't it?"

"Oh, I don't think so." She smiled as she said this, a sly disingenuous smile.

"Fine, be that way," I huffed.

Agnes patted me on the knee, the smile still residing on her beautiful face.

The sheriff arrived five minutes later and motioned for us to join him.

"I apologize for losing my temper yesterday." He looked over at Agnes, "I'm sorry, but I've forgotten your name..."

"Agnes, Agnes Duquesne," she replied.

We entered his office. He sat at his desk and Agnes and I in two chairs across from him. There was more light in the room than I expected courtesy of the large window behind him. Maps and certificates adorned the wall to our right, a file cabinet and a credenza to our left. His desk was organized and clean, a stack of reports on one side and a computer monitor on the other.

"Have you lived here long?" I asked. Curiosity and anxiety opened my mouth.

"I've lived here all my life. My great-grandfather ended up here after leaving Scotland. Having been to Scotland I don't quite understand why, other than opportunity, but my family stayed so here I am. Why do you ask?" He leaned back in his chair.

"Mostly to break the tension, but I also have some questions about Basker's farm," I said. "If you've lived here a while maybe you know its story beyond what I know."

"And what do you know about Basker's farm, Mr. Buttman?"

"I know it started out as a religious compound a hundred or so years ago, that it was later abandoned and then bought so people could use it as a retreat. Now it's home to DeBerry's people."

MacAfee smiled. "It was started by a man named Emile Basker and his sister, Hermione. They were Shakers. The men lived apart from the women. Obviously there are limitations, where relations, as my grandmother used to say, did not happen between men and women. Since there were no babies, for a time they took in orphans to sustain the flock, but most of the orphans didn't stay, and the property was deserted after the First World War. The Cox family later purchased the farm. I believe you've met Ashton Cox. It's his family, and yes it was used as a retreat for many years, but that ended some years ago after his grandfather died. Apparently, his father had no interest in it. Mr. Cox and Mr. DeBerry restarted the farm about five years ago, and it's my understanding that Mr. Cox has given the property to a trust established for the people there." The sheriff put his hands together and for a moment, I had an image of Marsyas Durant in my head. "What's your connection to all this, Mr. Buttman?"

"Call me Monk." Even I was tired of Mr. Buttman. "Our connection is Farrell Jenkins."

"That reminds me, where is your daughter, I expected her to be here as well?"

"Rebekah is at Basker's farm. There, I suppose, with Farrell. You released him, No?"

"Yes, we decided not to hold Mr. Jenkins for now."

"Can I ask what he told you about the man in the ditch? Can I ask if you know the man's name?" I leaned forward towards the sheriff.

"There was no identification on the man's body. Mr. Jenkins told me he only knew him as the ghost," he said.

"Have you heard of the ghost or seen the man before?"

The sheriff leaned back. "Only hearsay. Do you know who he is, Monk?" He made sure to accentuate the 'K' in Monk.

"Based on the information I received yesterday, his name is either Asa or Jeffery Peterson. He is Justin Peterson's uncle." I had hoped that name would get a rise out of the sheriff and it did. I was almost giddy inside.

"What do you know about Justin Peterson?" Colin MacAfee's angular features tightened.

"I was told, initially, that he killed his wife and then himself. The ghost assured me that that was a lie, that Justin had been framed. That it was a cover-up perpetrated by DeBerry and his people. What's the law say, Sheriff? Did he do it, or was it a frame?"

"Justin Peterson brutally beat and raped Amy Peterson before he strangled her in the field beyond their house. That's where we found her. There's no doubt about it, all the DNA and forensic evidence supports it. After he killed his wife, he went back to their house where he swallowed glass shards and hung himself on the inside of the front door. Again, all the forensic evidence supports our conclusion that he killed himself. It was one of the ugliest things I've ever had to deal with. What does that have to do with the two murders in the last two days?"

"It's the reason for them," I said. "What did Farrell tell you, about why he was there? Why did he run off?"

"He said he was there to meet the man and had arrived just before you did. Apparently, seeing his wife unexpectedly caused him to leave."

"Did he mention hitting Rebekah?"

"Only after I brought it up. He apologized, saying his emotions got the better of him. I'll leave it up to your daughter if she wants to press the issue. As to why he was meeting the man he called the ghost, he claimed he was trying to stop all the bad gossip going around. When I asked him about that, he said that Ashton Cox was a better person to talk to; that he was meeting the ghost at Mr. Cox's request. After talking to Mr. Cox, and admonishing Mr. Jenkins about leaving the scene of a crime, I agreed to allow Mr. Jenkins to return to Basker's farm with the understanding that he was not to leave the area. Mr. Cox said he would hold Mr. Jenkins to that."

"Did Mr. Cox explain the situation or the content of the gossip?"

A thin smile crossed the sheriff's face. "Mr. Cox assured me it was just a matter of foolish words being bandied about. He did not wish to waste my time with it and that he didn't believe it was relevant to the man's death. I'm assuming you disagree?" the Sheriff cocked his head slightly to emphasize the question.

"Since it may involve the deaths of nine people, then yes, I disagree." I thought the number would intrigue the sheriff. It did.

"Then explain it to me, Mr. Buttman." The smile was gone.

"Call me Monk—"

Agnes interrupted. She was pale. "May I have some water please? I don't feel very good." I think Agnes has had enough of our splendid little adventure.

"Certainly, Miss Duquesne. Would you like to lie down? There's a cot in the next room. I use it sometimes on long nights, like the last two." The sheriff went into the next room for water.

Agnes had tears in her eyes. "I'm sorry. Too many bad memories..." MacAfee handed a bottle of water to Agnes, "I don't need to lay down. I'll be ok, don't mind me..."

"Agnes..." I realized I was pushing too hard, being too glib. To me, it was something to finish. The dead were dead. I was much better at blocking them out. Agnes had slammed into the wall. "Maybe you should lie down for a minute..."

She stared at me. "And do what? Replay every time Jordan beat or kicked me? Replay his hands around my throat? No, I just need a minute. I don't want to be alone with those memories. I'd rather be here. I'll be all right." She drank some of the water.

"You're sure?"

She took another drink. "Yes..."

MacAfee returned to his chair.

I began composing my theory. "Did you talk to Lucian DeBerry or Ashton Cox about Justin and Amy Peterson?"

The sheriff sat back. "Mr. DeBerry was out of town. I learned from Mr. Cox and some of the other folks that there had been a history of domestic violence, that they had talked to Justin about it and that they felt he had made progress while he was away, but obviously something happened to set him off. What didn't they tell me, Monk; what is it that changes that?"

"Lucian DeBerry was having a sexual relationship with Amy Peterson that began when Justin was gone. That's what set him off. And it set off his father, Roger Peterson."

"How do you know this?" he asked. I had hooked him!

"DeBerry confessed the affair to me after we met him in Elizabethtown, Kentucky. I don't know why, other than he loved her and felt he needed to get that out, even to a stranger. The ghost thing bothered me. He seemed to be everywhere. He surprised me and Rebekah at her home in Virginia, and then was in Springfield, Missouri when we ran into Cox and his buddies. DeBerry said he was bothering the people here when I heard he was bothering a couple in Virginia, who later died, purportedly by suicide. How is it possible to be in so many places in so short a time or at the same time? Either he is a ghost, which is bullshit, or more than one of them existed, and I was certain they were a little different each time I saw them."

"How?"

"DeBerry said the man accosted him claiming to be Justin's uncle, knew his secrets, yet the same guy didn't recognize DeBerry's birth name when I talked to him. Secondly, they were different. The one in Virginia was cagey, playful, but the one in Missouri was angry, out of control. That made me wonder if there were two of them, so I had Art see if he could find anything out about Justin Peterson's father."

"Who's Art? Art who?" the Sheriff asked, somewhat perplexed.

"Art Devaney, used to work at the CIA. He now grows tobacco. I don't ask him where or how he gets his information, but he has a fondness for delving into the seedy underbelly of human nature. Anyway, he found that Justin's father was not a twin but a triplet and that he had given up custody of Justin at an early age to his brother Asa. Asa was found dead in the Mohave not long after the murder-suicide here. Something snapped within the Peterson clan and my idiot son-in-law, whether he knows it or not, is in the middle of that feud."

"So that's what you meant last night when you said the ghost had killed DeBerry even though the ghost was dead in the ditch," Agnes added, having perked up just a little. "But if that's true, who killed the ghost in the ditch?"

"Who killed Molly and Jonathan? Who killed the five people we found in Pennsylvania? Since Ashton Cox and his goons were there, in both towns, just before these people turned up dead, the assumption is they killed them. They were, after all, determined to keep the stories the ghost was telling under control."

The sheriff was incredulous. "Are you saying Ashton Cox had been out on some cross-country murder spree?"

"I'm saying that's what we're supposed to believe. As much as I don't want to say it, it's possible we're dealing with an honest to God lunatic, and it's not Ashton Cox. My worry is that he might be next. I mean who's going to worry about a dead man."

The sheriff shook his head. "That's quite a tale, Monk. If I'm following this right, Roger Peterson killed his brother in California, two people in Virginia, five people in Pennsylvania, and two here with more to come. And all because of what he believes Lucian DeBerry did to his son, someone he abandoned years ago. Is that correct?"

"It is." I knew how it sounded

"And Farrell Jenkins? His part?"

"I don't know exactly…" I could be wrong.

Sheriff MacAfee stood up, so did we, "Thanks for coming in. I'll be in touch." We walked to the door. "Are you going back out to Basker's farm?"

"Yeah, I need to find my idiot daughter." Agnes stuck her elbow in my ribs. "Oww! You need to stop doing that."

"She's pregnant, not an idiot," Agnes grumbled.

"Whatever you do, I don't want anyone in that church until the state boys are finished with it, understand?" the sheriff demanded.

"We get it." It was my turn to grumble. "Anything else?"

His eyes darkened. "Amy Peterson was pregnant."

• • • • •

Rebekah wasn't answering her phone.

Sometimes it's best to just stop thinking and go thinkless. Let the world do its thing, observe, but don't waste your time trying to figure people out. There are places where the chaos of human stupidity is beyond understanding, better to keep it out of sight, out of mind. It was time for me to find such a spot. Agnes was driving us back to Basker's farm, alarmed as much as I was that Rebekah wouldn't answer. Her fears were magnified by the violent means of Amy Peterson's death. That only brought Agnes a flood of bad memories and the fear that Rebekah was next. I wanted us safe in the truck on our way to LA. I looked out the window. A thin dirt road was calling to me.

"Turn right," I said.

"What?" she didn't understand. "Why?"

"Just up there." I pointed to the turnoff.

"Why?"

"Agnes, just do it!" I shouldn't be angry with Agnes.

She grumbled but didn't say anything. We turned onto the road and went another couple of miles. I asked her to stop the truck.

"What are you doing?"

"I'm going for a walk."

"You're going to leave me here?" I sensed a certain panic in her voice.

"You can come along if you want." I got out, so did she. We walked maybe a few hundred feet. A rock about five feet around and three feet tall provided a place to rest my weary butt. I sat down. Agnes sat next to me. A breeze worked its way past us. Not a mechanized sound could be heard, just the wind and an errant bird here and there. The land was scrub as it had been for thousands of years, stretching out nice and easy, no hurry, no need: it's what it is. My eyes wandered from one end of the horizon to the other. High wispy clouds dusted the sky comingling with the vapor trails of planes crossing the country.

I was tired.

I put my arm around Agnes. I wanted nothing more than to lay down for a while, to rest my weary bones. I wondered how many dirty dusty souls had come across this section of land and sat here thinking they must be out of their ever-loving minds.

"It's quiet out here," Agnes offered.

"Yeah, something other than non-stop noise. Sometimes it's good to take a break and listen to the world around you."

Agnes nodded, then turned and put her hand on my face. "Please don't leave me, Monk."

"Why would I leave you?"

She looked at me with those beautiful blue eyes. "You know why."

Except I knew it would never come to that. "You worry too much. Nothing's going to happen."

Agnes frowned. She wanted definition, not the blurry line I often danced across. "That doesn't make me feel better." She was pouting, which was odd to see in a forty-something woman. "Why won't you marry me, Monk?"

"I never said I wouldn't marry you."

"Then what's the goddamned holdup?" Maybe I was wrong; maybe it is kind of cute.

"Maybe we're just not ready yet," I said.

"You mean you're not ready yet."

"I didn't say that."

Here it comes… "You're a jerk, Buttman."

I leaned in and kissed her, catching her off guard. "I prefer to think I'm delightful."

"Uh-huh, how long are we going to sit here?"

"Until the end of time or fifteen minutes, whichever comes first."

Slowly we ventured back to the truck, then the paved road, then to Basker's farm. We parked, and Nathan came over. For a moment, I worried he might punch me. An irrational fear, sure, but given that I've become Monk Buttman, bearer of bad news, angel of death, I don't think it was that fantastical. Everywhere we've gone on this misbegotten venture, the dead have come to greet us.

I wasn't happy about it either. I was becoming morose and angry, all the things I fled in Virginia. We should have stayed in California. All my hopes of being helpful to my daughter were falling away, replaced by a consuming fear that I'd lose her, and the baby, to madmen lost to their own demons.

"How are you holding up?" he asked. That surprised me.

"I'm tired, and I want to go home. I should ask the same of you: how are you doing?" He tried to smile. Agnes wrapped her arms around me. I could tell she didn't want to let go.

"To be honest, it's been a very difficult night. It all seems so unreal. I don't understand why this happened. Lucian was so kind and loving, why would someone do that to him? It makes no sense."

I put my hand on his shoulder. "Why don't we go sit down for a moment? Maybe I can explain things. Are Farrell and Rebekah still here?"

"I think so. They were at the vigil last night." He stood there, lost in thought. "We can go to the dining hall."

Several people were in the hall. They looked up briefly as we entered and then returned to their own. We found a spot at the end of the table. Nathan took a bible from his pocket and held it in his hands.

"Why did this happen? Do you know? Ashton said something about asking you before he left for the church..." Nathan's eyes were wet, imploring.

"The sheriff told us not to go in the church," Agnes said, grabbing my arm.

"The police finished a couple hours ago, they were here all night. Ashton wanted to go. I saw no reason to stop him." He didn't care about the police. Nathan wanted a reason, an explanation, for why this was happening.

"It all started with Amy and Justin Peterson," I said. He just looked at me uncomprehending. "Tell me this, how did Lucian behave before and after their deaths? Do you remember?"

A different kind of sadness filled his eyes. "About what?"

"About Lucian and Amy?" I said. He seemed embarrassed.

"How did you find out?" he finally asked.

"Lucian told me. He felt the need to experience confession and inexplicably chose me," I told him. "So it wasn't completely unknown to those of you here while it was going on?"

He didn't want to answer. Nathan's wife, Ariel, spied us from across the room and came over, sitting next to Nathan and looking at Agnes and me. She was a sturdy woman with what was once called a ruddy complexion. Her eyes were a sharp green, and they drew you in when you looked at her. She wore her hair, a mix of light browns, pulled back in a ponytail. From her expression, I could tell she was worried for Nathan and not happy to see him cavorting with us.

"What's wrong, Nathan?" Nathan continued to stare at his bible.

"He wanted to know how this could have happened, and I told him it started with the deaths of Justin and Amy Peterson," I told her, " and I asked if he noticed a change in Lucian's demeanor after they died. I told him that Lucian had confided to me that he had a physical relationship with Amy and that he loved her."

Ariel put her hand on Nathan's. "I thought as much. I know it's not a kind thing to say, but I didn't care for Amy, and we all were concerned with how much time Lucian was spending with her after Justin left. I guess we shouldn't be surprised, she was what she was..."

"What was she? I got the impression she was Lucian's great love."

Ariel turned those green eyes on me. "She was what my mother called a flirt. She liked men and was always pestering them. It doesn't surprise me that Lucian fell hard for her either. I don't think he ever had a real woman in his life and he was gullible that way. To be honest, we were all a little suspicious when she stayed here instead of going back to California with her husband. I mean I know theirs was not a perfect union..." She put her arm in and around Nathan's. "We heard them argue and looking back I'm certain he struck her too..." I noticed her looking down when she said that.

"What happened that day?"

"Is it important?" Her eyes had softened.

"I think so."

"Who killed Lucian?" Nathan was still focused on the good book.

"Roger Peterson, Justin's father."

"Why?" Ariel asked.

"He blamed Lucian for his son's death. He believes all of you killed him in a conspiracy to protect Lucian."

"That's why you want to know what happened that day?"

"Yes."

Ariel shifted in her seat. She was clearly uncomfortable. Nathan spoke first. "I found her, out in the field. I'd never seen anything like it. I can't even begin to describe it..."

"There's no need, sheriff MacAfee told us what he did to her—"

Ariel interrupted, "It was my fault. I saw him taking her out towards the field. In the past, they'd gone out there to argue after Nathan had talked to them about how it was disturbing the children. I'd seen them go out before, but something was different. I could tell he was furious, calling her vile names and pushing her. He was yelling at her saying he was her boss and her saying she didn't have to go, but he kept pushing her. I watched as they disappeared down the wash. I went back and forth over whether to say anything to Nathan..."

He was holding her hand. "It's all right, Ariel, you didn't know," he consoled her.

"I shouldn't have waited. It wasn't much later when I saw him coming back alone. His clothes were a mess, and there were scratches and bruises on his face. He looked at me with a terrible face, like he didn't see me and went into his house. I ran to find Nathan."

Nathan continued, "Lucian and Ashton were away, so I went out there, into the wash with Bish Hanks. I had him wait by Amy. I went to call the sheriff. We gathered at Justin's door telling him we'd found his wife and had called the sheriff. I asked him to come out. I tried to open the door, but it was locked. I called his name several times. He only answered once, and I could barely hear him. He said..." Nathan stopped to wipes his eyes. "He said God will forgive me."

"Have either of you spoken to the man everyone called the ghost?"

They looked at each other.

"He started scaring people about two weeks after it happened, usually in the evening or at night, catching us off guard," Nathan said. "I only saw him once. I told him he was wrong about Lucian, but he laughed and said that I was wrong and that the truth would come out. Several of us were approached, and he seemed to be everywhere, so we decided to stay in pairs and report any contact with him to the sheriff. I didn't hear from him after that." Ariel nodded in agreement.

"Did you know Jonathan and Molly?" I asked.

"Yes, they had been here only a short time before Justin... I think they were frightened and they wanted to go home for a while. I told them not to believe the stories going around and that they were always welcome. It was quite a shock to hear they'd killed themselves." Agnes handed him a tissue. "Sorry, it's just been such a trying time. I know God tests us and I want to be strong, for all of us... but some days it's hard."

There was more I wanted to know, but I felt I was only throwing salt. I really only had one more question. "Do you have any idea where Farrell and Rebekah are?"

"Ashton would know. It was my understanding Farrell was helping him."

"No," I corrected him, "Farrell lied to him. I'm sorry about all this, Nathan, I truly am. You think Ashton is up at the church?"

"Yes."

We left them at the table.

I hoped we weren't too late.

33

My first stop was the truck. I wanted the shotgun. I also tried to convince Agnes to stay back with Nathan and Ariel.

"No!" was her answer to every argument I made, to my demands that I knew best, to pleadings for her safety, to all of them.

"Why won't you do this for me?" My patience was at an end.

"What part of *no* don't you understand? I'm not leaving you, Monk Buttman, no way, no how! We're in this together; got that! You're stuck with me!" She had her hands on her hips, which were shaking and not in a good I'm in the mood kind of way.

"Fine," I sighed.

I opened the breech of the shotgun and examined the shells. After assuring myself they were still good, I put four more in my pocket. I said a small prayer for their efficacy. Like some damned fool in a spaghetti western, I held the gun close to my side, so it wasn't particularly visible to those around us. Fortunately, there weren't many people out; most were in the dining hall or out in the fields. As we had the day before, we trooped up the hill to the church. Unlike the day before, the weather was turning foul. How appropriate I thought. Dark clouds were pushing out the sunlight and casting the colors of the scrubs and trees to their edge. Where the tree-lined path had once looked so inviting, it now promised nothing but trouble. The part of me that had run for California wanted to know what the hell I was thinking. I was getting into situations I had no talent for. I'm no lawman or gunslinger, I'm no aggrieved landowner pushed to the limits of his patience. *I'm a fucking nobody, man!* I should be at the beach with my trusty lawn chair and a cooler full of beer and fruit. That made me smile. I was always asked why beer and fruit? Wouldn't chips be more complimentary? Yeah, but fruit's better for you, that's what I'd say.

The clouds were bringing rain and maybe more. This was also tornado country. My mind kept pushing me west. I could feel that glorious California sun beating down on me as I lay on the beach with nothing else to do. I wanted to be anywhere but here.

Ashton Cox was sitting in the first pew on the left side, staring at the bloodstained pulpit. He looked over as our feet made the floorboards squeak.

"The sheriff doesn't want anybody in here," I told him.

"My concerns are not for the sheriff." His voice was soft and low.

"I came for Rebekah; I came for my daughter." I hung the shotgun over my left forearm.

"I imagine you did."

"Is she here?"

He smiled. "You know she is."

His smile faded as Farrell and Rebekah slowly came out of the backroom. The 38 was in Farrell's hand, pointed at Rebekah. She appeared to be okay other than the fear woven into her face. I turned to Agnes, who was as close as she could get to me, her hands on my waist.

"Now do you understand why I didn't want to give her that fucking gun?" She shied away as I said this. Farrell held Rebekah around the shoulder.

"Well, I have it now," said the fucking little prick.

I leveled the shotgun.

Cox spoke up. "Are we to have a gunfight inside a church, a church that has already seen too much violence? Put your weapons down both of you. They will not save you." I lowered the shotgun. Farrell hesitated. He looked back and forth between Cox and me. "You can't undo this, Farrell. You can't bring back the dead, nor can you lie your way out of it, but you can seek forgiveness. God's love is still here."

"We know you're involved with Peterson," I added. "All the way back to Jonathan and Molly. Nine lives, Farrell. The police are coming. Let Rebekah go."

Farrell's lips moved, but no words came out. The ghost emerged from the back room. He moved towards Cox, who didn't acknowledge him.

"He can't do that, Mr. Bohrman. Our Judas is stuck, aren't you?" Roger Peterson sneered at his accomplice. "You are with me till the end."

Farrell flinched. Fucking little prick!

The killer was more disheveled since we'd crossed paths in Springfield. Apparently, he hadn't had time to clean the blood off his jacket. He stood over Cox. "What's the matter, faggot? Mourning your cheap piece of ass? Sick! You're as bad as these worthless fucking whores." He sneered my way. "That's what they are, Bohrman, cheap fucking whores, all of them. That's what drove our boy Farrell here, his faithless whore of a wife."

"Like your daughter-in-law, Amy," I answered.

"Yes." The sneer was gone, replaced with hatred. "She and all these Jesus freaks killed my boy." He turned to Cox. "I'm merely repaying the favor." I moved towards him.

"He brutally murdered his wife, raped and strangled her," I said, "and then he swallowed glass shards and hung himself. Fruit doesn't fall far from the tree, does it, Peterson?"

"She deserved what she got," he snorted.

Lovely man. I hadn't fired the shotgun in some time. How about now? "And your brothers, did they deserve it?"

Peterson demurred. "What brothers?"

"Asa and Jeffery. Asa out in the California and Jeffery here in that ditch. That's how you seemed to be in so many places at the same time. What happened? Did they get cold feet? Too many murders? And Asa? You two went way back when he took custody of your son from you. Was this his chance at redemption from his psychotic brother?"

"You seem to know quite a bit about me, Bohrman."

"A man with a record such as yours is there to find," I said. Never mind that Art had done the digging.

Peterson shrugged. He didn't care, never would. "Asa was a coward and Jeffy lost his nerve. I can't have them dragging me down." He motioned at Farrell. "You understand that, boy?"

Farrell said nothing.

"Don't believe him, Farrell. There's still time to embrace goodness. Don't let this man corrupt your soul," Cox spoke without raising his head. Peterson drew closer to him.

So did I.

"What do you know about goodness, you cocksucking faggot? You and that goddamned faggot DeBerry talking about God, it makes me sick. You're fucking hell bound just like the rest of us!"

Peterson spit out his rage at Cox, but Cox didn't move.

"Your words cannot harm me nor can they take Lucian from the light of God." Cox looked up at Peterson. "God loves us, and his love is everlasting. Even someone like you can be redeemed. God will forgive those who seek salvation and embrace God's love. I know that and believe it in my soul. I do not fear you or your hatred. You are not the first person to despise me for who I am. I know what you've done and while I cannot judge you for what you did to Lucian, I can forgive." Cox's eyes returned to his hands, which he put together.

Peterson recoiled. We were all watching him.

"Your forgiveness?" He mocked Cox, "You and your loving God murdered my son. The last thing I'd ever want from you is your forgiveness."

Cox merely smiled. "I was angry once. Hateful, vengeful, much as you are, filled with an ugly self-righteousness. Innocent people were hurt because of me, but my conscience was clear for I had acted as an agent of God. But that was a falsehood, a lie, a story I told myself to justify my actions. In time I came to understand my failure before God. I know now that being an agent of good is not conditional based on my prejudices. You murdered a man I loved dearly, but I know that he is with God, and if it is my time to join him, I'm ready. You believe you can destroy that, but you're a fool. You are no more God than I am. I too know your history, Roger Peterson. Just like your son, you cannot run from it or change it." Ashton Cox stood up and faced Peterson. "Here I am ghost. You came here to kill me, did you not?"

Peterson pulled the knife from his pocket. It was an ugly blade, jagged and sharp, the kind paramilitary types use. "An eye for an eye, faggot..."

I raised the shotgun and drew back the hammers. "Put the knife down, Peterson."

"Or what?" Neither the knife nor Cox moved.

No reflex from the blade, but I couldn't stand it. I could see James standing there, beaten and uncomprehending, waiting for Miguel and me to slide the blades under his skin. "Or I'll shoot, you worthless piece of shit."

Peterson laughed. "Aren't we all, Bohrman? And what of your daughter?"

I looked at Rebekah.

That was my mistake.

With my focus on Rebekah, Peterson drove the knife into Cox. A hideous groan escaped from his throat as he fell to the floor. I turned the gun on his killer.

"What's the problem, Bohrman, you didn't shoot me, too bad. Now you all have to die." Peterson turned to Farrell. "The time has come, Judas. Kill him." We all turned to Farrell standing there with a gun pointed at my daughter.

Judas was wavering.

"What are you waiting for? Have you forgotten your zeal for this? All that talk of getting back at them, getting your revenge for this whore of a wife. Is that all it was, talk? We can't leave them, Judas, and we can't stay. Kill the man, then we kill the whores. You'll feel better, I promise." Peterson smiled at his protégé then turned towards me.

The shotgun was heavy and slick from the sweat percolating out of my pores. "Don't do it, Farrell, don't make it worse..." I was trying to think. It wasn't working. Why did I give her that fucking gun!

"But it's already worse, Bohrman, and it's not going to get better. My preference would be to kill these precious whores of yours and make you watch before slitting your throat, but the scattergun bothers me. So you have to go first, just has to be that way." He stepped towards me. I steadied the antique firearm. "Judas, I'm not going to wait much longer... it's time, let's go."

He stopped. The man with the knife heard what we all heard.

Sirens.

Farrell slowly aimed the 38 at me. His hand was shaking.

Rebekah tightened her face and pushed away from Farrell, causing him to drop the gun. Agnes screamed.

Foolishly, I moved in Rebekah's direction. Peterson lunged at me. I saw him out of the corner of my eye, turned and fired, but the shots were wild and only clipped his shoulder. He stood for a moment to check the wound. I was struggling to find the shells in my pocket. Agnes was trying to help Rebekah. There was too much shouting, too much noise. I got the spent shells out and had the new shells in my hand when Peterson came at me a second time. All I could think of was to use the shotgun as a club. I started to swing when the shots rang out.

The first bullet hit him in the chest. The second hit the side of his head. He staggered as Rebekah emptied the 38 into his torso. Rebekah kept pulling the trigger long after the last round fired. I dropped the shotgun and reached over and took the 38 out of her hand. She collapsed in my arms, dazed. Farrell got up, and Agnes promptly kicked him in the nuts. Farrell flopped to the ground moaning.

"Agnes!" I cried.

She backed away. Her eyes were wild and unfocused. She looked at me, trying to remember who I was. "Monk?"

Yes, it's Monk. "You gotta stop doing that!"

We watched the Judas writhe on the floor. I remembered Cox by the pulpit. "Get Nathan! Quick!"

Agnes went to the door and screamed for Nathan. I assumed they weren't far away after hearing the gunshots. Rebekah and I kneeled by Ashton Cox, who was holding his wound, bleeding profusely.

"We need to get you to a hospital," I said, stating the obvious.

"No hospital. I want to talk to Nathan," he whispered.

"He's on his way."

Nathan rushed over once he found us in the haze of the cordite and smoke. He began crying at the sight of Ashton Cox bleeding to death. Much as we tried to staunch the wound, blood continued to pour out. Ashton took his hands as he knelt down.

"Promise me you will not let our work falter. Promise me..." Cox was barely audible.

"The ambulance is coming, hold on." Nathan couldn't stop the tears.

"No ambulance, no hospital, Nathan, promise me you'll carry on our work..."

"I promise," Nathan assured him.

"Pray with me." He began the Lord's Prayer. Soon we were all saying it with him as he struggled to finish, the pain contorting his face and shaking his body. He closed his eyes as Nathan held his hands.

• • • • •

After seven days they let us go.

To fill the time between interviews and exhaustion, we helped clean the church as atonement for being a part, however tangential, to the mayhem that had occurred. The sheriff had taken the shotgun and the 38 with vague promises to return them at the proper time. I had no papers to prove ownership of the shotgun. It was a cash purchase from years before, and I produced Car's receipt for the 38 to the sheriff's disinterested grunt. The FBI wanted to talk to us and that took two days. What did we know beyond conjecture? You tell what you know, what you're willing to part with and hope for the best. With the suspect dead and his idiot accomplice in jail, it was all clean up anyway, something to close out.

Farrell, for his part, had confessed to being an idiot.

I already knew that.

Agnes didn't get it. "I don't understand what he was doing?" I think she was just talking out loud.

"He pretended to be helping Cox while secretly telling Peterson what they were up to. Maybe it was to get back at Rebekah or show he was his own man or having himself an adventure, but I doubt he expected it to become the mess it did." That's what I thought.

It didn't matter.

We were sitting on the bed killing time. I had a beer and she had a glass of wine. The hotel had become our refuge. Once word got out about the murders at Basker's farm, everyone knew who we were. Not that they were poor hosts, but conversations were minimal, mostly our orders, thank you.

Rebekah said little. When she wasn't sitting for interviews, she was sleeping. I saw no reason to push it. After all, not everybody witnesses a brutal murder and then shoots a man to death. Maybe the lull was a good thing, time to decompress before driving back to California. Finally, I asked her if she said what she needed to say to Farrell.

"Yeah," she said, "I told him it was okay to blame me and I told him it was over and to forget me."

That was it. All the miles, all this time for nothing more than that. I don't know what they did the night they were together at Basker's farm or how he got the gun. She got through it in one piece more or less. It didn't matter now.

My phone kept ringing. Ma and Pa Jenkins wanted to know, in the words of Chester, just what the hell was going on!

"Farrell's in jail, Chess," I informed him.

"I know that goddammit! I want to know why! They won't let me talk to him."

"Well, when you're an accessory to three murders and possibly seven more, the cops can be kinda tight-lipped. They won't let us see him, so I don't know what to tell you," I lied. I had no interest in ever seeing Farrell again.

"Then what the hell am I supposed to do?" he demanded.

"I'll leave that up to you. Oh, and by the way, Becky's divorcing his stupid ass." Chester Jenkins began shouting, but I hung up on him. Agnes started laughing. So did Rebekah. "You are divorcing his ass, right?"

"Probably." Her cheek was looking better.

"Probably? Jeez Louise, Rebekah!"

On the sixth day, we were invited to the services for Lucian DeBerry and Ashton Cox. I didn't think that was a good idea, but Rebekah wanted to go. The bodies had been released, and Nathan made preparations to have them buried at the cemetery not far from the church. Sheriff MacAfee called to say I could pick up the firearms at the sheriff's office. He handed me the 38, which I put in my pocket and then the shotgun. He admired it for a moment.

"My grandfather had one like it. A beautiful piece of art now, it would have been a shame if we'd had to destroy it."

I merely nodded. "I'm sorry for all the trouble, sheriff. Odd where life takes you sometimes."

"Then the next time you find yourself in one of these situations, Mr. Buttman, do me a favor and go to Kansas."

I don't think he was joking.

The road to Basker's farm was full. Curious townspeople mixed with community members and three very uncomfortable people I later learned were from Ashton Cox's family. I found Nathan directing people to an open area off to the right of the cemetery, away from the church. He called me over.

"I'm glad you came, Monk."

"How's everyone holding up?" I asked.

"Good. I took Ashton's words to heart. We have a good life here, and it's a good place to live. Losing him and Lucian was quite a blow and I worried that it might break our families apart, but we had a meeting a few days ago and we came together. I think that's the way they would want us to go. God presents challenges to us, big and small. You can't let them overwhelm you." We looked over the crowd milling about. He smiled. "God loves us, Monk."

I watched him move to the front of the assemblage. The three of us sat down towards the back. It was hot as we sat there listening to the eulogy for the murdered men. Ashton's love of Lucian wasn't mentioned, nor was the reason for their deaths. As different people rose to speak of the good they had done and how they served the Lord, my thoughts drifted back to the church. I took the crucifix Cox had given me from my pocket. I could still hear them speaking.

He loved her.

He loved him.

We stayed for a while after the service then left for our last night at the Comfort Inn.

There were messages on my phone. Joanie had questions, *a lot of questions*, and Judith missed me, wanted me to come over. Agnes brought up marriage again and Rebekah asked if I had a place she could stay.

It was time to go home.

Read on for a look at the next exciting installment In the *Monk Buttman* series:

Too Many Women, Too Little Time

"What the hell is this, Buttman?"

I played dumb. "What do you mean?" I knew what he meant.

"This?" He was pointing to the baby.

"It's a baby. What do you think it is?"

His mouth fell open.

Link Deal, yes, that's the name he used, seemed confounded by the specter before him: a man and a baby. He was nuts, but many of the wealthy people I had dealings with as a communications liaison (that sounded better than courier) for Aeschylus and Associates were nuts. Wealth gave them a nice veneer that papered over the fact that many of them had issues that wouldn't be tolerated in the rest of us. Oddly, many found a safe haven at Aeschylus and Associates and had formed an unusual attachment to me, and being nuts, would only have me as their liaison. This allowed me a certain carte blanche in our interactions.

"What the fuck is a baby doing here?" He seemed genuinely shocked.

Zachary laughed in that cute little baby way as I nuzzled his neck just below his ear.

"It's my turn to watch him and you can't leave a baby alone in a car these days, so he's tagging along." It's important to be a responsible adult.

"No strangers, Buttman; you know the rules!" Link Deal had a lot of rules.

"He's ten months old, besides, he's assured me he can keep his mouth shut. I mean look at this face..." I continued nuzzling my grandson. He continued to giggle. He was a boisterous little boy with big brown eyes and a head of soft brown hair.

"BUTTMAN!" Link Deal was beginning to lose it.

“Uh-oh, someone’s grumpy today. Hey, if I can’t bring him in then I’ll have to go. I can always have them send over Jeffery.” I knew he hated Jeffery, one of the other couriers employed by A and A.

“You know I hate Jeffery!” Deal considered his options while eyeing me and the boy. “He’s not stinky, is he?”

“Not at all, I changed him before we came over.” Zachary and I stood there smiling.

“All right, all right, you can bring him in, but I’m not happy about this.” As Link Deal was rarely happy about anything, I didn’t take it personally.

NOTE FROM THE AUTHOR

Word-of-mouth is crucial for any author to succeed. If you enjoyed the book, please leave a review online—anywhere you are able. Even if it's just a sentence or two. It would make all the difference and would be very much appreciated.

Thanks!
David

About the Author

An engineer for 40 years, David William Pearce, following open-heart surgery, decided to pursue his muse and write. After completing a debut novel, Pearce enjoyed the experience so much that he began writing the *Monk Buttman* series, which also include *Where Fools Dare to Thread*. When not writing, he is the accomplished recording artist, Mr. Primitive. He and his wife live in Kenmore, Washington.

Thank you so much for reading one of **David William Pearce's** novels. If you enjoyed the experience, please check out where it all began.

Where Fools Dare to Tread by David William Pearce

It's easy to be a nobody when you've got nothing to lose, but with his life and potential redemption on the line, can Monk be a somebody people will remember?

www.ingramcontent.com/pod-product-compliance
Lightning Source LLC
Chambersburg PA
CBHW011131100726
47898CB00009B/2937
9781684334131